The Antonym of Apathy

This work of fiction uses history as a guide. No character is meant to represent the beliefs, philosophies, values, or morals of any actual individual, living or dead.

Published in the United States by Antonym Publishing.
www.antonympub.com

ISBN 978-0-9816391-0-9

Library of Congress Cataloging
2008902179

Lura Kibler Kyle

1941-2002

Chapter 1

The warm dry day succumbs to the clear bright star-studded night, vigorous oranges and reds punctuate the end of a glorious day. The near still breeze allows the comforting smell from chimneys to soothe the onset of the night chill. Inside the small plain A-frame house, a new young couple plays with their cooing, giggling baby girl. Their first time at parenthood, the inexperienced couple caught on quickly, encouraged by the supportive child focused community. Built with urgency and functionality in mind, the cloned homes line newly paved roads. The colorless houses, stories not yet developed, await history.

Unsure, the new mom cradles the baby, rocks her, sings to her, does all she knows she's supposed to, in hopes her heart will soon warm to the child. She worries the alert, perceptive child in her arms will sense her apprehension, her puzzlement over the unanticipated new course of her life. The bright starlight pours through the window, highlighting baby Ava's delicate features, her pale skin, her cherry red cheeks, and those deep brown eyes. She looks nothing like me, her terrified mother thought.

Helen watched her child grow with more a sense of fascination than concern. She marveled at Ava's strong connection to her surroundings, her ability to assess, diagnose and anticipate situations from a very young age. An active child, Ava preferred crawling and climbing to being held. When Ava began talking, well before her first birthday, her mother had a very difficult time deciphering what her child was saying. For example, Ava's first words phonetically sounded like ay-noo-ew, after several days, Helen realized her daughter was saying I love you, mimicking the exaggerated tone Helen often used. Realizing Ava was using full sentences to express herself, and not solely reciting one word, Helen overcame her shock, communication flourished, and Ava became an active member of the household.

By seventeen months, Ava was setting and clearing the table and drying the dishes. Her sense of responsibility was not encouraged by her parents, nor could it be discouraged. Ava potty trained herself, dressed herself, and taught herself to read and write. Neither her mother, nor Frank, her father, knew much about raising a child, but from talking to other parents around the neighborhood, they knew Ava was different, and they considered themselves lucky.

With each new sibling added to the family, Ava continued to amaze. Her kind nurturing and intuitive sensibility became invaluable to the overwhelmed mother of five. As capable and charming as Ava was, Helen was acutely aware of her first child's dark periods. Helen would witness her daughter become focused and fixated for hours, sometimes days, when Ava would perform her tasks, but spoke little, and emitted an unmistakable aura of inapproachability. During these times, Ava was often drawn to the family's radio, but not to the music she enjoyed during lighter times, she was drawn to the news, especially talk about the war.

Helen, unobservant at best, had largely been unaware of her child's desire to have the radio on whenever she was indoors, which admittedly was virtually never during the daylight hours, until, the one and only time she saw Ava dance. Ava was four and a half years old, lying on her stomach on an oval braided magenta rug, chin propped on her hands, in front of the radio in the dull gray house. The special address came booming through the speakers, it was May 8, 1945, VE Day, the war with Germany was over. Helen, surprised and elated to hear the news, was shocked to see her darling little daughter jump up, scream wildly, and dance. Not the playful, goofy dance of a child, but a fitful spastic release, almost, it seemed to Helen, like an exorcism had occurred.

The joyous time of elation was matched in equal intensity nearly three months later, only this time sorrow was the profound emotion which consumed Ava. The atomic bomb was dropped on Hiroshima. Ava was still glued to the radio when three days later another bomb was dropped on Nagasaki. Ava listened, horrified, she stood up and addressed the radio with the last words she would speak for a month, "never again."

The month long "stupor," as her mother referred to the period of silence, firmly woke Ava's parents to the intensity of their child. Frank, much more aware and in awe of his daughter, knew stupor was entirely the wrong word. He knew Ava was planning, deciding what to do, way down deep inside her, places he, and certainly his wife, were not able to comprehend. Once Ava decided she was ready to join the world again, she was affable, but undeniably focused; she was on a mission, her life's calling had come to her.

As a young child, the now seven year old Ava spent most of her days exploring the dry desert with her next-door neighbor, Marty. Born three days apart, their resemblance and comfortable intimacy was uncanny, almost as if they had shared the same womb and were raised as twins. They had a private language; a way of interacting that was totally lost to others. They had no other friends, and it appeared it never occurred to them to join the other kids in games. Like Ava, Marty had fair skin, dark hair and brown eyes. They were both unusually tall and lean, with alert eyes, as well as uncanny coordination and ease of physical ability. They climbed the local foothills, uncommonly balanced and agile, adults rarely ventured after them for fear of being unable to make the climb. They were rare kids indeed, in essence they were able to create a private wonderland where they were free to roam and explore the local geography and environment. Insatiable curiosity and quest for experience drove the children to wander farther, look harder, and search deeper. They reinvented their surroundings day in and day out with their creative interpretations and assessments of the elements. Endless hours of wandering the foothills, catching lizards, tasting cacti, avoiding snakes, the pair grew up together as they constantly scoured the many barren miles of the surrounding landscape.

This particular day, the soft fall afternoon light lent a noticeable tranquility to their walk. Ava and Marty hadn't uttered a word since stopping for a bit of lunch. Their steps seemed more purposeful this day, as if their countless days of exploring now exposed their direction. Sure steps moving gracefully from rock to rock scantly looking around, they could close their eyes and imagine virtually every detail of the terrain, the pale sand colored jagged boulders with various hearty desert plants peeking out where they got a chance, the dark ridges that comprised the merging of peaked mountains, and the endless flat horizon laid out behind them.

The unusual arched ridge appeared first. Feeling the distinct presence, they both halted their trance like trek and looked up; they glanced at each other and smiled. They quickly climbed around a large boulder, exposing the entrance to the cave. Once inside, they realized they had found the perfect hideout. The arched, six feet wide by eight feet high, opening to the cave gave way to a dark, expansive space. Awestruck, walking with possibly the first apprehensive steps of their seven years, they walked until the edge of the light provided by the opening ended. There they sat, at the edge of the light, soaking in the new sensations of the sensory deprived space.

The two cross-legged still figures sat in the mouth of this unknown beast. Ava sensed the great magnitude of the space, its almost vacuum like quality, the cave's distortion of light and sound. The two sat for a long time, feeling the reverberations off the walls, it was Marty who spoke first. "Ava," he said as he softly touched her knee. "Ava, the light is almost gone."

Slowly, Ava opened her eyes, looked at him with the most peaceful sense of calm, and mused. "Marty, it can be done."

He, without knowing what she was talking about knew it to be true. "I know," he said. "I know it can."

The pair left the cave, but not before deciding on a name, they combined their names and declared their find, "Mav's Hollow." The knowledge that the presence of Mav's Hollow would be kept strictly between them could have gone unspoken, but still, they promised each other they would tell no one of their find.

They spent the next few months making Mav's Hollow more hospitable; candles, matches, wood, pans for cooking, blankets and pillows they sewed, a few of Ava's books, and paper and pencils for her equations. Ava's affinity for the cave proved to be much stronger than Marty's. He spent much of their time at Mav's Hollow studying the plant life in the surrounding area, checking in to make some tea, or heat up some soup, but for the most part he wandered the nearby foothills.

Ava used the time of inspiration at Mav's Hollow to devise countless experiments and preparations for her lab. Since the age of five, when the necessity of action became clear to her, Ava had read every math and physics book she could get her hands on. Her ambition and desire became so clear, the council decided to expand the science portion of the library to better meet Ava's growing needs. Now, with the recent passing of her eighth birthday, she had been approved for her own lab, complete with all the requested equipment. Ava had been applying for a lab every month for two years. And while the children were told no labs would be assigned until they were at least eleven, the caliber and exceedingly high quality of Ava's work encouraged the council to drop the age requirement. Ava had the distinction of being the first of her generation to have the honor of her own lab.

Marty cherished their last few days together at Mav's Hollow. He knew the opening of Ava's lab would mean free exploration for him, something he looked forward to, although he was sure to miss her terribly. He had loved spending the last year essentially alone together. But, he knew her focus and drive necessitated structured development, and she was ready. He also had hopes of getting his own lab one day. Plant biology had become his passion and he had learned so much about the distinctly hearty desert plants. He wondered why their ability to survive far surpassed most known species. But he did not share Ava's same sense of urgency, and was fit to remain innocently meandering in the foothills.

Their last days before Ava slipped even deeper into her obsession, dreamily passed by with less studying and calculations and more idle chat by the fire. The two giggled, shared theories about the potential impact of their respective studies, and speculated about life on the other side of the mountains. Their final walk back from Mav's Hollow was slow and deliberate, their usual pace tempered by their changing future. Marty knew Ava was eager to start the next phase of her research, but she too cherished their time together, and her affect hinted at a slightly detectable tinge of sadness, an emotion she was generally very skilled at hiding, but for now her protective intellect was resting, safe in the moment of comfortable companionship. Possibly, because of his intimate knowledge of her every behavior, only he could see the sorrow she carried with her into the escalation of her studies. But if others cared to look, they would find a burdened child struggling for meaning. For even the eternally focused scientist occasionally gives in to emotion.

Helen and Frank were pleased their daughter had been granted a lab. They earned praise from members of the community, and family points from the council. Ava was the child they had all hoped for, bright, self disciplined, determined and profound. The good news slightly eased the difficulty of raising five young children so close in age. While the twins, age six, John and Julie, proved almost as easy and self-sufficient as Ava, Thomas, age four, was apathetic and unmotivated. And Stevie, only two, was temperamental and highly dependent.

Ava's prolonged absences from the house meant less help with the other children.

But, thankfully for Helen and frank, the local Childcare Cooperative had recently built up operational capacity to accommodate any child in the neighborhood, anytime. Child focused programs, including educational training, allow for multiple sources for enriching interaction outside the home. Many parents, including Frank and Helen, were also educators. They taught many of the community programs, including character construction, body wellness, structural support, energy outlets, and the directed learning discipline. All children in the community have an opportunity to apply to, or create, a direct learning discipline of their choice. If highly motivated and of exceptional aptitude they may eventually qualify to join a lab, or as in Ava's case, head their own.

Educational opportunities were offered seven days a week, three hundred and sixty-five days a year, sun up to sundown. Members of the community must exhibit oral proficiency of material to gain education points. Education points determine when an individual qualifies for different levels of responsibility: directed research, discipline mastery, and skilled educator. Character construction in its most rudimentary form begins when a child starts to crawl and continues throughout the lifespan, with mandatory hours increasing throughout early adolescence to a peak of ten hours per month at age thirteen, and declining thereafter. All other community programs must be completed before directed learning may be approved. General education with hour quotas must be maintained until directed learning is qualified for.

The process for Ava to attain her lab was groundbreaking and somewhat surprising to the Council who had tried to anticipate all possible scenarios, but exceptional talent cannot be anticipated they found, only accommodated. Council member, Judith Delk, presided over Ava's oral proficiency attempt, a step necessary before being granted a lab. The precocious, then seven-year-old Ava, stood boldly, barefoot, in burgundy corduroy overalls, smiling and animated as the questioning began.

"Ava, can you briefly explain to me the principles of structural support?" Judith asked.

"Structural support applies all the components of a safe, equality based environment embodying the society's commitment to character construction, notably, the infrastructure to enact and provide development." Ava had never been particularly childlike; she spoke with the assured composure of a competent adult. Judith did not bat an eye at hearing the strong confident tone from the child she had always had such an affinity for; she simply smiled as Ava continued. "The childcare cooperative is an example of the community providing child care, to expand both the child's and parents' opportunities. Simple things like medical care, education, sources for income, food and shelter, are the products of structural support, but the theory behind it is the most important aspect of it. The foundation of security and goodwill underlying each individual encourages achievement, provides guidance for those who need it, and creates an overall strong sense of well-being."

5

"Thank you Ava, that was very well put," Judith said. "Tell me about body wellness?"

"Well, the name of the program is slightly misleading only because of the propensity of individuals to break the body down by emotions and thoughts, the heart versus the mind. The body is actually the synthesis of mental and physical health; you cannot have a healthy body without a healthy mind, and vice versa. A comprehensive plan for whole body health includes emotional, physical, and intellectual achievement among many others..." Ava paused, sure Judith was quite aware she had mastered the different programs. Eager to complete the proficiency test, she asked, "shall I go on?"

"I believe you've integrated the teachings," Judith stated. "I'm aware of your devotion to science, and you seem decisively certain to have mastered the understanding of energy outlets, but humor me will you?" Judith said, aware of the absurdity of the test for a person like Ava, but happy to hear Ava continue.

"The force a single person can generate when they put their whole being, whole soul, into the creation of a principle, or project, or relationship, has the ability to transcend all matter, all mass, all previously known principles, and make change, real lasting change, and whether individually, locally, or globally, the world is different forever. While I know the sole purpose of energy outlets is not to change the world, and they are simply meant to find creative and exciting endeavors to impact time on any scale, I believe I have one true calling, one choice, in my case there is no plural, I pursue one outlet entirely, and my goal is global change."

"Thank you, Ava. Now, I know you have expressed interest in your own lab to further your pursuit, and clearly you have shown competence in the community programs, while the Council has set eleven as the age minimum for a lab to be granted, the decision was a rather arbitrary one based on speculative predictions. We had not anticipated your passion and focus, and I must say you have shown the promise to exceed our wildest expectations when we began this program. If you continue to develop your knowledge and provocative insights into the world of physics, the council will acquiesce. Let your determination prove undeniable, we hope you succeed, if the task proves too much for you, we will embrace you just the same," Judith instructed.

"Concerning the oral proficiency of community programs performed by Ava Muller," Judith began, addressing the council later that day. "I can only say her understanding of principles, character, community and globally based, are profound. And furthermore, her ability to articulate her feelings, both eloquently and passionately, proves rare for an individual of any age. She demonstrates leadership and individuality along with internal fortitude which can only be deemed as remarkable. Her understanding of complex mathematical equations and many of Ipstein's most complicated theories astounds many of the country's top physicists. My concern is there will come a time when the council and government support will be unable to comprehend the direction of her work. Her reclusive nature, and lack

6

of interest in being forthcoming about her ultimate desire, could pose a security risk. While I am completely confident in the noble pursuit of her objective, we cannot be certain that we will be made aware of her intentions," Judith concluded.

"What do you propose Judith?" asked the council leader.

"I propose we establish a mentoring program with some of the top physicists in the field. A strong professional and personal relationship could be beneficial for all those involved. We could fly them in here periodically to share their expertise. We would set up briefings with the physicists involved to be better informed about Ava's findings. "

"Whom do you have in mind?" asked the council leader.

"Opalman, Cherkoff, and Steinman."

"From the Manhattan Project?"

"Yes, ma'am."

"What about the security risk?"

"These individuals, because of their enormous knowledge of previous government programs, are deeply invested in this type of research, and have proven trustworthy."

"And when do you envision this happening?"

"She certainly needs to prove her desire for her research and lab of her own will remain strong despite consistent short-term refusal from the council, but I see no reason for her to have to wait another four years."

"Report and recommendations noted. Thank you, Judith. We all have great hope for the potential Ava seems to promise. We will do all we can to aid her in her quest."

Judith smiled. "Thank you, Natalie," she said. Natalie returned the smile.

For one of the few times in her eight years, Ava slept soundly through the entire night. The comfort and security provided by being granted her own lab calmed her nerves and momentarily lightened her heart. She woke feeling refreshed, with a clear open mind, ready to devour the many unknowns which lay beyond her understanding. After years of compiling theories, and mathematically testing them, she would finally be working with the actual elements of her desire.

Judith and Ava arrived at the lab at precisely the same time, seven a.m. sharp, as agreed upon. They both were accustomed to utilizing time efficiently and precisely. The lab was located in a newly built, large beige, unassuming rectangular building. When Judith opened the door, it became clear to Ava her lab comprised the entire length of the building, and was not merely a subsection of it. Ava, seeing her dream equipment for the first time, felt a cold chill move up her spine, she shivered with anticipation.

"Now, as you requested, the enriched Uranium, Plutonium, and liquid Nitrogen will be held over here in the radioactive chamber. The other items you asked for including: the particle accelerator, heavy ion collider, vacuum equipment, inductor, electromagnetic alternator, and the Beryllium, as well as stored noble gases Krypton,

Argon, and Xenon, should all be here. Take your time and get acquainted with your new lab. At ten o'clock Dr. Opalman, Dr. Cherkoff, and Dr. Steinman will arrive to discuss your theories and help you adjust to the new machinery," Judith stated.

"And if I do not want their help?" asked Ava.

"Then they shall not return," replied Judith. "I'll be back at ten to introduce you to the doctors. Enjoy."

"Thank you..." Ava paused, walked over to Judith, squeezed her hand and said, "please let the council know I appreciate their generosity and kindness in providing me with the opportunity to conduct these critical experiments. I will not let them down. And to you personally, I am grateful for your trust."

"I am grateful for your trust, dear girl," Judith said without emotion. "Now get to it, we're ready to see what you can do." Judith closed the door behind her.

The large room, as long and wide as a football field, created its own unpredictable energy. The humming machines, the presence of all the heavy metal, the sense of freedom and hope was far greater than Ava ever could have imagined. The tiny eight-year-old girl, tall for her age at four and a half feet, but very thin, somehow maintained an imposing stature amongst the giant machines, like a lion tamer completely in control, seemingly outmatched in a physical sense, but able to remain untouched by the looming danger. She took a large deep breath and slowly investigated each machine. She smelled them, ran her hands slowly over each part. She laid her cheek against the particle accelerator, displaying an intimacy she had not as of yet shown any living being.

In seemingly the blink of an eye, the door opened and Judith walked in with three middle-aged men. The only man she cared to take note of, for the other two she immediately knew she could not trust, was a tall, lean, bright eyed man with closely cropped dark hair and a kind inquisitive face. The two made eye contact, he gave a quick knowing wry smile. Ava's eyes softened, she approached the men, never dropping the stranger's gaze. Judith began to introduce the men. "Ava, this is Dr. Cherkoff, Dr. Steinman, and last but not least, Dr. Opalman." Ava shook each of their hands and stopped at Dr. Opalman. She said, "I think you can help me."

"I believe I can," the Dr. replied.

Dr. O, as she called him, decided to stay awhile. He saw something in the little girl, that of a guided solace leading her to places of triumph and accomplishment he could not fathom. Ava and Dr. Opalman spent nearly a month theorizing about science, and finding ways to manipulate the machines to fit their theories. The insidious mistrust which had begun to overtake him in the years since the war melted away now with the same red and orange fury of the monster he had helped create. His once optimistic and limitless view of the potential of physics to create revelatory experiences in the universe had played out in the most lecherous manner. The aftermath had created a well of darkness inside him that four years of relentless repentance could not brighten. With her, he saw a way to become whole again, a chance to accomplish the profound, an elixir to the ravages of human domination he had helped further.

8

For Ava's part, she found a mind like her own, one she could deluge with thoughts and possibilities and talk about her theories in a way she had never done with anyone before. She knew what he had done, she saw his desire to make amends, and she knew there was no one else in the world more desperate, more talented, and more capable of helping her in overcoming human aggression than he. Their time together was limited, which brought her comfort, for the expansion that can come from communication can become a new direction of its own, and she knew there could only be one direction, her own. She pulled and pried at the helpful bits of Dr. O's mind. His experience with the machinery was timesaving. But she quickly found ways to alter and improve the output of the machinery, even he was unaware of, to suit her goals.

Dr. O. was like an exuberant puppy nipping at her heels. It was quickly obvious he had never thought about space, time, and matter in the ways she was proposing. This surprised her, and momentarily made her wonder about the sincerity with which he had attempted to undo his wrongs. Through their further discussion it became clear his mind seemed to have an invisible blockade creating passages through which his intellect could not travel. She saw where he was able to understand alongside her, and where he would have to simply trust and follow her along as she exposed luminous conceptual thinking unrestrained by pre-conceived limitations.

She gave him hope, and the freedom of creative expression he longed for. He gave her time and understanding, but now she needed reflection and space. As their month together at the lab was coming to an end, she looked forward to burying herself in all the possibilities running through her head. She felt his tinge of sadness as he smiled and walked away. His long gait, with knees slightly knocked, seemed to physically express the sorrow of a man who ended so many stories and created the greatest, latest act of infamy. Despite his height, his awkward physical presence emitted a harmless lack of agility that made his intellectual prowess his only chance at power. And he among the billions inhabiting the earth had unforgettably displayed the culmination of that power. His dominance over the elements had brought godlike wrath, the power to determine existence.

Ava's unyielding singular focus over the first month in her lab had left her invigorated but cluttered. After a dreamless night she woke early and headed to her beloved foothills. Under the expansive sky she felt her thoughts slow and localize, tranquility accompanying the mental reorganization. With every step the increasing emergence of her senses drew her back within herself. Her breathe, the subtle sounds of the terrain, the attention to her every step, they all brought her to the moment. The forward thinking of the lab had let the present obscure, and now she must find a way to bring herself back to the essential, this moment in time. Like walking the well-worn path home, her feet guided her without conscious thought, letting her quieted mind wander free. She thought of Marty and Mav's Hollow, of their time together, the uncomplicated dreamlike state they seemed to maintain. Her once streamlined sense of physics and research had blown up, expanding so rapidly she was unable to interpret all the possibilities quickly enough to find them useful. She had begun to see her mind out in front of her, limiting her in a similar way Dr. O's limited him; she had tipped the scale in the balance of her knowledge within space and time. She continued on the familiar path, the arch rose above her; she stopped, looked up, looked directly in front of her, and continued.

She entered the deep, dark space of the cave. Time slowed, she breathed deeply, slowly, her fingers tingled. She walked past the edge of the light. She placed her cheek against the cool smooth wall, a single tear rolled down the side of her face. She turned her face to place her other cheek against the wall, she spread her arms out wide, pressing herself gently against the cave, feeling the pressure, the temperature, the lack of life.

Eventually, she slid down the side of the wall to the floor and sat with her back against the side of the cave. Her eyes adjusted to the lack of light, she closed them, internal stimuli was all she craved. Ava could hear the swoosh of the blood rushing through her head subside as her pulse slowed. She rested her head against her knees, slowly letting her body sink into the supportive grasp of Mav's Hollow. Her jaw relaxed, her mind stopped for a brief perceptible moment, and then redirected itself to the burning question buried inside her for so many years. She envisioned engulfing bursts of energy taking away harmful matter as it dissipates. She imagined identifying, tracking, and attacking her enemy with a startling stealth and untraceable manner. She smiled slightly, she knows it can be done, she has seen the future, and she will shape it.

The sure quick footsteps revealed his presence before he arrives. She stood slowly, stiff after hours sitting on the floor. She walked to the edge of the light, "Marty?"

"Ava?" Marty replied.

He looked different in the subtle light of the cave, calmer, more self-assured. In the neighborhood he was more withdrawn, difficult to read. Here, there was no reason for him to protect himself; he stood taller, looked alert and carefree. He, like her, was at home among the elements. She too had changed. She was no longer the brilliant, inquisitive girl who people believed had potential. Her gaze was slightly more directed, deepened into the realm of wisdom, her potential was beginning to be realized.

They slowly walked through the foothills towards town, talking the whole way. She told him about Dr. Opalman and how he had shown her the entire process necessary to make the atom bomb. She described the machines, how they worked, what they did, and excitedly what she thought they would be able to do. He listened patiently as she recounted her experiences over the last month. After nearly an hour she stopped and looked back at Marty. "You look concerned," she said.

"Do you trust him?" He asked without hesitation.

"Not with everything, but I don't have to tell him everything."

"Why work with him at all?"

"He created the atom bomb," Ava stated, emphatically.

10

"Exactly."

"He has saved me years by sharing his knowledge and expertise with me. He's a good man who found himself deeply involved in an extraordinary scientific quest with a horrific outcome based on the decisions of others. If it wasn't the U.S. it would've been Germany, in a land of either or, we hope for the lesser of two evils. Or, like I'm trying to do, change the rules of the game, and undermine their ability to create devastation. Dr. Opalman did the best he could based on the information at the time. Now, he has better information, and he has made a better decision."

"You don't need him," Marty said.

"I may not, but for now he remains a valuable resource. Plus, he is capable of getting my notes to Doctor Ipstein for collaboration. Ipstein is a good man, and the best Physicist in the world. He is the one that informed Pelt about Germany's plans to create the bomb in the first place. Marty, It's important for me to have communication with the outside world," she said.

"The government supporters will never go for it."

"You're right, they don't have to know, and if they find out, I'll know I can't trust Dr. Opalman."

"But they'll know your intentions," Marty said, worried.

"I never declare my intentions. I discuss small bits of information like pieces of a puzzle for which only I have seen the picture. For everyone, except possibly Doctor Ipstein, all the pieces must be together to see the whole."

"Just take your time revealing yourself, sometimes ulterior motives don't present themselves immediately," Marty warned.

"I will, Marty, I will," she said, reassuringly.

Chapter 2

The passing weeks had gone from joyous relief to concerned trepidation. Urgency and necessity left many details of their voyage unsettled. Quota numbers were yet to be obtained, with hopes they would be issued en route, a temporary stay in Cuba may be required to procure quota clearance. Agitation of the crew and passengers was increasing, one death due to natural causes, and one suicide have been reported. The declining food rations are only of concern if quota clearance delays persist. The crew has been given specific instructions to treat the passengers humanely; thus far only seventeen have been relieved of duty.

Permission to dock off the coast of Cuba has been granted, request to disembark denied. Confused and weary, the passengers become more restless as family members in small boats anchor by the ship in hopes of communicating with their loved ones. Police patrol the water fearing the passengers may attempt to reach shore. The nearly thousand refugees docked outside Cuba have garnered worldwide media attention. After continual refusal to allow the passengers to touch Cuban soil, the SS St. Louis sets off for the United States, where democracy reigns, religious freedom is paramount, and hopes of safe harbor lights the way.

The crew no longer shares news of the transmissions and negotiations between countries. Promises recanted, soaring hearts clipped, the bottom sinks perilously beneath, lower and lower, darker and darker. Currents rush directly towards the southern tip of Florida, deliberately encouraging the St. Louis, tantalizing with thoughts of freedom. With the bitter taste of disappointment still lingering, fear during the short voyage from Cuba to the United States enveloped the passengers, crawling up their skin with a deep lasting chill. The scene which awaited them off the coast of the United States of America may have been a surprise weeks, even days ago. Now, hardened by the dominant presence of their impending death, the large navy warships firing warning shots matched the countless other surreal elements they had come to encounter with nary a startled flicker of the eye.

The slightly perceptible rise in tension did not escape the babies and children. They fidgeted, some cried, big sorrowful eyes looking to their parents for comfort.

Who look down only to say, there is no comfort here young one, yes we are unwanted, and yes, we are also afraid.

Possibly it was the look in the children's eyes, possibly it was the hunger, possibly the fog of death that could not be lifted, but seeing the United States of America shrinking behind them, there was an uprising. Mutiny spawned by sorrow, when control of the ship ultimately means there is still nowhere to go, is an easily squelched battle. Resolute, the next few days spent circling Cuba seemed like cruelly prolonging the inevitable. Listless, all options exhausted, the crew headed back to Europe, fate unknown.

*

"We have lost our authority to lead, for these are the decisions of closed door, backroom deals which reek of whiskey and cigars. No thoughtful man would come to this conclusion of his own volition, and Henry, I know you as a thoughtful man, there seems no plausible justification for failing to prevent certain death. We cannot plead ignorance; we cannot plead hardship, lack of resources… Are we to say this is within the acceptable realm of our moral code? Are we powerless?" Her intense pale eyes narrowed, her voice slightly raised as she asked her husband, a passionate, merciful man, the question that was sure to wound him most. "Are we apathetic?"

She calmed slightly, seeing him slump in his chair, revealing his discomfort. Tall and imposing, Maggie Pelt, had trained herself to speak calmly, almost soothingly to assure her message had a fair chance of being heard. The fact that she was a woman, that she knew may leave her at a disadvantage with some, but that was certainly no reason to leave her opinions unspoken. Dark-haired, pale skin, unguarded only among her most trusted few, Maggie was known for her intellect. Any physical beauty she may have possessed had long since been deemed irrelevant. Her presence was undeniable, quite possibly the only first lady for which that could be said. Her interest in the goings-on of her husband was at first perceived as charming, her persistence and competence quickly made her role essential. She became her husband's supporter, confidant, and now for one of the few times, his detractor.

Henry had long known the dastardly direction the decisions he had made would lead him squarely to this moment, where he quite possibly had lost the faith of his wife, and far more frightening, faith in himself. He had spent the last few months steadily sinking, trying to stay afloat, his eyes pleaded with her, but the elements don't you see? The elements were too much, and now he could only drown in the inevitability of disappointment. He spun out of control under the weight of the new reality. Shall he die? Shall he survive? Will he be able to live? His resolve leaves him, the room closes in on him, he takes his head in his hands and weeps. Her question answered, she walked behind his desk for the first time, and put her hand on his shoulder.

13

*

The committee had come to the same small room in the bowels of the White House every week for nearly a year since the refusal of the S.S. St. Louis. The low white ceiling and small round oak table provided the eight members of the committee, headed by Maggie Pelt, both the intimacy, and candor, close proximity tends to elicit. The secretive nature of the committee necessitated privacy, Maggie specifically chose the room for both its remoteness to the rest of the house, and its tendency to evoke frankness from its inhabitants.

The group, mostly close confidants of the first lady, except General Cartwright, the military liaison, was comprised of five women, including first lady Pelt, and three men. They spent their initial seven meetings brainstorming, discussing principles and theories, and deciding on location and numbers. The last nine months they had spent refining and enacting their plan. Construction on the project had begun six months ago, and its opening was expected next month. With the conclusion of today's meeting they will have three final meetings to draft the official bylaws. Then they will anxiously wait to see if the implementation of the plan matches their vision.

Maggie, high from the meeting, calmly walked into her husband's smoke filled office. He looked up from his briefing, "how's Project Redeye coming along?" he asked.

She mused, "oh Henry, it's just bliss. The energy, creativity, and the humanity this group brings to the table, there are endless possibilities."

He somewhat sarcastically asked, "are there any tangible possibilities among those endless possibilities?"

"Tangible yes, unpredictable maybe, but very real actions are being taken."

"It is a massive undertaking of monumental proportion," he said skeptically.

"That it is darling, great problems call for great solutions, hundreds of thousands of lives come with great inherent complication. Our commitment and dedication to Project Redeye is not timid or fleeting, nor is our belief in the preservation of life and the exploration of all options to prohibit the death of spirits and minds, of relationships and families, there is no greater course."

"I admire your vision."

"I hope not to be admired, especially for my vision, but to actively do all I can to further the prosperity and survival of many without regard to my role. I hope to achieve to whatever degree possible what every living person ought to strive for; peace and harmony within humankind. The focus should be on those who do not share that vision and how we can help to show them the way. Lead with deeds, unequivocal actions to better humanity, that is our duty as living, breathing, feeling beings. I can look the other way no longer as a person, and now we as a country, and hopefully followed by the world as a whole."

"Maggie my dear, many have come before you who have shared your ideals, great

14

leaders with great spirit and intellect, I hope you do not get your hopes up too high. Let's see how this plays out for awhile before you prophesize an unprecedented shift in the human paradigm."

"There is no better time than now. You have a man looking to exterminate a distinct group of people. Genocides have been far too long a mainstay in human culture. This is the time to actually oppose predation of one upon another despite the difficulties a strong stance brings. We have a responsibility to enact change in the manner that is afforded to us. I am the wife of the President of the United States, I dream without limitations, and this is what I've come up with."

"We shall see if it can be done," he said.

A progress report from the group about the Redeye Project left Maggie satisfied, but not without trepidation. "All of your most recent requests have been authorized by executive order. Of course, only absolutely key figures have been made aware of the existence of Project Redeye. I must say one hundred thousand troops, that's a lot of unsuspecting free Americans," General Cartwright stated.

"Yes, one hundred thousand is the agreed-upon number. How is their immersion training progressing?" Maggie stated plainly.

"Well, nothing they learned in boot camp has prepared them for this I'll tell you that much. The initial shock and sadness over being separated from their families seems to be dwindling. These are good American soldiers ma'am, proud men and women dedicated to serving their country. While it's not what they had in mind, they are honored to be involved in the noble project and are giving the most they can, ma'am."

"Thank you, General."

"Yes ma'am. Regarding the strict logistics, the buildings and infrastructure are all near completion. The soldiers have adapted quickly to the two session system consisting of building by day, and immersion training by night. They are a resourceful lot, and the camaraderie developing as the inception of the project nears is just what we had hoped."

"Thank you, General," Maggie said appreciatively.

"Welcome ma'am. It's a good thing you're doing here ma'am, somewhat peculiar with your different philosophies and all, but those people need help, and we are the United States of America."

"And every life is sacred," she added.

"That it is ma'am, that it is. Those folks love just like we do, they're scared just like we get."

"Yes they do, and yes they are." She paused. "Okay, we'll meet again next week," she said, addressing the rest of the group, "our last meeting here. Our final meeting will be held on the grounds of project Redeye." The group got up to leave. "Bea, could you please stay? I would love to go over some ideas with you," Maggie stated. Beatrice stopped, her assured athletic build dominated the small room, she turned, smiled and said, "yes Maggie, I have a few moments."

15

Maggie smiled. "Good, sit down please," she said kindly.

Alone in the room they dropped any formality. Maggie reached across the table and grabbed Bea's hand. "Oh Bea, do you really think it'll work?"

Soothingly Bea replied, "I do Maggie. Something needs to be done; we can't let our doubt paralyze us."

"But are we trading the lives of those hundred thousand soldiers for the lives of others?"

"Maggie, no soldier can ever be assured of a future, especially now, time is very uncertain, if not this assignment, then where, Germany?"

"We don't know about Germany."

"Oh Maggie, we can't bury our heads in the sand forever, the suits and the cigars will run out of hot air soon. Diplomacy, my dear, has its limitations."

"I am aware conflict with Germany appears inevitable, but frankly, I'm happy Henry has chosen not to rush to war. There are opportunities to influence matters without full invasion."

"Influence what?" Bea asked. "Hope Europe handles the Nazis on their own? Or possibly we'll allow every Jew in Europe to resettle here? There are no options, the maniac needs to be stopped, the sooner the better. A chain reaction of really sick events has begun, the longer it continues, the stronger the momentum, the more difficult it will be to stop. Don't protect your husband and his little pal Trindle. They know what he's building, what are they waiting for? Take him out."

"It's not that simple."

"Is that what your husband tells you? He's giving you this little pet project to placate you and you whistle his tune."

"That's enough Bea," Maggie said half-heartedly.

"We sit here like we are making a difference, we're fooling ourselves. This project is insignificant compared to the massive devastation that is occurring right now."

"Would you prefer we do nothing?"

"I would prefer we do more. I think I've made that clear."

"Bea, all options, in order to be considered a decent rational country, must be considered and exhausted." Maggie walked over to Bea's chair and leaned beside her still holding her hand. "Listen Bea, I know you or I would have rooted out the tumor of the movement spreading across Germany a long time ago. None of this is acceptable, this is not the best that can be done, I agree with you. Did you know Henry hardly sleeps at all anymore? He's a good man, he's doing the best he can, I assure you. But he is only human dealing with the very real frailties of other humans."

"No, he is only a man dealing with other men. That is only half of humankind, and the part that can't seem to figure out what's important until it's too late."

Maggie stands, throws up her hands, and for the first time in their decade old relationship raised her voice. "Don't you know I agree with you? Don't you know I hate playing these little games, acting like I'm not outraged by the political process, like it doesn't kill me to see how many lives are needlessly lost because it doesn't

16

serve our best interests as a nation to intervene? How somehow our best interests as a nation involve something other than the preservation of peace and the saving of human lives, which is the only thing that if lost, all is lost? As a country, and a world leader, I am sorry to say our priorities are first economical, then our own citizens, then everybody else, and believe me, we rarely get past the first priority. And I know it is men who have made these decisions most often, but not everywhere, and not forever. History is not over, and we will do what we can under the circumstances we have been presented. But mark my words, in the next century, this country will have a female leader, but now, we must exert our influence subtly and tactically. There are many reasons I'm creating this program. You have yet to see the true potential of a supportive environment for both boys and girls. The great leaders from our program have an equal chance of being a man or a woman, and they will be in a community that supports either. So while you are so dismissive of this feeble attempt to save a few lives, the course of history will be altered forever, and that is the best I can do."

Bea stands, grabs Maggie's hand and says, "I know my dear, calm down, I know." Bea can feel Maggie's body trembling as she hugs her and strokes her hair. "I'm sorry dear, I'm sorry I pushed you. The project is incredibly ambitious, to belittle it is disgraceful, and the lives saved are revolutionary. I'm sorry sweetheart, I know, I'm sorry."

Chapter 3

Four years into her lab work, the now twelve year-old Ava was more in awe of the complexity between science and the properties of the universe then ever, yet somehow, much more confident science could unlock the mysteries which would make her dream a reality. She routinely made trips to Mav's Hollow for quiet reflection even though she spent a good ninety hours a week in her lab. Time with her family had become virtually nonexistent. The distance she had always felt from her parents, even her siblings, seemed alleviated by her life away from the house. In a way, the more possessed and thriving her research life had become, the more comfortable she became with the unsubstantial role of her family in her life. She no longer lay awake at night wondering about every sound, feeling the tension within the house; she slept soundly, with visions of absorbing matter in her head.

The only entirely personal relationship Ava maintained was with Marty. Their brief interludes together at Mav's Hollow reminded her of the world she wanted to exist; a peaceful, carefree exchange of ideas and feelings between people who trusted and enjoyed each other, and a building of energy that incorporated the senses coming together to exist on a plane slightly higher than before. Ava explored almost entirely unutilized portions of her personality when she was with Marty. She was gentle, calm, sometimes silly, and in a rare dropping of the guard, she could even be funny. The serious and darkened world in which Ava walked seemed entirely lost when she lightened enough to laugh so hard she turned bright red.

Marty marveled at these humorous times the most. Marty could see the stored sorrow of years of deep contemplation release from her. After a laughing fit she was always still for a couple of minutes, reevaluating the world without her usual intense focus. He liked it, when he could see the slight peaceful smile she displayed. These were the times they both loved, when nothing beyond Mav's Hollow existed, time stopped, their lives meant nothing more, nothing less, than these exact moments, the brilliance captured between them, free to be their fragile and endangered selves.

Ava's time away from Mav's Hollow was spent almost entirely alone, in deep internal discourse constantly attempting to invent the unknown. She occasionally reported her progress to Judith. Who related with knowing amusement to the council the slow progress, as reported by Ava, of her research. Judith's meetings with Dr. Opalman shed an entirely new light on the wonder child's ability as a physicist. Aware of how fond Dr. Opalman had grown of Ava, Judith knew he would never reveal too much about the direction of Ava's research. And knowing Ava, Judith knew no one, including Dr. Opalman, would ever know her final mission until it was too late. This last bit of information Judith kept from the council. The leeway they had given Ava most certainly was contingent upon the possible gains the research could provide the country, and too much information to the contrary would jeopardize the future of Ava's support. Judith already had the power to stop the project at will and need not alarm the council unless she lost faith in the child, a prospect which seemed highly unlikely.

Ava eagerly anticipated Dr. Opalman's bi-yearly visits for two reasons: first, the theoretic scientific conversation she and Dr. Opalman shared, and secondly and most important, the response to the notes Dr. Opalman was able to exchange with Dr. Ipstein, securely wax sealed with Dr. Ipstein's famous $E=MC^2$ emblem.

It was her breakthrough collaboration with Dr. Ipstein which allowed her to find a way to coherently harness light's wavelengths to make a controllable stream with which to transport energy. Their discovery, the laser beam, would not filter into the general world of science until several years later. The tiny beam had enormous impact on Ava's project. From her readings and exchanges with Dr. Ipstein she knew a directed light cavity was theoretically possible, but the day she sent Xenon through the vacuum and watched the light stabilize, was the day her research transformed from dream to reality.

The hours and hours alone in the lab accompanied only by machines, swirled in thought and determination, steered the lab into an unyielding abyss of isolation. Her breakthrough, and Dr. Opalman, brought life and new perspective to the cold, gray environment. They spent hours debating the possible. He was always left gasping at the audacity with which Ava ignored previous convention. "But Doctor O, previous convention has not found an answer to the question I am asking," she'd say. "So humor me, Dr."

When Dr. O arrived for his most recent visit, Ava was buried in the back of the lab. She did not reply to Dr. Opalman's first attempt to track her down. "Ava?" he called several times to no avail. He heard the sharp sound of metal clinking in the far rear corner of the voluminous mostly colorless workspace. He stopped calling for her and followed the sound. After navigating through several machines he saw the slight dark-haired figure hammering at the pistons of the Ion Collision machine.

She had changed a great deal over the last six months. He noticed the elongation of her face, the slight rounding of her bottom, and the presence of budding breasts. He was surprised to see the larger-than-life child would not remain in the place he had saved for her in his mind. If he was lucky enough to continue to work with her she would become a woman right before his eyes. Her unabashed uniqueness as a child would become a resolute agenda as an adult, with unnerving implications, he thought. The innocence that can be imposed on a child because of the perceived inexperience which comes with youth would slowly be eroded as Ava progressed into womanhood. He looked at her lovingly, and knew her task would become immeasurably more difficult as her cloak of innocence was removed.

Ava finally noticed the doctor approaching and ceased her hammering to wave the doctor over. "Look," she said, "if I increase the distance the pistons travel, I'll be able to create more pressure in the machine, and consequently a more powerful collision will be created which will cause a bigger explosion, which means more energy."

"Great," he said, "not sure creating energy is the problem."

"I know, I know," she said. "But creating this much energy in a controllable, stable environment will allow me a chance to manipulate it without radiating the town," she said, with a wink and a smile. A couple of years ago she made a failed attempt at making light of the devastation caused by Dr. O's research. All the blood had drained from his face, and a wounded look of terror came over him, paralyzing him, and scaring Ava. She realized the pain and guilt he suffered walked with him just below the surface, haunting his every moment, waiting to overtake him. This wink and a smile were as close as she had come to alluding to the bombings since then. He saw the charm in her, and knew she meant no harm. He grabbed a hammer and started banging away.

They had a particularly cheerful visit this time around, with the exception of one early tense exchange. It began with a simple inquiry; Dr. O. was aware she was making some major progress and hoped to know more. "Do you and Dr. Ipstein talk about the same things that you and I do?" he asked.

"Why would Doctor Ipstein and I talk about the same things you and I do? You are two totally different people with entirely different perspectives and ways of interacting with the universe and matter. Don't worry," she continued, realizing he might be hurt, "you are both equally important in the advancement of the project."

Slightly startled, he replied. "Equally important? You haven't even met him."

"Our minds have met, and there are not many people I can say that about. So is it significant? Yes. Could I do the project without both of you? I'm confident I would find a way. Am I thankful for both of you? I am. Dr. Ipstein's distant physical proximity does not diminish my thankfulness, or his importance."

Dr. Opalman, slightly wounded by her comments, receded into his work. He had always relished his perceived superior status to Dr. Ipstein in regards to Ava's research. He felt that the allegiance and loyalty he and Ava created bonded the two beyond the letter exchange she shared with Ipstein. It seemed to him, Ipstein had always remained above the fallout created by the bombings, but the damage done to Dr. Opalman's reputation was immense and immeasurable. However, the professional consequences did not pervade Dr. Opalman's consciousness nearly the same way the personal damage did. In Dr. Opalman's eyes, Dr. Ipstein did not have either the desire or the courage to commit to a project that would forever alter the course of human history. It was us or the Germans. Doctor Ipstein encouraged the development, but took no personal risk in its terror. Yes, Germany was defeated without it, and its later application was debatable, but how was he to know?

Drawn away from her work for a moment, sensing his internal drama rise, Ava walked over to Dr. Opalman and put her hand on his. "Dr. O, you have meant a great deal more to me in a personal sense, of course, than Dr. Ipstein. I was speaking before strictly in a professional manner," she said. He smiled, his tension eased, their manner was casual and easy for the remainder of the week.

They spent nearly the entire week working on bettering the accuracy of the laser detection system. The system she had created was able to detect different nuclear components, including plutonium and enriched uranium, as well as calculate the velocity at which the matter was traveling. The detection proved basic, a simple matter of creating particles small enough and sensitive enough to respond to the large levels of nuclear energy surrounding a bomb. A master of electron manipulation, she created ions, which in the presence of radiation, set off an extremely short but powerful chain reaction. In essence, this highly explosive substance effectively could be used to launch anything within the presence of radiation. However, controlling the timing and size of the reaction proved difficult in the highly unstable environment. How many ions, the radiation necessary to elicit the chain reaction, and how to keep the large clumps of ionic matter from repelling each other, or worse, creating a massive explosion, were the questions of the week. Through modifications Ava was able to execute pinpoint coordinates based on gravitational pull. Sometimes late at night, the townspeople caught a brief, almost hallucinatory, glimpse of Ava's laser searing into the night. Emerging from the temporary hole in the lab created by the retractable roof she fashioned, the purple beam raced through the sky. Ava gave no hint of what the laser would be used to deploy, and Dr. O didn't ask. Yes, he speculated, quite frequently actually, but with too much information he knew he would become a liability to Ava.

He wasn't quite sure it was possible to accomplish what she seemed to be trying to do, but he was sure there was no one more capable. And there was nothing he would rather be doing than looking for the answer with her. He extolled her achievements daily, for they were greater scientifically than any he had ever seen, and if he had been free to share with his peers what he learned with Ava, the scientific community would be greatly indebted to him. He would be a hero in legacy, leaving his death emotionally swift and merciful. But he knew he was destined to die a pariah, the agonizingly slow, painful end which comes with the torment and guilt of a gruesome past.

These moments of unparalleled scientific creativity, and the reawakened love of the potential, had become more of an expression of life than anything he could have imagined. His time with Ava was the glory of creation he never knew existed, but drove him nonetheless. They had found so much of science's potential possible. The way she pushed beyond all barriers placed before her, she was both ruthless and

21

divine in their most extreme forms. He possessed neither in great quality. He was talented and smart, but his limitations were always present. She seemed absolved of all limitations, scientifically at least, her abundant limitations in the non-theoretical portion of life were evident, but necessary to achieve her goals.

His time with Ava was such a departure from his life. The pressure of a leading scientist in a power-hungry world was warping to the soul. He envied Ava's seclusion, her private lab in a remote untouched world free of tyrannical forces. Somehow, the government accepted his project with Ava as a compromise; he was not required to do any other government contracted work. He could study what he wanted as long as he visited Ava twice a year, and shared with them what he had learned. She had freed him, freed him from the demanding pressure of an overzealous world power, and lessened the torment of the burden of creating a device for mass murder. With her he could right his wrongs, he was indebted to her forever in a manner greater than family, stronger than religion, she was faith personified.

The week passed surprisingly quickly. Ava was usually eager for the isolation his leaving provided which allowed her more freedom to experiment with the true nature of her research. The temporary respite from isolation the Dr.'s companionship provided quickly dissipated as the hunger to reach her goal grew. And her goal was the pursuit of the unbound, she was a restless spirit who strives for accomplishment above all else. Consistent engagement with another, regardless of intent or context, proved to be a distraction pulling her off course. Her pursuit stood in the way of true friendship with Dr. O, but friendship was a known lab hazard, and her safety guidelines were clear.

Her frequent midnight walks home under the dark black sky shattered with the light of millions of stars, anchored by the Moon, returned her briefly to the land, free from the machines she used to manipulate elements and matter. Every night Ava was brought back to simple wonderment at the beauty of the elements in their still, natural state. The ten minute morning walk doubled in duration late at night as she peered into the darkness, listening to the calm still night, the cool air fresh and rejuvenating. During these twenty minutes under the stars, seemingly the only soul awake in town, she transformed from intense, eccentric, experimenter, to sedate, soothed young girl, comforted by the accomplishments of the day, ready for the rest that will fuel her for the next.

Nearly home, she stopped to follow some fireflies as they investigated a signpost. She watched as the glowing flies fluttered carelessly in the still night. The three glowing comrades noticed Ava and twirled around the young girl, their reflection gleaming in her smiling brown eyes. Her eyes wandered with the small moving celestial group as they surrounded their next play toy. She was startled as the tiny group of lights illuminated a familiar figure. "Marty, what a wonderful surprise, have you been following the fireflies?" she said, upon recognizing her friend.

He looked up, the light revealed glistening cheeks, he softly muttered. "I've been waiting for you."

She walked over to the boy of the same height and stature. She looked him in the eyes, cupped her hand around the back of his neck and brought him to her. And for the first time in their twelve years, Ava and Marty embraced.

Marty cried and cried. She held him, soothed him, stroked his back, breathing deeply she tried to align the rhythm of her heart to his, he eventually calmed. They sat on a curb; the fireflies had gone, leaving only the moon and the stars to illuminate the two young adults sitting in a silent embrace. Heads bowed, Ava wrapped her right arm around Marty and placed her left hand on his thigh as he rested his head on his arm folded over his knees. They sat that way for hours. Eventually, she nuzzled her face into his neck. They cocooned in a trancelike state, not sleeping, but a dream like imaginative energy hovered gently around the pair. Slowly, they were stirred by the light coming over the foothills, the soft yellowish green of the morning sun reintroducing them to their surroundings. Only the last of the most brilliant stars lingered in the sky, they exchanged glances as they stood and stretched their stiff limbs. Marty spoke first, "Ava, my mom died," he said solemnly.

"I'm sorry Marty," she said, grabbing his hand. "Come on," she said, as she led him into their beloved foothills. The two slowly made their way through the rocks and the cacti in the peaceful tranquility of the early morning light. Marty lost his footing several times, but Ava, right by his side, would not let him fall. She guided the broken young man to the entrance of the cave where they walked to the edge of the light and sat down. Ava, with a hand on his knee, not breaking the interlocking energy of their touch.

Marty eventually lay down, resting his head on Ava's lap, and slept. Ava, in turn, closed her eyes and took long slow deep breaths, concentrating solely on the emotion inside Marty's chest. She breathed her life into him, and exhaled out his strain. He slept soundly, restfully. She felt the weight of him on her thigh, she felt the softness of his thick dark wavy hair, she listened to the sound of the air passing through his pursed lips. She sat breathing deeply, holding him for hours even as the moving shadows left them shrouded in darkness.

He woke gently, cozy in Ava's arms. Ava stroked his hair and lightly kissed his temple. He sat up, weary and dazed, "what time is it?" he asked.

"It's almost noon," she replied calmly.

"Don't you have to be in the lab today?"

"No, I don't. When was the last time you've eaten?"

"Dinner, last night. I'm not hungry though." He paused, looked at her sheepishly, even after years of constant companionship and countless times excusing himself to run behind a rock to relieve himself, he was still shy about it. "Excuse me a moment."

They both got up and walked to the bright opening of the cave. They squinted and shaded their eyes from the intense midday sun. She went her way, he went his. After years at Mav's Hollow they both had their preferred "spots." They reconvened at the cave's opening and walked inside together.

They sat in the light, backs against the wall. Ava asked, "Marty what happened?"

"I found her in the bathtub, she slit her wrists."

"Oh Marty, I'm sorry."

"She had been going on and on for months about how she hated it here, she thought the travel restrictions were unnecessary, and that she didn't want to live with a man she did not love. I knew it was serious; I tried to help out around the house. Government support came to talk to her several times, they brought counselors. She wouldn't get out of bed anymore; there was nothing I could do."

"I'm sorry Marty, I didn't know it was that bad."

"I didn't want you to know, I was embarrassed by her…and now she's gone."

"She's not gone Marty. Energy is never lost, she's just changed forms."

"You know what I mean Ava. I can't talk to her, touch her, laugh with her."

"She couldn't be here anymore Marty, she gave all she could."

"I hate this place," he said angrily. Why couldn't they make an exception for her? They knew she was going to do it, so what if she went through the radiation field, so what if there was a chance she could get sick. She wanted to die, she wanted to die in Larkspur, and they let her."

"Sometimes suffering is greater than all else."

"I know Ava. I know suffering is real, but they should've hospitalized her, they should've helped her get through it."

"You're right Marty. No one should be left to suffer alone."

They spent the next few minutes lying quietly in the sun. They soaked in the reality of their new existence, letting the warm sun restart their shocked constricted veins. The awakening blood tingled toes and fingers, softening the core. They lay as the familiar dry, hard earth supported them, enveloping them with the safety of consistency.

They walked back to town slowly. Marty was more in charge of his senses now, still, he lagged some distance behind Ava. He shuffled through the dirt between the rocks, following the natural curves of the earth. Ava abandoned her usual rock hopping route, instead following the ground to accompany Marty. She expressed something she had been thinking about since before the death of his mother. "You know Marty, there's a large section of my lab that I haven't used for a couple years. If you're interested I could ask Judith if it can be converted to a biology lab. I mean, I would like having you around more. We can work together, eat together, I think we should be together if at all possible."

"You don't think I'll distract you from your work?"

"I think the worry of not having you around would be more distracting than anything else."

"I think it's a good idea," he said, shrugging his shoulders, then kicking a rock. "I've been missing you."

Chapter 4

The rising sun tickles the top of the mountain, darkening the depressions, illuminating the ridgeline under an expansive glowing cloudless sky. Rocky, barren terrain recedes to solemnly flat hardened soil. Silence pulsates, parades through the air, leveling the vast open space. Rays of light begin to reflect off the mountain, sending golden beams reaching outward, promising the hope of a new day. Earth's endless momentum propels the day's onset transforming the glorious into the ordinary in a matter of minutes. The small space in time when the collision of the atmosphere forces sparks of light from dark, new from old, present from history, the time is fleeting, retreating almost entirely unseen.

Hawks scream, restless to pursue their swift merciless plunges, in route to plucking their prey. A country lays sleeping, dreaming in black and white, gray extracted year after year, lesson after lesson, test after test, strained, filtered, dark from light, day from night, the immensity of all between engulfed by the predominant way of being, led trustingly through the passage by those bestowed the praised gifts of the multitude. The land spread before her like the hands of God, she breathes deeply as she takes in the scene, this is the place, she thought, now is the time.

"Thank you all for assembling on this monumental day. This project represents a fundamental shift in the evolution of how this country enacts its commitment to human rights. While we may not be in the position to openly advance our policies throughout the country, that shall not prevent our necessary mission from being fulfilled."

Maggie raised her arms up to the open sky as the thousands of plain clothed military personnel looked on.

"I understand the sacrifices you have made for this country. With great purpose comes great responsibility. And as sure as we witness this great landscape, so shall many thousands and thousands of individuals, who without your remarkable dedication, would be deprived of the right of existence we so cherish. This is a time in our history when humanity and the preservation of all life has taken on a sacred equality. We have the rare opportunity to be a part of something far greater than ourselves. When catastrophic circumstances dictate drastic interventions we hope as a society we rise to this call to action with a clear mind and open hearts, not clouded by judgments based on race, or religious preference, but on the humble plane of acknowledgment that every person has a perspective that they cherish equally and as vigorously as our own, and that perspective shall never be justification for death, and furthermore, should always be justification for life.

"And yes, these are times when we feel, as a society, a justification for life must be given. We live during times when the color of your skin or your interpretation of God is used as cause for the most severe form of degradation, cause for humiliation, cause for abuse, cause for death. Today, we accept no such world without a fight. We believe it is not just our role as U.S. citizens, but our role as humanitarians, and individuals with an unwavering conscience for our fellow people; that we will not watch another one of our people, the world's people, be persecuted without our diligent, determined effort to declare and decry this unjust and immoral perversion of the human spirit.

"Today, we go beyond declaration, today, we attempt to save, in the only manner I believe it can be done, with action, peaceful, and nonviolent. Albeit, an imperfect solution, as your sacrifice is testament to. But, because of you, today, we provide opportunity to those who would otherwise have none. Understand every life we take in tonight, and throughout the course of the Redeye Project, would be a life lost. And, we as a society cannot afford to passively condone the execution of a single person, let alone an entire race, and still attempt to navigate our lives with peace filled souls. For when we dare not speak our mind and stand against injustice, we are not free; we are burdened by the knowledge of tragic loss. Our hand may not deliver the death blow, but our collective passivity allows it. I for one cannot condone the slaughter we have begun to witness. And while we wait for the perfect solution, more and more die. While we attempt to make all sides happy, more die. Today is the day we stop waiting. Today is the day less people die. I wish I could tell you no Europeans would be slaughtered today. I wish I could tell you we had more support than we actually do. I wish I could tell you more shared the ideals of this community, but I cannot. They do not think it can be done. They do not think a society like this can exist.

"We are here to prove people wrong. We are here to say yes you can make the preservation of every life the top of any agenda. And how will it serve our interests they ask? Besides unifying the human consciousness and transcending any experience possible by having the opportunity to save a life, I say, let me tell you. We will raise people in an environment which supports and nurtures individual development in a community first environment. We will normalize excellence, expect greatness, and embrace diversity. No more are the days of the degradation of the human soul. No indoctrinated preconceived notions based on sex, or race, or any other characteristic that makes up the human experience. We will not tolerate abuse, the rape of our women, the emotional gutting of our men. We will guide by example and practice. We are a society based on the incomprehensible value of

26

each human life as an entity to be expressed to its fullest capacity with no hindrance placed upon us by our brethren. Community, family, achievement, freedom, these are the principles we strive for.

"The art of intuition and grace must be nurtured and developed. We are an active society, moving towards great endeavors, great understandings as a whole. We have the opportunity to dedicate ourselves to the development of an enlightened human consciousness, that puts all people, and their survival above all else; above land, property, money, pride, power, above all the reasons we use to justify the exchange of human life for something inherently less than. For there is no greater calling than the preservation of life, and no convincing justification for the taking of, these are the principles we proclaim to live by.

"Now is the time we rise above all else, now is the time we save lives, for in the process we save us all. Today, I dedicate our new town, and our new hope as a nation, and as a people. Today, we put all life above all else, and we serve this goal humbly with pure intentions, for one life is our life, today, all our lives are made greater. My sincerest thank you and well wishes. I assure you, your contribution to our community will transcend all space and time, and we will change the world together."

She bowed slightly. The massive flatlands covered with a sea of inquisitive figures erupted into loud applause. The tension of the event was gone, they were ready. The promise of a new day is upon them.

*

"All we can hope for is the best. We have attempted to create a community for optimal human achievement, including a peaceful, thoughtful, creative and nurturing environment for all townspeople," Maggie said to Bea. Back in the familiar intimate room where the inception of the Redeye Project occurred, Maggie raised her right hand for emphasis. "But you know, as well as I do, Bea, that one cannot instill values in a person if the foundation is not there. The military personnel must come to believe in the project as much as you and I do for it to be a success."

Bea smiled at Maggie. "Well that was one hell of a speech," she said. If they weren't ready to change the world before, they sure are now."

Maggie smiled shyly. "Oh Bea, I don't know, one speech?"

"One speech, yes. The leadership Maggie, the faith in humankind... I dare say we are believers at heart who are bogged down by the nonessential because it is propagated institutionally, religiously, educationally, and governmentally. You have dared to redefine the role of institutions. The people will follow."

"That's just it Bea, we need them to lead."

"That will come from the new generation." Bea stood and grabbed Maggie's hand. "Come on, let's go get something to eat. I haven't seen you eat for weeks."

"Where shall we go?"

"My place. Pasta, wine, you need a little time to unwind."

"I'll call Charlie," Maggie said. She walked over to the phone and picked up the receiver. "Charlie, could you please give us a ride over to Bea's?"

The two women snaked through the underground maze of the White House. They exited the building into a cold, rainy night, which despite the chill, in their excitement, they hardly noticed. They waited a few moments for Charlie to pull up. They stood close together, talking and laughing, glad to be out in the open air setting off for a private dinner with no particular agenda, no company, just the two of them, momentarily free of burden.

Beatrice Halsey lived in a brownstone ten minutes from the White House. A successful journalist, she bought the home thirteen years ago when she was first sent to cover Washington politics. She soon met Maggie, and they have been inseparable ever since. The modest home, built in eighteen ninety-two, still had the original hardwood floors, and was sparsely decorated with antiques, pieces handed down by her family. Bea preferred the colors of fall, with warm accents of burgundy, gold and brown throughout the home. The original kitchen, including a wood burning stove, tried and true, spoke to Bea of a simpler time, fewer options, fewer decisions. Bea had always made do, hardships had come her way, but that was the past. Now, she was in her basic kitchen, drinking a glass of red wine, making dinner with the person she trusted and loved more than anyone in the world.

"How do we encourage women to complete their degrees?" Maggie was saying. "Maybe we could just raise the legal age to get married to twenty-five?"

"Oh Maggie, you're so bad," Bea said, shaking her head.

"Well, they go to school, meet a man, get married, and drop out."

"That's what they know," Bea said earnestly. "The opportunities provided to women are laughable, expand their access to the work force and you might see some change."

"Well, you seem to have done pretty well for yourself," Maggie said playfully.

"Yeah, but I never had a choice, the standard convention never appealed to me."

"Yes, well I suppose that might make a difference."

Bea turned and lightly poked at Maggie's midsection. "Oh, I suppose, I suppose. Of course it makes a difference."

"I'm not much for convention myself, and look how my life turned out."

"Beyond convention, my dear. You completed your education, and married, rather well I must say, but as far as I can tell we're right here in the same kitchen. Damned be convention."

They raised their glasses for a toast. "Damned be convention," they say loudly.

Maggie asked, "how did you keep from getting married all these years anyway?"

"The only man I ever loved died in the Great War, and after that, I was rather underwhelmed by my options, shall we say."

Maggie laughed. "Well many underwhelmed women still get married, my dear."

"I need the whole show," Bea said. "I couldn't care less what people think about this old spinster. I'm not here to impress people with my well played out life. I do what moves me, marriage didn't cause a ripple, I left it alone." She paused. "I thought you already knew this about me Maggie. My god, I thought you knew everything about me."

"Yes, an unspoken understanding, but it's always nice to hear you express how you feel. I like to see your mind work."

"This has more to do with my heart than my mind."

"It always does," said Maggie with a laugh. "And who are you calling an old spinster? Do not demean yourself by falling prey to some simple invented convention of females beyond the norm." The two women laughed lightheartedly, enjoying each other's company.

"Dinner is served," stated Beatrice. They took a seat at the small round candlelit dining table, beautifully adorned with fresh old-fashioned sunflowers, begonias, roses and daisies. Both sleepy eyed from the wine, they relaxed with the slow satisfying comfort of good food, good music and good conversation. Their bodies revealed their unguarded natural state. The tension of the difficult days melted away with the warm glow of the candles and the air filled with love.

"We don't do this nearly enough," said Maggie.

"Life as the first lady doesn't allow for many personal evenings for you to relax with your loved ones."

"Truly, you're the only loved one," Maggie assured. "Being the first lady doesn't interfere with much else. I must admit, mostly I love the opportunities the position provides. But yes, our infrequent dinners are the most unfulfilled part of my life."

"Mine too dear Maggie, mine too."

The next morning Maggie walked into her husband's office, her head still full from the conversation and wine from the night before. She was lost in thought, recounting the sounds and smells of her evening with Bea. "Well how did it go?" She heard her husband asking.

"Pardon?" she said, her trance lifting.

"Project Redeye, how was the opening?"

"Oh, well, quadrant one was completed on schedule. The place looks wonderful, very quaint in those vast open spaces. The personnel seem to be adjusting to their mission. I'm confident General Cartwright is executing the directives competently. The numbers seem to be working out properly. The initial deployment of one hundred thousand should be able to accommodate twenty thousand new recruits a year as long as they have to, but frankly Henry, I hope it's not very long."

He quipped. "Recruits? Is that what we're calling them, seems rather uncivilized?"

"Security and anonymity, that's what you stressed, no one can find out about this, Maggie. This would set a terrible precedent, Maggie. Isn't that what you said, Henry?"

29

"How are the accommodations?" he asked, without commenting on her rebuke. "I know you're committed, but staying the night, really Maggie, the first lady staying with soldiers."

"I didn't stay there. I had dinner with Bea; I drank a little too much wine and fell asleep on the couch."

"Oh, I didn't know you had come back from the dedication."

"You were talking with Trindle; I didn't want to disturb you."

"How is old Bea anyway?"

"She's wonderful."

"So nice she gets to serve on the committee with you."

"Her input has proved invaluable."

"I'm glad. I really do believe in the project, Maggie."

"I know, Henry. You wouldn't have agreed to it if you didn't."

Chapter 5

The addition of Marty's lab to Ava's workspace proved to be a harmonious union. Marty, intrigued by his opportunity to study the plant structures he had for so long been fascinated with, proved to be the ideal lab mate, companionship without distraction. His early work on the heartiness of desert plant cell structure has encouraged him to explore the countless possibilities of plants potential contribution to the environment.

Marty didn't have quite the zeal and stamina for research Ava exhibited, but his gentle presence rounded out some of her rougher personal edges. He looked out for the people in is life. He made sure she stopped at some point during mid-day to have some lunch. After he completed his work, he would go home and make dinner for his dad and siblings, making sure the young ones were put to bed. Then, he would bring a warm plate back to Ava. Ava couldn't always be trusted to take breaks or eat, Marty insured that she did.

Marty eagerly anticipated his return to the lab in the evenings, his work complete for the day, but Ava still in the thick of it. She wouldn't be quite ready to speak yet, so her expressions were nonverbal and often highly physical. She would always smile, and look so kindly at him with her eyes. Inevitably she would squeeze his arm, touch the small of his back, even hug him. He craved these physical exchanges so viciously, his heart would race the entire walk there. As the night progressed, he would talk to her. He would tell her about what he was working on, talk about his family, about how he missed his mom. He sat high on the platform of the laser so he could follow her movements around the lab, and his voice would be able to carry over the machines into the space Ava occupied. He examined her, followed the light reflecting from her large capable hands, to her long, lean, muscular arms, to the curve of her neck, freely exposed by the tying back of her dark wavy hair, up to the sharp angle of her jaw, her delicate cheeks and lips, with her prominent profile defining nose, and finally, her clear focused brown eyes. He talked to her, he watched her, and he healed.

In the three years since Marty's mom had died, this had been the routine. They nurtured and took care of each other. Ava, with her caring, accepting way, left Marty free to bask in the glow of her warmth. And Marty, with his practical, non-intrusive adoration that nourished from within, encouraged Ava to flourish.

During this time, he had become a man, not merely in physical stature, although he had grown to six feet two inches, he was skinny, and maintained the thin fresh faced physique of a boy, but with his composure and competence. He had lost his mother, he ran the household and helped raise the kids, and at fifteen he was no longer afraid.

Ava had always possessed the qualities that came with knowledge and composure. Her previously gaunt frame had softened, widened and rounded just slightly in her fifteenth year. Her perceptible female shape was accompanied by a softness and openness which had not been present throughout her childhood. Her confidence and assuredness had blossomed with the progress of her research, and the consistent and loving presence of Marty. Her movements were freer; she stood up straighter and taller, chest out, calm and strong. She no longer worried about how someone looked at her; she possessed herself, undefined by others. The years between Ava and Marty, adorned with imperceptible growth, like the subtle inching up of a tree daily, constant attention and the differences go unseen, but allow years in between glances, and the change becomes apparent.

Dr. O was like the parent away from a small child for a few days, surprised upon return by how much their child had grown. He too had keenly observed Ava throughout the years, and he knew she was learning exactly what she wanted. He knew she would achieve everything she had hoped. This trip, the maturing pair would appear different to him forever.

He studied Ava and Marty as they walked through the open field to the lab in the soft light of the early morning. The brisk temperature seemed deflected by the power of the pair as they walked purposefully to their destination.

Ava noticed Dr. O, hands in pockets, mulling around the front of the lab. Cheerfully, she acknowledged him. "Hey Dr. O, I didn't expect you to come until next week, but I'm glad you're here. I need someone else to harass for awhile, Marty's getting sick of me," she said laughing, squeezing Marty's hand.

Marty had long ago lost any apprehension he had over Ava working with Dr. O. He had looked wonderingly at the conciliatory doctor's face, and knew the Dr. wanted redemption, and knew Ava could give it to him.

The doctor smiled and shook the hands of his two friends as they arrived. They quickly went inside the warm lab, blowing their hands noisily as they entered the warm gray bastion of the machines. "Ava, I have come early for a reason," Dr. O began. He paused, Ava looked up with concern. "Doctor Ipstein is sick, he's very ill Ava, it doesn't look good." Dr. O opened his coat and reached into a pocket. He pulled out a note, the familiar $E=MC^2$ seal intact. "He wanted me to give you this," he said, handing Ava the note. "There is not much time to reply. I'm leaving again immediately, and will be back for my regularly scheduled visit next week."

Ava took the note. "Could you please excuse me?" she said. Both the men nodded their heads. She climbed the metal spiral staircase up to the laser's platform. She sat back against the body of the laser, pulled her knees up to her chest, and opened the letter.

April 1ˢᵗ, 1956

Dear Ava,

Space and time seem to be exerting their relative force on my personal matter, lovingly called a body. The last equations you sent me proved to be exactly correct by my calculation; nothingness is within your grasp. The maintained secrecy of your project is more paramount than ever, and I encourage you to continue to propagate the slow difficult nature of your task, and give no indication to Dr. O, or Judith, about the advanced development of your progress. My dear Ava, physics teaches nothing is as it seems, and every particle of light and experience we have is comprised of so much more than we could ever know. There may be no finer human example than all which surrounds your life. Curiosity is essential to the expansion of human existence, in your case my dear, the parameters with which you live necessitates your curiosity have boundaries. Placing limitations on energy like yours is dangerous at best, with your power of combustibility unparalleled. I don't imagine you will be able to suppress your wanderlust forever, and I fear the completion of your project will only inspire the natural desire to see it through. Ava, there are perils and hardships to be faced shall you choose to subvert the government and their doctrines. I make no recommendations on the course of your life, as I know you need no such advice from me. I warn you of the danger of a life pursuing your passions and dreams, and as I know there is little choice for a restless spirit such as yours, I wish you safety and honor.

With fondness and admiration,

Dr. Benjamin Ipstein

Ava stood up, turned on the laser, and touched the tip of the letter to the thin purple stream of energy, she watched the letter burn. She walked down the stairs and calmly approached the two men who seemed engaged in pleasant conversation, both laughing and animated. Dr. O spoke first. "I'm sorry Ava, I'm not sure what the doctor said, but I know it cannot be easy for you to hear of his demise. I've watched you grow very fond of him, and he of you, despite the fact that you have never shared company."

Ava looked at the doctor calmly. "In our absence of the usual physically comprised setting, we have been able to share and explore theoretically without the limitations and confinement the presence of typical physical stimuli can undermine.

And I have loved every second of it. But now, I must request I accompany you on your trip to see Dr. Ipstein, I will return with you the following week."

Dr. Opalman, visibly stunned, looked over at Marty. Marty, not the least bit surprised, shrugged his shoulders. "What did you expect her to stay in this bubble forever?" he said.

Dr. Opalman stumbled over his words. "Ava, I don't think that's possible. Have you spoken with Judith about this?"

"No, I just thought of it. Surely if you travel here freely, the radiation field must be avoidable; an exception to the travel moratorium can be made."

Dr. Opalman took a brief moment to compose himself then stated in a clear and authoritative voice. "This is a matter for the government supporters. The plane leaves at noon, if Judith clears it, I'll see you there." Dr. Opalman turned and briskly walked out of the lab.

Marty coyly looked at Ava. "What are you up to?" he asked. "You know there's no way they'll let you leave."

"Well, it just occurred to me how absurd this travel ban is."

"Just occurred to you? When my mom was sick it was all I could think about. And when she died, you were the one who convinced me the ban somehow made sense."

"And at the time it did make sense, but it doesn't anymore. No, I don't suspect they'll let me go, but I must try; there are things I need to know."

"What did Dr. Ipstein say to you?"

"He said what I've always known, that nothing is as it seems."

Ava hurriedly walked over to Judith's office. Judith's office door was open, and she waved her in from behind her desk. The hexagon shaped room had a large navy and gold braided rug, and an oversized dark wooden desk, framed by the three nearest walls, which were comprised entirely of glass, with the all too familiar foothills cascading in the background. "Dr. Opalman said you were on your way down," Judith said.

Hiding her shock at the doctor's warning of Judith, Ava walked into the room, and sat in one of the two large chairs in front of the desk. The enormity of the wide, high backed, brown leather chair made the five foot, seven inch, Ava, appear dwarfed and childlike, with her feet dangling awkwardly as she pushed herself into the back of the chair. Ava immediately repositioned herself to the front of the chair. With her feet squarely on the floor, and her beloved mountains in the background, for the first time, Ava challenged the foundation of the Council.

"Judith, you have always shown me great respect and latitude when it comes to my research. Now, a man who has been instrumental in the scientific process, and one who I always hoped to meet when the travel moratorium was lifted, is very sick. I have come to question the sincerity of the government supporters in allowing the people of our city to leave at all, and I have my reasons. Dr. Opalman for one, he safely navigates the purported radiation field with no apparent harm. I ask your

34

permission, with the council's approval of course, to travel with Dr. Opalman to meet Dr. Ipstein during his last remaining days?"

Judith calmly placed both hands on her desk. "I've heard about the condition of Dr. Ipstein, and I am very sorry. And you are right, we can create conditions in which it is safe to travel to and from the city without chance of harm. However, the lengths, as Dr. Opalman can attest to, in which we have to go through are very timely and costly, and we are not in the position to make travel exceptions at this time. Many people in the community have very compelling reasons to leave; you are not the only one. I can assure you, we are making our best efforts to clear the contamination from the area, but it will take time. You of all people, Ava, should know the vile, toxic nature a nuclear explosion leaves behind, and the difficulty which comes with trying to remedy the consequences."

"I do know precisely of what you speak of Judith. I suppose you had this exact conversation with Marty's mom a few years back. I was under the impression this community cared more about life than about time and money, this appears not to be the case."

"The tragic death of Marty's mother was a very unfortunate situation. She was troubled, Ava."

"Is that what you call someone who doesn't want to live by your rules?"

"It's about safety Ava, and in the interest of your safety, I cannot let you visit Dr. Ipstein. Please trust me, I have your best interests at heart."

"I trust you believe that, but I assure you, my best interests are subjective, and your heart and my heart have some very different notions right now."

"I understand your frustrations Ava. I respect your feelings, and although you may not like it, this is the best decision I can make."

Ava stood, smoothly saluted, and said, "yes ma'am." She began to walk out of the office.

Judith called after her, "Ava?" Ava stopped, but didn't turn around. "I care for you like my own daughter, and I'd rather you were here, unhappy but safe, than off into the unknown with your life at risk."

Ava turned to face Judith. "Life is nothing without risk. We are not here simply to do what has been done before." She turned and walked out of the room.

Ava headed to Mav's Hollow to find Marty. She stormed into the cave where Marty was sitting quietly at the edge of the light. He stood as she entered. She stated loudly, "I've been so naïve, so wrapped up in my own pursuits, so coddled by their classes and their assurances, I've been blind to the web right in front of me which surrounds us all."

"Ava, consider yourself lucky. You have devoted your time and energy to something that can change the course of history. If you wasted all your time trying to get out of here, you wouldn't have a decent reason."

"So you knew we would never be able to leave?" she asked defeated.

"Ava, when I went through what I did with my mom, I was forced to think of all the possibilities, and those possibilities led down some very dark and scary roads. I had to wonder whether or not she killed herself, or whether she became too much of a liability and was taken out. Asking questions around here is highly regarded, as long as you're asking the right questions, ask the wrong ones, and anything could happen."

"I didn't know you had doubts about your mom's death?"

"I know. I still hope I'm wrong. I would like to believe we are not a society of killers."

"Marty, if my research is ever going to help anyone, we are going to have to figure out a way to leave."

"We will Ava."

Ava resumed her research with new zeal. For the first time, she wondered about new research beyond the completion of this project. She was now close enough to imagine accomplishing her goal, and determined that she must share her achievements with the world. She knew creating a system to clear radioactive elements from the air would allow her to appeal for travel. A request the council would undoubtedly deny. She also knew, once denied, she would have to take matters into her own hands, and that her dream of changing the course of humanity, may rely on betraying the town which raised her.

The network Ava had grown accustomed to was disintegrating, Ipstein being sick, fighting with Judith… The long days of anticipation before Dr. O's return were a test in concentration. Her normally stalwart mind was prone to distraction and irritation. The pleasure she received through her exchanges with Ipstein had fed her quest for other worldly possibilities. She was allowed to exist in the realm of abstract expressionism, a liquid lifestyle fluidly moving through the boundaries of comprehension. She experienced a freedom of thought, in conjunction with shared human understanding, which she didn't think possible. Ipstein had provided a safe haven for outlandish experimentation through supportive and intriguing feedback. He spurred her interests to reach farther, aim higher, her only limitations being lack of creativity and inflexibility of thought. She had hoped to spend hours in the company of the man whom she had spent so much time with on a theoretical limb. They were explorers in matter and energy together. He helped refine her sense that anything was possible. The strength she gained in the union would help carry her through the last trying stages of her project, and defiantly into the next.

The arrival of Dr. O, her genial liaison, brought an unusual tightness to her chest. "Ipstein is gone," he said.

"I know of his passing. But gone, really Doctor O, as a physicist I'm surprised to hear you utter those words."

"Yes, you're right. His existence has changed." They were silent for a moment, then he could not help himself from inquiring. "How did you know? I gave strict instructions I would be the one to inform you." he said regarding Ipstein's death.

"Don't worry dear man; your authority over me has not been usurped. I felt the moment in time, eleven thirty-six, Wednesday night."

Dr. O. looked up at her in amazement, with a tinge of fear. "Precisely," he said.

"There are many tunes surrounding us, filling the space, we can hear extraordinary things if we find a way to listen," she explained to the puzzled Doctor.

"Judith and I have spoken, and we both don't feel it would be prudent to absolve our relationship because of the loss of Doctor Ipstein."

"No, I don't see why our interactions should cease," Ava stated calmly. She felt the uneasy burn of insecurity. She understood the game had begun in earnest. She was being looked at as a potential rogue operator and she must do everything in her power to seem inconsequential and harmless. The misgivings which arose with her foray into coy deceit emerged inside of her as an unwelcome visceral response. She must control her emotions she thought, to tip her hand so early on would be disastrous, she needed her resolute composure now more than ever. She let the rush of fear pass through her, noticed and bypassed.

Marty joined them at the front of the lab. He grabbed Ava's hand. "I'm sorry to hear about Dr. Ipstein," he said kindly to Ava.

She leaned into him and smiled. "Thanks Marty."

Marty turned to the doctor. "Have I shown you what I'm working on?"

Dr. Opalman politely turned his attention to Marty. "No Marty, I don't think I know exactly what it is you do in that overgrown jungle you call a lab."

Marty walked over to Dr. Opalman and put his hand on his back. "Let me show you," he said, composed. The two men walked away. Ava, relieved, headed to the perch atop the laser to be alone.

The men entered the green cavern with branches and leaves snaking throughout the interior walls. The vivid color and life of the room displayed a vibrant contrast to the rest of the gray, lifeless lab. Marty's workspace was part rain forest, part high-tech lab. Small spaces carved in the lush landscape allowed just enough room for equipment to reside, and Marty to navigate. The oxygen rich, humid environment left Dr. Opalman momentarily breathless. They toured the, forty by forty, space brimming with a lush tropical canopy, and teaming with the sounds and smells of the jungle.

"You've created your own ecosystem here," Dr. Opalman said.

"You don't know how correct you are. As I'm sure you are aware, the only plants well suited to our desert environment are cacti and a few hearty wild flowers. Cacti have very unique, resilient cellular structures which allow them to go months, even years without water. The benefits of combining the hearty, almost waterless life of cacti with oxygen-rich tropical plants could be extraordinary. They could potentially restore oxygen to the atmosphere, without depleting the very finite levels of fresh water. I've created hundreds of these low maintenance air purifiers, albeit some with more success than others. For example, the Argemone Pleiacantha completely rejects all cellular material from pussy willows, but if you combine Argemone Pleiacanthia and Winterberry Holly, the new oxygen providing species will successfully grow using one sixteenth the typical water supply. Coreopsis Tinctoria thus far has proved entirely unsustainable, while I have had the most success with Castilleja Integra, probably due to its parasitic nature."

"Sounds interesting Marty, but it's hard to imagine an amazingly abundant planet such as Earth needing help to replenish its oxygen supply, but it is ambitious son."

Marty felt queasy under the weight of the patronizing dismissal lingering in the air. "Unfortunately there are foreseeable circumstances where man's devastating impact on nature may prove too much for our mother Earth to withstand on her own. Certainly you can imagine such destructive forces coming from mankind Dr. Opalman. You of all people should not be naïve to the ruthless power of man."

Dr. Opalman's face drained of color. "Point taken."

"You see, both Ava and I are attempting to protect the world, she with physics, and me with biology. You may not fully understand the necessity of our actions, but we believe the best way to show faith in humankind, to do good above all else, is to be the initiators of the world we believe in. Faith is nothing without action. Faith in a better world can only be expressed by actions to make the world a better place. The callous direction some choose to take has been evident throughout history. The willingness of a good spirit to work just as hard to anticipate and combat those whom bring tyranny has been lacking. War, genocide, destruction, they will continue to occur until we create an environment where those things are not tolerated, an environment where the glorious and brilliant possibilities so far surpass the perceived power gained by conquering, an environment where the inherent value gained by beauty and peace are so overwhelming, there is no other option. We are here to help create that environment, and while plants with the ability to stay alive in a waterless oxygen depleted environment that can restore the balance of the atmosphere may seem unnecessary to you, history proves otherwise. And providing solutions to problems that can be foreseen, changes the course of history forever. We prove the solution is more powerful than the problem. The problem becomes obsolete, and we become a society focused on solutions, how to fix things, make things better, a paradigm shift old man. A shift you had the opportunity to be a part of during the Manhattan Project, but instead of finding solutions, you propagated the problem, and therefore you became the problem. Here, we are about solutions, so I'm not surprised you cannot comprehend my work, but please have the decency not to belittle me in my own lab with your arrogant judgment and presupposition about what is worthy."

"Marty, let me assure you that the world looks a lot simpler when you're fifteen years old. When I was your age I had all the answers too, or the solutions as you're so fond of saying. But it doesn't work like that. You can't rely on others to do good and bury your head in the sand pretending the threat isn't there. It was us or Hitler, Marty. And believe me, Hitler was not out to do good."

"Exactly, Dr. Opalman. You can only rely on yourself, not others. If you spent your time at the Manhattan Project making their bomb obsolete, all you would have to do is rely on yourself, it wouldn't matter what Hitler did. If all the energy, money and time we spent creating weapons and opportunities to kill was spent on making the weaponry powerless, and creating opportunities to save lives, it wouldn't matter if people wanted to do harm, they couldn't. Because we would be a society which values the preservation of life in our actions and deeds more than a loss of life. Until that time, we are not good enough, and I for one will not stop working for change as long as that is the case."

"People like you don't last Marty. What you are asking for is a world which values and rewards talent and achievement but not the power that comes with it. You will always be undermined by the dumb and greedy who could not achieve power by any means other than vile and corrupt measures. They are highly skilled animals so focused on their preservation they smell you coming from a mile away. Fear and intimidation will always weed out the idealistic egalitarians. The same society you are trying to help will betray you in order to selfishly further its own interests. People don't share your ideals Marty. Here in your bubble world you think people care about honor and harmony, they don't. They will stomp on anyone in their path to get to the top, sacrifice any moral they thought they had. It's survival of the fittest Marty, not the most honorable; and in this society power and making the rules mean you're a lot more likely to survive. You may want to change the system, but they won't let you. They'll eat you and your ideals alive, they're ruthless, Marty, you might as well learn that now."

"There is nothing you can teach me. I don't share your beliefs, and I don't need anyone's approval."

"You don't? I'm sorry, who do you think funds your little rain forest? You are completely dependent on others. They can end you at anytime."

"I will not live in fear. Every moment I spend pursuing these interests the world's direction changes. It's worth it, whatever may happen, it's worth it."

"I hope you really mean it, because there will come a time when that belief is all you have to hold on to."

"That's the difference between you and I Dr. Opalman, that's what time has always meant to me and always will, an opportunity to change the world."

Dr. Opalman turned to leave Marty's lab then stopped. "I'll do you a favor and keep this conversation to myself."

"That is no favor to me Dr., I am not afraid of the content or implications of my beliefs. The favor is to you, because you can pretend it didn't happen, and then you don't have to examine the lies you've been telling yourself all these years to justify your own cowardly actions."

Ava, still high above the lab, could not hear the conversation between the two men, but felt the chill of the emotion exchanged in the air as she walked down the staircase. She intercepted Dr. O. as he was attempting to leave the lab. "Dr. O., what's going on?" she asked.

"I fear Marty's extreme and divisive views may hinder our ability to work together."

"Since when did our working relationship depend on your acceptance of Marty's views?"

"Since he so plainly stated his lack of respect for mine. I don't want to be subjected to that."

"Dr. O., I want you here. There's still so much more yet to be done. I believe you are an indispensable asset to this project. Marty has worked here for years without incident, do not let one contentious conversation ruin years of work."

Dr. O. visibly softened; he lowered his head and spoke softly. "Is there nothing I can do to make it better, to keep the world from seeing me as a monster?"

"There is, Dr. O, stay and work with me."

Later that night, after Dr. Opalman had gone, Ava walked into Marty's lab. She rarely set foot into his workspace, and was again stunned by the indomitable presence of life that overwhelmed the space. She saw Marty deep in concentration, hunched over a microscope. She gently placed her hand on his shoulder. He turned, a slightly mesmerized look of searching still lingered on his face. Ava knew the look well, the combination of amazement and determination he often expressed when working. "Ava, I'm sorry. I didn't mean to jeopardize your project. He..."

She put her finger up to his lips. "Ssshhh, Marty it's okay. I'm not mad." She leaned in and kissed him, slowly and softly, lingering like long time lovers. She pulled back, brought her hand to his cheek. "I love you," she said. Marty blushed and smiled.

Ava managed to make great progress in her work while appearing to all those interested, except Marty of course, that little was being accomplished. The transcendental nature of Ava's research lent itself to remaining mysterious. Only she and Marty had ever seen her nearly perfected illusory creation materialize.

Marty's fascination with Ava's project grew as she progressed, and he took to watching the culmination of her work with her routine experiments at the days end. To him, her creation seemed like the most natural evolution of Ava's experiences. Knowing Ava, knowing how she cared for things, he couldn't imagine how she could do anything else.

By age nineteen, the year 1960, fifteen years after the dropping of the bombs on Japan, all the necessary components for Ava's project were in place. Her work became about the mastery and manipulation of transient physical properties. She and Dr. O. created more powerful weapons than ever previously known. She sensed Dr. O's apprehension at bringing such horrific beasts to life. She knew he wasn't ever quite sure what she did with them, but he marched on like a good soldier, hoping his orders had merit.

Marty mostly stayed in his lab when Dr. Opalman came around. They sometimes exchanged pleasantries, but things were better left alone between them. Marty saw how close Ava was, he knew where those bombs went, he saw the whole picture and Dr. Opalman's place in it.

Over the years, Marty and Ava's research routines slowly synchronized. Their rhythms and pace developed natural break patterns where they would eat, chat and discuss the goings on with their projects. After Ava's daily experiments, the two would spend the rest of the evening together. Marty no longer had as many responsibilities at home, as his siblings were more able to care for themselves. The two spent their evenings in a lounge area they built in the lab. As their accomplishments grew larger and more secure, the frenetic research lifestyle they had thrived on became less essential. The twelve hour workdays became eight hour days, capped by an evening of leisure reading and listening to the radio. The restless longing inside the pair was being soothed by academic progress and personal fulfillment.

Ava put all her work focus into creating one great experiment every day, expanding on the previously known principles of her work. Marty, limited by the small environment of the lab, had created many new hearty oxygen producing plants, but could not test their full abilities in the confined space. Soon, he would leave the lab and return to the free open spaces bathed in the sunshine he adored, but for now, he was committed to helping Ava see her project through. Meanwhile, their sense of urgency with each other had begun to dominate their free time. Ava looked forward to the time after her daily experiment in an equally profound emotional way as she did the experiment itself. The girl thought to be entirely comprised of drive and will, had become utterly content in the moments she spent talking and laughing with Marty. A new ease and pleasure consumed her. The bitter struggle she for so long engaged in became simply a part of her life, seamlessly synthesized with a happy girl in love.

The three pieces of furniture they built for the lounge were all made for two. They built a standard couch, a daybed, and a love seat. They utilized various quilt work fabrics from around Ava's house for the furniture, and hung warm rich tapestries to make the space cozy and private. Dizzy and light with love, the lab was filled with smiles and flirtations which altered the heavy weight of their endeavors. For moments in time they walked like many others in the world, light and free, hopeful about the possibilities each day brings.

Dr. Opalman's regular, biannual, week long stays could do nothing to dampen the dreamy aura the teenagers moved within. He noticed the looks, the smiles, the gleam in their eyes. He couldn't help but comment. "Oh my goodness, you two are over the moon for each other. It's about time," the doctor said. "Saving the world is important and all, but if you yourself are not living a life worth saving then what's the point? Don't get all defensive and philosophical on me, Marty. I'm happy for you two. We've all been waiting for years for this to happen. I must say, you're a hell of a lot more patient than most teenagers." They both looked at Dr. O. and carried on. "What, no response? It must be love. No meandering explanation or discussion on the meaning of love and how your work won't be affected..."

Ava turned and kindly said, "Doc, drop it. Now get over here and build the best bomb I've ever seen." He laughed as he headed towards her.

Many weeks after Dr. Opalman's latest visit, the pair sat atop the laser perch marveling at Ava's most recent experiment. They sat in silence for several minutes before Ava spoke. "Marty, I think I've done it," she said almost shyly.

"I think you have," he replied.

41

"The strength of the bomb is irrelevant," she said. "It is a simple matter of detection, tracking and interception. I mean, of course the moment of interception being where highly theoretical inferences play out. But it works. Thoughts from the air turn nukes into thin air, can you believe it?"

"I never had any doubt."

"I think we're ready to perform a live test, with a very small bomb of course. We can't do it from the lab though. I must create portable equipment that we can carry out to the mountains."

"Okay, slowdown. Take a moment to enjoy this time, right now, all the work."

"Well, it's not totally done, but Marty can you believe it, the greatest amount of energy human beings can create, gone in a flash, like it never even mattered."

She ecstatically jumped up and hugged him. "Well done," he said, laughing and holding her, "well done." They walked quietly hand-in-hand down the stairs through the lab to the lounge. They lay intertwined on the couch exhausted. Dreamily, with a sense of the greater world to come, they fell asleep.

They awakened a couple of hours later, as the deep red sky of the setting sun flowed through the high lab windows illuminating the tapestries that surrounded them, creating walls of radiating color. They caressed each other, softly exploring the subtle contours of each other's bodies which had grown so familiar. Ava explored Marty's broad lean torso, the strong tight muscles of his back. Ava focused all her attention to the sensation in the tips of her fingers, the sound of his breath, the feeling of his body pressed against hers. Marty felt the small of her back, underneath her shirt; he touched her stomach, her thighs.

Shyly, they worked underneath each other's clothes, until Ava finally gathered the courage to remove Marty's shirt and then her own. They lay together pressing their warm soft skin together, locking the energy escaping their hearts between them. They kissed, slowly at first, then rapidly, growing with intensity as their tongues touched. They removed the rest of their clothes and slowed again for exploration. Marty took the side of his still baby smooth face and ran it up Ava's leg. He ran his face along her abdomen, her breasts, down her arms. He smelled her skin, kissed her neck, exploring her body with his hands. Ava squeezed and grabbed at his slender hips, his broad back. They followed the energy and heat between them, until finally, they become one.

Chapter 6

Henry and Maggie Pelt were having their weekly Wednesday dinner in the blue room. They sat at one end of a long wooden table large enough to seat twenty. Light blue walls, accented by white crown molding, with a thirty foot high, elegant ceiling displaying a mural depicting angels with young plump cherubs cascaded above them. Maggie, who hadn't touched her food, loudly played with her wine glass on the table. "Henry, General Cartwright confirmed the Nazis have completed another internment camp near the eastern border," she said intensely.

Henry grudgingly raised his head to look at her as he placed both wrists against the table still holding his fork and knife. "Maggie, can we at least get through dinner before you bombard me with questions," he said.

Picking up her fork she stabbed a small roasted potato. "Fair enough, Henry, we'll talk about religious persecution after dinner, I'm sure there are more pressing issues we can discuss."

"Maggie, you're so venomous tonight."

She softened. "I don't think we're doing enough. I look at the numbers for the Redeye Project, and then I look at the numbers coming from Europe, and I feel incredibly dejected."

"I know my dear, we all do. I speak with Trindle everyday and the reports are worse and worse. I encouraged them to form a large coalition to confront Germany, but they are not eager to send their men into another war when those being persecuted have yet to stand up for themselves."

"They are not an army, or a country, they are people Henry, like you and me... before you were the president anyway."

"I know Maggie; I can't say I agree with them. If this was going on in our backyard I wouldn't hesitate to get involved. But logistically it's a nightmare, and the surrounding countries need to show a great deal of commitment before we would ever step in."

"Henry, you know I think the whole world is our backyard, so that argument doesn't work with me. We are not defined by the space between us, oceans, mountains, air, we are defined by our community, and our shared human experience here on earth. I feel like we should be doing more, a paltry twenty-thousand a year."

"Don't get down dear. Where are the 'every life saved changes the course of human existence,' speeches I'm used to hearing? I'm sorry to say Maggie, your pursuit in trying to save every last soul is an endless one fraught with despair and disappointment."

"That's no reason not to try Henry."

The next morning, Maggie woke to find Henry had already left his sleeping room. Usually, she heard the fastening of the metal braces he used to support his legs in order to be able to stand for short periods of time when delivering speeches, but this morning, deep asleep in the predawn hours, she was not to rouse. She sat up in bed and watched as the first light appeared; a small green line gave way to violets and pinks. She stayed wrapped in her warm down comforter until the rising sun fully announced its presence. The realization of the contentious previous evening's dinner rose inside her, which led her to recall the lurid, haunting elements of her dream.

She often dreamt of her childhood home in upstate New York, last night was no exception. The unsettling physical vulnerability she always remembered feeling throughout her childhood played out in her dreams with intense war like scenarios. This particular dream involved intruders attempting to get into her home at night. She was a child of eight or nine and her mom was the only other person in the house, asleep on the top floor. Three men surrounded the house, each with pistols. She herself had a pistol and peered out the window to ascertain their positions. She ran from her room to the terrace and leapt onto a nearby tree to intercept the men before they entered the home. One of the men heard her. She aimed her gun, pulled the trigger, and nothing, the gun did not fire. She leapt from the tree to the ground and ran. She hid amongst the trees and tried her weapon again, still nothing. She thought of her mom alone asleep in her bed, she tried to alert the neighbors. She felt a burning sensation in her back before she heard the sound. She couldn't move, couldn't speak, she felt the presence, the burning. That's all she could remember.

Maggie shivered with the chill of the recollection. She left her bed for the warm refuge of the shower. Maggie allowed the water to pour over her face, her chest. She slowly rotated, letting every square inch of her flesh be smothered by the heat of the liquid. She sat in the corner of the shower under the heavy stream. She listened to the strange sound inside her head when the water poured over her, like her skull was the roof of a car in a rainstorm. The protection of her structure, the dimples her skin formed, the releasing of her muscles, she was keenly aware of her body, the part of her she tried to ignore; her womanhood, her sexuality, her wants and desires. She turned off the valve, dried herself, dressed, and headed for her husband's office.

She found him behind his familiar large wooden desk, talking on the phone. Taking a seat in a chair in front of his desk, she quickly ascertained he was speaking with Trindle. Her husband held up a finger to motion he'd be off shortly, and said into the receiver, "okay my dear boy, let's talk tomorrow after you have a chance to speak with Parliament. Let me know if you hear anything sooner." Maggie's ears perked up, surprised by the decisive tone of her husband. He continued. "Goodbye old chap, do try and get some rest tonight, this torrid pace you keep is bound to catch up with you if you're not careful. Okay. Good day." He put down the phone and cheerily greeted his wife. "Good morning Maggie, how did you sleep?"

"Well. Although, I had another nightmare, which left me slightly disturbed, but I am well rested nonetheless."

"Very good. I have some news I know you will appreciate."

"You and Trindle have come to some sort of conclusion have you?" she guessed.

"We have. While we don't totally agree on strategy, we do agree our presence has become necessary in the war."

"I hear that with great sadness and responsibility, yet with understanding that it must be so."

"You were ready to come to blows over our lack of involvement last night, Maggie."

"I, like you, had always hoped a peaceful resolution could be found, but in the wake of no preventative efforts to control an event like this from occurring, this option will hopefully save more than it takes."

"I know it is not ideal, Maggie, and you're right, maybe we could have done more sooner, but we will do all we can now."

"I'm glad Henry. So what needs to be worked out with Trindle?"

"Well, I have proposed a united front attack coming through France. Trindle would like to split forces and surround the enemy. I do not believe in splitting forces. He will discuss the plans with his counsel, and I with mine, but I've agreed either way, we will enter the war. Give us a month, maybe two, to make the necessary preparations, and we will declare war against the axis powers."

Momentarily startled by the sight through the window, Maggie stood and pointed. "Look Henry, it's snowing. Snow in early December, it's going to be a long, cold winter."

"Hopefully not my dear, hopefully it will be a short, productive, historically profound change in time," he said proudly.

"I hope so, that sounds like just what this country and this world needs. We shall see."

Maggie left her husband's office with a subtle queasy foreboding. She had nearly an hour before her Redeye Project year end review meeting, she decided to wander the hollow, familiar, yet unforgiving halls of the place she had called home for the better part of a decade. Still lost in the expanse of endless chambers, she was reminded of her time away at boarding school. A place with procedures and the pressure of grand history, she felt unable to measure up, a fraud even. Who was she, a lonely, scared girl, too tall, too severe to be revered, to be walking these fabled halls? The walls of expectation encapsulated her fear, her unworthiness firmly inside her seeking its way out, tightening her throat, blurring her vision, she panicked slightly now, as she felt her body slipping away from her.

The grand old door to the study moved slowly, unveiling the large roaring fire maintained at her request. She quickly scurried over to the chair before it comes, she curled up in the corner and listened to the popping, crackling of the blazing wood, her heavy breathing eased by the warmth and comfort of the room. She feels the tingling in her back, the pit in her stomach, the ache in her feet. She slowed her breathing, taking long deep breaths; she inhaled the pungent smell of wood burning, and exhaled the tension of her racing mind. The sizzling and cracking of the fire helps draw her out, the smells and sounds, her stomach releases, her feet relax, the tingles move into her head. She will be okay, it will not take her today. She rests her head against the side of the chair, and breathes, and listens.

She wakes to the soft stroking of her hair. Disoriented and weak, she makes no attempt to get up. She hears the fire, sees the books, the beautiful warm natural wood tones of the room, then she remembers, we are going to war. "Maggie, Maggie," she hears Bea saying softly, "sweetheart, are you okay?" Bea squeezes in the chair with Maggie and holds her. They sit for awhile cozy by the fire, free from urgency, settled in together.

Maggie, regaining her senses, repositions herself and turns towards Bea. "Is it time for the meeting?" she asks.

"Forget about the meeting," Bea replies, dismissive of the task.

Maggie, realizing she is unfit, does not object. In a concerned voice, Maggie asks, "I guess you've heard then?"

"Well, yes."

Maggie sat up, concerned. "Frankly, I'm surprised you know about it. Did Henry tell you?"

"Everybody knows. It's all over the news."

"The news? He said we were waiting for a month, maybe two."

"Maggie, the attack, Pearl Harbor, haven't you heard?"

"No, what attack?"

"The Japanese bombed Pearl Harbor, a complete surprise, thousands are feared dead. It's tragic."

"Oh my gosh, when did this happen?"

"This afternoon, well, morning local Hawaii time."

"What have we said? I mean what has Henry said?"

"Nothing yet."

"I must talk with Henry. Why did no one wake me?"

"Maggie relax. Your body is asking you for rest. You know how bad it can get if you ignore the warning signs. I came as soon as I heard, nobody knew where you were. Sit, I'll make you some tea." Bea rose. "Stay there, I'll bring your favorite cookies, just rest. I know it's not easy for you to take time for yourself, but you will break, Maggie."

Bea's advice was the only she would allow to occasionally supplant her own.

46

Maggie suppressed the little fight she had inside of her. "Could you bring peppermint tea please?" she said, as she settled back into the chair.

"Of course," Bea replied warmly as she left the room.

The two women sat together by the fire with their tea and cookies. "Henry had already decided to enter the war this morning. That's what I thought you were talking about," Maggie said.

"Well he certainly has just cause to join the war now."

"I guess this does make it easier."

"Yes. It's amazing how the loss of life makes it easier to justify the loss of more. The tragic cycle of events with such enormous momentum no one can seem to stop it. No one really seems to even want to," Bea lamented.

"They are unable to actually rely on each other," Maggie furthered. "They meet, and smoke and drink, and wonder suspiciously who'll stab them in the back. They cannot take each other at their word. The only sure thing is there will always be someone on the horizon clamoring to gain power, and the only effective way for the incompetent to achieve power is by force. Kill or be killed, the most ruthless rise, look at Hitler."

"I'm so sick of that explanation," Bea said. "We as a society decide the policies we accept, we always, as a collective union, can exert more power and force than any regime."

"I agree with you Bea. But that's the way they think, and we are a passive society, we absolve our power to those who want it most."

*

"There comes a time in the course of human existence when faith and reason have been broken. A time when no thinking, feeling man can ignore the course laid before him and refute the action he must take. We are a civilization of laws and morals. And when these underpinnings of society are challenged, the preservation of humanity is threatened. My responsibility as leader and caretaker for our union dictates I must do everything in my power to ensure the fabric of our society remains strong.

"We have been stripped of our security by a vile, unprovoked attack. Our role as peacekeeper of the world has been undermined in a farcical and cruel manner, defiling the very process meant to ensure the safety of mankind. A nation, so callous as to commit acts of murder on an unsuspecting, innocent democratic nation without provocation, has broken the most sacred code of a citizen of the world, and there will be no mercy for such action. Vengeance must be swift and strong. Without deference to the right of a sovereign country to live without fear of threat from imperialist governments, there can be no harmony, no world worthy of inhabitants.

"The ideological conflicts occurring throughout Europe are ones, I believe, are better solved diplomatically than with bloodshed. For the belief systems of the people behind the devastation are what drive them, and we cannot change beliefs with force. We have provided support to our friends in hopes all-out conflict could be avoided. We have done everything short of war to end the tyrannical persecution of our fellow people. Now, the fight has been brought to our doorstep. An immoral enemy has begged us into action. And I say here today, be careful what you beg for. We will treat you like the scoundrels you have proven to be, no questions asked. Today, my fellow Americans, with the utmost reverence toward liberty and freedom, we the United States of America, declare war on Japan. May our troops fight hard, secure their mission, and come home safely."

The flurry of reporters clamored to ask the president questions. "Mr. President, why declare war only on Japan when Hitler and Germany are threatening to take over Europe?"

"We have been attacked by one country and our military action has no contingencies or need for approval under such circumstances. The same cannot be said for our entrance into Europe. In order to fight an enemy surrounded by sovereign nations we must work together for the proper course of action. And as Germany has not successfully executed an attack on our homeland, I do not think Britain, or France, or any other European nation, would take kindly to us setting up major military operations on their land without permission."

"But it is not out of the question?"

"I think we can safely say after yesterday's attack on Pearl Harbor, nothing is out of the question."

"Mr. President, how could a United States military base be approached by hundreds of planes without being aware of their presence until it was too late?"

"We are first and foremost human beings. Our men believed we were at peace. Their unsuspicious minds were not alerted by the warnings. The attack against our country was unprecedented, neither you, nor I, would have responded any differently than the innocent men at Pearl Harbor. Lest you hold your judgment, at least until you have encountered the same situation, and I daresay, you would not be here to ask me such an arrogant question if you had. Good day, gentlemen."

As was customary, all reporters and nonessential staff members were immediately ushered out of the press room. The president was helped back into his wheelchair and taken to his office. Immediately he phoned Trindle in England. "Hello, good friend."

"Hello Henry, how are spirits over there?"

"Low as you might imagine. I must say, we have been made the fool. Sitting on our hands to be whacked upside the head conveys weakness, or stupidity, or both. Our enemy is emboldened."

"Until yesterday you had no enemy."

"Enough, Trindle." The President said forcefully. "Yes, by proximity you have faced far graver dangers than we have. But your insistence on protecting your people, your way, has stalemated our efforts, while the rest of the world moves freely. A lame-duck crippled by our allies."

"Spare me the analogies, Henry. There was never any reason to believe you would be attacked."

"What about now? I have to go out there and tell people we're only declaring war on Japan because our supposed allies wouldn't want us on their land."

"Henry, we are very close. Rolen's people have sacrificed more than any. We cannot lose his confidence. We are very close to coming to an agreement. It is rather unfortunate that your two strongest allies have the enemy in between them; the approach becomes that much more sensitive."

"I feel I've been far too sensitive to both your concerns. The Jews are the ones being persecuted, need I remind you. My patience is nearly gone. Baptiste will let us go through France, with or without you."

"I didn't know Baptiste had a say anymore. Surrender has consequences. Henry, we will come to an agreement. The Japanese attacks have changed the tenor of the conversation, I assure you."

"Good day, Trindle."

"Henry. I am sorry." The line goes dead.

Maggie entered his office and seated herself in a chair in front of his desk. "Henry, I think you are doing the right thing. You've proven yourself as a wonderful leader. You helped bring the country out of poverty and despair. Times are hard, but people have faith in you, they trust you. They will wait until you decide the time is right to invade Germany. They have not forgotten your strength and character. Henry, win the war with our allies and no one will condemn you for not going it alone." He leaned back from his position hunched over the desk. She softened her voice. "Henry, there is no one that I would rather have making the decisions for the fate of our country than you."

He looked up at her. "Not even you?" He asked quietly.

"That is not even a reasonable assertion."

"If it was?"

"The entire course of history would have been so dramatically altered we could never know. Henry, I believe in you. The country believes in you. Full fledged war will be upon us soon enough. We must succeed."

"It will not be easy," he said, speaking with more authority now. "Hitler's army, unfettered by intervention, is well organized and powerful. He has a stranglehold over his people like history has rarely witnessed. They want to believe in him so badly, and have become so afraid of what happens if they don't, he has become a god."

"They want to believe they are part of the most powerful country in the world," she said. "what they have to go through, or why, is irrelevant, it's the pursuit of power that blinds them. Domination in the name of religion, or race, or purity, whatever they call it, it always comes back to power."

"That's right. Somebody's got to have it, and no one will survive the type of power employed by tyranny. Benevolence through force, the cruelest oxymoron of them all, is our only option."

"Is the military ready?"

"It will take the effort of the entire country. The massive call up of forces will leave businesses and families strained. We are talking millions of troops."

"Millions?" she repeated.

"This war will determine the entire course of human history," he declared.

Chapter 7

Ava spent nearly a year creating portable components for her device. Final preparations for the first uncontrolled open-air test of Ava's device were made. Marty prepared a simple vegetable soup for the long night ahead. The two set out just after midnight under a cloudless brilliant starlit night. They took their time, savoring their eager anticipation. Ava's great excitement was expressed through a quiet confidence. If happened upon they would be mistaken for nothing more than two young lovers on a moonlit stroll. Their calm assured nature would betray nothing of the magnitude of their impending operation.

They walked hand in hand for most of the unfamiliar route. The test location was far away from Mav's Hollow. If they were found, they wanted to make sure to keep the secrecy of their hideout intact. The near fatal blow of the discovery of the project would certainly be unmanageable if they lost the security of Mav's Hollow as well. The hour walk in the brisk desert night air left them rosy cheeked and bright eyed, ready to test the limits of human comprehension.

Ava efficiently assembled the device. She set the coordinates for the nuclear warhead. After enabling her creation, she and Marty took their seats on a large boulder. Ava looked over at Marty. "Are you scared?" she asked him.

"Not at all. I have not one doubt."

She smiled. "Here we go," she said nervously. She pressed the button.

A narrow, three foot long, rocket entered the sky. The intense bright white light propelling the warhead shattered the tranquility of the night. Almost immediately after the warhead shot into the sky, Ava's creation emitted a thin, nearly imperceptible, ray of light into the sky. There was a large bright round flash of light, half a kilometer in radius, directly in front of the rocket. The bright light quickly turned into a totally black colorless mass. The rocket flew directly into the mass and disappeared. The whole occurrence lasted a fraction of a second, blink and you'd miss it. Ava and Marty didn't blink. They saw exactly what they had hoped, a machine generated black hole able to detect the presence of nuclear elements, intercept them, swallow them whole, and implode into nothingness.

51

Pure exultation overcame them as they leapt up victoriously. "oh my God," Marty said, "that was the most beautiful thing I have ever seen." He hugged her. "you did it," he yelled excitedly. She grew limp in his arms. He released her. She fell to her knees and wrapped herself in a tight ball.

She felt the cold, hard, smooth surface of the rock jab into her. Ava began to cry. Blood rushed to her head, heat rose through her body. The tears came quickly, violently overtaking her. She moaned and wailed like a wounded animal. She writhed in agony, slapping her hands firmly against the rock, she mimicked the devout during prayer, only she was offering, not asking.

She spent several minutes in the fury, a burning inferno of pent up emotion brimming over with grief and torment, the forces that had driven her for so long touching their ugly root, grown from a well of sadness. Her motivation and devotion had allowed the toxic fuel inside her to have productive means, the tight grip she used to maintain control over the forces that drove her were now broken with the culmination of her efforts.

Unguarded and overwrought, she lay curled up on her side, whimpering. Marty sat next to her and placed his head on her shoulder. After a few moments he laid down and wrapped her in his arms. Ava quieted, and stopped shaking. Exhausted, she was not quite sure if she could believe her senses when she heard a slight rustling. Marty sprang up alertly. "Did you hear that?" he asked.

She immediately jumped up. "I'll get the laser, you get the rocket launcher. Let's split up, go home, not the lab, they probably already checked there," she said.

"Okay," replied Marty. They jumped off the rock, grabbed the equipment and ran.

The moving group of beams of light breaking through the calm dark horizon was still several hundred yards away. Their pursuers communicated in hushed determined tones. The onrushing group slowly navigated the unfamiliar terrain with its changing surfaces and unruly cacti. The best way to travel in the low foothills was from rock to rock. If the men could flip a switch, and bring about day, they would have witnessed two gazelle like creatures bounding gracefully in opposite directions from the top of one rock to another.

Their silent escape greatly aided by their youth, agility, keen night vision, and their unsurpassed knowledge of the land. The distance that took Ava and Marty an hour to walk, was covered in twenty minutes with leaps and bounds. Running up to their street nearly simultaneously, they acknowledged each other's safe passage, and quickly snuck in their neighboring houses.

The next morning, Ava and Marty were up at dawn like usual and headed for the lab, with two new additions. Ava had fashioned two large pillows to hide the portable devices for the walk to the lab. The couple moved quietly through the sleepy town. They arrived at the lab, relieved to have not been intercepted. Ava quickly tore open the pillows and placed the devices in the hollow chamber of the heavy ion collision machine.

Marty made some eggs and toast, and they sat to eat. Before Ava took a bite, she softly spoke to Marty. "We were at the lab till eleven, then went home, we were asleep all night, heard nothing, saw nothing. No, our family didn't check on us, they're always asleep before we get back and not awake when we leave. That's it, do not speculate, less is best."

"Got it," he said, "now eat."

A couple hours later the expected knock at the door came. Too distracted and tired to work, they had been hanging out with the plants in Marty's lab, chatting, and soaking in the life of his creations. Judith opened the door to Marty's lab, no door is locked in Larkspur, crime is unheard of, the community, so close knit, the perpetrator would be exposed immediately. Judith stood alone. They had expected more people, possibly the entire council, but the presence of only Judith was a welcome surprise. "Good morning Ava, Marty," she said cheerily.

"Judith, nice to see you," Ava said equally as cheerful.

"Do you think we could have a seat? There's something I want to talk to you about."

"Sure," Ava replied.

"Marty, I just need to speak with Ava," Judith said to Marty as he began to follow.

"Oh, okay, I'll be here if you need me," he replied casually.

"Thank you."

The women sat down in the comfortable room created by the two young researchers. Judith's previously austere long blonde hair had turned into a generic gray closely cropped style, indicating the time that had passed since she was a vibrant woman eager to face the challenges of the world. Now, she seemed beleaguered, worn by the burden of her responsibilities. "Ava, we had an unusual event last night. I'm not even going to ask if you were involved, because you will either deny it, which will be of no use to me, or admit your participation, which will force grave consequences neither of us wants to deal with. Your relative anonymity is over. The council is suspicious and will be attempting to ascertain information through various means. I am one, which will probably not prove very fruitful. The codes of the community will not be broken, for, if we have no honor, we have nothing, but their curiosity is piqued. Watch yourself."

"I will."

"Very well then, I'll show myself out. Say goodbye to Marty for me."

"Thank you, Judith."

"Thank you, Ava. You are hope and inspiration through some very dark days."

Marty heard the door to the lab open and close. He walked over to the lounge nervously to join Ava, his heart pounded through his chest, causing his vision to blur, and his gut swirled with paranoia over the thought of losing her. Life without Ava was incomprehensible, and until this point, something he hadn't dared to consider.

He was visibly trembling as he reached her. She stood firm and hugged him tightly. "It's okay, Marty." she said. "Come, sit down. Let's not work today." She led him over to the couch. They curled up together, and slept until late afternoon.

They woke to the golden glow of the afternoon light, basking in the glory of the momentous night. Their nerves settled by the gentle interaction of their bodies, previously taut muscles released the strain of the emotional weeks leading up to the test. There was an overwhelming sense of calm, things had changed, life was new again.

The lovers, in each other's arms, spoke softly together of the future. "I saw and felt everything inside you shift last night," Marty began. "It was like your whole being had been geared for one purpose, and you achieved that purpose, and nothing will ever be the same. You self-destructed in a way, the crying, the heat coming off you. Now, there is space for different parts of life to develop. It's great actually, you spent the first twenty years so obsessed and focused, you've been able to accomplish your great life pursuit. You knew what you wanted, and never wavered, you made it happen. Now, I know there is still a great deal to be done, and the quest you are on will always be a part of your life, but the rapid trajectory of your physics knowledge is unsustainable. Not necessarily because you can't handle it, but because the community will interfere, and you will be forced to live a life of such deception to keep your research private, that your life will cease to be your own. I fear the only alternative is to come back into the fray a little bit, slow your research down, come back to the community, ease their fears. You have the opportunity to fine tune your black holes, if it even needs it, everything seemed to work perfectly last night, but you can investigate some of your other interests, maybe teach, have a family. I believe you could be the most accomplished twenty-one year-old in the world, and that's a pretty great starting off point for the rest of your life. I'm going to start teaching and I want to petition the council for housing. I want us to live together."

Ava kissed him. "I've been thinking the same thing. I know what you're saying; last night was like a transformation. I've been this person who read, and studied, and figured out how to make life safer for everyone, because I've been so affected by this deep fear inside me that my life was not my own, and people could take it from me in the blink of an eye. I didn't want to wait for that, I wanted to change it, make that feeling go away. I did what I set out to do. I mean, you're right, not everything; I'm determined to share my work with the rest of the world so that the threat of nuclear warfare is no more.

"But now I've realized there was so much more to that feeling than the threat of nuclear warfare. I somehow thought the key to my sense of belonging was all wrapped around this one project, but it's not. There is a whole complex range of emotions which comprise the burning hole in my chest, that's what I tapped into last night. As hard as I've worked to complete my goal, it has always been the easy way out, a way of ignoring any other emotion I may have been feeling. A singular focus is just that, one which rises to prominence above all else, at the sacrifice of all else. Great for making something as crazy as controllable black holes which swallow

54

nuclear weapons, and I wouldn't change a moment, but there has been room for nothing else.

"I needed every ounce of that desperate pursuit to survive the longing inside me. But now I need to know more, more about who I am, where I come from, why I am like this. The lab, this project, it's wonderful, but it's not everything. I look forward to the process. I'm no longer running scared, trying to stay ahead of my feelings, they are part of me, I need to understand why. Yes, I think it's time to slow down, I wouldn't mind doing a little teaching myself. And yes, we should live together. Marty, I could not have asked for a better person to walk through life with, we will be together always."

"I'm ready," he said.

"Me too."

They were granted one of the new houses in quadrant two. The single-story, thousand square foot, ranch-style house, white with blue trim, was just the domestic sanctuary the couple had been seeking. Not one remnant of either of their work lives entered the home. Their taste was simple and functional, a couple of oversized chairs in front of the fireplace, some books, a dining table. The two spare bedrooms were outfitted with two twin beds and dressers. The walls throughout the home were covered with pictures of people in natural settings from all over the world. Through pictures, they brought into their home the people and the places they themselves could not go see.

They split their days between teaching and research, and spent quiet nights together at home. They cooked together, read together, listened to music, and sometimes when Marty could convince Ava, they danced. Marty did plant the most unusual garden the desert had ever seen. He tried to keep it rather tame as to not upstage the neighbors, but he created a sustainable, nearly waterless, oasis for he and Ava to enjoy.

Teaching brought them closer to the community. Marty attended many community socials and maintained relationships with acquaintances. Life seemed downright ordinary for Marty and Ava. As the years passed they became upstanding citizens of the community, not solely for their research prowess, which was well known to be extraordinary, but for their warmth and kindness in dealing with the issues of the community and the people.

Chapter 8

"Lay down sweetheart," she said tenderly, "let me hold you." He carefully positioned himself on the bed, slowly she removed his braces. He began to relax as she stroked his forehead and lightly touched his forearm. He laid on her soft, plush bed, inhaling her aroma, slowly taking in her distinctly feminine smell. He ran his hands over the sheets. "I love it here, so warm and relaxing. I don't know how you do it," he said.

"I love you, Henry," she said, as she takes him in her arms, "the best I can. For all your bravery and heroism, I know sometimes the best thing I can give you are these quiet moments. After all, how can a man hold together a country if there is no one there to hold him?" She brings him tightly to her, kisses his forehead, he snuggles in. "I love you," he says, returning her affection. She holds him tight, all night, soothes him when he stirs, despite it all, he is forever hers, and she forever his.

Her modest house near the river indicated nothing of her importance to the president. His deepest, truest love, the one he nearly gave up his family for, his political career, all else that mattered, to be with. But he did not, could not, would not, so he lived in this silent state of compromise, partially having everything he ever wanted, wholly having nothing at all. Through it all, he has consistently remained the picture of what they wanted, not his mother, not his wife, but the country, those so desperate for greatness devoid of human folly. He faces a grave disease and perseveres, he loses a child and struggles on, he gracefully holds up the legacy of one of the country's greatest families, he is widely revered and respected by a multitude of world leaders. He does not know which drives him harder, the fear of letting down his family, himself, or his country. But somehow, right here in the dingy brown house on a hill overlooking the tumultuous waters of this country's history, he feels no fear, only hope and desire.

She wakes, rested and calm. She drains his catheter and returns to bed. He turns to her and reaches for her hand. "Ruby is it worse than you imagined?" he asks.

She smiles, she hugs her wounded bear. "Every moment with you is more than I ever could have hoped for with my life. Everything it is so far outweighs everything that it is not." She squeezed him tightly. "I know exactly what is between us, I wouldn't give it up for the world, not for anything, or anybody, not for public acknowledgement, or kids, or marriage, and I'm not willing to ruin you to have any of those things. What we have together is all I could ever want, it is not a sacrifice, Henry, it is what I enjoy most about my life."

He kisses her deeply, forcefully. With her he is everything he wants to be, virile, self-assured, adored, meek, callous, flawed, deeply, deeply flawed and still loved, simple, unwavering love. He lets the physicality of the moment overwhelm him. He is no longer the crippled dependent man he has been forced to live inside. He is strong, able, in charge, and alive. Blood rushes, sweat pours, and everything he feels for one brief moment releases, he has left himself, warm and glowing, in the fleeting world of acceptance and enchantment. He opens his eyes, he is back, he hears his breath, then hers. She removes herself from him, he feels the sweat that has formed between them, he leans back into the pillow and laughs. He is happy after all, right now, he is exactly sure of how he feels, he smiles and he laughs. He lights a cigarette, she gets up to make the coffee, she leaves him smiling and laughing as he smokes.

They spend a rare leisurely day together. The ever present winter snow sedates the landscape, covering its vibrancy, the life beneath waiting, gathering strength for its time. They eat breakfast, still in their sleepwear, they read the paper. He is mostly dismayed by reporter's frivolous interpretations of events. She assures him it is of no matter, history is not told at the time by journalists, it stands the test of time and many men's interpretations. Only the juvenile among us judge so swiftly and so coarsely. Their opinions, while seemingly relevant today, will be lost in the abyss of inconsequential narcissistic diatribe which so commonly afflicts the media. He is soothed, she does it effortlessly. Her mind is the solvent to his insecurity. He gently looks at her. "Ruby, you are God's gift to me," he says.

She quickly replies, "we are God's gift to each other."

Henry arrived back in his office mid afternoon, relaxed and refreshed. He was quickly jarred out of his peaceful solitude by his wife's abrupt entrance into his office. "Henry, how could you?" She exclaimed.

For a brief moment he thought she might be talking about Ruby, but they had long since left each other alone in that regard. Then everything that had washed away at the humble house by the river came flooding back to him. A wartime president, he thought, how has it come to this?

"Relocation camps, Henry," she said almost violently.

Startled by the despair in her voice, his blank stare sharpened. "I must make difficult decisions," he said resolutely.

"I know Henry, but you never even talked to me about it. Maybe we could have figured out a better solution?"

"There is no solution, dear. The country is terrified. What other country would let the enemy walk around their streets when they are at war?"

"The enemy? Everyone of Japanese ancestry is the enemy, not the government who made the decision to attack? Certainly the Japanese government did not ask for the consent of its own people before the attack, let alone the U.S. citizens of Japanese descent. U.S. citizens Henry, locked up, it's disgusting."

"It's temporary, Maggie. We can't possibly flush out all the potential spies with surveillance and covert operations. It's for our safety as well as theirs. You know the dangerous level of hostility out there. Besides, creating a separate living situation for those in danger is not unprecedented in this administration, need I remind you."

"Please, Henry, your pathetic attempt to justify imprisoning innocent people by comparing the threat of people of Japanese heritage to the rounding up and murdering of a whole religion by a ruthless dictator is so absurd it exemplifies the desperate thinking behind your current decision-making."

"Maggie, I want you to leave my office."

"With pleasure." She turned and slammed the door behind her.

Henry, exasperated, let out a heavy sigh as he returned to his desk to read the day's briefings. Since the passing of his mother nearly three months ago, he had been less willing to engage in spirited debate, even with Maggie, but he had expected a reticence after the watchful eyes of his mother had been lifted. He did not expect other relationships to dull. Possibly it was temporary, he thought, but he seemed less inclined to mull over strategy with Trindle, or defend his position to Rolen. A certain malaise had overcome him, with all except Ruby that is, the constant pulse of their relationship was not flattened. Only Trindle seemed to notice. He had said, "the fire in your belly has dimmed to that of a candle. For we all must find a way to regain our strength when the light from the being that birthed and nurtured us is extinguished. Don't take too long to rediscover your life source my dear friend, the world is counting on you."

*

The pre dawn banging at the door quickly migrated within their minds from all-out terror to resigned relief. The dull droning fleeting pangs that come with the acknowledgment everything they had feared, they had dreaded every moment for months, sleepless nights, dreamless days, the endless pitfalls of the mind, would now be replaced with the true terror that awaited them. They listened a moment longer, unsure what to do. They discerned a small group of men, the boot shuffling, stifled low whispers, they rose.

Lying in bed fully clothed for weeks, the simple act of rolling over, sitting up and putting on their shoes was complete before they heard the kids' cries. Quickly the pair soothed the three small children, tied their shoes, found their jackets, lit a candle and opened the door. The darkness revealed little of the three figures huddling at the door. He noticed the full beard of the man who spoke first. The movement of the man's lips and accompanying sound of his voice seemed out of sync. The man grew more hostile. "Do you speak English? I said, by authority of the United States government, you and your family are required to come with us." The definitive words penetrated his very body, he dutifully bowed his head.

They made no sound as they crossed through the cold, dark morning to the waiting bus. The pungent smell of urine soaked seats struck the family first as they entered the vehicle. The youngest began to whimper; his mother quickly shifted him in her arms and quieted the small child. Two families occupied the two back rows of the bus. Fearful parents with sleeping children scarcely glanced at the newcomers.

They spent the rest of the day witnessing the rounding up the last of the central California group. They could relieve themselves whenever the bus stopped for more families. No diapers for the babies, no food, no water, no talking, especially in Japanese.

After sundown, they finally came upon the plain barrack like structures diligently aligned in rows. They shuffled off the bus and joined the long line leading up to a table with two men in uniform dishing out a goopy white mush. An older kindly woman made eye contact with him. She smiled, and quickly said in Japanese, "they are not cruel, you will not be harmed." His eyes softened, he bowed.

The bare essentials, that's all they were given, freedom to move within the barbed wire of the camp, to shit in a hole, to kill time. No explanation was given, nor was one needed. They had become the scourge of the earth. Treated with verbal disdain, but without physical assaults, they grew listless and despondent. Casual relationships outside of the family could be maintained, but any evidence of a bond was spurned by watchful guards. They were the enemy, potential co-conspirators in the atrocity at Pearl Harbor. Unable to contact extended family, their loneliness was compounded by their isolation. But still, they were lucky; many had been separated from their immediate family, grandmothers in their eighties without a loved one to care for them, parents without their children. Yes, they were lucky; they at least had each other. Their unanswered questions did not include where is my wife, my child, my mother?

The long cold nights interspersed with sniffles, coughs and whimpers did more to brutalize the soul than the dull, aimless days. A mind left unsatisfied, without stimulation, is a troubled mind indeed. The wanderings of the soul guided by fear and loneliness lead to a path so eerily idle, the silence begins to echo, leading to reverberations of melancholy. A melancholy so thick and pervasive, all emotions get caught in its sticky surrounding, trapped in a world of expressionless misery. The activity and noise level of the camp gradually declined to a whisper. The kids rarely played, the adults rarely met. The camp of several hundred became a ghost town of shattered dreams and lives derailed.

*

Her swirling mind led her farther and farther away, deeper, through the mass of regularity, past the intellect, below knowledge, to the guts, the visceral uncontrolled experience of the unmistakable emotion of a full mind and body engaged. Her breath, her warmth, the way she slowly explored the dips and curves of her body. The locked energy emanates, and circulates between them. Heat rises off them, changing the physical structure of their surrounding, leaving an enchanting and dreamlike state of mystery and wonder. They enter willingly, unguarded, searching the warm golden light, touching its soft radiant glow, succumbing to the grand peacefulness of the present. Altered, the world appears undaunted free of questions and insecurities, freedom flows, overwhelms and restores. Senses flaring, an entangled mess of sounds and smells, touches with fingers of fire, the brilliant bounty of love holds and releases. They forage on, through the deep thickets, unafraid by the strong presence of the surrounding life, excitement rushing, guiding them through the harrowing passes, rewarding their perseverance every step of the way. Engulfed and unfettered, they glide, above reckoning, beyond revolution, they have found transcendence.

The avenging presence of Bea in her life left Maggie tireless and sharp, confidence high, focused and strong, able to attack life, deplete her energy, and know she would be replenished. Maggie feared less, strove for more. She had a tried-and-true resource, Bea, a foundation solid and withstanding. The aches and pains of experience were eased. A beating, thriving drive swelled through her, pushing through the murky water, purifying and enriching. A spiritual source of guidance, of comfort, longing ceased, travails overcome. She was not alone, her body knew it, her mind knew it, she glides.

Their trips to the country house were among Maggie's most cherished memories. The quiet and solitude enhanced the intensity between them. The simple, turn-of-the-century, two-story cabin served as both a resting place and a house of worship for the revered natural setting. Tall, luscious maple trees surround the cabin. The soothing sound of the rushing river accompanied by bird calls and rustling leaves became the soundtrack of their love. Sometimes, briskly, they carry on talking, burying themselves in the old spirit of the unchanged land; other times, they explore slowly, taking in every unusual tree hollow, marveling at the audacity and triumph of the un-impeded life. Hours upon hours they explore together, the parallel universe that is their country life.

This weekend, Henry at a conference in Europe, they spent their days fishing. Trout were plentiful this time of year and Bea had caught Maggie's contagious enthusiasm for the hobby she grew to love as a child. The river, swollen with the runoff from melting snow, rushed by as they stood perched on the large rocks at the shore. "Maggie?" Bea called over the roaring river. "Did you read that letter from Schumann yet?"

"Not yet, I'm planning to read it tonight," Maggie replied.

"What do you think it's about?"

"Well, I know her local work with women and children has expanded to reach most of southern India and she's expressed interest in creating an international program."

"Really?"

"Yeah, along with Rosa, Amelie, and myself, we are hoping to create an international doctrine on human rights, including women's rights."

"Oh, that sounds amazing," Bea said enthusiastically.

"After all the time and energy spent creating the framework for the Redeye Project, the seeds have been planted. It would be a waste not to share some of the principles with the general population."

"I was wondering how big this pursuit would get. I'm really glad you're taking this farther."

"Sometimes I feel like it's taking me. Like I tapped into the power of a belief system so much greater than myself, and while I keep reaching and searching for meaning, the direction and scope continue to grow."

"A vehicle for greatness, that's what you are."

Blushing, a large smile came over Maggie's face. "Hardly," she said shyly.

Bea smiled back. "Come on, you know what you've done and continue to do, helping people of all kinds. And now, working with women from all over the world, it's pretty amazing."

"Really, I'm simply refusing to ignore a massive and underrepresented part of the population, which I happen to be a part of, and certainly have a vested interest in the empowerment of. Truly, it's rather self-serving."

"Oh please, Maggie. Manipulating stock prices is self-serving. Intellectually and emotionally engaging yourself to demand fair treatment for others to the point of clear personal sacrifice and strife is quite far from self-serving, regardless of any personal benefit that may result from your work. Nothing you are doing is easy. Creating an international collective with the talents and bravado to challenge the structure and hierarchy of not only the U.S., but around the globe, is an extraordinary feat not to be belittled. Self-serving," Bea scoffed, "I think not."

Maggie looked at Bea intensely. "I love you, Bea."

"I know you do Maggie. Now why don't you say we get out of this cold and fry us up some fish," Bea said lightly.

"Sounds good." Maggie said. They gathered up their gear, smiling playfully, and walked shoulder to shoulder back up to the cabin.

The soft light of the setting sun enhanced the serene candlelit interior of the rustic cabin. The two women cheerily prepared dinner with the sounds of Beethoven stormily filling the room. The delicate ease of familiarity, the light touch of a hip when passing by, a space with no tension, they were at home together in the cabin. The wine, the music, the food, sensuality on form, the charming dinner turned into cozying by the fire. Maggie quietly spoke into her lover's ear. "These are life altering days," she said dreamily.

"They are," Bea replied enchanted.

Maggie continued. "The type of days that assure you life is good, in an honest, spiritual human connectedness sort of way."

"What we are all searching for," Bea furthered.

"These glimpses of life coming together, the struggles, the heart ache, the joy, they're all here, these intense waves flash over me, like, I got it, I see it," Maggie says.

"I personally think kissing can tell you everything you need to know about the potential of a relationship," Bea says seriously.

"Kissing, the key to life," laughs Maggie.

"No, really, virtually every human emotion can be communicated through kissing: anger, fear, boredom, impatience, lust, longing, passion and in some cases, between those rare connections, transcendence. Kissing is a conversation with the addition of touch and smell and the constant exchange of energy. I'm sure not everyone you've kissed you've managed to see the limitless potential of human relationships. Some kisses lack range, lack growth, I daresay that relationship lacks as well. Without the beauty kissing your true love can expose, the world can seem a little bleaker."

"So a kiss is not just a kiss."

"Not between us."

"Prove it," Maggie says leaning in.

Chapter 9

The cold gray fog rolled in over the dark green foothills. The uncommon silence momentarily transported, still, serene thoughts grow with the color transformation. Dawns trepidations, the precursor to cracks and whirring, engines roaring, the ground below frightening with vibration, are slightly eased by the merciful covering of voluminous moisture. The visually impairing blockade brings reprieve to the young, homesick infantry, shivering through the night, posturing during the day.

Slowly they wake, thankful as they look up, they smoke, smiling and jovial. Frozen feet, soiled trousers, dirty faces, not the boys their mamas raised. But they were still here, braving through another day in a foreign land with so many strange sounds. There they lay, with the best friends a man could ever make, surrounded by the worst enemy they ever could imagine. The enemy unseen, faceless, voiceless, ever present, all powerful, and just like them, fighting for their lives. An enemy with no home to return to, more afraid of what happens if they don't stay and fight, than if they do; Somehow, the vile battlefield seems less troubled than the tyrannical leader they try so hard to please.

Some of the men take the opportunity to write, some try to clean up, some sleep; asleep or not, they all dream. They dream of a better time, the home they left, or the future they hope to see. A dark, resolute spirit has taken over the troops in recent days. The constant shelling, lack of supplies, and loss of life, have begun to take their toll. Worn, but not broken, they have managed to make it another day. These moments of bomb-less daylight to the soldiers is an average person's two-week vacation. A game of cards, a silly practical joke, their youthful humanity nurtured for a moment, scared men become boys again, oh so briefly, boys again.

Trenches, like the encapsulated maze of an ant lair, defines their space. Close, narrow walkways loom over them like controlling parents restricting their movement. The walls that protect them also enclose them. Weeks turn to months, the same hard dark bread, nuts and dried fruit. The canned meat and chocolate gone long ago for all accept the hardiest of conservationists. Those who expect the worst seem to fare much better, the most pessimistic possibly, the men who planned for months despite rations for weeks, the ones who expect the horrifying screams to fill the air, grateful it is not their own. The sight of a dying comrade, or enemy, for a human dying, whether a friend or foe is a tragedy that never leaves the mind; as unseemly as it is, they've already made space for it in the realm of possible experience. Always prepared, better able to anticipate the ravages of war, those are the ones who survive through will and grit, not happenstance. They seem to maintain an impenetrable aura of aloneness, a defiance to the surroundings which helps them get through. Wariness beads up and rolls off of them like water against an impermeable surface. Tormented, the constant subtle undercurrent that embroils them never boils to the surface. Time control, and measured release, makes these warriors seem three parts human, one part machine. Necessarily callous and contained, incredibly loyal, reliant and competent, but often alone in the corner during times of leisure, as if an emotional bond would snap the spell of survival. Wars make them; societies berate them, castigate them and subjugate them.

This platoon, comprised entirely of men younger than twenty-two, had its stalwart, its version of the perfectly composed warrior. Little was known about the tall lanky redhead, a quiet, freckly, eighteen year-old with a furrowed brow. He mostly kept to himself, the way they do, the men so focused on survival they leave little of themselves to be found. Not arrogant or off-putting, he was well-liked by the unit. Secretly they admired him, his unyielding commitment to stay alive. They were glad he was on their side, and particularly glad he was in their platoon. His will carries men through, he instills confidence, the battle will end, he will survive, and they can too. Late at night, when the silence is so heavy and death itself seems like the only thing that could break it, they realize they need this man more than they have needed anything in their life.

The affinity they have for their troop mate carried over into a quiet respect. They always left the best sleeping spot for him; he got first choice on extra supplies, when cleaning their own gear they always offered to clean his. He takes care of them in his way; they take care of him in theirs. Practical jokes among the men were common, but never on him, they had no interest in unsettling the man. For now, he fought hard for them; they know he could easily fight only for himself.

Strangely, for all the respect this man has earned within the platoon, he was utterly despised by the commanding officer. Few institutions hold so steadfastly to the blind conformity to a hierarchical structure than the military. Talent does not circumvent it, nor morality, nor justice, order and rank above all else, power or no power. The imbalance reeks of insecurity, arrogance, and dominance for all but the finest of men, for few can handle the responsibility of legions of followers, their life, their blood, their fearful eyes, without crushing any semblance of their own humanity. Any disruption of the hierarchy threatened the entire system with which they have committed their lives. Those who are elevated know better than to stake too much importance on any fledgling placed before them. Their survival and advancement relied on maintaining the discipline and order which rewards their decisions, their interests. The interests of the men below them were too varied and inconsequential to factor into the direction of the hierarchy. Few make decisions for many, no input, no assurances, no questions.

It is not uncommon for hierarchies within a unit to be created. Some men are simply more charismatic or more domineering than the others. Leaders within platoons have their place, keeping morale high, troops bonded and wayward soldiers in line. The danger comes when a member of the platoon rises to such popularity, the power of the superior officer is usurped. Orders are given, plans are made, but in battle, they notice the betrotheds strategy and more closely adhere to his plan than that of their leader. Dangerously, to the commander that is, they start thinking, using their instincts; they are guided by something other than the law of their superior.

Sergeant Pierce began to notice the shift in his troop two weeks into their deployment. They had faced fierce battles immediately upon their arrival in Europe. They took casualties their first day, three soldiers lost, the men were shaken. Quickly an unlikely star emerged among them. A man they jeered in boot camp for his loner tendencies and flaming bright red hair, now, always seemed to be in the right spot at the right time and know exactly what to do. They started to call him Ace; they said he always seemed to have a trick up his sleeve. If a bunker needed to be taken out, he'd do it; support for surrounding troops, he provided. He had an uncanny ability to predict the enemy's movements and know when his fellow troops were in trouble.

Ace's legendary status among the men was solidified in a week long battle with axis forces. His steady aim picked off dozens of the enemy. Every time the enemy seemed ready to advance, he took somebody out. He was catlike quick and chameleon like in his ability to blend in with the terrain. He always came at the enemy from different locations; he was one man whose skill and speed made him seem like many. While at war, killing is a revered form of protecting, there is no higher regard than that of being a savior. Even with the constant peril and risk of war there were few chances for a man to be a hero, the type of hero that risks his life to save others. Some men encounter those situations and balk in the face of mortal danger. Ace was not one of those men. It is not that he thinks for a moment he will be killed, for thoughts like those have no place in battle, it's that he sees men who need help and he finds a way to help them.

The first time Ace saved a life, it was actually that of the sergeant himself. The platoon was engaged in heavy fighting, as was his customary position, the sergeant was buried deep in the rearmost trench with his usual accompaniment, his right-hand man, the company kiss up, Private Gunderson. Mostly observers and commentators of combat, the high-minded pair seemed to have little interest in the day's proceedings. The battle seemed a stalemate, likely drawing down over the next few hours. In fact, the perceptible decrease in gunfire seemed to corroborate the sergeant's belief. He shouted rather absentmindedly, "maintain positions, looks like this one's almost over boys." The tired group relaxed slightly.

Ace did not share his commander's assessment of the situation. Keenly aware of every firing point, he noticed an atypical pattern to the stand down. The perimeter of the enemy's position had stayed intact, as well as its central point, but firing from the intermediary positions had ceased. Generally, a phased withdrawal will consist of the unit slowly shrinking back to the middle to track back tight as a unit. Rarely, if ever, as Ace had never seen it happen, does the unit track back in a spread formation.

As Ace was working out possibilities in his head he grew increasingly leery of an ambush. He pulled back from his position, stopped and listened. Firing was sporadic now and the men were calm and complacent. Ace turned and surveyed the area; he saw them, four men running from directly behind the unit to overtake the commander's bunker. Quickly he rose, firing as he ran, first-round, kill, second round, kill. Sergeant Pierce startled with fright as the whizzing bullets interrupted his daydreaming. Private Gunderson hit the deck, burying his face in the ground. Ace, nearly upon the attackers, fired a third round, kill, fourth round, jam. Sergeant Pierce fumbled to pull his revolver out of his holster. The last of the oncoming men recovered from the shock of Ace's attack, pointed his weapon at Ace, and fired. Ace had anticipated the soldier's shot and began a diagonal run moments before, the bullet missed. Ace quickly darted in before another shot could be fired to gouge the man firmly in the abdomen with his bayonet. He quickly twisted, pulled up and removed the bayonet, the soldier crumpled to the ground.

All four attackers lay dead before the rest of the platoon was aware of what happened. Silence overtook the field, a couple heartbeats later a barrage of gunfire aimed at the American hero filled the air. Ace quickly scampered into Sergeant Pierce and Private Gunderson's bunker. The rest of the troop returned the enemy's fire. The enemy immediately began to regroup and pull back; in a matter of a few minutes it was over. The sound of the wind rustling through the trees returned to the war-torn field.

Private Gunderson picked himself up off the ground. Covered in dirt, he sheepishly explained, "I thought a grenade had been thrown into the bunker, I was looking for it."

"Give it a rest Gundy. I suppose you're going to tell everybody that you fell in a puddle and that's why your pants are all wet," exclaimed Sergeant Pierce. Private Gunderson looked down, not realizing what the captain was talking about. He saw the dark stain on his camouflage pants, he grimaced and turned bright red. "Come on, let's fall back and set up camp. Ace cover the point," Sergeant Pierce ordered.

With slightly stunned looks on their faces, the men gathered in file formation. Glancing at Ace through the trees, some occasionally tipped their head to Ace, a few whacked him on the back as he passed. Ace took up the least coveted position, because of the increased danger, the point, at the front of the file, the first man to happen upon the enemy, almost always the first to be killed. An assignment usually rotated amongst the men as to not fray the nerves of the chosen, Ace would remain there for the rest of the war. Because, according to Sergeant Pierce, "well son, you've proved that you can handle it."

The slow, lethargic trek to camp was occasionally broken up with low grumbles and snickers, nervous pressure released by juvenile taunts. The fragile psyche of the men elevated through degradation. The usually untouchable Private Gunderson was now tainted in the eyes of the captain, and the shift was perceptible. Slowly, the spirits of the troop rose as their increasingly vile remarks went unpunished. They exalted over their new whipping boy, a smile here, an extra spring in their step; the timid, frightened bunch which had begun the walk transformed into a scheming vengeful squad on a hunt.

For his part, Private Gunderson kept his head down, ignoring the wisecracks and objects thrown his way. At times he appeared to be visibly shaking, possibly mentally recounting some of the more horrifying hazing stories he heard throughout basic training; sodomy with foreign objects was a common tale, excrement also seemed to be high on the list of preferred weaponry.

One fine example of predatory humiliation which quickly entered Private Gunderson's mind was executed by his very own commander, Sergeant Pierce. The sergeant shared the heartwarming tale with every new troop he received. With pride, the sergeant recounted the day he and fellow soldiers weeded out an unworthy member. The sergeant's story raced through Private Gunderson's head now as the men homed in on him.

Sergeant Pierce's story of military justice, as interpreted by Gunderson, went like this: the "fairy," as the sergeant put it, exhibited none of the qualities a true soldier should possess. The fairy was slightly built, with a whisper of a voice, he was meticulously groomed, private about his body, and generally kept to himself. He refrained from the usual tits and ass talk the men thrived on. He didn't smoke, didn't drink, and didn't grope the women in the local bars. The fairy had made the mistake of telling the men he was a virgin. Still trusting, he answered sincerely when on the first day of training the commanding officer asked if there were any virgins in the group. He, unsuspecting, was the only to answer in the affirmative. Although not such a strange thing for men of nineteen in the early part of the century, he was chastised and ridiculed from that point forward.

Pierce, however, did not share many of the particulars of the story and there was much Private Gunderson did not know. As it turned out, the young, unassuming southern boy, Pierce called the fairy, was both physically and mentally resilient. Despite constant harassment, the fairy never grew upset, never reacted, and never retaliated. He managed the brutal regimen of basic training seemingly with ease. The troop grew more aggressive and resentful of the charmed fairy they couldn't rattle. They were determined to break him one way or another. Sergeant Pierce and a small group of determined tormentors planned the assault for weeks. The usual methods of degradation had proven ineffective in regards to the fairy. Shit in his bed, nothing; piss in his canteen, nothing; cockroaches in his food, no response.

The boy's unwillingness to join the fray left a looming cloud of judgment in Pierce and the troops mind. The fairy threatened the comfortable homeostasis created by unchallenged groupthink. The men felt no compulsion to understand their enigmatic counterpart. They saw weakness, they saw difference, they saw contempt for their ways. When life is risked, the investment and trust the men must display in each other is unparalleled in life outside of the military. What exactly causes a breach of that trust is incalculable. Often times the tone of the platoon is set by its most dominant member. In this case it was Sergeant, then only a private, Pierce, and the fairy had no chance.

Typically, a quiet soldier who bothers no one and shows competence in the drills would not draw the full ire of his fellow soldiers. The usual pranks would suffice to pacify the group's ego. But the fuel that led this troop's fire burned hot from the dark pit of self-hatred which festered inside one, Private Pierce. He impregnated the minds of his fellow troop with poisonous anecdotes about the peculiar sexual proclivity of the fairy, stories of masturbation to male erotica, blow job rendezvous' with other suspected queers behind the barracks, and the most incendiary, the secret fondling of fellow troops as they slept. None of it ever witnessed by anyone but Pierce, regardless, venom spread through the other men. And soon new stories rose like ghosts, from nowhere, unsubstantiated, unseen, but given credence, presence, and power. Like any hate fueled fear, its legend grew to irrational proportions. Their hate became a climate, sometimes torrential, sometimes mild, but an undeniable component of every day.

Private Pierce did not start out hating the fairy, quite the contrary actually. Pierce found the boy's innocence in admitting his virginity charming. He noticed the boy's surprising physical prowess, his stamina and determination. He noticed the boy's modesty and couldn't ignore his own curiosity. The fairy made it a habit of showering at night after the other men were asleep. Pierce secretly watched the boy who rose quietly from his bed in his usual sweatpants and long sleeve heather gray cotton shirt. The secrecy and composure of the boy fascinated Pierce. How does someone no one likes, who clearly has something to hide, never get rattled, never blow his cover, Pierce wondered?

Pierce, like the rest of the troops, suspected the boy was homosexual. Lots of guys called the slight soldiers queer and all sorts of derogatory names: cock sucker, faggot, ball licker, but few of the men truly believed those they harassed were homosexual. The fairy was different, he never defended himself, never denied it, he never seemed to care what others thought about him. His silence was deemed as confirmation. But he was a good soldier and that counted to most of the men, so their attacks, in contrast to Pierce's, were relatively mild until the night Captain Pierce describes with merciless clarity to every new group of men he receives.

The tenor of Private Pierce's attacks on the fairy grew considerably fiercer nearly a month into basic training. The troop didn't know exactly why Pierce became more vicious, and he offered no explanation, but the men followed his lead, and when he presented a plot to put the fairy in his place, it seemed like the logical conclusion to the mounting virility of their emotion.

The events leading up to the incident, things commander Pierce did not share, were these. After several nights observing the fairy's shower habits, which included the unyielding presence of darkness, much to Private Pierce's dismay, the private decided to follow the boy to the showers. Pierce hid in the darkened hallway, examining the slightly feminine silhouette of the fairy's body. Moonlight glowed through a window high up the wall of the large rectangular room with ten showerheads coming from the walls, slightly illuminating the young boy. Pierce noticed the small of his back, the shape of his buttocks. He thought about masturbating, thought better of it, and began heading towards his bunk. He quickly changed his mind, returning to the shower stalls, disrobed and entered the showers. The boy had his back to the door and could not hear Pierce over the sound of the rushing water. Pierce violently grabbed the slight man, wrapping his upper body around him, pinning the boy's arms to his sides. The boy did not start or struggle, he simply asked, "what do you want?"

"I've been watching you," Pierce replied. "I know you want it."

The boy calmly assured, "I'm sorry, there seems to be a misunderstanding, I'm not homosexual. Listen, I haven't even seen your face, I won't tell anybody about this, just let me go and we'll forget it."

Pierce tightened his grip and harshly penetrated the boy. "Shut the fuck up fairy." The boy grimaced with pain. Pierce snorted and grunted, he whispered, "feel-good queer boy, feel good?" Pierce groaned, it was over. The boy crumbled to the floor. Pierce took the boy's towel, dried himself, dressed and went to bed.

Both Pierce and the fairy lay quietly in their respective bunks on opposite ends of the room. The fairy burned inside, seething with the betrayal. Pierce stayed up, wondering, he had never had any homosexual tendencies before, how could he have done that? Was it the Army, the close proximity, the lack of access to women? What was it about this boy, why did he get to him so? Pierce felt ill, queasy, dirty. He wanted to go back to the shower room and scour himself raw. But he was trapped, not wanting to implicate himself; he was forced to lie quietly in the dark with the fairy.

All night Pierce listened to the breathing, snorting and snoring of the men, wondering which ones were those of his nemesis. He heard whimpers and moans and wondered if he was in pain. He wondered if the boy was really not a homosexual like he claimed. Why didn't the boy defend himself? Why didn't the boy try to stop him? Would he have stopped? Did he just want to know how the boy would respond? He hadn't the pride to fight back, the fairy really was a coward just like he thought, acting better than everybody else like he couldn't be bothered to know the swine in his troop, like they were beneath him. Well, make no mistake Pierce thought, he won't go around acting like some big shot now, he's the one that needs to show some respect, give the troop the treatment they deserve. They're all in the U.S. Army, he was no better, the fairy had to be brought back down to earth, that type of superiority brings derision, it had to be done Pierce told himself.

The merciful dawn finally arrived, teasing Pierce with its yellows and oranges until finally the brilliant bright blue began to wake some of the troops. He waited until a couple of guys headed to the latrine and then headed off himself. He was surprised by how well he felt, alert, invigorated even. He didn't dread the day's drills; he actually looked forward to the physical effort. He felt so good he broke the typical early morning silence with a joke. "What's the difference between a dog and a fox?" he asked. "Eight beers," he said laughing. The two men also laughed. As more and more men filed in for bleary-eyed tooth brushing, he kept them coming. "How are blondes like cow pies?" Pierce joked. "The older they get the easier they are to pick up." The men laughed.

One of the men called out. "Pierce what's got into you, you're a regular funny guy?"

"I just feel good today, gentlemen, it's the beginning of a great new day."

He goofed around some more and had to scramble to get his uniform on to try to make line up in time. The fairy was the only other guy in the room, seated on his bed, slowly lacing up his boots. Pierce saw him, and yelled, "Come on fairy, what are you going to sit on your ass all day? Come on, it's time for roll call. Plus that, it don't look like sitting feels to good right now do it fairy?" The boy did not respond. Pierce didn't care now if he knew it was him, he didn't know why he was so worried in the first place, no one would believe the fairy.

Pierce ran quickly to roll call just in time, followed several moments later by the fairy, who gingerly made his way late to the lineup. Drill Sergeant Grant, a stickler for time, but fond of the boy who said little and did exactly what he was told, a good soldier he thought, watched the private limp up late, and decided to give him a break. The tall, deep voiced man was considered the fairest of all the drill sergeants, a respected hero of the Great War. He continued to be loyal to the country that wouldn't let him eat in certain restaurants, which berated, heckled and belittled him. The honorable man had a way of getting the most out of a soldier, and he liked this kid, he recognized a little of himself in the boy. "Gentlemen, mark this day," the sergeant said. "This is the first time many of you have arrived anywhere before Private Lisack." The men moaned, one coughed under his breath, "fucking fairy." There were a few muffled laughs. "Settle down, gentlemen, save it for the obstacle course," the drill sergeant said.

After a morning run and breakfast, the men began obstacle course training. It was clear from the run the fairy was bothered by his injuries and didn't exhibit his usual pace. During breakfast the sergeant had come over to the fairy's table, the quiet table of outcasts, and gave him a pat on the back. "You doing okay today, Lisack?" The drill sergeant asked.

"Fine, drill sergeant," the soldier responded without lifting his head.

"You injured or something, running a little awkward?"

"Must've slept wrong or something drill sergeant, just stiff that's all."

Pierce looked at the two men across the mess hall intently. He wasn't worried exactly, more like curious.

The drill sergeant placed his large hand on the back of the boy's clean-shaven neck. "Keep your head up son, you got a bright future ahead of you," he said reassuringly.

Private Lisack glanced sideways at the drill sergeant. "Yes, drill sergeant."

Private Lisack had been the only man in the unit able to navigate the obstacle course the first time they had attempted it. The course demanded both physical strength and mental problem-solving capabilities. There were mazes, climbs, crawls, leaps, and runs, all involving planning and coordination. Most of the men needed the experience of several attempts to untangle all its challenges. Now they ran the course to build stamina, to grow comfortable maneuvering with their weapon, and to increase their agility.

The day began as a typical course run through; the men were staggered two minutes apart, the better times started first. As usual, Private Lisack was the first to begin. The Private knew the obstacle course would not allow him to favor his injuries, it was going to be a long painful test of his will, but he didn't give it a second thought, he'd been in pain before and always persevered. He ventured into the all-too-familiar space, the space his mind drifted to when he both had something to ignore, and something to prove. The private slowed his brain, focused on his heart, his chest, the source of his fire. He heard only his own breathing, saw only the task directly in front of him. He was both completely in and out of tune with his body, seemingly only firing healthier neurons, temporarily turning off those pesky damaged nerves. He involuntarily grimaced at certain points, but he did not get passed, and he completed the course.

The second soldier appeared shortly after the fairy, Private Dunny; he had blood staining the front of his uniform. Pierce was the third to arrive; he also has blood on his uniform. Lisack was resting in his usual spot under a nearby tree. Drill Sergeant Grant noticed the blood on the two soldiers. "Did you guys take a spill or something?"

Pierce responded, "no drill sergeant, there's blood on the equipment."

The drill sergeant grew concerned; he left the two men and walked over to Lisack. "Lisack did you see blood on the course?"

The Private was just re-engaging his senses, downgrading from trauma to vigilant. "No drill sergeant, I didn't see any blood."

"Let me look at you son." The drill sergeant said. The boy appropriately raised his arms out wide and slowly twirled. From the waist down, the back of his uniform was covered in blood. "Shit man, what happened to you?"

Lisack turned his head and peered down at his backside. "I thought it was sweat sergeant."

Pierce knocked Private Dunny on the shoulder. "Check it out, the fairy's finally burst." Pierce yelled over to the two men. "Hey fairy, guess you ran into a dick to be reckoned with."

"Shut it Pierce," said the drill sergeant. Quietly he said, "Lisack, you're done for the day. Go get yourself cleaned up."

"Yes, drill sergeant."

The drill sergeant waited for the rest of the troop to complete the course. No more men arrived with bloodstained uniforms; the young private's blood seemed to have been absorbed by the first two men. Word passed through the troop quickly, the fairy's legacy as the most despicable kind of homosexual, the kind that gets caught, was cemented. Even those who had been withholding judgment gave up on respecting the man. All those, except for Drill Sergeant Grant, he'd been the man they had wanted to break for too long to miss the signs.

"Gentlemen," the drill sergeant beckoned. The distracted men barely noticed the commander. "Attennnnntion!" the drill sergeant commanded. Drill Sergeant Grant rarely used his full booming voice in an authoritative manner, as he did the men quickly came to attention. "Gentlemen, today we will forego our midday meal in order to reiterate some of the morals and codes of the armed forces that may not have fully integrated into your consciousness in the short time we have had together."

No one stirred. For many, his tone became the first recognition something was wrong, terror began to build inside them. Most platoons had experienced an overzealous spell of anger from their commander. Most other platoons had been run into oblivion, puking, shitting themselves for the sake of character building. But they were lucky, they had Drill Sergeant Grant, he was fair, he respected their minds, their bodies, he believed confidence and skill building were more important in becoming a soldier than breaking a man's spirit. But now it was clear, the ethical inner sanctum of Drill Sergeant Grant's tactics had been penetrated.

In that timeless moment when they realized life as they knew it was sure to change, they quickly wondered, was it the beer they smuggled into the barracks? Was it their course times? No, couldn't be. It had to be the fairy, that fuck had gotten them all into trouble. Maybe a few, for one brief moment entertained the notion that something had happened to the fairy, that maybe it wasn't as it seemed, after all, he wouldn't have been able to leave the base, someone must know something, a few actually wondered what had really happened?

"It is clear to me," the drill sergeant continued, "there are men among us who lack the basic decency to allow a man to walk the earth without the fear of threat from those who are supposed to be on his side. Being a member of a unit is far more than being teamed together; it is about men relying on each other. And you have proven to me that you as a unit are unreliable. I would be remiss in my duty to allow a group who preys on its own members, and devalues the soul with humiliation and intimidation, to go unpunished, action must be taken. We have amends to make gentlemen, today we begin the journey from ignorant to informed. Let's run the perimeter, gentlemen, you have two and a half hours."

The men squirmed, one spoke up. "Serge, that's less than eight minute miles."

"You will address me properly as your commanding officer, private."

"Yes sir, Drill Sergeant."

"All right, time starts now. I'll join you in my jeep, get going."

The men began the twenty mile trek. Only one other platoon had been sent to run the perimeter, and they had started at dawn, and had until lunch to complete the task. A mostly dumbfounded group started the run. One man asked, "what was he talking about? What did we do?"

"We fucked up," Private Dunny said.

Pierce interjected. "We didn't fuck up, the fairy fucked up. He wouldn't step in line, and now he brought his faggot ways to training and Grant has had enough."

"Why did he let him go then? Why isn't he out here running twenty fucking miles?" Dunny asked.

"Oh, he'll get his, don't you worry," Pierce assured.

Dunny said, "I don't know man. That guy is one tough hombre. That kind of blood, that wasn't from no consensual homosexual intercourse, something fucking happened man."

"I'll tell you what fucking happened," said Pierce, "the fairy had some big cock up his ass all night, nothing's supposed to go in there shithead. The only time he's tough is when he's so into taking it up the ass, he don't even know he's ripping his guts out."

"I don't know man?" Private Dunny questioned. "I ain't never seen him do nothing wrong, and he takes all that shit you give him and doesn't even flinch. Hell, I ain't that tough, I could never run the course with my asshole all split open. That boy been running scared a long time, and he's still here, I'd rather he's on our side than against us," Private Dunny said.

"You sound like a fucking queer Dunny. That boy is so scared of us finding out he's queer, he doesn't even say anything, he doesn't even fight. Only queers don't fight," Pierce said. Another soldier yelled, "shut your trap, here comes the Serge."

They run. First hour, no problem, these are military men after all. They run. No water. Sun. They run, many still mulling over the cause of their predicament in the first place. The longer they run the more excruciating it becomes. Their standard military issue boots, uncomfortable during normal PT, were creating more blisters and gouges every second. Knees throb, shins ache. Some men fall off the pace. "If you do not finish today, you can try again tomorrow," the drill sergeant assured.

With every painful step the platoon becomes less aware of reason. Could they be here because someone harmed one of their fellow soldiers like the drill sergeant said? Or, is Lisack a low down fucking faggot like they thought? The more they run, the less they attempt to understand. Now they feel the pain, they feel the hate. Do they believe in the truth? Do they care? All they know is they're running, and the fairy has something to do with it, what, they'll never really know. They're too tired to look at anything but the obvious. They drift, they're lost. This is not the experience they thought they'd have. This is not the army they wanted. They didn't want to choose. They didn't want to see the gray between the black and white. They wanted to be told, this is right, this is wrong. Now it all seems so wrong. What do they believe? Who will guide them? How do they know who to trust? Is it each other? Is it the drill sergeant? Themselves?

The run finally over, depleted, aligned, and listening, wary eyes gaze upon the man vying for their trust. The drill sergeant begins, "there are many reasons a man chooses to enlist in the army. Some men enlist because of national pride, some financial need, some family lineage, some anger, some fear, some join to belong. But it is not why you join that is important, it is what you do when you're here. And I know, no matter why you've come, all of you are scared, every last one of you. I don't care if you act like the toughest guy here. I don't care if you're the funniest, the quietest, or the prettiest; nobody here walks without that constant reminder in the back of their mind that they have joined something, voluntarily, that could very well kill them. All of you have taken that step with your life. Few of you understood how dependent your safety would be on your fellow soldiers, strangers, men you probably wouldn't even say hello to if you passed them on the street. Maybe they're not your color, maybe they don't act like you, maybe they're just dumb. But gentleman, you are now involved in something beyond thought or judgments. Now, you are involved in life or death.

"Look around, I don't care if you like the man next to you, all you need to know, is if you like your life. Because, if you like your life, you need to know that man next to you has just as much power over your future as you do. And every bit of disrespect you show that man is the same disrespect you show your own life. This is the United States Army, gentlemen, this is not your schoolyard, your neighborhood, your backyard; we are representing and upholding the freedoms of our country. If the people sent to defend our country are unable to honor its possibilities, there is no reason to defend it at all.

"Right now I would be embarrassed to tell a single soul you represent the United States of America. We are not a people who prey on the innocent. We are people who help those in need, who bring everyone up with us, not step on them on the way by. We do not believe in oppression or superiority, we believe in equality and the power of a free majority. We have not fought so hard for our sovereignty to prevent others from experiencing such, that would be the ultimate perversion of justice.

"As men, I cannot force you to believe anything. As your platoon leader, I can demand that things are done a certain way. There will be no mental or physical harassment of your fellow soldiers. We are here to train to be the best soldiers we can be. A fragmented company is weakened by its separation. The united company is empowered by the bonds of that union. Gentlemen, I don't plan on letting pettiness put me, or my platoon in danger. Any distrust you may have in camp will only amplify in combat. So, anything that's going on within the platoon needs to end immediately. I don't care what it is, it ends now. It is time you understand exactly what is on the line, it is not popularity, or power, or pride, it is survival.

"If the gravity of the situation you have placed yourself in does not become clear in light of this conversation, I will find another way to make myself clear. And I assure you, in so doing, you will quickly find out everything you are made of, and if the Army is the right place for you. As it stands now, this platoon has brought shame to the unit, Armed Forces, your families, and your country. The only one of you I'm proud to call a fellow soldier is back at the barracks now, suffering. Suffering at the hands of those he entrusted his life to, the same people he would surely die for. So while you think you embarrass him, the only person you embarrass is yourself.

"War has a way of finding corrupt men and breaking them, leaving them a victim of their own devices. The unit which stands together, tall and proud, will fight wholeheartedly and is worth ten times that of a fractured group. We fight the way we live; we lead the way we hope things will be. And I will not sit idly by and turn a blind eye to a platoon of mercenaries and cowards. When one among you is mistreated, you all bear the responsibility. We protect everyone in our troop, no questions asked. A continuation of this intolerance will nurture the worst qualities in the human spirit and leave only a thin shell of a platoon, easy to break; the hollow center provides no resistance to those who pass the initial layer. Look around, every man out here relies on everything that's inside you. If you are a façade of bravado and brawn with cowardice and conniving intentions, the enemy will know. He will look at you and instantly be able to tell you are less of a man than he. He will see it in your walk, and in your lack of camaraderie, just as I see it today. And no platoon I lead will be comprised of men I'm not proud to call soldiers and men I would not choose to risk my life with. Today, I would rather leave the Army than go to battle with this platoon. Tomorrow is a new day, a new opportunity to value the life next to you as you value your own. You are dismissed."

The beleaguered men stumbled into their barracks. Pierce immediately yelled, "where is that piece of shit?"

"Fuck off, Pierce. It's over," Private Dunny said.

"Fuck you, Dunny. That piece of shit is going to get what he deserves."

"He deserves our respect, asshole. He hasn't done anything."

"You saw him today, he's a homo. Maybe you're the reason he was bleeding all over the place? You didn't seem to mind plowing right through it. Maybe you're a homo too?"

"Fuck, I ain't no homo, Lisack ain't no homo either. Somebody did that to him. We should help him, man. What the fuck's your problem? You want to ruin this guy's life, what the fuck did he ever do to you? Let it go man."

"We're a disgrace. Every other platoon laughs at us. We have some smug fucking fairy walking around and we just let him get away with it."

"Get away with what Pierce? You fuck with him all the time. They think he's shit because we treat him like shit. We made him a big deal, you made him a big deal. There's nothing wrong with him, he's a good soldier, fucking leave it alone."

"Fuck you."

Another man piped up. "Yeah Pierce, you heard the Serge," he said.

"He's nothing but a nigger. A stupid power-tripping nigger should be shining our boots, not telling us how to be," Pierce yelled.

A different soldier broke in. "Pierce is right. That nigger had no right to make us run like that," the soldier said.

Dunny jumped back in. "It ain't about him. It's about how you fucks treat Lisack.

A man in this unit just like you, a man that's never done anything to you, just fucking drop it," Dunny demanded.

Pierce spoke. "We can't fucking drop it. The whole base has probably already heard about the queer who made his whole platoon run."

"Fuck 'em, it's over," Dunny replied.

"I'm not having every guy in the company laughing at me. We'll be considered spineless the rest of our careers. Something needs to be done."

"Yeah!" several of the men yelled in unison.

"It's him or us," Pierce quipped.

"Yeah!" some of the men yelled again, riled up now.

"I want no part of it," Dunny said.

"No problem," Pierce replied.

So, they plotted the wicked horror of a night Pierce would mercilessly recount to all the fresh faced men sent his way. A group a dozen strong, nearly half the platoon, brainstormed their most wicked torture plots. Weeks passed, exemplary behavior by the platoon eased tensions with Sergeant Grant. Lisack was left alone; other platoon's gave him a hard time, but nothing compared to how his own men, the men he spent every moment of every day with, had treated him.

The nightmare of the first few months in the Army seemed over for Lisack. He had heard the speech Drill Sergeant Grant gave the platoon. From behind the barracks he listened to the poetic voice of the humble man echo off the buildings. He watched as the turbulent sky turned from pale blue to vibrant orange and then a deep dark red. He listened as a man came to his defense, not because he had to, but simply because he was human. It was the first time in his nineteen years somebody took the time to notice. Lisack had listened as tears quietly ran down his face. He cried, not for everything he'd been through, but for the joy of feeling respected for the first time. Meaningful words of grandeur were being spoken on his behalf. The slow, warm burn of hope had flowed inside of him. His throat grew tight, heavy with emotion. He could take anything they dished out and not bat an eye, but this selfless kindness opened the taps of his heartache. His chest tightened, breathing became painful, a labored necessity. The drill sergeant stood up and spoke on his behalf, declaring his life as worthy as all others, it was almost unbelievable. His legs stiffened as he sat stretching them before him, rubbing his chest with his left hand, gripping his head with his right, trying to keep it together. There he remained as the color in the clouds receded, the sky grew darker, his resolve grew stronger.

The uneventful weeks that passed were the most tranquil in Lisack's life. The training was rigorous, but offered the physical exertion his mind cherished, as the complete engagement of his body allowed distant and free thought. His body grew firmer, stronger, more his own. The lifelong tension trapped inside him started to sense the change. His decision to join the army, which at first seemed a furtherance of everything he had known, now seemed to be the fresh start he was looking for. His breathing grew deeper, slower; he stopped glancing over his shoulder so much. His finely attuned hearing, like that of an animal in the wild, noticing every oncoming footstep, able to discern pace and intent, and anticipate the anger level of an on comer through fine gradations of sound, dissipated. He began to slowly relax, declining to attend to the unyielding focus of his surroundings, the force he used as an attempt to stay one step ahead of terror.

Lisack had three weeks of this near bliss, the joy of no longer being hunted. But the fragile fortress of fearlessness that had been hastily constructed tumbled quickly with a warning wind. Fittingly enough, his state of equanimity was brought to a halt on the obstacle course, the first time the platoon had run it since that bloody day. He heard the sound of a man gaining ground on him. Surprised, but not alarmed, he believed he must've gone out a little slow and the second to leave must've caught up. So, when Private Dunny came up running alongside of him, he thought nothing of it. But then hearing the strained and labored breathing of the private, he realized he had caught up to him for a reason.

"They're coming for you," Dunny managed to squeeze out before dropping off the pace. Lisack's heart immediately sank. Long ago trained against disappointment, the weeks of complacency had left him particularly vulnerable to such news. He ran faster, and faster, ahead of his fear, trying to leave behind his torment, racing to catch up to the future he had only recently allowed himself to hope for. But no man can outrun what was coming for Lisack, what had been coming for him since the moment of his conception, the slow meticulous deconstruction of the human spirit.

The course ended. "Forty-three seventeen, well done private, a new personal best," the drill sergeant called.

Lisack stopped running, gained control of his breathing, and walked up to Drill Sergeant Grant. "Drill Sergeant Grant, I want to thank you for what you said to the men that day. I'll remember it as long as I live. It's been an honor to serve under you," he said stoically.

"You aren't going anywhere private, save the pleasantries for another time."

"Yes sir, drill sergeant."

Lisack began to walk over to his favorite tree when the Sergeant called after him. "Lisack?"

"Yes, drill sergeant," the private replied.

"You've made me proud son," the drill sergeant said.

The private nodded his head in a slow exaggerated manner resembling a bow, and walked over to lean against the tree.

That night he awoke with five men surrounding him, one holding each limb, the fifth covering his mouth with tape and quickly binding his feet and hands as they carried him out of the sleeping hall. They continued past the stalls and sink to the shower room. They placed him face down, arms bound tightly behind him. He felt the cool hard tile pressed against his face. He saw the familiar moonlight pouring through the one window and he felt no fear, as if his entire life was leading up to this moment, and either he would survive or he wouldn't, but he had tried his hardest, he had done his best, he was not afraid.

The men poured hot sauce into his eyes. The searing pain made him clench his teeth, which probably saved him from biting off his tongue when the first jarring blow came. They pummeled the man they thought of as the fairy, kicked him with their steel-toed boots, beat him with the butt of their rifles, stomped him until he lay silent and listless. They ripped off his pants; his pale white skin glowed in the moonlight. A man shoved a large carrot up his asshole, violently penetrating the young private. When the carrot broke, they grabbed another, and another. They eventually turned him over. They thwacked his balls with their rifles. They warned him to stay still as they carved into his penis with their bayonets. They laughed and taunted, Lisack made no sound.

They ripped his shirt off and began to carve into his chest. Suddenly the lights came on and the men froze, first at the shock of being discovered, then at the still boy on the floor. Partially covered in blood, battered and bruised, the gruesome scene was enough to startle the attackers. But the naked uncovered body in between the blood was the most disturbing vision of all. The boy was covered in perfectly circular scars, raised round bumps ran from just above his knees to his neck, covering his chest, his arms; perfect round scars covered nearly his entire body.

"Leave him alone," private Dunny yelled. The group of men quickly ran from the room. Private Dunny carefully removed the tape from the now shaking man. He took off his shirt and tried to stop the bleeding from Lisack's nose. He helped Lisack sit up. "You're going to be okay," he said. "I'm going to get help."

The drill sergeant was awakened by the ringing of the phone, it was nearly three a.m. "What, what is it?" He asked.

"It's one of your men drill sergeant. He tried to attack someone and they beat him pretty bad," the voice on the other end of the line said.

"Lisack?" He asked.

"Lisack, drill sergeant."

Grant hurriedly put on his uniform, for the first time in his life completely uncaring of the lines or creases. He ran to the infirmary, boots untied, buttons undone. "Where is he?" he asked.

The prone figure he happened upon in no way resembled the stalwart, courageous young man he had watched blossom over the past three weeks. The boy's face was so swollen, a myriad of purples, blues and blacks, he reminded the sergeant of a monster in an old horror comic magazine he read as a child. The sergeant took the boys hand, gently emitting the love he felt for the boy with his touch, envisioning a warm, soft light passing from his body through his fingers into the battered boy. He brought his cheek down to the boy's hand, breathing deeply. And as the night wore on he heard nothing, thought nothing, felt only a raw burning inside of him. He stayed there through the sunrise, which for the first time in weeks was unspectacular.

After what seemed like years beside the boy there was a tapping on his shoulder. The company captain had come to talk with him. "Why aren't you with your men drill sergeant?"

"I am, captain."

"I mean the men in your platoon, drill sergeant."

"So do I, captain."

"Listen Grant, I heard about what happened. This homo tried to get at one of your boys, Pierce, and he defended himself. He's got a right."

"Does this look like defending yourself, captain?"

"He was pretty upset, quite angry by the looks of it, but it's understandable considering the circumstances," the captain replied.

The previous afternoon's conversation he had with Private Lisack suddenly flashed in Grant's mind. "He knew," the sergeant said out loud.

"What are you talking about Grant?"

"He was attacked, sir, unprovoked. He is the kindest most respectful soldier I've ever witnessed, he'd never go after anybody."

"Sounds like love Grant. Didn't figure you for the type, but you never know with you people. Anyway, the other soldiers corroborate Private Pierce's story. Lisack, if he survives, will be shipped off the base. You would be best served to get back to your men, business as usual, you hear me."

Drill Sergeant Grant dropped his head into his hands and remained in his chair. "I can't do that captain," he said.

"What are you talking about Grant?"

"I mean, there is an injustice here sir that must be addressed."

The captain looked over at the disfigured man lying in bed. "Seems like justice has been served to me, drill sergeant."

"You got it wrong, captain."

"No, you got it wrong Grant. I order you to get back to your platoon or there'll be hell to pay. You understand me, boy."

"I understand you, captain; I'll get back to my platoon when everyone is assembled."

"You stupid Grant? I said that boy is being shipped out of here." The captain grabbed the sergeant under the arm to lift him to his feet.

"You best not be grabbing me, captain," the drill sergeant warned.

The captain reached his other hand out to take hold of the drill sergeant. The drill sergeant rose, shook free of the captain's grasp, and punched him very, very hard on his upper cheek and temple. He knocked the captain out cold, and as the man fell heavily to the ground his left eye plopped out of its' socket and dangled, swinging up, then resting on the bridge of his nose as he lay unconscious on the floor.

Chapter 10

The cool winter air mellowed the heat rising inside her. She hummed as she worked the rich dark soil through her hands. When the currents rose inside her she momentarily stopped, her hum took on a slight groaning quality until, inevitably, the voices and giggles of her two children brought her back. The pain subsided, she worked and hummed.

This her third, she was familiar with the cycles. She knew soon gardening would not be enough to keep her occupied. A walk generally seemed to keep her engaged just enough to float through the pain. This she learned with the birth of her second child, Benjamin. There was no urgency, the process played out in its own time; she was more of an observer than an actor.

Her first was quite desperate really, unsure if anything was as it should be, a muddled mess of screams and pain. Despite the chaos, little Oscar joined the world quite sheepishly, calming an anxious and excited crowd. Now, the two boys waited eagerly for the arrival of "my" new baby, as they both liked to say.

Conscientious Marty had the living room transformed into a veritable transitional womb. He built a spherical birthing tower for Ava to hold, lean, and garner support from at a variety of upright angles. Ava preferred to stay upright during the delivery, noting gravity pulls down, not sideways, and she needed all the help she could get. Marty felt strongly soft light was the best light for keeping both the mother and newborn soothed. The deep burgundy printed fabric surrounding the birthing tower filtered the daylight and glowed with the candlelight at night. He felt if one relied too heavily on the visual elements of a birth, many of the emotional and intuitive elements may be overlooked. He didn't look for the head to come, he felt for it, he didn't wait to see Ava's Perineum tear, he felt the skin for tautness and flexibility, massaging and repositioning to prevent damage.

Ava roamed around the garden taking in the beauty of the moment, her boys playing, the beautiful lush garden landscape, and her body, the serenity of an ingeniously executed design exploring its full potential. She gently rubbed her large protruding belly. She felt the warm synthesis of her body and the being inside of her, their energies merging. This had been her most difficult pregnancy; she suffered far greater nausea for far longer than with the boys. She was forced to stay away from many of her favorite foods, the sign of a strong-willed child Marty said. "If the baby is determined enough to overcome your strong will, we got ourselves one determined kid," he would say half jokingly. Ava wasn't so convinced, possibly an inherent incompatibility she thought, or the even more feared possibility of extraordinary similarity. Either would be a challenge, the former had the potential to dismay, the latter to consume.

It was time she thought; the contractions had grown stronger and more frequent. As the shift in light of the early winter evening brought a chill to the air she gathered the boys. She found Marty heavily engaged in the kitchen with both the evening's meal and the loud outpouring of the radio. She came behind him, warmly placed her hand around his head, bringing her face to his, kissing his strong jaw muscle below his ear. "It's time," she whispered. He turned, smiled, embraced his wife, washed his hands, and led her to the transformed living room.

The boys emerged from the bathroom scrubbed, wet around the collar, they took their father's discussion on cleanliness for the baby seriously. Anywhere you might want the baby to touch you he had said, scrub it well. They had particularly washed their faces; they wanted to bring their face close together with the babies like their parents so often did with them. They entered the "baby's tent," as they called it, and headed directly for the small fort of pillows and blankets their dad had built them. They saw their mother in a short, thick cotton gown, breathing heavily. Beads of sweat formed on her forehead and glided down her temple dripping down her cheeks, collecting at her chin and dropping to the floor. Occasionally, their dad would wipe her face. He squeezed her hand, rubbed her back and felt for the baby. He sometimes left his hand down there a long time, explaining to them that he had to help mom's body get ready to open up for the baby.

Her moans grew louder and more intense as the evening wore on. They weren't exactly scared, at six and four they still funneled many of their emotions through their interpretation of their parents, and they saw a calm and composed man confidently engaged with a focused and determined strong woman, exactly as it should be they thought. They witnessed the enormous intensity of the onset of new life, and their parent's assuredness to participate in it, and the freedom of accepting the intensity as necessity.

The boys watched transfixed for what seemed like just a few moments, but what must've been hours, because the candlelight had been glowing for some time now. "I feel it now," they heard their dad say. They heard loud animalistic groans intermingled with their father's encouragement. They saw the physical strain of their mother's now naked body, her muscles taut, jaw clenched, hands gripping the odd structure in the middle of the room. They saw the baby's head, then they saw their dad competently rap his large hand around the baby shoulders and back, gently supporting the tiny baby's torso. Their father quickly scooped the baby's mouth out with his finger. Then the baby came quickly, he grabbed the baby's legs down by the ankles, and in one failed swoop caught the baby and swung the child up to its mother as a gush of fluid flowed. A slight gurgle was followed by a decisive loud cry. The boys temporarily worried, for they surely did not associate crying with anything good, but were comforted by their parent's quick smiles. "Sounds hearty," their father said. "Look at this," he said as he held up the umbilical cord. The boys had to squint to see in the dim flickering candlelight, a large knot had formed in the middle of the cord. "She's a fighter," their dad said.

The baby cried and cried, at first the boys thought it was because they cut her cord off, but she just seemed to keep crying and crying and they weren't sure what was wrong. Their dad said it was because she had such a tough time getting any food through the knot, and she was just letting them know about her struggles, but they weren't so sure. "It's a good sign," he said, "if this baby wasn't crying she'd be dead boys."

"Did we cry dad?" the oldest boy asked.

"No, you boys didn't cry like this, but you didn't have to."

Finally, she stopped crying, she even started nursing, mom said she would when she was ready, and they guessed she just had to get all that crying out before she felt hungry. It was late, their dad said, "go on boys, get to bed, mom needs to get some rest now." They scurried away, not all that impressed with the new baby, but happy everything seemed to be okay.

Marty looked lovingly at his wife and new baby girl. The warm light glowed off the baby's bald head and tiny button nose. The golden light and enormity of the moment made Ava look more radiant and alive than ever. He embraced the pair and kissed Ava passionately, their warm mouths and soft tongues entwined in a state of heightened ecstasy. They closely hovered over their newborn, who was resting soundly, they explored every inch of her perfectly completed form. They touched each of her ten fingers and ten toes, her legs, her knees, her small round belly, her shoulders, her face. They kissed, they laughed, relieved to be holding each other and their healthy baby girl. Eventually, they headed carefully to the bedroom, Ava holding their girl, leaning heavily on Marty as he slowly led her to their room. Ava abruptly stopped. "What should we call her Marty?" she said, as if it just occurred to her their daughter needed a name.

"Gloria," he said, "for surely unmistakable glory pours from her."

"I feel it Marty, Gloria, yes."

Gloria proved to be less than a glorious baby as far as her brothers were concerned. It seemed their parents sometimes felt that way too. "Maybe we should have named her colicky or cria," they would say, because she always had an upset tummy and cried all the time. The boys grew more and more disenchanted with their fussy sister and after the first few initial hugs and kisses they completely lost interest in her. Those first few terrible months the baby would only stop crying when their mom was holding her, the boys didn't like this at all, they were mad at that baby, they didn't want to be nice to her at all.

For Ava, Gloria was an immense test in patience. Ava grew quiet and despondent, always at the beckon call of the small child. She couldn't put her down for a second without an onslaught of wailing, not even to shower. Marty did the best he could to support Ava, but he was dealing with his own strong sense of rejection from the combustible child. Months passed, the baby rejected anything but breast milk, and even then showed persistent food allergies to many of Ava's food choices. They almost lost her to swelling and congestion caused by an allergy to dairy. Gloria proved to be a physically and mentally trying baby, but just when they were at their breaking point, everything changed.

The savior was physical mobility. By seven months, Gloria began to crawl, and that little bit of independence seemed to pacify the girl. Her dependency on breast-feeding waned, and while she still didn't care to eat much, which was of some concern, Ava's burden was eased tremendously. Then the strangest thing happened, it took them a couple of days to notice. "Do you hear that?" Ava asked.

Little Ben chimed in, "yeah, the baby's quiet. She likes crawling so much she doesn't feel like crying anymore."

Marty and Ava smiled at their son. "That must be it," Marty said. "Sounds good doesn't it?"

"I'll say," Oscar replied in a slightly sarcastic and exasperated tone.

Gloria quickly changed from the baby always around to the baby they could never find. She took to crawling like a duck to water. Within a week she had shimmied herself over the backyard fence by climbing on various shrubs and branches, and crawled out to the foothills behind the house. Once Marty and Ava realized she was gone, they searched the house and yard turning it upside down trying to find her until Oscar finally told them he had seen her climb over the fence and head 'that way,' as he pointed to the foothills. Ava and Marty took off running, the boys lagged behind following them nonchalantly. Nearly one hundred yards into the hills, high atop a large rock formation, they saw Gloria scooting her little naked self, save for the diapered booty, up the rock. Marty gracefully executed the climb and grabbed his stealth girl. Ava was right behind him as he picked up their little girl. Gloria looked up at them and playfully giggled, the first time they had heard her emit the sound of pleasure.

Relieved, they headed back home. "I guess we shouldn't be that surprised," Marty said, further alleviating the tension. "Although, she is starting a little earlier than we did," he said lightly.

Ava bellowed, "oh man are we in trouble. I've been letting myself go a little; I'm going to have to get back in shape just to chase after our little mountain goat."

Marty placed his free hand on her firm butt and playfully gave her a squeeze. "You seem in plenty great shape to me," he said.

"You're biased." Ava responded.

"On the contrary, I consider myself a highly qualified expert."

She laughed, stopped and kissed him. Gloria giggled. They both looked at her. "Well you are just full of surprises," Ava lovingly said as she rubbed the baby's chest.

They arrived back to the house calm from the frenzied panic which temporarily besieged them, and found the boys already back in the yard playing. "Oscar, Ben, come over here," Marty called.

Ava took Gloria from Marty. "Come on, let's get you cleaned up," she said to the child, who in the process of the great escape became smudged with dirt from head to toe.

"Boys, have a seat," Marty said. They obligingly sat on the edge of the brick patio. "Now I know you haven't always gotten along with your little sister," he began. "But she's growing up, and I can assure you she will start being a lot more fun. She's going to start walking, and talking, and just think, she'll be another person to play with."

"We already got enough people to play with dad," Oscar said grudgingly. It was true; the neighborhood was teaming with kids of all ages.

"That's true Oscar, you do have plenty of friends, but you've only got one sister and as big brothers it's important you look out for your little sister. She's too young to know she's not supposed to be doing something. Like Oscar, when you see your sister climbing over the fence, you know that's not safe, you have to say something. Now your mom and I are trying to look out for her the best we can, but sometimes we need your help. So if you see your sister doing something that might get her into trouble, you come and let us know, okay."

Ben quickly popped up. "Okay dad," he said.

Marty raised his hand, then gave him a quick solid high five. "Good boy, son. Oscar how 'bout you? I need your help in this too. You're the oldest; I expect big things from you."

The boy slowly looked up. "Oh, okay, dad," he said reluctantly.

Marty sat down next to his oldest son and put his arm around him. "I know it's been tough son, we haven't been able to spend very much time with you because of the baby, but that's changing now. We're going to spend so much time together you'll be sick of me," Marty said as he poked the boy in the ribs.

Oscar laughed and got up. "Okay, dad," he said, then ran off.

As Gloria matured from a crawler to a walker, she innately developed her own sense of boundaries. Still one to wander off into the foothills, for no contraption barring her outright caging could keep her confined, she seemed to understand unfettered exploration within reason. She understood every place she roamed, she not only had to get herself there, but get herself back. Ava or Marty would wander the foothills with the girl, staying within sight, but mostly leaving Gloria up to her own devices.

As adventurous as the small child was, she was no daredevil. In many ways, despite her willingness to put herself in seemingly precarious situations, she was much more cautious than most. Gloria did nothing without thought; she quickly assessed a route, planned an approach, and maintained mental engagement throughout. Her parents marveled at her focus. Gloria knew exactly what she could not do, and she was on a journey to figure out exactly what it was she could.

After those first few labor intensive months, Gloria became the most independent, self-sufficient baby Ava had ever seen. Gloria knew what she wanted to eat and when; she bathed herself in the bath with the boys, she used her own little potty Marty made her, a mini version of their own complete with working plumbing, she dressed herself, put herself to bed; really, her parents were feeling a little left out.

As if caring for herself was not enough, Gloria began to clean up after the boys. One particular afternoon Ava was asking Ben to clean up the toys in the living room. Gloria overheard, left the project she was engaged in, walked over to Ben, muttered something, patted his head, and proceeded to pick up the toys. She'd prop up a chair by the sink and help her parents do the dishes. She seemed to have boundless energy, never one for a nap she was up at seven in bed by nine, like clockwork, a child of rhythm.

Now don't mistake Gloria for an unhappy, stoic child, quite the contrary, she radiated vibrant energy with an easy, wide, infectious grin. No more was her playful spirit on display than with Ava's parents, gramma and grappa, she called them. She let them hold her, she would sit with them, "talk," with them, which Ava found particularly amusing because Gloria had been babbling away since she was six months old, and had now finally found a willing audience. Marty joked that Gloria would go over to her grandparents just to sit and hold court; the only time she ever sat still. Often times Ava or Marty would arrive to pick up Gloria and it was clear the three of them had spent the whole day sitting and "talking." It seemed about right for Ava's parents, who by now were in their seventies, but they were amazed Gloria didn't need more activity. Every time Ava's parents spent time with Gloria they would express what wonderful company she was, how funny, how charming, how engaging and how much they adored her. That's great Ava and Marty would say. Sure, Ava's parents were slightly senile, but Gloria seemed happy, so all was well.

One day, Gloria, fourteen months old, was helping Ava do the dishes. Marty and Ava had become increasingly more concerned their daughter was taking on too much responsibility. They were attempting to clearly define their parental role. Ava began saying things like, "let mommy do this," or, "don't worry about wiping the table, mommy can do that." Gloria would often look up at Ava puzzled and continue on. So, Ava took their time at the sink as an opportunity to talk with the girl about being a kid. "Gloria honey," she began, "I think you're trying to do too much." Ava raised a dish, pointed to it, shook her head, and said, "you don't need to wash the dishes. You don't need to set the table, or clean up after your brothers, or water the plants, or any of those things. You see, you're just a little baby girl who needs to play, and grow, and be silly. These things are for adults to do. Now I know you don't understand what I am saying…"

"Ni unnerston mom," the little girl rattled off.

Ava startled, looked at her child. "What did you say?"

"Ni unnerston mom."

"You understand?"

"Yes mom, ni unnerston."

"You talk? How long have you talked?"

"Ni lally's tak."

It suddenly occurred to Ava; Gloria had been speaking in complete sentences the whole time. Ava was so set on hearing the customary one or two syllable occasional word the way most kids begin speaking, she mistook Gloria's babbling as unintelligible baby talk. "Well, I'm sorry I haven't been able to understand you. I will listen more closely," she assured her daughter. Ava chided herself for her ignorance to her child's somewhat obvious communication. It made perfect sense; she didn't know how she could have been so oblivious. Ava called her parents. "Mom, I have a question about Gloria," she said.

"Yes dear, what is it?" Her mother replied.

"Do you talk with Gloria?"

"Yes dear, of course I talk with Gloria."

"I mean does she talk with you? Do you understand what she says?"

"Oh, yes dear. She tells us all about her time in the mountains, all about Benny and Oscar, and you too, she adores you, tells us all about you. She's very insightful you know. She says you have a lot inside you don't let out. She says you have the power and no project. You know how you are always talking about her little projects; she says mommy nees nabeeg projet. Mommy needs a big project. I mean, she's a little hard to understand, but after a couple months we got the hang of it."

"After a couple months? How long has she been talking to you?"

"Oh, I don't know, probably six or seven months. You were the same way."

"I was?"

"You were. We thought that's how kids were we didn't know, but then your brothers and sisters didn't talk like that. But when we heard little Gloria talking like that, we knew, we thought you did too honey."

"No, I didn't know."

"You listen to her dear; she'll tell you what's on her mind."

"Okay, momma, I love you."

"Love you too."

Gloria's independence eventually led Marty and Ava to become increasingly more hands-off with their child. Soon after Gloria turned two they had their fourth child, a girl, Audrey. Shortly after that Gloria found painting and was nary heard from again. In an attempt to keep the kids nearby, particularly with the addition of their fourth child, for they were always out of doors, Marty constructed a large easel which he situated on the deck in the backyard. The boys set up paper and splattered paint all over. Gloria watched the chaos, waited until they were through, then she cleaned the easel and surrounding area, and began to draw. She had always loved playing with crayons but now she experimented with chalks, pastels and paint.

She spent much of her third year glued to the easel exploring color and light, attempting different shading techniques, and watching the interplay between light and dark. Ava and Marty were relieved. With a newborn they couldn't keep chasing Gloria all over the foothills. Ava continuously complemented Marty on the pure genius of providing Gloria the perfect outlet right outside their back door. They immediately recognized the child's focus and passion. "She's a lot like you," Marty said to Ava. "No need to talk to anyone, dead to the world."

"Look at me now, never a quiet moment," Ava mused.

"I'm not fooled. I know you're just taking a break; once a revolutionary, always a revolutionary." Marty said.

Ava, reading a book with Audrey sleeping on her chest gave Marty a sly smile. "Well, there's a lot of work still yet to be done."

He smiled. "There is indeed."

Marty, more than anyone, possibly even Ava herself had witnessed the increasing fire smoldering inside his childhood companion. Since Gloria's birth Ava seemed more expressive of the longing inside her. Back in the days when they worked in their labs, she had given everything she could during the tumultuous time. He recalled the desperation, the yearning, the gnawing in her to get beyond the hopelessness of powerlessness. He knew she could not begin her life of comfort and family until her fears had been pacified. And for a time they were. She created a device to neutralize nuclear weaponry and diminish the power of tyranny. That was the best idea she could come up with, a way to end the nuclear reign, she had the knowledge, she had the ability, monumental at the time, but not enough for now. Now, she must bring the information to the outside world. She had regained her balance, spending nearly as much time as a family woman as she had an avenger. The prying eyes of the council had turned the other way. She was trusted again, free to rejoin the world of science. He knew the time was coming.

Marty knew the danger, but also knew that she must go; finish what she ached for with every fiber of her being. Life with Ava was better than he ever could have imagined, and everything that made it extraordinary was shared between them, and her dedication to changing the world through science was a part of it. If he ever knew her at all, he knew her time to return to the lab was coming, and it made every moment until then even more meaningful.

Watching her first daughter spend her days enraptured struggling to express herself, Ava felt her own passion rise. And she knew this young one, the most like her, would never really know her, for two energies, no matter how powerful, on divergent paths, will never see the beauty of their counterpart. And as she watched her daughter falling further and further into unknown space, she began to long for her familiar space. The baby suckling at her breasts did nothing to squelch the fury inside her. It was Marty she worried about most. He considered her an essential part of his whole. His picture of life always included her presence, and she knew he worried about her so. Without him she would not have pulled back when she did, risking detention or death she would have pressed on. He helped her see the time for attack is not when the enemy is alert, but when they are lulled into submission by their own arrogance and complacency. She must prepare, she must plan, nothing can be left to chance.

Chapter 11

"There is a protected personal space each of us possesses," she heard her teacher say as her attention shifted from the landscape beyond the window to her Constructive Community class. "Why do you think this might be important, Gloria?" her teacher asked.

The gruff girl with disheveled long thick dark curly hair sat up in her chair. "I don't know," she said casually.

"Oh, I doubt that," the lively sixty something-year-old man they called Bugsy quipped. A favorite of the students, not only for his propensity to incorporate creativity, especially when it came to bugs, into his lessons, but for his provocative and animated lecture style. "More likely your mind has wandered off to a place you enjoy far more than class and you dare not disturb it by entertaining our discussion," he said. She smiled with her newly grown adult teeth that looked far too large for her mouth. He continued on addressing the entire class. "Imagine an environment in which you have no claim to your own body. Where others are free to intimidate, harass, and ridicule your vessel of life. How might that make you feel?" Bugsy gave a quick glance over to Gloria, hoping he had engaged her enough to provide a response, but she was staring out the window again. Another student called out. "Unsafe."

"Unsafe. Why?"

"Because they might hurt you," the student responded.

"Yes, that's true. But what have you done to an individual by raising them in a state of fear? You have already harmed them, have you not?"

"What do you mean?" a young boy in the back of the class asked.

"You have asked that person to protect his or her self, guard against an unknown ever present enemy, and what do you think that does?"

"Makes them paranoid," the boy said laughing.

"I know it is a difficult concept to understand Johnny. You have grown up in an isolated town where there is no threat of physical violence and every person is treated with dignity. You have not come to understand the concept of the soul through your own tests, through your own trials. You have been taught how to treat people because everyone around you has agreed that fundamental respect and sanctity for the body is essential to spiritual freedom, because without movement free from terror we are not without impediment. And why is this important?" Bugsy asked. The class was silent. "For one, it is important because the power hierarchy that emerges when intimidation is tolerated is one that breeds a ruthless and violent perpetrator, an aggressor who is allowed to rise at the expense of others. Without intervention those most willing to abuse this neglected safety of the self will rule over those whom choose to cherish it. In fact, verbal and physical intimidation can be used to undermine the standing of an entire group of people. The premier example of such a practice can be seen with male dominance over females."

The entire class was paying attention now. They had never heard anyone say men dominated women. Sure, they knew boys could hit a baseball farther, and carry more, but those things meant so very little when perspective was maintained. A woman's body was designed to bear children, to bring life; any difference when compared with men was considered essential and regarded with respect.

"There are cultures," he continued, "that have neglected to uphold and honor the differences between people. There are cultures which choose to exploit those differences for the ruling party's personal gain. Now class, while we do not see it in our town, it is safe to assume a man could overpower a woman, an adult a child, a child an animal. The potential for abuse is endless. Furthermore, it is conceivable people who have more money for example, could exert their influence over those with less. I do not share with you the horror of what is possible to show you all the ways to gain power. I share the possibilities with you so you shall be able to recognize in your own life the danger of neglecting to maintain the balance between people, so you know the importance of protecting that balance, and what is lost if it deteriorates.

"It comes down to you, each individual here, deciding that person next to you has no more, or less right to success than you. And a corrupt act by one, without condemnation, without your swift disapproval, leads to more such acts. And it will be only a matter of time before that treachery comes for you. So you need to decide for yourself whether or not to respect others, not because you have been told, or it's the right thing to do, but because it's what you believe. Because you are going to encounter, probably every day, a moment where you can gain something for yourself by taking from others. You need to decide if you want to live in that environment of threat, or if you believe we all have an equal chance to succeed or fail based on our own merit, not to lose out because someone's bigger than us, meaner than us, or richer than us. And I'm talking about the times when it's not easy, when you thought you wanted something so badly, and you're so close, and all you have to do is one silly little thing, tell a lie about someone, ruin somebody's work, whatever, because you wanted this so badly and you're so close and you've decided that person doesn't deserve it, you're better than that person, that's when it happens. The moment you think you're better than that person you are now entitled and you believe you deserve power. Lose sight of our equality and perspective shifts, if you allow it in others, you allow it in yourself. We are a culture founded on equality, but what do you believe? Are you willing to stand up to a culture that discriminates? Because, that's what it takes to maintain this freedom you enjoy. There is only one law, one moral code, and that is the one you choose to practice. Ideology without its people is nothing. Statements and declarations mean nothing unless people are willing to dedicate themselves to the enforcement of. So I ask you again, is your personal space, and I'm talking both mental and physical, of such value that it should be unimpeded by others?"

"Yes." The class loudly declared.

"Is your neighbor's space equally as important?"

"Yes." The class declared.

"Show me," Bugsy implored.

*

The Saturday fair was in full swing. The Hampton family band, complete with upright bass, piano, saxophone, trombone, drums and trumpet were playing their rendition of, "When the Saints Go Marching In." The families dancing, the smell of fanciful food wafting through the air, this is what Gloria conjured when she thought of happiness. The laughter, the bright neon lights bursting from the dark sky, a complete visceral sensation overload, another land even. Removed from usual thought and typical intake, she wandered around watching the people play. Young eyes wide with glee, broad smiles, handholding, a singular purpose; enjoyment, pleasure, no lessons, only living. Still, Gloria mostly observed. Although she was only eight, she struggled with many kid ventures. The rides made her sick, the food was too rich, the games, she just didn't enjoy. She loved the music, the lights, the sounds, the smells, and although she didn't dance, hardly ate, rarely laughed, she loved the fair; she loved the people loving the fair. Often, the noise and the images would reappear to her throughout the following days, visit her dreams and tickle her mind with playful loving reminders.

Another reason she loved the fair was because it was there where she was able to spend time with Bugsy. Gloria adored the old man, hated being in class, but loved the old man. They talked about everything, especially life beyond the foothills, for he was one of the few in the community who had been granted relocation status. She thought he was the most fascinating man she had ever met. He had deep soulful eyes, and nothing about him, not one thing, scared her. Gloria felt calm and free to express herself, her loves, her passions, her fears. He would listen to her talk about her paintings for hours; he was the only one she would share with in this way.

Gloria's curiosity about the outside world was insatiable. While Bugsy mostly told tales of caution and woe, she managed to extract and cherish the occasional beautiful detail, marveling at its' mystery. Like the pearl pulled from the thousandth oyster opened; she never lost faith the pearl of intrigue was just on the horizon. She believed in the good, the potential, and in the aggressive sometimes merciless society Bugsy explained, she found the grains of justice, the truth and the sorrow, the longing and the loneliness. For surely she didn't believe everywhere was like Larkspur, the clockwork, the predictability, the harmony. She believed in conflict and strife, in anger and volatility. His stories filled with turmoil intrigued her, not scared her like he may have liked. They differed so, he had grown so wary of the tricks and uncertainty, she craved them. He told of lush, tree filled landscapes, vast oceans, grand lakes, canyons, mountains, so many of the things she had only seen in pictures. The images she constantly dreamed about, imagining their presence, their quiet vastness. The images she interpreted time and time again on canvas, interpreting their liveliness with her own color and emotion. He had seen them all, and she wanted to know every last detail.

She worked many of her emotions out through the canvas. Away from town, away from Bugsy, she came to learn about herself in her most pure form, restricted by no one. Gloria was not a typical plein air painter. After a couple years of capturing the local landscape, the cacti, the foothills, the rocks, the dirt; she had stopped painting what her vision displayed. She set up her portable canvas at the base of the foothills and painted the land she had never seen. She painted from memory, recalling the emotions that swirled inside her when confronted with a world so unlike her own. Her visual reference so limited she had only her instincts to guide her. The life of a painting was limited only by the life inside her. The colors, the scale, the movement, it was all conjecture, all feeling coursing through her veins. Her greatest collaborators were not only nature, but also the vivid descriptions provided by her teacher. She heard his words run through her head, listened to his tone, what moved him, lured him, compelled him to nearly jump out of his skin when describing the gravity of his experiences. Gratefully, she had found a man similarly intrigued by his surroundings, who had witnessed many of the great natural treasures of the world. She listened so hard, she tried to hear what he heard, see what he saw. His gift of oratory was her indulgence.

*

Ava left her family when the youngest was only five. Left, not in the literal sense, for she usually still slept at home, and occasionally ate a meal at home, but her work became her life, she spent virtually all of her time, just as in her youth, at her lab.

She had spent many of her family years teaching and mentoring students in her lab so the equipment was well maintained and her skills still sharp. Now, her mentoring stopped, the students used the general lab, and she, alone again, navigated through her mind to give her hands the power to change time. Her mind exuberant at the thought of getting back to work after all these years was flooded with ideas. Whereas in her youth she had the patience and time to chase each of her thoughts

92

down, now she must rely on her instincts and experience to guide her efficiently through the theories. She knew all she was giving up, and it pained her, a frivolous endeavor would be salt in an already gaping wound.

Ava witnessed her kids change from afar. The boys, possibly because they were older and were so close to Marty, seemed unaffected by her absence. Baby Audrey became more dependent, needy, clingy even. Audrey smothered Ava when she was home, and called her when she was gone. Ava always made time to speak with her, not out of guilt or obligation, but out of love. Certainly, simply because she was gone, did not mean she had any less love for her kids than when she was home. Ava constantly assessed the strength of her love for her children. While the love in her heart proved strong, she knew love was more than a feeling, or expression, it was an action. There was no way she'd ever be able to convey to her children that her undying love for them, and the rest of humanity, demanded her presence elsewhere. She could not hold them when they ached, sooth them when they cried, cheer them when they triumphed, and she suffered, she writhed with the painful separation her life called for. There was no denying it, only the strong travel the path of desolation with no sure knowledge of the outcome. For only the truly brave among us sacrifice for uncertainty, because they know the journey is noble and true, and there is no greater travesty than the path of glory shunned out of fear.

It was her third child who struggled the most. The one who had seemed like she didn't need her at all, her little sunshine, Gloria, became cold and reticent. Different from the self-sufficient child of before, she was now angry, touchy, entirely unapproachable. She rejected as defiantly as she felt she had been rejected. Gloria, while always intense, had become stern and easily provoked. She no longer enjoyed playing with her brothers; she ignored her father, and lashed out at her mother whenever she was around. Their laughing, active, emotive child once again transformed. This time, she much more resembled the colicky, crying baby she first entered the world as than the wide smiling, friendly girl of her childhood.

Not surprisingly, Marty had proven remarkably resilient. He thrived in the role of fatherhood. He was no longer the boy whose life revolved around Ava, they had built a life together, and now her focus was work, his was the home. He seemed to effortlessly manage the kids, of course, with invaluable help from the community structural support. The family worked hard to maintain the family's point productivity, all except Gloria that is, she virtually stopped participating in classes, workshops, and community events.

Community members had noticed the change, they commented to Marty, and attempted to draw the child back to class, inventing specific lessons for the increasingly introverted child. They discussed art, nature, music, anything they could think of to get the girl to talk, to share her opinion, that although usually made the group uncomfortable, they loved hearing for the passion, the train of thought, the beauty of an engaged, alert and searching mind. Provocative, and well-founded, Gloria's opinions truly her own, they longed to disagree with her fervently, for the general passive unanimity grew tiresome. Nothing, no opinion, or discussion of controversial painters, the policies of the community, the travel embargo, nothing riled Gloria to participate; it was as if she was lost to them.

Marty began fielding questions daily, distraught teachers, program leaders, "what is going on with Gloria?" they would ask. At first he was slightly concerned, then flattered by all the attention the community was giving his child, then it started to seem pathological, the frantic inquiries, the beleaguered pleas. He realized they needed her, not the reverse. She gave them a sense of hope, a bright spark in the vast doldrums of redundancy. They needed her fire, her restless energy questioning the security of their well manufactured lives. They needed her fight, her speculative insights, the great meaning she attached to possibility. Marty knew Gloria didn't need them for insight or inspiration, but they needed her, and they wanted her back. Marty listened patiently to the town's outpouring, he respected their feelings and statements, but he assured them his daughter was fine, and no her behavior wasn't because Ava was working all the time. "Why then?" they asked.

"We'll see," he said. "Clarity sometimes comes with time and distance, and judgments about both Gloria and Ava should be withheld until we have both."

"Marty," Ava said, crashing into the house one afternoon.

"Hey Av, what's this, home during daylight hours, stop the presses," he joked.

"Marty, what are people saying about Gloria?" she asked concerned.

"Oh, it's nothing."

"That's not the impression I get. I walked to Tucker's to get some supplies and three people stopped to ask me what was wrong with her."

"You know there's nothing wrong with her."

"I hope there is nothing wrong with her."

"That seems a little cold Ava. I seem to recall a young girl just like Gloria once, quiet, reclusive, focused to the point of alienating. Don't you remember your childhood? I mean, you got your lab at the same age Gloria is now. Nobody asked questions then because they were in awe of you, they never knew you, never presumed to be able to understand you. Gloria is different, she gave herself to them, she expressed all her hopes, her desires, her fears. They envy her honesty, her willingness to put everything she has into everything she does. Now it's gone, and they want to blame something, or someone."

"Me?"

"You. But they're wrong. Don't you see, this is what Gloria needs, it's not about you, or them, it's about her. You are driven by a focus so great it cannot be ignored, so is she, Ava. She has purpose, and I'm surprised you of all people ever doubted her for a moment."

"You're the only one who never doubts. You're the one with the faith. I had my pursuit, that's different. I never had to believe in anyone other than myself."

"That's not true Ava. You had to believe in everyone, all of humankind. It's easy for me to believe in you, or Gloria, but humanity, that's hard. You've sacrificed not for your ego, or recognition, but to make the world safer for everyone. That is faith
94

you extend to all people. Take a moment to realize; sometimes the people closest to home get overlooked. Look at your daughter Ava, she's brilliant, no doubt about it. So what are people saying? They're saying we fear she will leave us, that she will find a way out, and then they will have only themselves to turn to. And for them, Gloria represents such beauty, such proclivity for the profound, they want to keep her Ava, keep her here all to themselves. But like you, she wants more, she feels the pulse beyond these foothills, and like you, she will stop at nothing to be part of it."

"So she's okay?"

"She's okay Ava. You didn't ruin her. Forget what people are saying."

"So confident, how do you keep it up?"

"I've seen things nobody thought were possible. I've witnessed the indelible ability of the human spirit. It's not confidence Ava, it's understanding."

Gloria stopped going to class. She loved to read and explore, and felt that would be enough. She stopped all community programs, all volunteering, she even stopped going to the fair. She spent her days painting and her evenings talking and reading with Bugsy. Her paintings transformed from the slightly surreal interpretations of nature, to the unrecognizable abstract musings of the mind. Her images grew darker, emotionally charged and reckless.

She set up at many locations throughout the hills, but found herself favoring one more than the others. There was a small bluff, twenty feet by thirty, accessible only through a complicated maze of various rocky inclines. Even she had some trouble navigating the steep terrain with her painting supplies strapped to her back. Some days the trek seemed too taxing to attempt so she'd stay within the relative comfort and ease of the foothills, but she knew her best work, her most free work, came up on the bluff. The bluff overlooked the eastern section of town. Upon her favored bluff, she looked out now on the horizon, about a mile out was the large rectangular building of her mother's lab.

The strange glows and bursts of light shining through the windows of her mother's lab intrigued Gloria. She had no idea what it was her mother did in there, it was like a mysterious land solely inhabited by her mother. Gloria wondered about the smells, the sounds, the colors, and what caused the thin concentrated beam of light she would see release from the retracted roof when she stayed deep into the night? Most importantly, Gloria thought, what was the purpose of this deep purple beam which invaded the sky? What was her mom creating? She had never expressed a particular affinity for any field, Gloria was puzzled. Gloria's curiosity spurred her creativity, and all her lingering questions about her mother seethed through her and forced their way onto the canvas.

Gloria writhed with dissatisfaction, stuck in this hovel with its mundane regularity and frictionless interactions. Gloria longed for the desperate fear she saw in Bugsy's eyes, his lack of security, she thought, it's what makes him intriguing. The insanity he must have faced out there left him deep and contemplative, far more so than anyone else in the community. She questioned the lack of strife in the lives of her cohorts; she simply couldn't relate, always feeling unsettled and underutilized, like there was all this energy on the other side of the foothills that never made it over the peaks. There were all these injustices and inhumane acts that she could never counter. Surely the limited scope of behavior displayed in Larkspur wasn't all there was to the world. She felt the anger, the rage, the fury of the oppressed, and the paranoia, desperation, and ignorance of the oppressors. The unknown world beyond the foothills constantly rushed through her body, and she felt helpless to pacify the energy. She was in a constant state of upheaval, with painting, Bugsy and books, her only recourse. This unknown land living inside her drove her, teased her with the inciting presence of need. Consumed by the limitless potential of devastation and transcendence that only others faced, her sheltered and sparse reality had become her prison.

Only brief moments of freedom came with the transference of her emotions to canvas; more so, anguish and sorrow besieged her, for everything she could not do, everything she could not experience. The miniature, just town, was like the only house left behind in a storm ravaged land. Who would care to live in the only untouched place surrounded by the reminders of suffering? Either the beauty is shared by all, she thought, or none enjoy the spoils without working to bring everyone else along.

Gloria loathed her existence, despised its hypocrisy, its non-involvement; the horizon reminding her real life was living all around her, steaming ahead without her input or her influence. She had grown fundamentally bored of the tireless predictability of Larkspur. She wanted out, she didn't know how, she didn't know when, but she had seen it. She envisioned herself in a large open park speaking to hundreds of thousands of people, the words were unfamiliar to her, but she was there, living it, breathing it, she was there.

As evening approached, Gloria left the bluff overlooking her mother's lab. The cool, late afternoon, fall air snapped her concentration with its chill. She slowly navigated the steep terrain, already lost in her non-painting self listening to the nocturnal insects welcome in the evening, smelling the slightly piney smell of the cacti brought on by the slight escalation in moisture from the drop in temperature which awakened the plants' cells. She knew the name of every plant species she passed. She occasionally recited their names and talked to the familiar friends along the route. She sometimes sang them little songs, incorporating their color, size and blooming habits. Tonight was an ode to Verbena Maedougalii. "Oh sweet verbena," she sang, "purple cones of rain. Tall, spiky, strong, purple cones of rain."

She was in a jovial mood after her vision, the one that took her beyond this place, and euphoric from painting and breathing the cool, crisp, clean desert air. She felt sure, composed, like for the first time her future was in her hands. There would be a time when her decisions were truly her own, her direction without limits. Following her desire to leave would be the first, most essential part of her plan. Over the past few months, many visions of a life not yet lived had flooded her head. She had elaborate dreams, murky and unrecognizable, but undoubtedly it was her life, she was older, calmer, more confident, the person she hoped to become. So she sang, happily, assuredly, willing to hope, indulging in a future imagined.

She hummed and skipped herself all the way over to Bugsy's house. She heard him playing his harmonica, smoke wafted from the chimney of the tiny adobe structure. Two rooms comprised the four hundred foot, partially submerged structure, the bathroom and "the everything else room," as Bugsy called it. There was a small area around the wood burning stove which he cooked on, with a few dishes and pans, a small sink, and a round wooden table just large enough to seat two. He built a cocoon like loft walled in on three sides, with a four by four opening that he managed to squeeze a mattress into. There was one small window in the elevated sleeping cocoon for light and ventilation. The pane had the remnants of hundreds of candle drippings along the base of the sill. Every wall of the main room was covered three quarters high with books, magazines and records. The final quarter of each wall had a long horizontal window running across the entire length. Bugsy had one high-back plush, soft, burgundy velvet chair tucked into a corner, with a stained-glass lamp hanging over it from the ceiling above. In another corner of the room, resting on an old trunk, he had a tuner, receiver and turntable. Four small speakers were fixed into the ceiling at each corner of the room. In the center of the room he had a, five by eight, dark mahogany table. He used the large table to sketch the many blueprints of the dream homes he created in his imagination.

Gloria opened the door and burst in on the harmonica playing Bugsy who was sitting cross-legged on the mahogany table. He jumped hurriedly off the table, surprised by the barging presence. "Jeesh Glor, you trying to give me a heart attack?" he said.

"Just testing those catlike reflexes Bugs. You still got it old man," she replied playfully.

"Yeah, yeah, give an old man a break, you sounded like Armageddon storming in here."

"Armageddon wouldn't even bother showing up in Larkspur," she said dejectedly.

"Oh, come on, Gloria, Larkspur is exactly the kind of town you would want to live in if you had the choice. I can live anywhere, and there is no where I'd rather be."

"But it's so boring, everything is always the same."

"Yeah, safe. Safe and full of opportunity."

"Opportunity to do something in Larkspur, big deal. That's not opportunity, that's serfdom."

"It's the opportunity to study, learn, and become whatever you want."

"But not anywhere I want to be."

"Gloria, you have this glorified image of what the world beyond Larkspur is like. Trust me; there are not eight year olds who spend every day off in the mountains painting. Everybody has their prescribed place, some arbitrary identity based on the circumstance they were born into. If you are poor, female, black, that shapes your possibilities out there. Here, everyone's got a shot, everybody starts with the same potential, and the world doesn't systematically conspire against you to strip you of your ability."

"But what do we really have a shot at? Living out our merry little life and fading into oblivion, not impacting anything, not changing anything, why bother?"

"That's just it, in Larkspur nothing needs to be changed."

"Life is not Larkspur, Bugsy. While I acquiesce this is the best place for you, it is not for me. I want more out of life than to eat, sleep, paint and die. I want to change things. I want to fight against those who wish to control others. I want to help create a world that won't stand for abuse, one where everyone can explore their capacity to the fullest. Larkspur, in its isolation and irrelevance, is equally as treacherous as a world rife with injustice."

"You're wrong Gloria. Larkspur is an example of every principle you believe in exemplified. There is no way this can be accomplished on a large-scale."

"So, there's no hope."

"Yes, there's Larkspur."

"Well, that's not good enough."

*

The long days in the lab, while less invigorating than earlier years, still provided a vivid mental spectrum for which Ava to engage. Only now, Ava's psyche was replete with contradictions, worries and doubts. She no longer had the singular notion that she alone would be able to carry out her objective. Ava had always believed she would be able to create the nuclear interceptor. She could not live with herself if that had not been accomplished. But now, she progressed with a constant unsettled feeling deep in the pit of her stomach even though her work creating a radio activity shield was progressing quite smoothly. It's not that she felt unable to complete her goal of creating an environment in which to move through a radioactive field so they could leave Larkspur, it's that she didn't see herself capable of leaving. Not that she didn't want to explore life outside the town; it's what her family would be subjected to in the process. She would not leave without her family, she knew that. She feared the harrowing process involving council approval. More and more she considered the council's explanation of unsafe travel conditions due to radioactivity entirely made up. In spite of this mistrust, the travel embargo bothered her less and less. While their reasons for the embargo seemed audaciously implausible, she began to believe their reasoning for the embargo may have merit.

Ava no longer felt entirely deceived by the Council. Like a rebellious, unruly adolescent who when aged looks back at their parents with a softer lens, she believed some of the council's policies came out of the desire to protect its people. She no longer harbored the anger and resentment of the uninformed. The community had been good to her, allowed her freedom in all aspects, except the freedom to leave. After years of speculation on the possible reasons for the travel embargo, the sting of its reality had lessened. Possibly, reconciling her stationary fate was necessary to enjoy her existence at all. Somewhere along the way, her make do mentality and trustworthy optimism merged into a less confrontational frame of mind. Nonetheless, she devoted hours upon hours, days upon days, and years upon years, to creating a safe way to leave the isolated town.

With the youngest now ten, Gloria thirteen, Ben seventeen, Oscar nineteen and a fully commissioned quadrant regulator, Marty's duties with the kids were minimal. He again joined Ava in her lab, reinvigorating his corner space which had weathered some over the years of neglect, but was still a ringing testament to Marty's ability to make robust, and enduring maintenance-free plant life. Ava would marvel at her husband's still lush forest in the corner, surely the plants will die one day she thought, neglected but resilient, only Marty could master that combination. Marty typically worked the middle of the day in the lab, spending his mornings working at home, and teaching his typical evening classes on botany. He knew Ava was getting close, working out the last challenging elements of her equations. She hardly entertained the lunch Marty attempted to persuade her to eat, and there were more yells of fury and exaltation filling the lab these days.

Ava had stumbled with this project in the same area she had excelled in her last, what to do with the radiation? Creating an energy bubble which envelops its living entrants was easy. Creating the outer layer of the protective shield to absorb radiation was easy. Creating an impenetrable wall several layers into the shield proved a little more challenging, but she found a way to keep the bubble's inhabitants radiation free. But how to rid the absorbed radiation from the shield without dissolving all surrounding matter, notably the living matter inside, proved elusive. She was working on a way to detach the outer contaminated layers of the bubble from the inner impermeable layer. This would allow the radioactive structure to collapse, similar to her nuclear absorption device, and render the environment harmless. Detaching compounds she worked so hard to attach seemed an unlikely problem to be stumped on considering they didn't want to stay together in the first place. However, the process used to bind the unstable layers together had to provide such alarming stability, deconstructing them led to the collapse of the entire bubble, a major problem for Ava, at least thus far.

Ava came home a little later than usual, nearly three a.m., intense and agitated after a frustrating day at the lab. Marty, used to staying up until she arrived home, had fallen asleep seated on his reading chair in the living room. The sight of her sweet, devoted husband melted the fury of her frustrating failures. She sat on the arm of the chair and slowly rubbed his chest. "Marty," she whispered, "Marty, sweetheart."

He roused slowly, looking sleepily at his wife. "You look good," he said. "Did you figure it out?"

"I'm stuck, I have no idea what to do, no idea," Ava replied. "I've never once at any point in my research not had a multitude of ideas to fall back on. I've explored everything I can imagine. I've constructed and destructed the entire sequence by element. I've replaced, combined, divided, heated, cooled, vacuumed and exploded the bond in every state, nothing. The bonds cannot be broken without complete collapse."

"That's a compliment to your work isn't it? You've created a unique force which has no dissolution," Marty encouraged.

"I appreciate your sentiments, but there is little solace in a complicated problem half solved. Getting it half right is all wrong in science, that's part of the reason I love it, the clear proof of success."

"Maybe it can't be done," he said. Something neither of them had uttered before.

"Don't be silly, of course it can be done."

"Just not by you."

Her hurt look quickly was replaced by a resolute stare. "Of course by me, who else?" she said.

"Isn't that what you're telling me? You're out of ideas, you're beat, you're ready to quit."

"No, that's not what I'm saying at all. I just thought I would've figured it out by now."

"So what are you going to do?"

"Nothing. I'm going to figure it out."

"What's stopping you?"

"I don't know, it's strange, it just doesn't feel right. The closer I come to unlocking the code, the worse I feel. It's as if the mystery I'm trying to solve will only lead to greater and greater unknowns. My mind is convoluted with thoughts of terror about what this project will bring. My work is paralyzed by my fear of the unforeseen consequences of my actions."

"When have you let thoughts like these rule your decisions?"

"That's just it, I've never had thoughts like these, I've never felt doom on the horizon like I do now. I mean, I set out to create a device to make nuclear warfare obsolete, and I did it, yes, understanding people might be upset, and I've kept my secrets, but this feels different. This feels more subversive, underhanded shall we say."

"I don't understand?"

"My shield, if I ever get it right, will ruin everything this town is based on. People will leave, it's a betrayal. I never intended to do harm with my inventions, only bring peace. I will dissolve the sanctity of the community."

"Ava, that's bullshit. The sanctity, that's delusional."

"I don't know? Everybody has been so good to us here; it's like turning your back on your family."

"No, it's like turning your back on all of humankind. That's what you'd be doing if you don't share what you've created."

"Maybe there's another way? Maybe we could smuggle it out, or tell Judith…"

"What!" Marty said rising from the chair. "Unbelievable, a little creative block and you've crumbled entirely. Where is your resolve? If you weren't in this to see it through you should have never dragged any of us along. We didn't ask for this, but we've done it, because we believe in you. If you're ready to back down and let others, whom you know you can't trust, get involved, it's over, just give up now." Marty gathered his things and stormed off to the bedroom.

Gloria just managed to run back to the room she shared with Audrey before her dad rushed into the hallway. In her thirteen years Gloria had never heard her parents speak like this. Worried, she spent an especially restless night, even for her typical insomnia filled evenings, fighting off the troubling thoughts which invaded her head. What did her mom mean when she talked about the unforeseen consequences of her actions? What did her mom have to do with nuclear warfare? And the most intriguing of all to the wanderlust child of thirteen, did she really think it would be possible to leave?

Gloria woke up some time around eight to a strange noise, her mother's voice in the kitchen. Gloria was exhausted, she had fallen asleep sometime after the stunning orange sunrise, and even then her sleep was conflicted and filled with restless worrying of all she had heard the night before. Her mother was startled when her oldest daughter walked into the kitchen. "Oh, I thought I was here alone," Ava said.

"Why? Where's dad?"

"He had some work to do." What Ava didn't mention was that Marty had been unable to sleep at all. She spared her daughter this detail as she continued. "I mean, why are you not in class?"

"Mom, I haven't gone to class for years."

"Years? And they let you get away with that?"

The prickly teenager roared back. "They let you get away with whatever you want."

"I resent that."

"Yeah, well I resent a lot of things mom, that doesn't change the fact that it's true."

"What do you do all day?"

"Isn't it a little late to be asking me that, I'm thirteen mom, if you didn't bother to care by now, I can't help you."

Ava hadn't spoken with her daughter in so long the onslaught of anger was hard to stomach. "Gloria, I've always cared about what you were doing."

"I don't believe you."

Ava felt a searing pain rise through her chest. "You don't believe me? You don't believe I love you?"

"No, I believe you love me out of some trite parent/child obligation that you seem to hold onto. I don't believe you really care, all you care about is your lab and your stupid projects, you don't really care about me, or this family."

101

Ava had not been accused of not caring about anything in her life, let alone the people she had spent countless tormented moments worrying about, hoping for their safety and happiness. Now her worst fears were realized, she had lost the love and respect of her beloved minder of justice, her pulse of decency, her daughter who only wronged when wronged. And it was she who had left this sorrow, this wounded, blighted child. Now, she realized more than ever how important it was for her to finish her task. Failure would mean her entire life was for not, and not just her life, that she could handle, but the lives of her entire family who endured and sacrificed. "Gloria, I will never presume to know how hard it's been for you. I will let you know, I also have struggled."

"Spare me," the teenager said rolling her eyes.

"Wait, let me finish."

"You will anyway."

"Yes, I will. Because I believe what I'm doing is important, important for more than just me, or my family, or this town, but for all people. I do not spend my days in the lab trying to come up with just the right color lipstick, or the most beautiful fragrance you have ever smelled, I'm trying to solve the pressing problems of the world."

Over her mother's shoulder Gloria noticed her dad entering the house but didn't acknowledge him as her mother continued speaking.

"I'm working to conquer the conquerors, to bring power to the powerless, to change the world as we know it. So when I'm not here, when you feel lonely, or abandoned, or betrayed, know I have left you for something so just, so monumental, all your hardships and sorrow will seem worth it one day. I will make sure of it."

"I hope that's true," Marty said.

Ava turned to her husband. "It's true." She turned back to Gloria, hugged her and kissed her forehead. The stiff, raging girl relented for a moment then abruptly pulled away. "I love you, Gloria. I wouldn't have put any of you through this unless I thought I had to."

"Whatever," the child said as she left the room.

"What was that about?" Marty asked his wife.

"Gloria doesn't go to school?" Ava asked, deflecting the question.

"Not for years."

"I can't believe I didn't know that."

"You did at some point."

"I did?"

"Yeah, a long time ago, forget about that. Why was she so upset?"

"She thinks I don't love her."

"No she doesn't."

"She does, she just said it."

"She wants to know she's important. She's accepted how little time you spend at home, but something needs to be done when you are around to make her feel remembered. She loves you, she adores you, and she respects you have something you are so passionate about. She admires your dedication; she wants to know you feel the same way about her. She has a complete life of her own that you know nothing about. That makes her feel like you don't care."

"But I do admire her. I think she is an extraordinary girl, smart, capable, charismatic, people flock to her, idolizing her and she shuns them. I don't get it, she seems unapproachable emotionally, I never know what to say to her."

"Let her figure it out. Spend time with her, hike with her, go with her when she paints one day, she'd love it."

"I don't know if she'd let me."

"Ask her. She wants your company even if she's pissy about it."

Ava grabbed her husband's hand. "Let's go for a walk," she declared.

He immediately knew where they were going. It had been years since they walked to Mav's Hollow together, their childhood meeting place replaced by the practicality of cohabitation. As they slowly walked the route, Marty felt a pang of regret that they had let this part of their life languish. His fingers began to tingle as the magical moments they spent in the cave flooded back to him. The burgeoning of their romantic love, the crystallizing of theories, thoughts, fears and desires, all nurtured in the small remote secret locale. "I miss this," he said, "the two of us hanging at our old haunt."

"Me too, but times change, we are not kids anymore."

"Says you," Marty laughed.

They walked to the center of the dwelling. Ava breathed in deeply, slowly taking in the cool serene air. She lit a torch and took in the sandy, earthen tones of the walls. "Marty do you remember when we promised never to tell anyone about Mav's Hollow?"

"Yes."

"I want you to break your promise."

"You do?"

"Yes...Marty I've been hiding things in the cave. For years I've been transferring documents, my work, Marty, it's all here. The portable device, the equations, everything one needs to build the interceptor is here."

"Where?" He asked befuddled. She led him back to a small crevice in between two rock walls. "I didn't even know this existed," he said. She stepped through the jagged entrance, he followed. What he saw surprised him. A medium-sized red and black hiking backpack leaned against the wall. "That's it?" he said.

"That's it."

"The interceptor and everything you know about stopping nuclear weapons fits into one backpack?"

"It has to, Marty, if it's going to get out of Larkspur."

"Yeah, I'm just surprised. I mean I knew you were good, but not this good," he said, grabbing her around the waist.

She laughed, then grew serious again. "It's funny," she began, "I always thought I'd be the one carrying this out of Larkspur. But even with all the time I've spent trying to leave, I never had a plan for when I left. I could never imagine myself there, you know, part of the world. And then a few years ago I had this dream, so vivid, so lifelike, I was overcome. Then I'd see it during the day, the images were pestering me, nagging me, so I came out to Mav's Hollow. I was drawn here, as if this cave was the apex of all my hopes."

"What did you see?" Marty asked.

"I saw Gloria."

"What do you mean you saw Gloria?"

"I saw her there. It was beautiful, Marty."

"Where?"

"She's the one, Marty, not me. She's the one who will bring the interceptor to the world. I have seen her high above vast canyons, swimming in the ocean, walking amongst the skyscrapers."

"Where are we?"

"We are not there, none of us. She is the only one I see."

"Why didn't you tell me?"

"I thought I had time. I didn't want you to treat her any differently. I didn't want her to find out. And, I wasn't exactly sure it was the right thing to do, she never asked for this. But the longer I have these images in my head, the more I realize this is far greater than you, or me, or Gloria. We are all the future, linked by our past as a collective humanity, and this is our part, if many pieces of many people's path's merge, what we envision is possible. And Gloria, just like me, and you, and all the people along the way, are going to have to seize the future laid in front of them for the imagined to become reality. I'm doing my part, but it is only one small part. I used to believe I could do it all, but I see now there is far more to this journey than what I can do alone."

"So you want me to tell Gloria about your project?"

"Marty, I want you to bring her here when you think she's ready, I trust your judgment. Tell her I've seen her there, she will leave. Tell her about what I've created. Let her know what she does with the device is entirely up to her, I thought she should know. Tell her I believe in her, always."

"Why don't you tell her?"

"I think I've figured out how to dissolve the radio active material without compromising the structure. Everything I was trying before was based on destroying the bonds, now I realize I simply need a stronger one on the preceding layer that will hold its integrity through the matter absorption. I mean, there's a small threshold to work with, and it will mean improving upon the most solid merging of matter I've ever created, but I know it's the right direction. It can be done."

"That's great, I'm really excited to hear you're hopeful and the resolve back in your voice, but I really think you should be the one to tell Gloria, I mean it is your life's pursuit."

"Well, I might change my mind, but just promise me if I can't do it, you will?"

"Okay, of course, I promise."

*

"I was planning to go somewhere else today Bugsy, but I'll take it easy on you old man."

"G, I can handle anything you throw at me."

While the seventy year-old had shown quite remarkable agility and balance for someone of his age, she was not convinced he could traverse the steep, rocky terrain to the bluff overlooking her mother's lab, so she decided a simple hike into the foothills would be best. "I'll bet, but today we'll take it easy."

The midmorning spring sun warmed them. They breathed heavily with the exertion, sweating through the serene landscape. They silently worked their way through the desert brush. Bugsy was right; he did not struggle at all. Maybe Gloria would take him up to the bluff next time, she thought. The clear blue expansive skies surrounded them as they settled upon a spot just before noon. Shrouded in the bright white light of the desert they prepared their easels. The two of them stayed that way, Bugsy drafting a house, Gloria painting the abstract, for the remainder of the afternoon. They packed up as the sun fell low, and headed back.

Gloria, ever curious about Bugsy's life outside Larkspur, began asking him questions. "What happened to you Bugsy? Why do you hate it out there?"

"We've talked about this Gloria."

"No, we've talked in a broad societal sense. You've never shared your story, what you went through. I don't know anything about your life before you came here."

"It was nothing special."

"Tell me about it anyway."

"You know I'm not really allowed to talk about it, the specifics that is."

"Oh please Bugsy, if they haven't thrown you out by now for all the crap you bring up in class, you're safe."

"I'll tell you one day G., just not today."

"You're not getting any younger," she joked.

"Not true, I feel younger today than I ever have. There's something about this place that has turned back the clock for me."

"We'll, don't wait too long, because dead men don't tell stories."

"Some dead men's stories live on forever."

"Not if nobody knows them."

"True. Well, I don't plan on living forever, literally or figuratively, but I'll tell you soon, okay."

"How soon?"

"When the time is right."

"Oh geez, you're never going to tell me."

"Patience my child, the time will come."

They continued on as the pale lavender sky eased the day into night. They were quiet now, except for the steady sound of their breathing and the even pace of their footsteps. The lavenders gave way to greens as they approached the earthen adobe dwelling Bugsy called home. They removed the canvases strapped to their backs and placed them in the watertight storage shed Bugsy had built at the side of the house. He was in the process of building another, as the several hundred paintings by Gloria necessitated further protection.

They walked down the small stairway, four steps to be exact, to the small arched door of the partially submerged home. Gloria washed up at the sink as Bugsy lit the candles. She then pulled out a record by one of her favorite artists, Johnny Cash. The familiar sounds of the deep voiced crooner filled the air. Bugsy washed up and began prepping for dinner. He rinsed, drained and butterflied shrimp, a rare luxury for Larkspur, only shipped in once or twice a year, a little salt and pepper and they were on the grill. He trumpeted up a salad with pears, brie and walnuts. He poured his tequila and waited.

Gloria sat cross-legged on the mahogany table in the center of the room. She listened to the music and mused, "you think the reality of their love was as great as the song's idea of it?"

"Greater," he said, sipping on his tequila.

"How could that be? The confident longing in his voice, proximity usually snaps that spell. I mean, when they were apart he wanted only her, but what happens when he gets her, that's what I'm interested in. The promise is always better than the reality."

"Sounds like a woman who's never been in love," Bugsy replied.

"I'm fourteen."

"That doesn't matter. Truly, I've considered you in love your whole life."

"What do you mean?"

"You're in love with life, the colors, the sounds, the people, the emotion, you're living on high. You seek the greatest experience, accept nothing less than the extraordinary, and what love truly is, is not necessarily meeting that bliss, but still believing it's possible, caring enough, and believing enough that you will find your way to the supreme. Love isn't always a person's desire to be with another and certainly at fourteen that is not your understanding of love, but your devotion, your desire to see the world, that hunger you possess, I've never heard the likes of it expressed in any song. And I can assure you what you will feel when you find true love will be far greater than any that can be conveyed through music."

"So you think I will find it?"

"I do. And then you will know love is far more than the longing for, or the desperation of, it is the synthesis of all those feelings into action."

She smiled and returned to the music as he removed the shrimp from the grill, and they go on.

Both seated on the table they enjoyed their dinner. "You see those two, Johnny and June," Bugsy said returning to the discussion, "they became inseparable and he longed for her even more. Together, the reality of their potential became so much greater. Like you, and what you will achieve after you leave this place. Speculation and hope do not measure up to accomplishment and triumph, they are what helps us in the battle until we achieve our desires, and the truly great achievements always make you realize there is so much more that can be done. Great accomplishments beget great possibilities. Here, you could not truly understand the possibilities which await you. An unaccomplished mind is a limited one, and while you give every ounce of your emotion and beliefs to your paintings, you have yet to fulfill those emotions outside of the imagined world. And as creative and thoughtful as you are, there are limits. For some, the limits never cease to rule them, for others, with every measure of achievement they want more and more until they see no limits placed before them. So as good as love can seem from afar, for those willing to continually push the boundaries of possibility, the actuality of love is transcendent. That's what I see for you, because you believe so strongly, and you've seen so little. For the visions that will fill your eyes will open your heart and mind so wide nothing will stop you, and the burgeoning delirious emotion of possibility inside you will continue to grow."

He gulped down the rest of his tequila and banged the glass loudly on the table. "Amen, hallelujah, praise the Lord, I do be given a sermon tonight," he said loudly.

She laughed as she took the plates to the sink and washed them. He filled his glass of tequila and moved to sit in his high-back burgundy velvet chair. She finished washing the dishes and put on another album, this time Chopin. She knew Bugsy loved Chopin, which made him drink even more, which got him talking, and that she loved the most.

They settled in for awhile, absorbing the revelatory vibration of the concerto. Gloria, for possibly the thousandth time, poured over Bugsy's collection of National Geographic. She loved the creatures, the colors, the people; the magazines were an amazingly diverse representation of everything still unknown to her. She admired the beautiful photography and the discussion of cultures. She had read and reread every issue from the nineteen twenty's, when Bugsy was about her age, until the early nineteen sixty's when he arrived at Larkspur.

"It's a shame you still can't get National Geographic here," she said.

"They wouldn't want to make the rest of the world seem too appealing. Only the doom and gloom of the outside world gets in here, that's why they let me in, they knew this sorry example of an outsider was sure to halt any desire to leave."

"Oh please Bugsy, stop feeling so sorry for yourself, you're the most thoughtful and inspiring person in the community."

"To you, Gloria, only to you. Plus that, if you had any sense you'd see your mother is the most inspiring person in the community."

"Now you really must be drunk," she said dismissively.

He looked at her wounded, then quizzically. "You really have no idea who your mother is, do you?"

"Why would I, I hardly ever see her?"

"A poor excuse coming from a girl who paints the most beautiful waterfalls

107

although she has never seen one, brilliant living trees even though there is nary a tree near here, valleys, peaks and oceans, she paints them all even though she has never laid eyes on them. And how does she do it? She feels, she imagines, she uses her intuition. Yet, when it comes to her own mother, she is baffled, stifled by everything she believes her mother is not, instead of enraptured by everything she is."

"What do you know Bugsy? You've never even talked to her."

"Long-ago Gloria, before I came here, I was befriended by a very powerful woman, one who knew the inner workings of this community. She would tell me stories about a girl, Ava; how she was the most brilliant, determined girl she had ever seen. And just you wait, this tough little thing was going to change the world."

"Change the world? You can't change the world if you spend all your time in a lab."

"You're right, not alone, but your mother is not alone."

"That's all she ever is."

"She is with you now, you are breathing her name, speaking of her, she lives through you now."

"Who is this woman who told you about my mother?"

"She was legend personified."

Gloria rolled her eyes. "Oh gross, spare me the details."

"No, nothing like that. She was my friend in the truest sense of the word, honorable, giving, and kind. But more important than her kindness was the extraordinary leadership she showed in reaching out to all people. You see, she was a humanitarian, one who believed in freedom for all. I was lucky enough to know her personally, but her work was with the world. She did more to ensure rights for all people than possibly any person who came before her. And in your mother she saw a kindred spirit, someone as dedicated to a world of equality as she was. She's the reason I'm here, and I thank her everyday."

"What did my mom ever due to be called a humanitarian? She hasn't done anything."

"Gloria, when I first came here it was nineteen sixty-two, your mom was in her early twenties, married to your father and had already finished her work in her lab."

"Finished what?"

"Well no one knows exactly, she's kept it a secret."

"So you just think she might be great, you don't even know?"

"Yes, just the way I think you will achieve greatness, even though, to date, you have not. With the exception of some perception shattering paintings, of course. Yes, I believe your mom has accomplished something extraordinary."

"But what do you think she's working on?"

"Now, I'm not sure, but I have a pretty good idea of what she was working on. When I first came to Larkspur your mother was a much discussed figure, rumors ran wild about, "the physics girl," or, "the science genius." She had been working in

108

her lab since she was eight years old and no one knew for sure what she was doing. Most thought she was working for the government, or the Council as you call them here, in an attempt to make the greatest weapons of warfare ever known. Well, I had heard a very different story from my boss."

"Your boss?"

"Yes, the woman I was talking about. According to her, your mother was not working to create weapons, but destroy them. My boss was never entirely sure because most of her information came from a physicist, who although he worked closely with your mother, readily admitted he could not from a physics standpoint, completely understand the direction she was headed. but his estimates of her intentions closely matched that of my employer's beliefs about your mother's goals."

"Well, I'm convinced," Gloria said sarcastically.

"The impatience which drives you also does you a great disservice," he said with frustration in his voice. "I am not finished, there is more. Back when your mom was twenty-one, there was a strange event right before she stopped working in her lab. Members of the security board reported seeing very bright, swift flashes of light late one night. They saw something launched into the sky, and then vanish. They sent men into the desert to investigate but they found nothing. They suspected your mom the whole time, but she gave up work in her lab and started a family so they never pursued the matter."

"What do you think happened?"

"Well, you are aware the surrounding area is used for nuclear testing, as a matter of fact, the first atom bomb was dropped not too far from here."

"Yeah, the reason for the high radiation levels, the reason we can't leave."

"I believe your mom did her own nuclear testing, only, her goal was to stop the missile from exploding. Gloria, the only person other than your mom and dad who possibly have the ability to know what she created, because of her depth of knowledge of both the government and Larkspur, my boss, believed your mom created a device with the ability to intercept nuclear weapons. You see Gloria, her creation has the potential to make nuclear warfare obsolete."

"I don't believe it. I'm not calling you a liar, because clearly you believe what you are saying is true even though you may be piss drunk, I just don't believe my mother is involved. I don't believe she's some secret nuclear avenger working for the safety of all humankind."

Bugsy quickly jumped to his feet, staggered a little, then regained his balance. "You are a silly little insolent child sometimes," he yelled angrily. "You look far and wide for the answers to all your questions and you ignore what is directly in front you. You believe in nothing but the unknown. Right here, right in front of you, in your own home, is the one person in the world who shares your ideals most, and you refuse to see it. Go, be gone, I've had it with you," he said, waving her away.

Gloria gathered her pack and left.

The next few months she didn't see Bugsy at all. She felt betrayed, belittled; she wanted nothing to do with him. Every day since angrily leaving Bugsy's she climbed to the bluff overlooking her mother's lab. Some days she painted, some days she just sat and stared at the building so rife with enigma in her mind. She wondered, could it be true? Could her mom really be what Bugsy says she is? Gloria no longer saw all the reasons why her mother couldn't be a great inventor, but searched for what evidence there was to disprove the possibility. She could not come up with a single reason why Bugsy's story couldn't be true, other than she just couldn't imagine that was what her mom had been doing all these years. So, she sat there, watching her mother's lab, imagining everything she might be doing, imagining the machines she would use, the light she created, she imagined her mom in there trying to change the world, and slowly, skeptically, she began to believe.

Tensions at home dissipated. For Gloria the mornings were even jovial. Her mom even made it a point to stay home for breakfast. Since longer than she could remember Gloria was consistently sitting at the kitchen table sharing a meal with her mother. She was surprised by how funny her mother was, how full of life. They shared stories; for the first time she heard her mother express similar frustrations with Larkspur. It could be true she thought, my mother the revolutionary. She watched her mom smile, beautiful, bright and knowing. She watched her contemplate over questions about her past. She watched her flirt with her husband. Gloria watched and watched, talked and talked, and grew to love her mom for much more than a parent, but as a person, independent of obligation or necessity, a bona fide, deep, profound love, respect and admiration for an endearing and talented woman, whom happened to be her mother.

The transition from summer to autumn was late and abrupt. Unusually warm weather characterized all of September and much of October; this final week of October proved different. Huge, bright white puffy clouds interspersed with low lying dark gray clouds began to dominate the autumn sky. The clouds lingered, teased the parched desert plants with the tantalizing cool drops of life held tightly overhead. The strange weather was so ominous Gloria was afraid to paint. She feared the damage done by the insidious, unpredictable deluge of a desert storm on her canvas.

Gloria felt naked traversing the steep ledges leading to the familiar bluff without her painting pack. No canvas strapped to her throwing off her balance, she was agile and undaunted. She enjoyed the relative ease of the challenging climb; a brief vacation at her favorite locale, she thought. The unusual weather bringing temporary respite from the ordinary.

Light and free, she managed her way up to the bluff. She sat and dangled her feet off the edge, something she had been too scared to do until recently, mesmerized by the sheer cliff hovering over jagged rocks hundreds of feet below. She rested, happy, swinging her feet, singing to the plants, the rocks, the sky. She laughed to herself about something her dad had said before she left. "These clouds are here for a reason; maybe they've come for you. Think hard enough and they'll beam you right out of Larkspur," he had joked. She laughed, not because it was funny, despite his best efforts her father was corny at best, but because she had thought the same thing. She herself had wondered about the clouds, and if there was some impending special celestial event that would lead her away from this place.

Growing tired, surprisingly even sleepy; she moved away from the ledge and leaned against one of the large rock formations on the bluff. She looked out over the town, past her mother's lab, to the perfectly aligned characterless neighborhoods, each row as mercilessly precise as the first. For miles, there was nothing but right angles with forty-five degree roofs. Boring, she thought. Bugsy should've been allowed to design the new community buildings, he would've brought personality and life to the dull artificial skyline.

She missed her friend. Still smarting over their recent fight, she hadn't seen him for weeks. She had seen Bugsy drunk plenty of times, even angry, but this time she had felt his contempt for her. He spewed out judgments she hadn't even begun to realize existed. He disliked things about her, this was new, and she wondered if she could again regain the confidence to walk freely in front of him.

Her vision meandered from house to house, building to building, until she worked her way back to her mother's lab. She looked at the ever darkening clouds looming and back again at the lab. It was the smoke she noticed first, a small spiraling trail releasing from the drawn back roof. She had never seen smoke coming from her mom's lab before. She stood up hoping to get a better look, then, in what seemed a timeless moment, she saw the swift, colorless implosion of the building. She heard the loud boom in strange slow wavelengths, and watched with horror as the flames and smoke rose.

She immediately ran full force down the steep terrain. Despite her tremendous speed and momentum she managed to keep her feet. She hit the bottom of the hill in a flat sprint and headed towards her house. The clouds burst, the rain came pouring down, relentless and hard. The sheer terror that roared through her body was staggering in its ferocity. Unsure if her body was still her own, she pushed forward, there was no sound, she was aware only of the terrain directly in front of her. She demanded of her body like never before, running harder and with more meaning than she had ever thought possible. Maybe she's at home she thought, she's home, she must be at home.

At first she didn't recognize the figure running towards her, then the familiar gait came to her, it was her father, running in the same maniacal manner as she. They came upon each other, almost unable to stop the entirely consuming pursuits of their body. "Is she at home?" Gloria yelled, grabbing hold of her father's arm.

"No, she's not at home. Is it her lab?" her father asked.

"Yes," Gloria said tortured.

"The rain," he said, "maybe there's a chance?"

They sprinted to the smoldering lab. The rain had squelched the fire and they began to scavenge through the rubble. Large pieces of machinery were strewn about. There was no sign of Ava. They searched for hours, hundreds of townspeople

111

joined in. No trace of her remained, not a scrap of her clothes, not her flesh or bones, not her wedding ring, nothing, gone, she was gone.

Hours of frantic searching left both Marty and Gloria dirty, bruised and bloody. The torrential rain finally subsided as night fell. Heavy equipment and floodlights were brought in to help with the search. Marty, exhausted and trembling, staggered over to a small city park a hundred yards from the destruction. Gloria followed, noticing the pristine, untouched park mocking her with its smug lifeless presence striving on. Marty fell to his knees, sobbing, groaning under the strain. He placed his forehead on the ground, he pleaded. "No, not yet. Don't take her from me yet." Gloria kneeled by her father and placed her hand on his back. She cried. Silent scolding hot tears tumbled down her cheeks, freeing themselves from the deep, dark depths from which they came. They never did find Ava's body, hypothesizing she had been eviscerated by the energy of the blast.

Chapter 12

They joined several other platoons back at base camp. The men lined up for hot potato and onion soup, cheerful, eagerly anticipating the soothing warm liquid and relatively cozy sleeping conditions the tents at the base provided. The increasingly lively troop shared stories of the week's battles with other units. Private Gunderson pissing himself soon became common knowledge. The long line of hungry soldiers extended far out into the cold night from the large tent of the mess hall. The end of the line relegated to the unpopular or unseemly among them. Many men cut in front of the lowly, shivering soldiers, willfully ignoring the unheralded. The second to last man in line, Private Gunderson, received his share of jeers, usually involving his need for diapers or the reassurance they didn't allow girls on the front lines maybe he'd get reassigned. The other men at the back of the line went unnoticed, occasionally getting splashed by the clever soldiers who doused Private Gunderson with water. The cold night grew more bitter as the sun mercifully ended the dreadful day of Private Gunderson's humiliation.

The men at the end of the line finally wound their way to the soup after frustratingly witnessing some of the more highly regarded soldiers jump the line for seconds, even thirds. Military order and discipline suffered under the inept and petty leaders of the battalion. Chaos had seeped into the war weary group, leaving a power struggle amongst the men. And as the new power hierarchy emerged, leverage and bargaining tools were coveted. The men in the mess hall were gods. Controlling the food supply brought many gifts, and unparalleled battleground protection, for a favored portion provider had many angels on the battle field. So, when lowly Private Gunderson arrived for his ration, the cocksure cook couldn't let the moment pass. "Gundy, little girly, Gundy. Tough day hey, did the big bad wolf scare you, make you tinkle in your pants. Didn't you know we don't let little girls like you play with the big boys, hey Gundy, why you hear?"

"Could I get some soup please?" Private Gunderson asked meekly.

"Can't you hear me? We don't want little girls around here," the cook said.

"I'm very hungry, please, May I have some soup?"

The cook grabbed a bowl, ladled some soup into it, and then from the depths of his nasal passages hawked an enormous loogie and spit into the soup. He then put his briny index finger into it, stirred the soup, and handed it to the private. "Here you are little miss," he said. The private stood still, looking at the cook through his large doe eyes. The cook continued. "You said you were hungry. This is what we got today, chicken shit soup, special for little pansy asses like you."

"Please, I'm hungry?" the private asked again.

"That's what you get, it's a shame to waste any food on you at all, take it, consider yourself lucky."

In his protracted state of misery not even Private Gunderson had noticed the man behind him, the final soldier in line. But the man who hadn't uttered a word during the hour-long wait, interjected now. Gunderson immediately recognized the slow southern drawl as the man spoke. "I do believe the man deserves a proper portion of soup," said the last man in line.

The cook, not accustomed to any challenge to his authority, lashed out. "I don't give a fuck what you believe."

"It appears you don't give a fuck about anyone other than yourself?" the soldier said as he lifted his head slowly, exposing his face from under the bill of his cap.

"Oh, Ace, didn't see you there," the cook said sheepishly.

"I think you should give Private Gunderson a proper portion."

"Sure, Ace," the cook said obligingly. He ladled a bowl of soup and handed it to the private, who quickly grabbed the bowl and found a seat in the nearly empty mess all. "I was just giving him a hard time," the cook said as he ladled Ace some soup. "Toughen him up, you know. He's going to get somebody killed..." Ace said nothing. "Heard about what you did today, saving Pierce, heard he ordered you to patrol the point permanently. What a fuck."

Even with all the extra protection the cook received he knew Ace was the best soldier in the brigade, and keeping him well fed and happy was the only rational thing to do. What the cookie and other soldiers failed to take into account was Ace fought the best he could regardless. He didn't care what he had to do to protect his troop, he didn't care who he saved, he fought equally as hard for every soldier in an American uniform. "Hey, I was just kidding with Gundy, I was going to give him a different bowl of soup," the cook assured as Ace walked away.

Nothing like a group of war torn men with a little time on their hands and few thoughts as arousing as rousting the boy who couldn't hide his fear to brew up trouble. There were few greater reminders of the perilous fight they were in than a boy, not that different from themselves, soiling his trousers. They must set him apart from the group, he could not be one of them, they are not all little boys so scared they might pee in their pants. It couldn't be any one of them; it was him, only him. And any acknowledgment of understanding would imply they felt as scared as he, that they could possibly be so immersed and awed by the end of life, they were rendered helpless. Not possible they thought, and certainly not a possibility they wanted to be reminded of.

As the night wore on, and the soldiers became drunker and drunker, there was less and less chance Private Gunderson would get any sleep. He heard every rustle of the leaves, every snap of a twig. Any bit of skill he possessed as a soldier he now utilized to anticipate oncoming attackers. He lay in a sleeping tent twenty yards from the drunken gamblers. He tried to read, even write home, but he mostly prayed. Prayed that they would leave him alone, prayed no military justice of the kind their sergeant espoused would be enacted.

He wanted to do better, he wanted to be the kind of soldier they admired, but his skills lay elsewhere. He tended sheep back home. He loved the open prairie, mounting his horse with nothing but the earth and God's great creation set out before him. He longed for the silence and stillness of those days, when he laid in the tall green grass watching the clouds roll by. He cared for and loved those animals as if they were his own brethren, for that's the only way he knew how. He'd been at war now almost a year and had never raised his gun at another man, couldn't imagine a time when he would, he had accepted he would rather die than kill.

He must've fallen asleep some time past three in the morning, not long before the card game broke up. The inebriated men made their way into the sleeping tent without deference to any of the sleeping soldiers, and certainly not Gunderson. One of the men immediately started slapping the private awake. "Did you wet the bed Gundy, let's see?" He pulled the covers off the sleepy private. "I don't think you should be sleeping on our good sheets, do you gentlemen?" the soldier asked the ravenous crew.

"Sure don't," one of them said as the private quickly sprang up out of bed.

"Maybe he ought to sleep outside where his pissing problem won't affect anyone?"

"Hey guys, I won't..." Private Gunderson started to say before someone slapped him on the back of the head. The rest of the men picked him up and threw him into a puddle of mud outside the tent.

"Looks like you're all wet again little Gundy," one of the men said.

The private got up and tried to make his way back into the tent. The men kept him out, toying with his lack of physical prowess, like a big brother picking on the youngest without any sense of fairness, simply bullying because he can.

Gunderson awoke shivering, huddled in between a tree and some bushes. His clothes were still wet, and dried mud covered his face. The sun had just reached the dark shell of night as the weary soldier picked himself up, thought for a moment, and headed for the mess hall. The smell of bread baking, and the promise of warmth spurred the frozen, numb soldier.

He stumbled into the large tent rousing the curiosity of the three cooks preparing the day's meal. Private Gunderson headed directly to the ruminating warmth of the large stoves. The three cooks, including the one involved in the incident from the night before, ignored the desperate soldier. They worked around the feeble man who was attempting to reengage his circulatory system. Gunderson groaned with pain as the feeling returned to his hands, he shook his legs, and tried to squeeze his body back to the living. Only after the terror of his body's near paralysis had subsided did he notice the solitary man reading in the corner. He couldn't quite make out the face but the glowing tufts of red hair unfolding from under his hat betrayed his anonymity.

"Bout time you quit rustling around," the cook from the night before said to the private.

Private Gunderson, still foggy from the cold replied. "Sorry?" he said not hearing what the cook had said to him.

"They throw you out?" the cook asked.

Private Gunderson looked at the cook suspiciously. "What's it to you?"

The cook smiled, nodded over at Ace in the corner. "Do he know about it?"

"No, he wasn't there."

In fact, the men weren't quite sure where Ace spent his nights. In the field Ace often slept at a distance from the platoon, choosing the risk and freedom of isolation over the security and conformity of the group.

"Well, you best make sure he know, he's the only chance you got," the cook concluded.

"Sergeant Pierce will make sure I'm safe."

"Sergeant Pierce. Oh, you Pierce's new boy, should've known. Boy, he ain't going to help you when the time come, he only cares about his self, you's a dime a dozen to him."

"Well, I ain't dead yet," the private said assuredly.

"Yeah," the cook said pointing towards Ace, "and if you want it to stay that way, you better make sure you can see that head of fire at all times."

"Why are you being so nice to me, I mean talking to me and all?"

"We all want to survive, and he's the best chance we've got. He says hands off, I listen."

The cook sent Private Gunderson off with warm bread, sausage and gravy, a veritable feast. Also, carried close to his chest, he held a large canister of boiling hot water. As the rest of the men filed in for breakfast, Gunderson headed to the latrine and took a bath in the most luminously warm water he had felt in months. He chewed his scrumptious meal while letting the warmth of the water loosen his taut muscles. He sat in the metal soaking tub, marveling at the events of the last twenty hours; nearly being killed, made the laughingstock of the brigade and now, a king high on his horse. He sat back and recalled the days before the army; the soothing recollections brought him peace for a few moments, the first time in over a year.

Gunderson leisurely dressed, alone in the bunk, clean-shaven, and refreshed, he crawled into his bed and enjoyed a deep pleasurable sleep. He felt the weight of someone sitting on the edge of his bed. Unafraid, basking in the warm glow of his dream filled sleep, he rubbed his eyes to see Sergeant Pierce filling his vision. The sergeant placed a hand on his leg. "Just wanted to see how you were doing after yesterday. Checked the mess hall, boys said you had a rough night, nightmares and all, said you left the tent."

"I'm all right now," Gunderson said, sitting up.

"Listen, Gundy. I know battles can get rough, and the aftermath isn't always pretty, but you're still my guy," the sergeant said, squeezing the private's leg. "You're my right-hand man, nothing's changed."

Ace entered the tent and Sergeant Pierce quickly stood. "There's the hero himself," Sergeant Pierce said.

"Sergeant," Ace replied.

The sergeant began to walk out of the room, stopping at Ace. He tapped Ace's chest with his pointed index finger. "You know son, war can change people, make them selfish, unwilling to sacrifice. I've seen it in the likes of men like you, big hero's one day, cowards the next. Don't you think you're some hot shit because you got lucky. Remember, I write up the reports, the battles go how I say they go."

The sergeant gave him one last poke to the chest as he walked away. Private Gunderson sat staring at the quiet exchange. Ace raised his head to meet the private's gaze; the boy blinked and stared trying to understand what had transpired.

The days of rest served some soldiers better than others. Most enjoyed the warm meals and cozy barracks, the American oasis in the middle of a European war. Others found no solace in the time between death and life. The difficulty that comes with exchanging the death of war, with the life of the base, left some un-pacified. The girls, the cards, the booze, the buffers between life and death, they held little interest to these men. In some ways, the time at camp was more excruciating, because of its degradation of life's values, than the war's unpretentious singular pursuit of death. War made no exceptions for morality, the blurring of the acceptable was entirely complete, an agreement furthered by both sides. The base, where wars egregious philosophies accompany every entering soldier, was a land caught between ideologies. The erosion of laws and rights synchronized with leadership degradation. Every base had its ethics, and for Ace, the base was more unbearable than the ravages of war.

Now, back on patrol, Ace, walked through the thick wooded landscape with a familiar sense of duty, a duty he only questioned back at the base. It didn't start out that way, the men seemed noble and earnest, hopeful they could squelch the axis uprising. They understood it was a war for power, a war for domination, a war brought on by aggression deserving of aggression. What they didn't know was the extent their necessary aggression would infiltrate their psyche, their vision of the army blurred, power and domination seeped into warless encounters. They happened upon the hamlet nestled in the hills by the river during a particularly nasty cold storm which teetered between freezing rain and snow. The village was entirely serene. Several trails of smoke could be seen from the less than a dozen structures which comprised the entire village and its inhabitants. Ace cased the village, encountering no men at all, only women; mothers, grandmothers and children, he relaxed. They offered him coffee and a seat by the fire, he declined, occasionally rustling the hair of an adoring child, or leaving a baseball card in the palm of a doe eyed onlooker.

Ace dreamed of being a professional baseball player when he returned. He had caught glimpses of a few of the profession ballplayers stationed in other units but had been too shy to introduce himself. Baseball, similar to war, he thought, demanded his extreme focus and concentration. When he played, nothing else in the world mattered, as if time ceased to exist, and all of life's concerns patiently waited for his return. The feeling of squaring up a pitch, there was nothing like it. Snaring a hard-hit line drive out of the air, a small hard round object, hit so hard one could barely see it, stopped dead by a web of leather, it seemed to defy the laws of physics. He didn't know how it was possible sometimes, but he was more addicted to that feeling, flirting with impossibility, than any he had ever known.

Wandering through the village, caught up in the allure of the sounds of the crack of the bat followed by the roar of the crowd, Ace peered through the cloudy window of a tiny hut nestled between two large trees. He saw a small baby crying on the floor, and several men from his platoon stacked into the small home. He opened the door. "What are you doing? Get off of her," he said as he lunged across the room and pulled a fellow soldier off a crying woman.

"What's your problem man?" The soldier said pulling up his pants.

"You must have a problem with a man getting his needs met," bellowed Sergeant Pierce from the corner of the room. The sergeant inhaled then exhaled the smoke from his cigarette. "Maybe he doesn't have needs like us gentlemen, maybe he has different needs?" he said.

Ace pushed the soldier out the door. "Go on, get the fuck out of here." He turned to the other soldiers. "Go on, get out," he said. They quickly scampered away.

Sergeant Pierce leaned casually against a wall, puffing the last of his cigarette. The woman covered herself and picked her crying baby up off the floor. The sergeant threw his still lit cigarette down. "It's best you mind your own business son. You think you've seen things, you ain't seen nothing 'til you see what we do to canaries around here. You ain't seen nothing, hear me boy," the sergeant warned.

Ace stood calmly and stared at Sergeant Pierce as he left the shack. Ace turned to look into the scared and wounded eyes of the young woman. He straightened up the small table and chairs the men had knocked over then returned to his unit.

Things grew increasingly worse after that. The unit became divided into those willing to play by Pierce's rules and those unwilling. For many of the men fighting the war, all experiences became moments of war. Walking through villages, getting supplies, getting their boots cleaned, the longer they were under threat, the more these activities became volatile, filled with angst and retribution. Balanced perspective became lost, skewed by the ideas and concepts of war, kill or be killed, what you have to do to survive along the way was irrelevant. Few men were unchanged, a good strong leader could usually keep them in line, but those were in short supply. The raping and pillaging, either outright encouraged, silently condoned, or snuffed out, seemed to Ace to occur in thirds according to the leadership, which made for two thirds bad, and it got bad, real, real bad.

A man like Ace would fight hard forever for what he thought was just, but he had never imagined having to fight a just war, with unjust men. He was caught between loyalties, the love for his country, his beliefs in democracy and respect for human rights, versus the complete degradation of those principles by his fellow countrymen. The same men he must fight beside, who by uniform represented the values of the country he so cherished, the same men that raped women and girls, young girls, raped them, stole their food, made them clean their clothes. Could he remain loyal to a cause fought by those men? Is that what he had become? Is that the man this war had made him?

For months Ace agonized over the direction his platoon had taken. He chided himself for consistently witnessing the aftermath of his rogue platoon, seemingly never able to prevent it. He began to realize, in a way, he was enabling the atrocities. Sergeant Pierce ordered him to sweep the village for combatants, and their faith in his ability, his thoroughness, would allow their unmitigated action without consequence he so despised. He would find women beaten, crying, fearful of his presence. He would soothe their crying children, put on a pot of tea, tend to their wounds, but he could not undo what had been done. He would rejoin the unit. "Find anybody Ace?" Sergeant Pierce would ask.

"No sir," Ace would reply, sick with guilt and torment over what he had seen. How many times could he be a part of this? How could he endure? What choice did he have?

For Ace, battles were moments of clarity and decisiveness, assuredness and competence, the simplicity of survival. But, as the moments away from war wore on him, he began to hesitate, doubts and thoughts seeped in. Should he risk his life and limb for a man he knew to be corrupt? Should he protect the life of someone bringing such harm to others? These questions began to plague him. His focus and concentration were waning; he felt an unfamiliar vulnerability rising inside him. His belief in the cause determined his ability as a soldier, and he could no longer believe, he could no longer pretend.

The revered and tireless man-of-war became a wary, tormented man of conflict. He no longer wanted anything to do with this war; he wanted either to be a casualty of it or, to escape from it. He no longer fought with the same conviction; he lost the respect of the men, of himself. They no longer heralded his keen ability, for his cunning was lost in a perilous world of betrayal and disappointment. Ace pulled further and further from the men, sickened by them, as they were by him, he a reminder of the reality outside of war, a dose of conscience they would rather forget. For him, they were a reminder of his new reality, a stain on his existence that could never be removed. Their faces, their disgusting smiles, their untouchable laughs, all seared his brain, injuring the soft tissue, scarring his psyche.

His only hope was the end of the war. Rumors swirled that the end was near and their advancement on Germany was yielding success. After several harrowing battles, Ace's nerves were frayed and his resolve low. They had been stationed at a base on the outskirts of France for a week. They were to take part in a massive, and hopefully final, offensive in the coming days. Ace had set up his pup tent away from the other men. He generally grabbed some food from the still sympathetic cook before the rest of the men ate. He stayed in his tent and read, neither attending role call, nor explaining himself. The platoon and Sergeant Pierce were equally pleased by the redhead's absence. "The fire?" The sergeant would ask.

"No fire here, sergeant," they would reply.

Ace heard the footsteps of someone approaching, it was nearly two a.m., he was long beyond caring if he would be killed in the middle of the night. The bespectacled face of Private Gunderson poked his head in the tent. "You awake, Ace?" he whispered.

"Go away, Gundy."

"Ace, there's something I think you should know."

"Fuck off, Gundy."

"There's a woman. Sergeant Pierce is holding her in his tent."

"What do you mean holding her?"

"I mean he took her from her home yesterday. He's got her tied up; I'm supposed to stand guard when he's gone."

"Why are you telling me?"

"I can't stand it. Her mouth's covered, she's whimpering, it's unbearable."

"Why don't you do something about it, Gundy?"

"He'll kill me. He said if anybody found out he'd kill me. He'll do it Ace."

"Might as well be dead, Gundy, watching that happen."

"I'm not like you Ace, always doing what's right. You're strong, you can stand up for yourself, I'd of been dead a long time ago if it weren't for the sergeant, he protects me."

"He uses you. He does whatever he wants, and you protect him."

"What choice do I have?"

"When did participating in the torture of women become an acceptable choice? What life do you have to go back to if you've given away your honor? If you have to give up everything you believe in to survive, what's the fucking point? You're just going to go around feeling like an asshole for the rest of your life."

"I'm going to do what I have to do, and yes, it's horrible, and I'll never forget it, but I'll be alive. And no, I'm not going to spend my whole life feeling like an asshole because I chose life over honor. Honor isn't going to make my mom feel any better when I'm dead, and it's not going to make the war end any sooner, and honor isn't going to keep those men from attacking me at night. So, until you are in my position, fuck you and your judgments. There's a woman over there being tortured, I thought you should know, do whatever the fuck you want," Private Gunderson said and walked away.

Ace put on his gear and spent the rest of the night walking through the trees surrounding the base. As the sun came up Ace was perched between two trees

120

surrounding Sergeant Pierce's tent. Soon after the first light the sergeant stumbled out of his tent to pee. Seeing the snorting and sniffling man made Ace sick to his stomach. He wondered how this man had come to lead his platoon. What was the lesson he was supposed to learn from this man's immoral and corrupt leadership? Was there some revelation he was missing, some golden value lost on him, or was this just a futile effort in mediocrity? What strength was there to be gained by freezing in a forest, watching callous irreverence, still hoping to change one atrocity one time, only for more and more to occur, ceaseless, senseless, they rise like ants flocking to the sweet injustice of war.

Ace watched the sergeant take out his tiny little cock. He didn't feel hatred, but pity, sadness even, for a man so far from loved, he was so far lost. He wondered how long the wounds festered inside this man before he acted, what finally set him off, was it a broken heart, abuse, or the silently insidious peril of neglect? Was he the type who tortured animals as a child, beat up kids, taunted girls, was he born evil? Does Satan really work through people the way they say, without mercy, pervasive and chilling?

Ace had studied him, observed every movement, every inflection, every look. The past year displayed little variance in the sergeant's emotion, but Ace had witnessed tenderness from Pierce on two occasions. Once, when they happened upon a toddler crying in the woods. The sergeant tenderly picked the child up. "This child should not be without his mother," he said. They searched the nearby village for the baby's family. They finally found the mother in a small house with her seven screaming kids unaware her second youngest had wandered off. She thanked the sergeant. He smiled, patted the oldest boy on the head and left. The second act of tenderness, only Ace witnessed. It was a few months back, a warm spring day, the men were leisurely patrolling a well secured portion of northern France. The sergeant was leaning against a tree smoking a cigarette when he suddenly sprang to life, quickly running up to a branch on a nearby tree, mesmerized by what he saw. Ace watched silently as the sergeant giggled with delight. "Look," the sergeant said aloud to no one in particular, "a cocoon, it's opening." The sergeant quickly looked around, seeing no one, not noticing Ace in the periphery, he returned to the cocoon. Pierce oohed and awed as a butterfly slowly emerged from its protective shell. Ace could easily make out the brilliant gold, green and blue of the new butterfly's wings. The weak butterfly staggered off the branch onto the uneven forest floor. Sergeant Pierce dropped to his knees and lowered his face close to the butterfly. In a sweet, barely audible, almost nurturing tone, he said, "come on little guy, you can do it." The sergeant tenderly watched the weak and limp butterfly struggle to navigate the tiny peaks and valleys. Pierce then gently cupped the butterfly in his hands and raised it from the ground and opened his hands, gazing adoringly at the awakening creature. The butterfly slowly tested its wings, clumsily opening and closing them. Then, in a flash, the butterfly quickly rose in the sky, fluttering its wings erratically until it was out of sight. "I'll be," muttered the sergeant as he lifted himself off the ground.

Ace wondered about these times now, if there was some sense of decency he could appeal to? Could he risk confronting the sergeant and rattling the vicious blood of an attacker? Ace decided against appealing to the gentle side of a maniac.

Ace waited for the sergeant to wander off to breakfast. After a few minutes he stealthily entered the sergeant's tent. She was a tiny woman, no more than five feet, one hundred pounds, tied face down on the bed. Ace slowly approached the bed. "I'm here to help you," he said in French, a phrase he had learned out of necessity. The woman turned to try to look at him then screamed into the cloth tied over her mouth. He reached for her wrist, untying it, and then the other. She stopped screaming, he removed the rag from her mouth, then he took off his jacket and placed it around her shoulders. She looked up at him quietly, cautiously, hoping he really was there to set her free. He untied her feet, helped her to the side of the bed, she was injured and had difficulty standing. He realized he must carry her, find some villagers to help.

Ace gently lifted her in his arms. She groaned with pain but managed to wrap her arms around his neck. He left the tent and headed straight into the woods, he ran flat out as far as he could. After a few miles he smelled wood-burning and happened upon a small clearing. There were several small stone houses spread over a few acres. He knocked on the door of the first house he came to. After a moment a very old woman came to the door, she looked at the girl, then looked at him. He looked the old woman straight in the eye; she motioned for them to come in. The old woman guided them to an open chair by the fire. He gently placed the injured woman down. The old woman found a blanket for the girl and put a kettle on top of the stove. Ace stayed with the injured woman for a few minutes, holding her hand until she fell asleep. The old woman patted him on the shoulder, he rose. "Merci," he said. She raised her weathered hand to his cheek. "Merci," she said.

Ace jogged back to the base and circled around to the other side of camp to his tent. He quickly grabbed his combat jacket and headed to the mess hall. The large tent was still filled with soldiers. He saw Sergeant Pierce, some officers, and Private Gunderson seated at the end of a nearly empty table. Relieved they were still eating, he went to the beverage table to get some coffee. The cook noticed him and yelled out. "Hey Ace, missed you this morning. Can I get you a plate?"

"Slept in today cookie. No, I'm fine with coffee for a while, thanks though."

"I didn't think you ever slept, must have had some company, hey Ace?"

Sickened by the morning's events, the pains in his stomach grew fiercer. Ace almost doubled over as the cook addressed him, he quickly composed himself. "Naw, just tired that's all," he said. He noticed both Pierce and Gunderson staring at him.

"You ain't been tired the entire war Ace and you don't look tired now," the cook said bluntly.

It was true; Ace was keenly alert and surely emitted the essence of a man fully aware of his senses. He knew the overslept rhetoric was possibly the most implausible explanation he could've given. Ace laughed. "My momma raised a gentleman," he said drawing on his affable southern accent.

"I knew it. You did get laid. 'Bout time, some of us were starting to wonder."

Ace picked up his coffee and sat at a nearby table. He felt the intent gaze of Pierce and Gunderson following him to his seat. He saw Pierce look at Gunderson and the scared private turn away. Pierce rose and quickly left the tent.

Later that day they received orders they would be marching into Germany the next morning. The camp bustled with activity: weapons preparation, packing, planning, strategy meetings, there was little time to worry about Pierce and his reaction to the woman being gone. But Ace was on alert, he watched his sergeant, but he never saw him break character once. The consummate officer, battle strategy, formations, war, that's all he conveyed, there was no hint of turmoil, no moment of wandering thought. Possibly, the battle would save him from Pierce's wrath; possibly there would be no time for revenge.

They set out before dawn; several hundred men from dozens of platoons comprised the largest unit formation Ace had been a part of. They arranged laterally by platoon, with Ace finally relieved of his traditional duty at the point, he meandered towards the back of the pack. The cool, crisp morning stiffened the groggy soldiers. Faces ached with the cold, lungs tightened at the unwelcome shocking bitter air. There was no sound other than the men tramping through the forests, no birds singing, no animals to be found, all life was leery of the passing group.

The soldiers were concerned, heading into possibly the last great battle of the war, the time the enemy would surely fight till death or capture, no retreat, no stalemate. Somber, but focused, they moved through the damp green land of their discontent, no idle banter, no jokes, just thoughts, pondering the possibilities. The pace was slow, hindered by the cold and the dark. They expected a two-hour trek from which they would never go back, but the journey appeared as if it would take far longer, leaving more time to anticipate their ultimate fate.

"Berlin will be the site of our next camp gentlemen; our mission is coming to a close. I need everything you can give for a short time longer," the brigade commander had said before setting out.

It was too soon to entertain thoughts of civilian life, but many of the soldiers felt the twinges of apprehension at the idea of integrating back into peacetime. The level of investment, mental and physical, the war demanded created so much space between now and then, the life of old, their fear of war dissolved into a fear of peace. Relating to their fellow soldiers, the men going through the same terror and trials as they, had been their only resource. An irreplaceable bond and camaraderie creating inter-reliance, even dependency, had formed. The first phase of war was the tremendous fear of the war itself, but somewhere along the way the war seemed bearable, almost usual, as long as they were there with their fellow soldiers. Soon, the only fear became being without those men, the one's standing by their side throughout, proving anything, even fighting a war, was possible. Those moments they thought they could never get through, the hunger, the cold, the violence, the gory reality of battle, the death, they had passed, and they had survived. Without each other, they were not sure if any of it could have been done. An allegiance of life and coping replaced a lonely determined field of doom. Between the men grew a love affair of companionship, everything was bearable, together.

But after the war, as unknown to those who leave war as war to those who have never been, all the shared experience, all the trust built, crumbles under the weight of geographical isolation. They will leave this war and they will go home, their old home, the one without the people who got them through the un-imaginable plight of the perils of war. Home becomes a matter of being alone, alone in a world that can't relate, can't possibly comfort them, and will never understand, a world that has no place for them because their only place is with each other. But now, there is no time for the gut shot of nervous emotion that rises inside them, now, they have a war to fight. The sun begins to peek over the mountains, they know they are close, they know the end is near.

The thud, like a watermelon dropped on the ground from high above, was faint, almost weightless, but so out of place in the cool dawn air Ace turned to follow the sound. Preparing for an ambush, he carefully navigated toward the strange noise behind him. After fifty yards he heard another thud, then rustling in the leaves, he dropped to his stomach and peered out from behind the trees. He was surprised to see American uniforms; he squinted and caught a glimpse of Sergeant Pierce's profile as he struck the soldier cowering on the ground. In one motion Ace sprung to his feet, ran a few steps, and pounced on the sergeant, knocking him to the ground.

"What the fuck?" the sergeant said. The sergeant looked at the man who had interrupted him and ruefully smiled. "Boy, this has nothing to do with you. This is between me and Private Gunderson."

Ace turned to private Gunderson and said, "Gundy, get out of here."

"Stay right there private," Sergeant Pierce ordered.

Ace looked at the Sergeant. "Sergeant, we are soldiers of the United States Army with a duty to fulfill, and you are hindering our ability to follow orders, we will be going now," Ace said.

The sergeant pulled out his pistol. "I don't think so Ace. You see, I'm your commanding officer, and I say when you go."

"Not any more sergeant, you don't hold any power over me, not anymore," Ace replied.

The sergeant laughed. "Oh, you think you're a big man now, you think you can do whatever you want?"

Private Gunderson slowly backed away from the two men. The soft early morning sunlight illuminated the two figures, giving them a slightly ethereal quality. Gunderson relaxed with the soft beauty of the light, feeling no harm would come to him. He watched as Ace dropped his rifle, removed his ammo, his jacket, and stood in front of the sergeant in his T-shirt, bare fisted.

"You want to fight?" the sergeant asked Ace. "How fucking noble of you. Okay, let's see what you're made of."

The sergeant threw down his gun and removed his jacket. Private Gunderson noticed a second pistol tucked into the back of the sergeant's belt. Ace, fists tight, knees bent, began to move forward.

The sergeant laughed. "You're still a fool who thinks people play fair," he said as he pulled the gun from his belt. "It's about time you learn those beliefs only get you one place, dead and buried," Pierce said, as he pointed the gun towards Ace.

The shot rang out before Private Gunderson realized what happened. Amazed, he saw the sergeant's right forearm split open and the gun go hurtling to the ground. The sergeant dropped to his knees in pain. Gunderson raised his own right hand and looked shockingly at the smoking pistol he gripped tightly.

"You fucking shot me, you stupid fucking piece of shit," the sergeant said in disbelief.

Ace looked over at the private. "Nice shot Gundy, didn't know you had it in you."

The private said dryly, "I was aiming for his head."

The sergeant, now pleading, said, "you stupid fucks, help me, I'm bleeding all over the place."

The two soldiers looked at each other almost playfully and broke into a smile. They heard the sound of men approaching. Ace picked up his gear. "It's time for me to go, Gundy."

"I think it is. Thank you, Ace," the private said humbly.

"Hey, you saved me pal."

"Thank you, for helping me finally stand up for myself."

"Give 'em hell, Gundy."

And with that he was off.

The private shook his head, then straightened up and stood tall. A few seconds later, half a dozen men from another platoon arrived. "What happened here?" a soldier asked.

"One of my soldiers attacked the two of us," the sergeant said. "He shot me and took off that way."

"Who was it?" The soldier asked.

Private Gunderson replied. "It was Ace. But it was the sergeant who attacked us." The men look stunned. "forget Ace, he's long gone, you'll never find him," Gundy assured.

Chapter 13

His frailty stopped alarming her long ago. After all, it had been over fifteen years since he had lost the use of his legs, and his decline over the past few months seemed more to do with the war than his health. He recently had begun discussing his goals for his fourth term as if he might be unable to complete them. She scoffed at the idea. "Tell it to the VP," she would say.

"He has an agenda," Henry would say. "I need someone without an agenda."

"And who's that, Henry?"

"You, Maggie."

"I absolutely have an agenda."

"Yes, but it has nothing to do with attaining power."

"It has nothing to do with oppressing, that's different than not wanting to be powerful. You must separate your power from betrayal, for they are not symbiotic."

"Only to you dear, only to you."

So, he talked about projects, life after the war, everything he wanted to do but couldn't because of the country's commitment to war, a vacuous vortex of international responsibility. Like the murder investigation in a small town only accustomed to an occasional fistfight, the country was overwhelmed by the distasteful venture. Resources allocated to the important, utterly necessary, and entirely unwanted pursuit of war. She would listen, not believing she would ever really have to know, messages ignored in a fit of eternal optimism.

Ruby listened. She listened hard to everything he had to say even though she would never be able to do anything about it. The years of loyalty and trust die when he dies, never recognized in a world where certain relationships are only given certain meaning. And the true meaning of their relationship will be lost when he goes, secrets underground forever.

Ruby watched the enduring spirit of the man she so admired wane, yielding to the physical and mental agony of a life faced with constant suffering. The war, his health, his love, devastated his strength. He fought for so long, more than anyone should ever have to, he did it willingly, courageously, but the battle had taken its toll. When he spoke of the end, she knew he meant it; it was coming, not because he wanted it, but because he had reached the limitations of being human. There are struggles which can't be overcome, only endured until the end. Henry's existence, filled with a lifetime of such torment, was spiraling. A life under full duress, in time, eventually becomes a life that fades quickly. Ruby recognized the dimming of the bright light of a great man. She mourned for all that will be lost when he goes, and reveled in the freedom and lightness that will be his soul without hardship.

The frenetic war obsessed energy of the White House drove Maggie to spend most of her days at the cabin in the country. She greatly preferred the clear, simple sounds of a world untouched to the tones of a world relegated into delegated distraction by its occupiers. The war was far more difficult to endure than Maggie ever could have imagined. The toll on the soldiers, the families, the land; she was unprepared for the utter completeness of the devastation.

There was also an enormous strain on her relationship with Henry. The distance between them was greater than it had ever been. A lifetime of back-and-forth had never seen them apart for so long. Once or twice a month was all they were seeing each other now. Henry stayed at the capitol, visited his beloved Warm Springs, or traveled to conferences for yet another friendly display of united force. She would call when she had congratulations, advice, or rebuke about policy or speeches. But their personal relationship propagated only in the light of concerned parents and shared history, building a future was a thing of the past.

Charlie, Maggie's driver and right hand man, kept informed about the president's health. He had quite a strong personal relationship with the chief medical examiner. Maggie trusted Charlie would let her know when it got bad. Charlie had been her travel partner for several years; after she had that little fender bender. Henry's advisers thought it would best if she have accompaniment, Charlie was the perfect choice.

She had first met Charlie not long after becoming First Lady, when he was a very young soldier. She had taken to him immediately, and had brought him to work at the White House having no idea he would ultimately become one of her dearest friends. And although she initially objected to the idea of a chaperone, even in those early days before she had really come to know Charlie, she knew she trusted him implicitly, and quickly relented.

At first she was very shy with Bea in front of Charlie. But the more time she spent with him, the more she was free to be herself. Charlie was very good at being essential and independent, leaving the women whenever seemed necessary, and being enjoyable during their time when together. He was witness to a more complete picture of Maggie's life than anyone. He saw her at the White House, with the president and without. He saw her life with Bea, and all she meant to her. Neither Bea, nor Henry had that kind of access to her, each giving way to the other.

Both Bea and Henry appreciated Charlie's role in Maggie's life. Henry, because it took the pressure off him and made it less likely what he suspected was between Bea and his wife was reality, Bea simply enjoyed Charlie. Beatrice found him sweet, reserved but charming. She felt an almost maternal affection for the boy barely out of his teens when they first met. She immediately sensed his gentle manner and went about rousting the playfulness out of him. She slightly prodded the boy out of his protective shell, safely teasing and engaging him, letting him know she saw him, she knew he was there no matter how silently he hid. The shy Charlie warmed to Bea, offering more and more of his opinions, consequently increasing his openness with Maggie.

When he began to work for Maggie, he was quite a meek young man. For a boy so clearly consumed with awe at the devastations of ordinary life, working for the first lady seemed a natural complication. Still recovering from the injuries which ended his military career when he arrived, he was frail and skittish, often jumping at the smallest of unexpected noises. Charlie would only sit in a chair with a view of the entryway, never wanting his back to the door, if one was not available, he stood. It was years before Maggie figured out the reason for his peculiar seating habit, his constant need to be on-guard, and many more years before he finally relaxed these restrictions.

Charlie never explained himself, nor was it expected of him. He was free to divulge as little or as much as he wanted, as Maggie reserved the same right. They joined together in a silent solidarity of understanding and deference to the unsaid, for they learned enough with the intimacy of proximity, and idle intrusion can dispirit the timid. He continued to trust and flourish, all his previous misfortunes melting into the warmth of their friendship.

Maggie and Bea took pleasure in Charlie's evolution into a comfortable and composed, if still, private man. Now in his thirties, they chided him about marriage, hoping he would introduce them to his special someone one day, knowing most likely he would not. He said he'd be happy to live out his life with peace and solitude. "What about sex?" Bea would ask.

"It's not for me," he would reply.

"We'll maybe you haven't met the right woman," Maggie would say.

"Or man," Bea chimed in.

"I'm just fine on my own, thanks," he would say.

"Just our luck, you can stay with us forever," Bea joked.

The three of them had spent the last week together at the country house. Beatrice had taken a rare hiatus from covering the progress of the war, but with news of the U.S. advancement on Germany, she decided it was time to get back to the capitol. Charlie and Maggie, enchanted by the early spring weather, decided to stay on a couple of more days. The past few weeks had seen the returning of the leaves and blossoming of the flowers, the land new again, with cold and stark days lingering only in fading memories.

Charlie drove Beatrice to the train station, they embraced. "She should come back soon Charlie," Beatrice implored.

"I know, I'll try," Charlie replied.

"She can't hide out here forever pretending it's not happening. What does the doctor say?"

"The President has been down at Warm Springs the past week gaining strength."

"Now, he's at Warm Springs now? We're about to invade Berlin and he's in Georgia? He is not well, Charlie. Does Maggie know he's down there?"

"She knows."

"What does she think?"

"She thinks he wants to be alone with Ruby."

Bea looked concerned and saddened. "Just get her back soon."

"All right," he said as she turned to board. "Have a safe trip, see you soon."

She returned to lovingly kiss him on the cheek and then boarded the train.

*

Henry loved the south in April, before the oppressive heat and torrential afternoon thunderstorms of the summer, the brief, mild transition from cold to hot. The temperate air and lush green landscape accentuated the allure of the place he had grown to love. The warmth and kindness of the southern people seemed to enhance the healing effects of Warm Springs.

He'd been coming to Warm Springs nearly twenty years, since shortly after losing the use of his legs. He had read an article touting the healing properties of the warm, buoyant spring water and decided to investigate himself. Whether it was the restorative nature of time away from the White House, or the genuine therapeutic quality of the water, his strength and coordination improved. He bought the place a few years later, and watched many hundreds of lives transformed. Some achieved physical change great or small, some came to terms with their abilities, all were accepted, possibly the greatest gift of Warm Springs.

He spent hours in the water, floating, swimming, helping his body live the way it used to, long ago. Out of the pool he was often found rocking on the porch, smoking, and playing a friendly game of cards. Here, he wasn't the President of the United States, he was a man struck with a disease which altered him forever, he was coping, hoping, working like all the rest. He dined with the guests, laughed with them, suffered with them, he was not the demigod of the rest of his life, he was as flawed, as humbled, as human as them all.

Unable to get to the springs as often as he would like during the climax of war, he felt its absence had contributed to his declining health. The past week away from the White House and all the meetings had helped. The water was invigorating, and Ruby was nurturing. Ruby accompanied him every trip to Warm Springs. She loved the wide open spaces and simple accommodations. The pretentious, demonstrative tone of the White House wore on her. If it weren't for her fondness for Henry and everything he stood for, she would have long ago stopped working for him, preferring a quieter, simpler life than the ballyhoo of the Capitol. Here, they lounged, relaxed, talked, the lightness afforded them by the Warm Springs seemed their only luxury in a fast-paced world, but it was enough, it was everything they needed.

The slow, saucy, southern summer afternoons brought things to a standstill. Over the years that's when their relationship developed, no work could be done, no running about, only sitting, sitting and talking. And that's what they did many afternoons, year after year, and pretty soon they yearned for those times more than any other, the adventuresome, playful conversation, the moments of unbridled silliness, time chosen for them, by them, a time for only them. The time dragged on and on, a festoon addiction growing in beauty. Time not altered by the cooling evening, the setting sun, the inclement weather, time that continued in their hearts forever. That slow, slow time of the beginning, oppressive heat swirled with cold hard reality, quickening time, robbing moments, hastening complacency. Until now, when the loss of time appears, and it slows, it slows again to warm afternoons on the porch, sitting, sitting and talking.

Ruby noticed the weariness, the over-engaged smile, the hidden sorrow; they appeared in the silent moments, the moments between the next and the last. He was still for longer periods now, harmonizing with the quiet, tuning the calm. There was acknowledgement of what he will leave behind, and acceptance that he must go. Heavy eyelids over blazing bright eyes, eyes resigned about the future, but eager for the present. She watches him move nearer and nearer every day, no longer fighting his fate, the mammoth effort drawing to its only conclusion. The inevitable prolonged, but not averted, a formidable foe, faced admirably with a brave, bold, spirit, every ounce of life squeezed out of dying. She watched, hoping not to forget any of it, dreaming it, smelling it, breathing it. She wanted to see the last, of it all, the last laugh, smile, yawn, capture and keep those times when he was still here. Languishing privately, thriving publicly, she soldiered on, her cause his cause, separated only by outcome.

The nights, oh the nights, don't let it happen during the night, she thought. She needed to know the moment, the last one he knew. She listened to his breathing, each part, the inhale, and exhale, were they getting softer? shorter? shallower? Reason for alarm, moment by moment, assessing and guessing, the strong and constant dialogue of his demise overruled her existence. Dispossessed, on her own, the drone of death devoured, slowly, wholly, completely, the unrecognizable commonality of life left her fooled and neglected. Friends fled, comfort decidedly absent, she was led with him down a path with unfamiliar sites and sounds, terrified at every turn, there was no going back, a barren island, left to fend for herself, only one of you will survive, for death was coming, though she'd rather it he than she, she'd rather it almost anyone than him. So through it she will go, the loss, persevering on, because she can, and he cannot.

And what he wants for her is pure and true. If only she was really that good, she thought, able to be what he sees in her. Hoping he will not be disappointed with her in the future, she does her best not to do it now. Anticipating every move, flinching at every cue, she becomes a well-trained meeter of needs, a crash course in caring for the initiated of the members of the club of the dying, a new form of life unto itself, defined parameters, unimaginable emotions, the least desired trail on the course, the path that ends. Peaks, valleys, forks, bumps, all contextualized by the finite, but never let it be known, for once known, the uninitiated places the burden squarely on the dying, and the only thing worse than dying is having to make the living feel better about it. She smiles and listens, tries 'til it hurts, because she knows nothing it is for her is near what it is for him, suffering is a privilege of the living only the dying envy.

Henry cared deeply about the war. More than any relationship in his life, the unfinished business of the war haunted him. The most volatile and essential relationship of the time, the least settled, the least predictable, the least understood, the reason he wanted to stay the most... his devotion to Maggie unquestioned, his love for Ruby unquestioned, his commitment to the war unfulfilled. He staggered on, bludgeoned by the reality, burdened by the unknown.

He had long since stopped living for himself, the welcome weight of the nation spurred him on. An idle life would have mercilessly ceased long ago, but he was not ready, he was not willing. Death must pry his passion from his grip; feeble halfhearted attempts shall not do, with only great honor and great trial will the great succumb. For if it is today, or tomorrow, or the next, the only way to live is as if it were not coming at all, to wake without fear, to lead without trepidation, to love without limits. He vigorously pursued the present with reverence for the past and an unyielding respect for the task ahead, each accomplishment greater than the next, simply because it exists at all, despite how easy it would be to not. The power of existence leveled against him in jerks and spasms, pulling at the final threads of his shelter, rotting, destroying, savaging the capsule of his logic, leaning on his mercy, the one reserved for the self that recognizes when enough is enough.

Exertion his norm, it was a matter of degrees, all of them worth it, most of them anguishing. He created the world around him, the one which predicted his outcome. If the U.S. had not been able to repel the Japanese in the Pacific he may not have lasted this long. The most harrowing moments of the war were the most delicate moments of his health. He nurtured every ounce of diligence and strength to overcame because his country needed him, not because he needed to live, there are times when purpose is greater than life itself. Both wars, the war of his body, and the war of his country reached their climax together. His outcome was certain; his country's was in doubt. He worked every day to eliminate that doubt, so he could face his last day, certain to come soon, with bold appreciation free of bitter regret.

Decades become years, which become days, distilled into hours, which eventually revolve around moments, the lingering moments of the dying. He sees them, skates by them, thank you, not today, he declares through gritted teeth; you will not be my last today. They are miraculous, they are profound, they are inconsequential, they are stubborn in their severity and presumption, their claim on his presence defined by these lasts and leasts.

He hoped his last week would be full of his greatest achievement, the end of the war. He wondered should any man be so lucky as to leave basking in the glory of his finest hour. Surely in matters of health he had been far from lucky, and expected no such grace as a death infused with completion and peace. He was not a man of peace, and would never find life complete. But there were others to carry on; he peppered them with insight and wisdom, the lessons of the dying. He stayed in hopes of learning them all, his final act of leadership.

He could only be here, surrounded by the fiery water that gave him hope. The state of his birth, the place of his work, neither of them approached the land that gave him back his life. His birth was happenstance, the devastation of his existence was noteworthy, the awakening of his determination was revelatory. Dark, depressed and in despair, he nearly withered away with the decaying of his legs. The water gave him will, the presence of potential. Every truly great day he ever lived came after his paralysis, for until then he had no context, no great valley to contrast his peak. Now, no accomplishment came without sacrifice, no achievement without suffering. Life had become a sweet elixir trapped in a bitter pill, and nothing that came before had ever tasted so fine.

"Ruby, how did we all happen to agree upon this?" he asked her on the porch that evening.

"What do you mean, Henry?" she replied lovingly.

"Well, you, me, Maggie. We came to this understanding about what's important to us, staying in the marriage, but still having our own personal lives. And Maggie knows you come right along with it. And you, you staying with me even though you know I won't leave my marriage. And then there's me, dumb enough to think it all makes sense."

"Maybe that's what love really is Henry, accepting it on its own terms, understanding the limitations of it and deciding to stay. I accept what is best for your life as a whole, and my role in it, I love you all the same. When I say limitations I am not speaking of limits on emotion, I am acknowledging the limited scope with which I get to share them. I miss wonderful, wonderful moments in your life, and I stay anyway because I would miss them all if I go."

"That's sad you have to compromise so," he said.

"It's not compromise, it's understanding."

"Well, I shouldn't have made you do it. A stronger man would have left, or at least ended it."

"Henry, you cannot look back at your life and say any of it was worth risking. This country needed you more than I ever could. The decision to stay was right then, now, and throughout history, because you've determined history, you've helped shape a period of time. None of it would have happened if you left your

132

marriage. And as far as ending it, that was just as much my choice as it was yours. Maybe neither of us was strong enough to end it, or maybe we just couldn't imagine life without each other and we accepted love on its terms."

He smiled and placed his hand over hers as they rocked in their chairs. Warmed by her devotion to their love he sat back puffing on his pipe. "I never thought my life would be like this," he said.

"It's hard to know everything life may bring until you've stuck around for awhile. I bet there's a lot more surprises out there for you if you care to stay."

"Oh, I care to stay, at least my mind does, my body is not so sure. And this old body of mine, it's getting to me, I don't know how long I can hold it off."

"You keep trying Henry, that's all you can do, keep trying."

"'Till my last breath Ruby, I promise."

Exhaling deeply, lifting both hands up and smacking the arms of his rocking chair he stated. "Have you ever seen colors so pretty in all your life?" Ruby looked into the magenta sky. Traces of purples, pinks and auburns infused their color into the malleable hanging clouds, swirling to bring a coral effect to the light. She turned to look at him as the playful light created a rosy tenor to his cheeks. She loved him for that, the constant look of an exploring school boy chasing down the next adventure. The colors drifted slowly, subdued by the earth's rotation. With it, his bright colorful face turned from the glowing oranges and red of the setting sun to the ashen green of a dying man. A few tears slid down her cheek. "Beautiful," she said, "indeed a sight to behold."

They had met when she was in her early twenties, fresh out of college with her Bachelor's Degree in Political Science and eager to get involved in his campaign. He had a burgeoning political career and was assembling his staff. A child of the Midwest, she had come to New York specifically to help his gubernatorial campaign. She volunteered every weekday while earning her living as a waitress at night.

It was several weeks before he noticed her, the timid, awkward, freckled blonde with a knack for organization. She, on the other hand, had many of his idiosyncrasies memorized by the time he approached her. The way he nudged his glasses in place with his left forefinger, his wry smile with the right side of his mouth lifted higher than the left when he playfully teased his staff, the way he leaned in close when he listened. She stared unabashedly, purposefully, and the few times he met her gaze she was surprisingly unself-conscious in front of the man she so revered.

When he finally did catch the young girl making eyes at him from across the room he was briefly embarrassed. In his forties, married, a father, he had long since stopped believing a woman of her age would show any interest in him. He tried not to notice, diligent and spirited he carried on, drafting speeches, discussing policy, but there always seemed to be that memorable moment when he caught a glimpse of her out of the corner of his eye. Transfixed, it became a game within a game, her staring, feebly trying not to get caught, him loving it, feeling her presence, wanting her to continue, until finally he gave in and sent a quick glance her way. And then the silly faces she made, she held his gaze for a moment or two, then turned away, but not without a slightly goofy contortion of her features. At first he wondered if he had seen correctly. Was that an eyebrow raised? Did she just frown? Scrunch her nose? Cross her eyes? He nearly laughed out loud at a couple of her silly glances. His enthusiasm for working at his campaign headquarters quickly grew from two indiscernible main motivators, his political desire, and his physical desire. Those stolen moments between them brought energy to his work and secret pleasure to his life. He found himself picturing her adoring face more and more, until it was the one he hoped to see most.

She reminded him of a carefree time, love for the sake of love not soured by obligation and expectation, still free, undaunted by the burden of responsibility. He had decided on Maggie so young, and for awhile with her that's what it was like, free. But there came a time when he was swept up by attraction, moved by the ferocity of need, and it was no longer Maggie he wanted. There had been times when he acted without fear of repercussion or sense of consequence, he had let himself be carried away. But he was a much younger man then. He was less inclined to act hastily in recent years, but he wondered if he had found that urge again with the young volunteer. Grotesque in its mind altering possession and uncontrollable consumption he painfully indulged. After a brief time he forgot all his fears, he felt only the pulsating burn of desire swarm through him.

When his fantasy became too intrusive to ignore, he approached. Closing in on the election many staffers were putting in twelve, even sixteen hour days. To his dismay she stayed late only Monday and Tuesday. Several months into the campaign, a cold blustery Tuesday night, he was determined not to let her go without a word or two, a simple introduction he thought. He confidently sauntered over with his competent athletic gait. "Hello," he said, "my name is Henry Arthur Pelt. Despite your consistent presence in my campaign I am quite certain we have not been formerly introduced. I am sorry for my neglectful inattention. I have come to say hello, and give thanks for your kind contribution on my behalf," he said confidently.

"Well, I was wondering if you would ever have the decency to come over and say hello, or if you were one of those self-absorbed politicians too busy to notice the little people," Ruby said.

Surprised by her directness, he stammered. "Um, no, I most certainly have noticed you." He internally admonished his clumsy admission and quickly continued in an attempt to cover it up. "I most certainly am aware of the hard work and dedication of all my staff."

"I know, I was just giving you a hard time," she said as she smiled. He relaxed, hoping to regain the casualness with which he first approached. She continued. "I wouldn't be here if I thought you were like that, but I was getting a little worried. I have been here nearly three months."

It seemed like years, he thought, she was so imprinted on his mental palette. He stiffened at the rapidity of her infiltration into his psyche. "Three months, really?" he said, adjusting his glasses with his left index finger.

"You do that when you're nervous," she said.

"Do what?" he asked, quickly followed by, "I'm not nervous."

"You adjust your glasses. I guess I'll have to take your word about you not being nervous. Although, I've seen you do it when you discuss changing diapers, prohibition, sexual education, and lobster. All of which I believe make you nervous, although I'm not entirely sure why, especially the lobster. I mean diapers; essential, prohibition; idiocracy, sexual education; practical, and lobster? Well I don't know what to make over your precarious feelings about lobster."

"All right, all right," he said, astonished by the girl's insight. He had not once changed a single diaper, and while Maggie had plenty of help with the children, it remained a source of contention between them. A drinker himself, he had frequently visited various friends speakeasy's and couldn't shake the shame no matter how silly the law, the guilt endured. He agonized over his own teenage daughter's sexual identity, and he was allergic to shellfish. "I may be a little nervous," he admitted. "I'm unaccustomed to silly faces being thrown at me from across the room," he said charmingly.

She looked away, her cheeks turning a dusty rose color. Worried he had embarrassed her, he reached out, lightly touching her arm. He noticed a heavy hollowness as the sensation ran up his arm and throughout his body. "I quite like it," he said, "the attention you pay to my conversations."

"I'm trying to learn as much as I can," she said plainly.

"What is it that you do?" he asked.

"Anything they ask me to. I type, file, clean, sometimes summarize documents, but I don't think they show you those."

"What do you do for money?"

"I'm a waitress over at Milo's Café."

"Well, do you think you could give it up, come work for me full time? I need an assistant, someone to take dictation, organize my schedule, things like that? I know it's probably not your dream job, but it's yours if you want it." Still, clear, and calm, he felt more sure about her than he had about anything in a long time. He anxiously waited the agonizing seconds for her reply.

She smiled widely, gazing up at him. "Sure, I'll do it, I'll work with you."

"Great," he said. "See you tomorrow, eight a.m. sharp." He turned to walk away and then stopped himself. "I never did find out your name?"

"Ruby."

"Ruby, it's been a pleasure." He nodded. "Until tomorrow."

She nodded back, grinning, cheekily lifting her right brow. He chuckled slightly, boyishly, freely he walked away.

Now, he remembered those times, the heightened arousal, the looks, the smiles. He was healthy then, standing tall, confident, blissfully unaware of the rigors which lay ahead. He flirted, sometimes shamelessly, almost daring his staff to confront him. What a fool he had been, butting up private betrayal with public reality. He had been risky in those initial years with Ruby, still convinced he might leave his wife,

135

hopeful the more everyone knew, the easier it would be. He had wanted to leave, he tried, Maggie would have agreed, he was certain of it, if not for his mother he would have gone. She made the move untenable, the disgrace to the family name, the end of his political career, and, of course, he would be disinherited. He could not stomach the loss of everything he knew no matter how engrossing his love for Ruby had become. So, he became a respectable gentleman, no longer publicly flaunting his affair, private matters kept private.

She almost left him then. He did not know, but Ruby's disappointment at his inability to leave his marriage was so great, she nearly left the love behind. She too had hoped for a life together, a public life. Her heart was torn when he came back and said he could not leave his family. She had allowed herself to dream, she envisioned holding hands together walking down a crowded street, being introduced as who she truly was, not merely his assistant. That danger of wanting more devastated her, annihilated her belief in love. She left his side for a while, she traveled, visited friends and family. She wasn't sure if she'd go back, but no one moved her like he did, nothing intrigued her like this man so full of contradiction and doubt able to harness every bit of his energy to inspire. She longed to hear him speak, to watch him move, she adored the way he invigorated a crowd, changed the mood of every room he walked into. Never had she met a man with such presence, and he wanted her, of that there was no doubt. So she returned to be with the only man she had ever loved, accepting the circumstances in which that love could appear. She accepted she would be considered a woman without love, she would not have a man to bring home to her parents, or someone to gossip about with her friends, no kids, no wedding, a woman without her role, she defined her own life, on her own terms, not exactly everything she would've wanted, but her chosen destiny nonetheless. Her job, it was the job that saved her, no one dared call her a disgrace working for the President of the United States of America. They thought she had sacrificed a lot for her career, possibly too much, and if it was solely for her career she would have agreed with them, but her sacrifice was far greater and far less than they ever could have known.

She sat on the porch now, holding the hand of the man she could not live without, and she felt lucky, blessed even to have walked through life, albeit somewhat covertly, in the presence of such greatness. To have walked through history while it was being made, meeting the great leaders of the time, being in the room where the great debate over the country's future took place, quite often the only woman in the room, she had been trusted with everything, a rare life indeed. And when he was away from her with his family, she foraged on, she even relished her time alone, reading, drawing, playing the piano. What she had thought at first she only needed, was actually what she wanted. She felt important in a way another life may not have afforded.

She did not fear living the rest of her days without him, she was grateful to have lived so many with him. An extraordinary life they had managed to live together, and despite it all, his marriage, his paralysis, it had all been worth it. She had experienced such profound loyalty and dedication, the kind that only comes when two people risk everything for each other. She had never worried about her future, not a single moment she was with him; he was the answer to all her questions, with him there could be no wrong. The feeling that had carried her through every day with him was impugnable; his absence would not jeopardize it. She lived a lifetime of confidence and great experience next to the man she cherished, nothing could take that away from her now, not even death.

The buzz of the swirling bugs, a southern serenade he called it, as familiar as the sounds of a partner's nighttime routine, had become the backdrop of their romance. He could not hear the swarming life around him and not think of her. Some loved the sound of a rushing river, the cars bustling in the city, or the waves of the ocean crashing; he loved the sound of wings fluttering and frogs croaking.

It was the insects that alerted them to on comers, their quick threat assessing silence drew the couple to attention. Prolonged pauses usually meant groups, not simply one of the president's men, cause for concern, they would stiffen, look politely engaged, a perfectly harmless business relationship to the casual observer. Sure there were some who looked twice, but they were off again in a moment, not given privy to the private time of the president. Tonight, it was a comfortable brief pause in the humming as Henry's chief war adviser approached. The couple maintained a relaxed intimacy around the president's loyal confidant, having nothing left to hide and no reason to do so. "Stewie, my good man, what news do you have for me tonight?" the president asked cheerfully.

"I do believe it is good news indeed, Mr. President. We are advancing rapidly on Berlin. The Germans are buckling under fatigue and failure; it shall not be long now, sir."

"The camps, Stewart, have we found any more camps?"

"Not today, sir."

"And the progress, the Jews, are they getting care?"

Ruby patted Henry on the hand. "I'm going to get settled in for the night, gentlemen." She leaned in, placed her hands on the side of Henry's face and warmly kissed his cheek. "Goodnight," she said.

The men nodded. "Goodnight," they said.

Stewart sat in the now open chair by the president. "I'm afraid we're having a great deal of trouble relocating those imprisoned. Some are very sick sir, unable to walk, we are having difficulty finding the personnel and care necessary. Our own forces are entirely dedicated to fighting, local infrastructures are devastated, many are still dying."

"Freed only to be betrayed again."

"Yes, sir."

"What about our nurses, our medical staff back here in the states?"

"Everyone we send over there is kept very busy with the sick and wounded soldiers, I fear we have none to spare."

"There must be more we can do?"

"Well sir, there have been a great deal of inquiries from women wanting to do their part, wives, sisters, mothers asking how they can help. Until now it has been too harrowing to send nonmilitary personnel over there."

"I've seen what they've done here at home, quite frankly, we found out more about the depravity of the human conscience in the exterminating of Jews and the remarkable ability of women who have admirably faced every new challenge thrown their way through this war than I ever thought possible. Sickness and beauty revealed together."

"It's true, sir."

"Let's get out there, I want massive recruiting drives for the American Red Cross, send our women over there."

"Yes, sir."

"And the battles, how are the casualty rates?"

"Slightly lower over the past few days. But we are gearing up to take Berlin, and while the Germans resolve is low, an injured and cornered animal can be the most dangerous."

"I want you to wait until our men are ready, let the Germans worry about it, hear the breath of our army blowing at the napes of their neck. We will see how they enjoy being the prey."

"I believe that is exactly what the general intends."

"Give him my regards and praise."

"I will, sir."

"Well Stewart, now I must be off to bed."

The loyal aide immediately hopped up out of his chair and retrieved the president's wheelchair from the side of the porch. Stewart aggressively lifted the president's upper body and transferred him from the rocking chair. "Thank you, Stew."

"You're welcome, Mr. President."

"Stew, there will be a day, maybe not tomorrow, but soon, when we will wake and the terror of the Germans and the war will be a thing of the past, a terrible and haunting past that will be grieved over forever, but the past."

"I am convinced of it Mr. President."

"Goodnight, Stewart."

"Goodnight, Mr. President."

Henry rolled into the house and poured himself another drink. He ached all over, his neck, his back, his shoulders. His stomach and intestines were an array of knots and blockages so bogged down by the years of stress and paralysis they no longer functioned like that of the living. An adventure in pains and cramps, he looked forward to eating like the pulling of a tooth without anesthesia. His only relief, drinking, smoking, and Ruby, the constants that helped him maintain.

A shocking pale green had recently overcome his complexion. Possibly his liver the doctor had said, or his ever decreasing circulation, but do not mention the liquor and tobacco, the doctor knew better than that. A man with so much strain and so few pleasures, who would deny him the comfort of his few remaining indulgences. Henry long ago stopped striving for tremendous longevity, just long enough and as painless as possible.

He rubbed out his forearms hoping to relax his overwrought wrists and hands. He drank and muttered, hopelessly searching for the source of pain. He drove his hands into his trapezius, his pectorals, his biceps, triceps, hoping each muscle would hurt less than the one before, that somehow his merciful touch could convince the pain it had been wrong to stay, to burrow in him so long, that now he shall be released. This will be the key, he thought each time, each time he delved into a sore, stiff, aching muscle; this will be the touch which unlocks the healing inside him. His hands gravitated towards his head; he rubbed his temples, his forehead, the base of his neck. He slouched over in his wheelchair, suddenly feeling drunker and wearier. He rested his head on his hand, slowly gripping his head tightly, then releasing, hoping for relief. Ruby walked out of the bedroom in her dressing gown. "You look beautiful," he said. For a moment he thought she was an angel.

"Come to bed," she said.

"I have a terrible headache," he said.

She kneeled beside him taking him in her arms, resting her head against his, kissing him gently.

*

The phone rang at half past three. Maggie woke immediately, her pulse jumping. "Maggie?" the voice on the other end of the line was saying. "Maggie?"

"Yes doctor, what's happening? Is he okay?"

"He has slipped into a coma, it doesn't look good. I think you should get here right away."

"Okay. I'm on my way."

She jumped out of bed and opened the closet door, frantically pulling clothes out of the dark closet onto her bed. Charlie appeared in the doorway and turned on the lights. She raised her arms to her face to protect herself from the harsh glare. "Ma'am, I already have our bags packed, just put on a traveling suit and we'll go," he said.

"He's in a coma," she said desperately.

"I'm sorry, ma'am."

"You'll get me there Charlie, won't you, before he dies?"

"I'll do my best, ma'am."

Charlie left to ring the train station where they had been warned to be on alert for such a call. They had set aside a driver and an engine at Charlie's request. The train would be ready by the time they arrived. He quickly gathered some food, a banana, an orange, some raisins, and loaded the car. By the time he returned, Maggie had managed to awkwardly put on some clothes. She tentatively stepped out of the bedroom. Charlie efficiently unbuttoned her misaligned coat, tucked in her blouse, and properly buttoned her up before she had a chance to blink. He reinspected her, handed her an overcoat, her purse, and he shuffled her out the door. She sat staring blankly straight ahead the duration of the car ride. At ten after four they arrived at the train station, they boarded and headed to Georgia, hoping the churning wheels would catch time long enough to see him again.

The treacherous passing of light from night, day to night, tormented her waking moments. She firmly gripped the arm rail in an attempt to hold herself upright to combat the forces weighing against her attempting to bring her to her knees. She spent the first thirty-six hours of the train ride in that forced, rigid, upright posture, clenched, unflinching, staring out the window. Charlie eventually persuaded her to lie down. He pulled the shade to shelter her from the ever present reminder of the passage of time. They had stopped once for supplies, the news from Georgia remained the same. Maggie had barely batted an eye when Charlie informed her of the president's continued comatose state. He could not possibly know she was holding out hope for more, for any sign of improvement. The thought of arriving by her husband's side as he lay in a coma was only slightly less unbearable than arriving to find him dead.

She lay on her side, curled up like a child. Occasionally, Charlie came in to encourage sips of water, a bite of fruit. Charlie could not be entirely sure, but he became increasingly concerned she had not used the toilet since their departure from New York days earlier. She seemed to have stopped functioning. He brought her blankets when she shivered, removed them when she appeared too warm. He tried talking to her, no response. He tried reading, but the only available script was the daily paper, and upon hearing the news she grew agitated. He finally began to sing, at first quietly, absently to himself, then as her tension seemed to dissipate he grew more confident, eventually singing boldly. His clear, sweet falsetto filled the room, drowning out the heavy metal noises of the train. He sang hymns he learned as a member of the church choir when he was a boy, the only activity his father allowed. "For God almighty will strike you down if you are not devoted to the pure actions of his word," his father would say.

Charlie sang for what seemed like only a few moments, entirely engrossed in every word, every melody, occasionally spying on the increasingly soothed first lady until finally it appeared she had fallen asleep. He slowly, so as not to wake her, lifted himself from the chair. He gently covered her with a blanket, tender and kind. He left her sleeping quarters and was surprised to see it was daylight yet again. He walked over to the kitchen in hopes of getting some food; he was quite suddenly extremely hungry. The cook respectfully acknowledged his presence. "Bacon and eggs?" the man asked.

"I don't like bacon," was all Charlie could think to say.

"A nice omelette then?"

"That would be greatly appreciated."

Charlie sat at the counter where the cook was pouring him a cup of coffee. He drank down the warm liquid, feeling it pass through his chest, opening his tight, worried throat. He warmed his hands on the mug, unaware of how cold he had become.

"That was the most beautiful thing I've ever heard," the cook said.

"What?" Charlie replied.

"Your singing."

"Oh," the weary man said. "Just a couple of hymns I know from church."

"Yeah, a couple of hundred, you were singing for hours..."

"Hours?" Charlie repeated, surprised.

"Yeah, you're a darn hero getting the madam to fall asleep."

"How did you know she fell asleep?"

"One of the men come to check on you two, see if you needed anything, you was singing, and there she was sleeping like a baby, he said."

"When was that?"

"'Bout an hour ago."

"I had no idea, seemed like no time at all."

"It was like you were possessed by an angel, the most beautiful singing I've ever heard. I'll never forget it as long as I live, the man who serenaded the first lady to sleep."

"Thank you."

"God sometimes has a way of looking out for us in our time of need. The madam got you, that's God's work."

Charlie, not wanting to be rude, gratefully accepted the food the man prepared him, but he couldn't help but scoff at the notion of God's mercy. A woman lay writhing in pain, heading to the bedside of her dying husband, and after several miserable days she is finally lulled to sleep, that's mercy? Does he mean without God it would have been worse? And as far as him being sent to her by God, the only mercy ever shown him was that by the first lady herself. She took him in broken and beaten, nearly mute from his experience in the army. Him being here now had nothing to do with God. Any mercy brought to Maggie Pelt on this journey was the mercy she herself was responsible for. Charlie thanked the man for the omelette and headed to a different car to be alone. "How much longer we got?" Charlie asked the cook as he was leaving.

"We'll be there before nightfall."

"Thanks again."

"My pleasure."

The hot, humid late afternoon air rudely greeted Maggie as she stepped off the train. The heavy, thick air clung to her as she passed through it, bogging her down, pushing against her as if she were walking through water. She carefully made the final step down to the platform. She saw dutiful Stewie waiting for them, he did not look good. She tried to breathe, she choked slightly on the moisture, unaccustomed to the water infiltrated air; she coughed, clearing her lungs.

Charlie grabbed her arm, Stewart grabbed the luggage. She led them to the automobile, Henry's favorite nineteen thirty eight, royal blue Ford glistened in the sun. No new cars had been produced in four years, a necessary war time sacrifice; she frowned at the old beloved car. Henry had always loved to drive; losing the ability was one of the greatest hardships of his paralysis. Eventually, a local mechanic, a great admirer of Henry, devised a system whereby he could operate the car with his hands. The broad smiles that day, indeed, part of life lost, found again.

"How is he?" Maggie asked Stewart as they arrived at the car.

He put the bags down beside the auto and placed his hand on her shoulder. "I'm sorry ma'am, he did not make it."

The blood drained from her face, she looked slightly perplexed but mostly frightened. "This can't be happening," she said.

Her mind wandered as she gazed at the countryside. She was seated in the passenger side of the open air car, the wind rushed by her undaunted, reminding her of the many times she had made this journey by her husband's side. She had always felt the landscape was rather drab, stubby bushes, and plain, less than glorious trees. Now, as the setting sun reflected the earth's deep purples and pinks, the flat green came to life, breathing with her, bowing into her on the inhale, and pushing away from her on the exhale. She heard the frogs croaking, celebrating the evening, and the crickets warming up their legs for the night ahead. She noticed the tapping of the woodpeckers, even the hoot of an owl, strange she thought, she had never heard any of it before, only the sputtering of the engines exhaust and the squeaking metal parts as her husband changed gears.

She smelled the sweet spring air swiftly rushing past her; cherry blossoms, jasmine, and gardenia filled her senses. The warm wind tickled her ears, brushed by her neck like the breath of a lover. She felt water dripping on her face, looked up to see if it was raining only to realize she had started crying. She sat perfectly still, legs crossed, hands folded on her lap as the tears rolled down her neck and chest under her blouse. A flash of lightning bolted through the sky followed by a distant rumble, another flash, and another, the bright pink sky pocked with pockets of incandescent hollows illuminated above her. She felt more drops, this time on her hands, her lips, now it truly was raining. A rapid deluge of water poured down, she listened to the ssshhhhhhh of the heavy rain hitting the ground.

"Sorry ma'am, this is unexpected," she heard Stewart say. "Don't worry were almost there."

She opened her arms to the rain, embracing its powerful presence. The rain somehow made the drive more bearable, eventful, even entertaining; she noted the wicked humor of it all.

They arrived as the last wisps of brilliant pinks were leaving the sky. The thunder rumbled low as she approached the porch, the door swung open and her oldest daughter came to greet her. Her daughter grabbed her by the hand and led her to Henry's bedroom. In a blur out of the corner of her eye she saw Ruby seated in the living room, her heart sank. It became clear to her now, the role she had given up in her husband's life, the part she wasn't willing to play. She felt like a guest in their home. The place had changed in the years since she'd visited, not dramatically, but subtly, little personal touches, the fabrics, the linens, the smells. Her daughter stopped her just before they entered his bedroom. "Mom you're drenched. Do you want to dry off and change before you see him?" What does it matter what I look like, she thought. "You might be more comfortable," her daughter added.

A deep burning feeling began to rise inside Maggie; she looked at her conspiratorial daughter. "Sure sweetheart, why don't you grab me one of Ruby's towels and then maybe one of her suits out of the closet? I'm sure then I'll be more comfortable," Maggie said, more out of self protection than anger.

"Mom," her daughter said in a conciliatory tone, "I just..."

"No, that's enough. I've put up with enough. Now leave me alone to be with my husband."

Maggie opened the door to her husband's room. She saw him lying there on his bed, more peaceful than she had seen him in years. He looked gray, gone, not the least bit present, his lifeless body emitted none of the power it once had. She grabbed his hand, kissed his forehead, felt the clammy cold reminder of a new reality. She was surprised by how different he was, how complete death was, she looked at him for reminders, but all she saw was loss. The desperate tension of his face that pained her so had slackened, he lay before her expressionless, emotionless, a void. She was so accustomed to his bountiful energy when they interacted, she couldn't relate to this man at all, the body of her former husband. The small room, with one small window, lit only by a single bedside lamp which he had so entirely overwhelmed before she could not bear to be in, now seemed empty, hollow, even cavernous. A shiver went up her spine, shaking her, she wasn't sure if it was the cold seeping in or her fear sneaking up on her, but her body began to break down. She started trembling, her teeth began to chatter, she felt a more ominous sense of dread than at any other time in her life.

She staggered out of Henry's bedroom into the expectant stares of the small group gathered in the living room. Only Charlie looked at her plainly, not as if her next move would be the most important of her life, like her whole existence was pared down to this one moment, her response to her husband's death. Would she be affected enough, or disappointingly detached? She entertained their feelings for a fleeting second, their hopes, their fears, and then she left them, she left them free of influence over her life. What she felt, and what she was experiencing was a dialogue open only to herself; discussion, judgments, opinions, there would be none. She loathed their unity, the separateness from her they had created. The three defenders of the president, his lover, his right-hand man, and his loyal offspring now seemed her arch nemeses robbing her of her freedom, the freedom to grieve the death of her husband and not the extent of his betrayals.

She composed herself for a moment, smoothed her wet, wrinkled blouse. "Charlie I would like to stay at," she slightly grimaced as she said the words, "the sunshine house if it is available."

Charlie rose. "It is Maggie," he said as he reached his hand out to her.

The others slowly rose. Stewart spoke. "Don't you want to stay here Madam First Lady?" he said, emphasizing her formal title, reminding Charlie of his place.

"No, I do not. And I'm no longer the First Lady, Chief Adviser Pleahy."

"Well, technically the Vice President hasn't been sworn in yet. He's been acting as commander since the president took ill. But he doesn't even know he's dead, thought you should know first."

She looked at Ruby and then back at the adviser. "How understanding of you Stewie. I thought keeping me in the dark was your game, they say death changes people, with you the changes seem to be immediate."

"Madame, there is not a person in this room without secrets. While you condemn me, you also condemn yourself. I understand you are grieving, but we all loved Henry, and all want what's best for him."

Charlie stepped in. "It's been a really long few days, everybody's nerves are frayed. We should go clean up and get some rest; I think it's time we leave."

"I guess we can talk about some of the arrangements tomorrow," Stewart said.

Maggie's daughter got up to hug her mother. Maggie stiffened in her daughter's grasp just like the little girl used to when she was young. Maggie pulled away after a moment, grabbed Charlie's elbow and led him out the door.

The severe rain had subsided to leave a calm, exceptionally clear night. Thousands of stars burned brightly above Maggie and Charlie as they walked to their accommodations. The muddy path was slippery and perilous; they walked slowly, Charlie holding Maggie high on her arm to keep her from falling. He could only manage one of the suitcases and would have to come back later to retrieve his, probably after she was asleep. The moon peered down on them from above the treetops, misshapen, three quarters full. The odd oblong tipped one's attention away from the brilliant stars to the large, bright, slightly demented, glaringly obvious dominant light. They came to the clearing on which the house stood. The strong light of the clear night radiated off the bright sides of the house, yellows and oranges, like the sun resting on earth, waiting to rise another day.

The small two-story house, where Maggie used to stay during the dark days of winter stood slightly elevated off the ground. Situated on top of a four foot crawlspace with a deck wrapped around the entire first floor and an enclosed sun room on the second floor, the house, less than a thousand square feet, seemed sprawling. The deck gave off the informal welcoming invitation only a southern home can. They climbed the porch steps, leaving a trail of muddy footprints behind them. "We better take off our shoes madam," Charlie told Maggie.

She plunked down in a white wicker chair on the porch. "Okay, Charlie." He bent down and pulled off her soaked muddy flats, she stood. "Might as well take off my stockings, and this blouse." She began haphazardly taking off her clothes.

Charlie slowly approached and put his arms around her. "Let's get inside Miss." He kicked off his boots and led her upstairs to her room.

Half-dressed, she threw herself down on the bed and began to sob; she trembled violently as she howled. Charlie sat with her on the edge of the bed for a few moments, not saying or doing anything, there if she needed him. The loud sobs slowly turned to whimpering. Charlie eventually put his hand on her bare shoulder, she was cold. He got up and began to run a warm bath for her. He waited for the hot water to run through the pipes, he adjusted the taps until finally settling on a temperature. He left the bath and returned to her adjoining room. He sat close to her, leaning in to her, he spoke softly. "Come on, let's get you warmed up, let's get those clothes off and get you into the bath." She managed to sit up on the bed, still whimpering, limp and listless. He helped her to her feet. "Can you manage ma'am? I'm going to turn off the tap."

Maggie did not reply but started at her skirt. Charlie turned off the tap, checked the temperature and lit several candles that lined the window ledge. He turned out the light and returned to Maggie. She was back seated on the bed, sobbing. "Come on," he said, lifting her to her feet. He unzipped the zipper at the side of her skirt and shimmied it off of her. She stood there crying in her bra and panties. He led her to the bathroom. "I'll be right downstairs if you need me," he said.

She reached her hand out to him. "Charlie, stay."

He nodded. She reached behind her and snapped off her bra. She placed her left hand on the edge of the tub to steady herself as she tried to pull down her underwear. She managed to get one side of her panties halfway down her thigh and stumbled; she steadied herself and tried again. Hopelessly stuck and unsteady, Charlie stepped beside her, wrapped his left arm around her waist, her hip firmly against his, he reached around her with his right hand and pulled the left side of her panties down. They came down rather easily, and Maggie obediently lifted one foot and then the other as Charlie removed her underwear. He slipped her still dangling bra off her shoulder. Maggie placed her hand squarely in his and stepped into the bath. Charlie sat casually on the floor as Maggie soaked in the water.

At first the water seemed entirely too hot to Maggie, scalding and dangerous against her frigid skin. But then the first few moments of burning shock eased into a penetrating, luscious, soothing warmth. Her head was spinning, caught up in the whirlwind of the last few days. She stretched out one leg, and then the other, taking it slow, still slightly wary of the heat but trusting enough to remain. As the warmth began to enter into her system, opening her veins and vanishing the goose bumps, she began to breathe deeply. She let out a couple of large sighs and forcefully inhaled and exhaled. She turned to see Charlie sitting on the floor. "Hi Charlie," she said innocently. "Are you taking care of me, Charlie? I think I need someone to take care of me?"

"I'm taking care of you Maggie," he said sweetly.

"You're a good boy Charlie. You're a good boy," she said like a mother to her son. She scooped up water with her hand and brought it to her shoulders and back, slowly acclimatizing her upper body to the water. After a few minutes she was comfortable enough to lay herself down, resting her head against the slanted edge of the bath.

As he sat in the candlelight with his naked boss laid out before him, he became keenly aware of how he had never been attracted to her. He loved her, respected and admired her, but not for a moment had he ever felt the rush of desire for her. That's not to say he wasn't curious, the intimacy of an unclothed body always provoked intrigue within him. Her breasts were small, cone shaped with very faint pink aureoles. She was curvier and more feminine nude than she appeared in her clothes. Despite her emotional frailty and prone position she seemed uncommonly strong to him, more physically capable than most of the women he had seen naked. Maybe it was the wood he had seen her chop, or the fish he had seen her catch, but her body oozed competence. He was proud to see her naked, honored by the rare privilege. Maggie appeared to be breathing easier, soothed by the warm candlelight and the quiet intimacy of the moment. He knew there would be much about this time in his life that he would remember forever, but few would be more lovingly recalled than this one.

A greatly subdued Maggie stood, declaring herself ready to leave the bath. Charlie handed her a towel, happy to see her lucid. She carelessly patted herself dry and tied the towel around her waist. Charlie blew out the candles behind her and they entered her bedroom. She grabbed her suitcase, opening it; she rifled through the neatly folded clothes, then emptied the contents of her case on the bed. "Charlie, did you pack my yellow nightie I like so much? I can't find it."

Charlie reached into the pile of clothes and pulled out the faded yellow dressing gown. Maggie had purchased the gown in college; the soft worn cotton made it her favorite. Charlie placed the rest of her things back in the suitcase as she threw the gown on overhead. She returned to the bathroom, finally, thought Charlie, sheepishly wondering if she had peed in the bathtub. She came out, kissed Charlie on the cheek, and crawled into bed. Satisfactorily snuggled in, Charlie began to leave the room. "Charlie," she said, "have you talked to Bea?"

"Yes," he replied.

"Can she come?"

"I'm sorry, Maggie. She has to be in Washington to cover the story of the president's death when it is announced. And with the war, there is just no way she can leave right now."

"Can we call her in the morning?"

"We can."

"Okay, thank you Charlie... for everything."

"Sweet dreams," he said.

A ray of light approached her eyes as the rising sun announced the day. She woke passively, momentarily without knowledge of the day to come. Did I sleep she wondered, unable to believe rest could be had with everything going on. She had slept, soundly, exhausted from the emotion. Her thoughts, at a tame speed for the first time since the middle of the night phone call, the night she was awakened to be thrown into a nightmare, began to organize. Her mind rested, she stepped away from her nightmare long enough to realize her place in it. Gone were the days of worrying about him dying, now his death begins. There were many things still to be done, a funeral to be had, she must make it through them soundly before she could allow herself to fall. She had her time, her time on the train, last night, now she must collect herself and move on. For the nightmare will be lengthy, and she was only at the beginning, if she gives in now, she will never make it through.

The sun peaked in the window through the trees, the streams of light picking out the shapes of particles in the air. She breathed deeply, stretched mightily, her stiff, sore body growled with the effort. She placed her bare feet on the cool wood floor and relied on them to carry her. She gently walked downstairs, peaked in on Charlie, who was sound asleep, and headed to the kitchen to put on some water. She made herself a cup of hot tea and headed to the sunroom. There, she curled up in her favorite soft, white wicker chair covered in yellow fabric with a red hibiscus flower print.

She let the early morning warmth of the glass encased room seep into her. The warm sunlight poured over her skin, slightly easing her body's tension. Her toes uncurled from their panicked state. She drinks in the warm liquid, keeping the mug close to her face letting the steamy air draw up around her mouth. She watches the branches sway in the breeze, noting the bright green color of new leaves. She flexes her hands open and closed, wondering where they had been, why she felt they no longer held strength. These few moments, only these few moments would she give her body. Tea time was over, she dressed.

Charlie thankfully continued to sleep as Maggie made herself breakfast. She cooked up an asparagus, artichoke heart and mushroom frittata with the groceries the caretaker had stocked the house with, and left enough egg mixture for Charlie to cook one when he got up. She sat at the table, feeling alone for the first time in years, nobody else's anything. She sat in silence, quiet with her thoughts and her fears. The feelings arising inside her both frightened and intrigued her with their endless possibilities, the unparalleled sorrow of losing her oldest, dearest friend, and the freedom to explore life on her own. Her husband's goals, which had entangled and overtaken her own, began to unwind. She felt them drawing back, leaving space for her to fill. Although his mark and pattern would remain everywhere, and undoubtedly some reminders of his former presence will cripple her to her soul, others will cheer her on, and she knows enough now to believe in herself.

She washed her plate then slowly turned the knob to the front door letting the fresh air pour over her. A short walk on the grounds would do her well, she thought. She leaves the open landing of the sunshine house and enters the damp terrain of the woods. The former muddy surface now caked into dry patties by the warm spring air crunches under her feet. The morning birds call to each other enchanting her way. She walks a hundred yards, maybe two, far enough to feel like the only person in the world. No one within sight or sound, she looks around for them, below her, above her, feeling her size, she stands still for a moment, one small person in a big world. Long enough, she thinks, the day is getting away from her; she must call Bea and then join the others.

Charlie was up cooking when she returned. "Nice to see you," he said upon her entry. "I worried for a moment, then saw the teacup and the food, thank you by the way, figured you wanted to be alone."

"Yes, good morning, Charlie."

He finished cooking the frittata and slid it onto a plate. Charlie walked over and gave her a warm hug, the first hug he had ever given her. "Did you get some sleep?" he asked.

"I did, thank you." She pulled at the fabric of his shirt. "Aren't you hot? Always in long sleeves, even when you sleep, you're a true prude, Charlie." He blushed slightly. She smiled. "Oh, Charlie, am I making you nervous?"

"No. I just feel more comfortable in long sleeves."

"All right, all right. You eat your breakfast; I'm going to call Bea."

She returned to the sunroom to make the call. Bea answered alertly. "Oh dear Maggie, how are you? I talked to Charlie last night, he said you weren't holding up very well."

"I'm doing better now."

"Are you eating, sleeping? You've got to take care of yourself."

"Yes, Bea, I'm eating."

"I'm sorry I can't be there with you."

"I know you are. It's fine, I always knew I was going to go through this without you."

"Still, it's worse than I ever imagined."

"I know, there is no anticipation thoughtful enough."

"When are you coming back?"

"I don't know. I'll know more later. Has word reached Washington?"

"Yes, early this morning. People are devastated, staffers, journalists they're crying. The strongest figure in the current identity of this country is gone, they are utterly devastated."

"He never wanted to leave them. He had so much more he wanted to do." Crying now, Maggie continued. "He kept telling me about things he wanted done, how to go about the war, the recovery and the triumphant return to a peaceful country. I couldn't listen, I couldn't hear it. I missed so much Bea."

"You saw more than any first lady, Maggie. You stayed involved in his life, and his life was the presidency. You were there for him, always."

"Not in the end."

"You both made your choices; he died suddenly, what could you do?"

"It took him three days to die. I knew he was dying for a long time, months, years, he's been dying for years."

"And you were supposed to spend every moment by his side, waiting there in case he died? That would've been two of you dying." Maggie cried softly into the receiver as Bea continued. "Look Maggie, I know you wanted to be there when he died. I'm sorry you weren't. But you have been nothing but a loyal and faithful wife whose ability helped her husband preside over the country. The final moment is no measure of all that came before."

A slightly composed Maggie declared, "I've got to go."

"Maggie, his love for his country can live on through you."

"Only if I can remember."

"You will. Call me soon, I love you."

"I love you, too."

Maggie and Charlie walked the crackly path back to Henry's residence. The house was busy with activity and strange men going through the rooms. She found Stewart. "What's going on?" she asked.

"Oh, hi Maggie, how are you feeling this morning?"

"Fine. What are all these people doing here?"

"They're coordinating."

"Coordinating what?"

"There are many arrangements that must be made to care for the president."

"He wanted to be buried in his hometown, not Washington," she said, as they walked onto the porch to get away from the crowd.

"I know Maggie; his loyalties go far deeper than the capitol. I talked with Henry at great length about his wishes. And if it is all right with you, we all plan to ride the train to Washington for a formal viewing and public ceremony, then on to New York for the private funeral. These men are here mostly for documentation, security and safety. I know it is less than intimate, I'm sorry."

"What will he be buried in?"

"We're shipping in a casket from Atlanta, the finest they had available."

"Where's Henry now?"

"He's with an undertaker."

"When is the train leaving?"

"Tomorrow morning, eight a.m."

Maggie began to step down the ramp of the porch when she heard the clip clop of horse hooves. She, an avid rider in her life before the White House, swooned at the long missed sound. Turning the corner was a horse drawn wagon steered by a man she recognized. He was the local auto mechanic who had spent countless hours with Henry talking cars. He tipped his hat solemnly to her as he arrived. She hadn't seen him for years, but nearly cried at the site of a familiar face Henry was so fond of. Maggie immediately approached the horses and began to stroke them lovingly. The driver stepped down. "Ma'am, I'm very sorry for your loss," he said.

"Thank you, Sammy," she said warmly; grateful the kind man's name had come to her.

"Me and the other townspeople have something we'd like to give you. We don't know if it's suitable for the President of the United States, but when we heard he fell ill we took up a collection. We hoped we wouldn't need it, we prayed for his recovery. Sorry I couldn't be here any sooner, I just finished it now." The man looked over her shoulder into the busy house. "I might need some of the gentlemen to help me if you don't mind?" he asked.

Stewart went into the house and brought three men out. Sammy pulled a large quilted blanket out of his wagon and spread it on the ground. He signaled for the men to come to the back of the wagon. They carefully pulled out a beautiful hand carved casket and laid it on the blanket. Maggie gasped at the sight of it. She walked over to the casket and began to feel the smooth wood. The rich tones of the mahogany shone deep against the light of the sun. It was a plainly enough shaped casket with flat edges and a rounded top. But the glistening that came from it as the sun passed over displayed the beautiful detail in the ridge connecting the rounded top to the body of the case. Around the entire edge of the ridge were various inlaid stones; pearls, jade, obsidian, quartz, all smoothed and polished, giving the casket a distinctly personal touch.

Sammy walked up to the casket and opened it. "Ma'am, I know how he loved the warm light of sunset, we wanted it to be special for him inside." Set down two inches from the top, a glistening three inch inlaid strip of copper surrounded the edge inside the casket. The copper reflected in the sunlight giving the inside of the casket a majestic golden hue.

"Sammy it's beautiful. But the rations, how did you get the material?"

"Well ma'am, when the folks around here heard about Henry," he paused and lowered his head, he blushed slightly. "Excuse me ma'am, the president."

Maggie reached out her hand placing it on his forearm. "Sammy, you go ahead and call him Henry, you two were friends."

"Thank you ma'am. When people heard he was sick they brought every bit of copper and stone they had. Women brought their jewelry, family pieces ma'am, everything they could. There were men that traveled a hundred miles to bring me a bit of copper no bigger than a pea."

She leaned into the man and kissed his cheek. "Thank you Sammy. You tell those people it is the finest gift our family has ever received, and thank you."

Sammy, noticeably blushing, said, "you're quite welcome ma'am. We know it may not be suitable for the President of the United States, and you might not want it, but we feel like he was our family, and we want to send him out right."

"Thank you, Sammy. I know my husband would be honored to be buried in such a fine casket made with so much love."

Sammy smiled and lowered his head; he got back on his wagon and rode away. Maggie walked over to Stewart. "I want him buried in this." Stewart, with a look of mild horror, began to open his mouth. Maggie interjected before he could get a word out. "I don't care who it will offend, or who will think it's inappropriate, this is the one thing I ask as his wife."

Stewart closed his mouth, composed himself, and said, "yes Maggie."

"Thank you."

Maggie spent the rest of the day at the sunshine house. She asked Charlie to inform Bea of the funeral plans and indicated she would be spending the day alone. She again lounged in the wicker chair in the sunroom, quite aware she would never visit again. Warm Springs was strictly her husband's endeavor despite her appreciation for the strength and courage the springs provided him, that desperate pursuit was now over and she knew she would not return. The resort always reminded her of how perilous life was, those stricken with polio flocking to even the most marginal sign of hope. It's not that she didn't believe the water held power. She had seen cripples walk again. She saw her husband arrive defeated and leave triumphant, but that so little could be done, so very little, for so many in need, that's what this place reminded her of. The children she saw, how it pained her so, never to take a sturdy, pain-free step in their lives. At least her husband had time, almost forty years of life before he began his fight with the disease. This was the place he walked again for the first time, drove again, laughed again, this was the place he learned to live again, but now, it was time for goodbye.

At sunset she emerged from her room just as Charlie was finishing preparing dinner. "Ah, I hoped the smell of freshly baked bread would draw you out. I know how you can't resist," he said.

"Well, I do suppose I could eat a little," she said warmly. "Charlie there's something I need to do tonight. I would like it if you would come along?"

"Of course," he said, placing a warm bowl of vegetable soup in front of her. "There you go, see if you can get some of that down."

She leaned down to inhale the rich aroma and smiled. "Smells delicious, thank you, Charlie."

After she had taken a few bites of the soup Charlie inquired about the evening. "So what is it you want to do tonight?" he asked.

"It's time for me to go swimming," she replied. Charlie turned pale as fright overtook his face. "Don't worry," she said, laughing at the horror to which his loyalty would take him, "you don't have to swim. I know how modest you are," she said, all the while knowing he would, no matter what it would cost him emotionally, if she asked him to.

They set out a couple hours after dark, assured the springs would be empty. The clouds hung low and the lightless night made it difficult to find their way. They used a lantern to navigate through the trees onto the main path that led to the springs. The night was calm, particularly quiet, the kind of night it seemed everyone decided to stay in. Even the frogs, crickets, owls and various other music makers were lulled into complacency by the starless evening.

They arrived at the dark pool- like structure which had been built to contain the warm springs to find it deserted as hoped. A shiver ran up Maggie's spine as the familiar musty salt smell passed over her. She had spent many a day inhaling the acrid air as her husband fought valiantly for independence. She remembered how the smell remained, lingering on her body, a constant reminder of her husband's need.

She disrobed down to her bra and panties. She had no suit, hadn't had an occasion to wear one for years. Her bare feet rested on the still warm, smooth cement she had only dared to approach during the day with shoes, for the hot southern sun turned the cement surface to a pit of coals. Charlie sat back on one of the poolside chairs keeping an eye out for on comers like she asked. She approached the top step of the main pool, the one her husband fought to allow those afflicted with polio to enter despite other guest's objections before he decided to buy the place and set his own rules. She stuck her toes in the water, for the first time exploring the liquid element her husband so believed in. It was never clear to her why she had not been more curious about the water before. Perhaps it was her own doubts about its powers? Perhaps it was her anger at the way the disease had altered both their lives? Perhaps it was jealousy that the water could provide greater solace to her husband the last twenty years of his life than she ever could? But now, with her toe submerged, she felt no more reservations. She retracted her foot, headed straight for the deep end, and dove in head first.

She was surprised by how light she felt, incredibly buoyant, returning to the surface like an emerging submarine. She dove deep, fighting the force that wanted her back to the surface. She lunged into a powerful underwater breaststroke, gliding just above the bottom of the pool. She could see very little, and relied solely on touch and feel to navigate her way. She began to keep her eyes closed, imagining the dimensions of the pool, coming close to the edge then reaching out to find her way. She glanced over at Charlie, illuminated by the lantern, he was smiling broadly. She felt free, like a trusting child in the soothing world of the innocence. She swam to the shallower part of the pool, and bound herself off the bottom, exploding through the surface reaching her hands high in the air then crashing back into the water. She did handstands, testing her balance and the limits of her breath.

She played for a long time. Finally exhausting herself, she lay on her back and floated. She let the water support her as she gazed up at the clearing sky. The sky was now half full of stars with a strong breeze moving the clouds quickly to uncover the rest. The moon lay somewhere behind the gray matter, she floated patiently waiting for the light to make its arrival. One sliver at a time the moon revealed itself, glowing, cratered, marked by its passage through time. She eventually grew sleepy and decided her time in the healing water had been fulfilled. They walked back silently, this time without the aid of the lantern, letting the light pouring from the sky guide their way.

Maggie boarded the train without apprehension, the final journey of her former life, she thought. She smelled the coal burning, she heard the whistle blowing, and felt the train lurch as it began moving forward. Shortly into the ride she walked to the compartment in which her husband was being held. He was situated in the middle of the train so certain passengers would not cross paths. The two halves of the train were quietly being referred to as Maggie's side, and Ruby's side. She entered the cold, windowless room wanting to make sure everything was in order. There were two guards watching over the president's body. They stood and saluted her upon entry.

"May I have a few minutes alone?" she asked.

They agreed and exited the room through the door behind her. She stood for a few moments admiring the casket. She ran her fingers around the trim of the inlaid stone, feeling the smooth cold surface. What would her life be like without him, she wondered? Would anyone take her seriously? There was the Untied Nations conference in San Francisco in a couple of weeks, how would they treat her without her title? The bringing together of world leaders, would their commitment remain strong without her husband's influences? There was so much yet to be done, visions they both shared still unseen.

She reached out with both hands and lifted the top half of the casket. It was heavier than she expected, solid wood, sturdy and strong. The copper trim gleamed up at her, reflecting an auburn glare around her husband. He looked swollen, filled with fluids attempting to make him look better than the sunken, hollow of a man he had become. He wore a fine navy blue suit with a navy blue necktie. The gray hues of his face covered tastefully by a rosy powder. He looked better than he had in years, even then, the deathly stillness pervaded, sinking into her pores like a toxic gas leaving her momentarily paralyzed. She closed the casket gently and returned to her box car, awaiting the end to the shifting ground beneath her.

Midway through the first day of the trip the train began moving painfully slow, slower than it started, and slower than necessary, Maggie thought. She removed her gaze from the open fields of lilac and headed to the dining car to find Charlie. She found him seated at a table reading a newspaper with a large salad and a glass of white wine before him. Amazed by his relaxed state, she was temporarily sidetracked. "Really Charlie, wine in the middle of the day, I'm shocked."

He smiled, sensing her playfulness. "Thought I might unwind a little, seems like we're in for a long trip," he said, pointing to the row of windows behind her. She turned to see scores of people, men, women and children running alongside the train. They were waving and holding up signs with messages; I love you, thank you, and we'll never forget you. "They found us about an hour ago," he said. "Word must have spread because they just keep coming. We have slowed out of respect for the people who have come to say goodbye."

"Very well then," she said stoically, despite the profound rush of emotion rising insider her. "May I join you?" she said, hiding her emotion.

"Certainly."

She looked over towards the kitchen and yelled. "Cookie, I'll have what he's having."

After the slow train ride everything became a blur. She joined her kids and family. There was a massive public ceremony, speakers, bag pipes, gunshots, entirely overwhelming. She found herself relieved to be stepping back onto the train for the final leg of the trip to New York. She had plenty of company this time, with family and friends along for the ride. Again, the crowds gathered to give their respects; the outpouring was truly a sight to behold.

She had hoped her husband was respected for what he had given the country, but to be loved in this way, she had no idea how deep the people's passion for their president had run. Their silent tribute encouraged her to carry on, to honor him the best she could, with pride, humility and love. Their faith in her husband turned some of her darkest hours into whimsical lessons of kindness, the outreach of emotion that helps keep one from feeling alone.

She saw him, that last time, in the church they both attended as children. She remembered him swinging his feet off the grand, long wooden benches, swinging earnestly as if the emotion he put into it would decide if God would hear him or not. The beautiful stained glass windows which diffused and colored the light, leaving the lingering heavenly air, the high grand ceilings full of the booming echoes of the word of God, she remembered it all, the place her husband had found his faith in God, and she in him. She remembered the post-church playful games, high on sweets and juice, full of thoughts of grandeur, the life of long ago.

He lay there now, upfront, separated from all he had ever known, looked at, cried over, something to be fawned over. She looked at the man she had known so well, she saw the copper glow from the casket linger in the air above him, she saw the purity and truth of who he was and the life they made together. She could have hoped for nothing more. She walked away not noticing the aisles and aisles of mourners staring at her, she was looking slightly upward at the golden light above.

Chapter 14

Gloria hadn't left the house for days, couldn't stand the sight of anything to do with the town. The stupid houses, the gawking people, the charred remains left by the blast all haunted her. Not even the open desert with its loving foothills could draw her out. She ate little, didn't paint at all, truly, she did virtually nothing. She would sit in the living room for a while, maybe visit the kitchen, then head back to her room, mostly staring, quietly camouflaging into nonexistence. Her brothers would rumble by, sometimes she noticed, mostly she didn't. Marty tried sweetly and subtly to bring her back to life, but resigned to her course, he could do nothing.

The only moments she seemed coherent, almost present, were the times Audrey came around. The little sister, who had always loved her mom so, idolized her in a borderline co-dependent way, occasionally, if Gloria could muster, she would come around long enough to check in with the little girl. Their interactions were minor and shallow, the only type Gloria could manage, clouded by the forced casualness which can overcome the grieving, part preservation, part incomprehension.

The mind simply cannot grasp death, once a lifetime together, now a future lost. For surely that person still invades every part of one's psyche, one can still hear their voice in their head, imagine what they look like, convinced they cannot be gone, they are here, right here in the mind, every moment. The insidious smell of her clothes, her lotion, they sneak up on Gloria, tricking her into imagining the person who belonged to those smells, believing she must still be here.

Gloria wondered how her family walked around at all, like they were still living their life, like it was somehow still the same. Was she really supposed to keep on existing when her mother could no longer do the same? Shower, why? Wasn't that just greedy? How could she care for herself so completely when the person she cared for most could do nothing? No moment lingering in the sun, no sound of her children's laughter, no whisper in her ear from her lover, for her mom it was over, everything was over. How could Gloria selfishly continue attending to her own needs, keeping her life in order? It seemed wrong, it seemed like a betrayal.

So she languished in a melancholy of apathy. Without desire, drive, or decisiveness she sat around wondering if she would ever come back. She retreated to the base of her brain, the slow, basically formed functions which expressed only a small part of her. She had no critical thought, no wonder, no pursuits. Time stopped for her, like it didn't even count, if she gave nothing, nothing would matter. Noise seemed intrusive, conversations seemed trite, eating seemed disgusting, she couldn't find a moments comfort. Gloria agonized into a state of submission, resigned to the hopelessness of it all. No, she would never feel good, her greatest fear turned out to be true, life was nothing but misery. There was only confirmation of greater depths of despair to be condemned to. No senses made it through her brain stem; there they remained trapped in rudimentary evolution not even hoping to survive.

Her dad finally convinced her to get some fresh air. She couldn't keep fighting him. After weeks of cowering at the thought of going out even for a moment. "But I can't," she would say. She had no more energy to fight his requests, so she succumb.

She had looked so frightened, so unsure of the consequences, Marty had not really pushed her. But he rejoiced when one day, nearly a month since her mother's death, Gloria finally relented and agreed to step outside. Marty held his daughter under her arm as she shuffled into the open air. Unstable and squinting at the light, it was clear she was sacrificing the sense of safety the indoors had brought her. He took it very, very slow, only a few minutes, a stroll around the garden. He pointed out the plants and insects. She looked lost, like she couldn't understand any of it, as if she didn't know what was going on.

Gloria and her dad didn't head out again immediately. But a couple of days later, another walk, a day or two after that, another. In a matter of weeks the walks grew longer and more frequent. She began to eat a little more, talk a little more. Her insomnia began to subside; she slept six, sometimes seven hours, waking up only on occasion. Gloria eventually began to go on walks on her own. She grew less timid, maybe this was the worst, she thought, maybe she was facing the worst, and while not unscathed, she was still here.

Gloria's prolonged silence began to amplify the emotion of the internal which eventually led to a rejuvenation of her senses. Most of the feelings terrible, the gut wrenching sort, but sparks of intrigue began to burst through. And as her listless sorrow was lifting a tumultuous terror arose, equally as frightening, but vastly more inspiring. She began to loathe, even deplore the space around her. Hate seemed slightly better than nothing, she grabbed on like a hobo grasping a train hoping it would take her to a better place, knowing she could no longer remain where she had been. The day was too bright, the night was too dark. Her skin crawled with dissatisfaction, a seething squalor of unsettledness. She gnashed her teeth, clenched her fists, snarling at the world. What raged in her was the uncontained delirium of trauma, directionless and consuming.

She walked all the time now, trying to cool the fire burning inside her, hoping to pacify it just enough to harness its energy. Gloria walked far out into the scorching hot desert under the blazing sun, no water, no plan, simply pushing the boundaries of existence. She would scramble home, sometimes late at night, crazed like a wild animal, her worried father there to lick her wounds. It was more revelatory than reckless, a test of her spirits triumphant will to stay alive. If she was going to stay it would have to be on her terms. She ripped and tore at the excesses of existence, and searched for meaning from the scraps left behind. Extraneous be damned, immaterial be forgotten, her purpose was formulating in the tragic fallout of death, in a place where primal pursuits still reign. An untapped ferocious energy welled inside her, what she would become, where she would go, she did not know, but a life without purpose had nearly killed her. There must be change.

The flood of anger that broke through her dam of sorrow allowed other emotions to trickle in behind. A glimmer of interest here, a dash of wonder there, she began to recognize again the complexity and subtlety of life. She couldn't bash it in with a stick like her anger demanded, but she could reroute, alter its flow, like a river pinched and squeezed into a new direction. So she explored new ways to get what she wanted, tuning her presence to her surroundings. She studied carefully the impact of one thing on another, hers upon others. Everything left some sign of its presence, the ant with its hill, the smoke with its trail, even the unseen, the wind with its swirling of dust, plant seeds able to travel within a clear gale to take root somewhere entirely unpredicted. She watched these occurrences, found relationships in the seemingly unconnected, and reimagined the limits of possibilities through the fiery stare of a girl inspired.

Gloria again climbed deep into the hills. She reached higher and higher, less afraid to separate herself from things below. She had already fallen so low without ever reaching great heights; the uneven trade did not seem fair. If it had to be so hard, why not see how good it could be?

The weather had turned brutally hot, no rain since the day her mom died almost six months ago. She synthesized her internal struggle with her fight against the elements. Her body grew stronger, her mind sharper. She began to read the layout of the land in front of her, anticipating its resources and perils, where edible cacti could be found, where boulders large enough to find shade would likely reside. She could pinpoint by elevation and proximity, certain land masses: foothills, plateaus, ridges, exactly where life sustaining forces could be found. She fine tuned her desire to live so sharply she needed nothing but nature to survive. This extraordinary relationship with her surroundings brought her back to the living. She was forced to use her insight, and her intellect on top of her rudimentary base instincts. She became more complete, more competent, more potent through time, rising above the darkness which had swallowed her whole and threatened to dismember her, render her useless. But now, she had been drawn out, intent upon building the sensibilities she nearly lost.

Aware she hadn't seen Bugsy for months, she began to wander closer and closer to his adobe. Hurt he had not cared to check on her, she fumed at his insolence. Her only friend, absent, salt in the wound of her already unbearable pain. She would have suffered with or without him, but the respect she had lost for him burdened her further. Fuming and cursing in the hills overlooking his house, his prolonged neglect tortured her sense of friendship. She felt an unspoken loyalty, she thought he felt it too, but where was he? She never got close enough to his house to be noticed, but she hoped to catch a glimpse of him, sear him with her gaze. She saw the smoke from the chimney at night, and the flicker of candlelight through the windows, but nothing else, no comings and goings, the place was eerily still.

Her curiosity about Bugsy replaced the anger of his betrayal. Her pride tempted her to continue the silence, but it was not silence from Bugsy she wanted and she knew how misleading pride could be. She set out to talk to him. Bringing a little fun into the endeavor, she plotted a strenuous loop into the hills beyond Bugsy's adobe to mentally prepare for her arrival. She hoped she would arrive tested and exhausted, free from judgments. The day was slightly cooler than the previous weeks, hovering in the nineties; perhaps the heat will finally break she thought. The typical end of summer had approached and passed with no sign of relief. Despite the ever-present heat, the hike seemed easier than she had anticipated. Maybe it was the adrenaline at the prospect of seeing Bugsy, or the resolve of her determined body finally rising above physical reproach in the familiar hills, but she arrived fresher and sharper than she wanted, still with plenty of fight.

Gloria rapped gently on the small sunken door. She heard a cough and then a pained groan of exertion. Hangover, she thought, Bugsy still searching for redemption at the bottom of a bottle. She heard a slow shuffle to the door, the unbolting of the latch, and finally the slow creek of the door drawing open. She laid eyes upon the only person to intrude upon the desperate thoughts of her mother. He was far from the man she had last seen. He was pale, with sunken eyes, hunched at the waist, something was very wrong. She realized how wrong when he lifted his hollowed eyes to meet her stare, he was dying, and they didn't have long.

He weakly nodded his head for her to enter. She leaned against the mahogany table watching him shuffle slowly back to his chair. Laboring, he grimaced as he sat, silently conveying the strain the simple action created. He began to explain himself. "I'm sorry I have not been in contact." He paused, regaining his breath, "I am sorry about the loss of your mother. I had suffered a nasty fall earlier that day, the day of the explosion. I had been having dizzy spells and one finally took me down," he stated, then pausing again to regain his breath. "I haven't really been able to get back on my feet since then, I'm sorry."

She remembered every mean thing she had thought about him and redirected it at herself. Like a dagger, her unforgiving emotion pierced her heart. "Why didn't you send word? I would have come."

"The loss of a mother, your life source, can cause the understanding of your derivation to be so dramatically impacted it can be as if you are born again. It is a time of great soul searching and the pursuit of great meaning. I would have robbed you of the purity of one of the greatest trials a person can face if I had interjected my own misfortune into yours. And you are here now; you have made it in time."

158

She returned every day after that. From sunrise to sunset she would stay. She would have stayed longer but he said he was at peace in the dark and there was no need. The owner of the local market had taken to weekly deliveries of his food. She ventured into town for the first time since her mother's death to set up an agreement with the market owner. She was apprehensive, but resolute, and managed to navigate her return to the public realm.

Every Wednesday, just before dawn, she would stop by the market and retrieve a pack full of groceries from the front of the store. She enjoyed the weight of the pack on her shoulders, reminding her of the countless hours she had spent trekking through the desert with her paint supplies strapped to her back.

She cooked for him, read to him, and talked with him. They often talked and talked the days away, the most soothing way to pass the time. Her favorite subject of course, life beyond Larkspur. She wasn't sure which of them needed the talking more. Trapped alone with their thoughts for months had left a reservoir of ideas and inquiries to be explored. He saw a final opportunity to share the life lessons he had learned with his most eager pupil, his life lived, now left to the memories of others.

She left him as he grew tired each evening, only to return each day to a refreshed listener ready to engage. She imagined the difficulties he endured alone with bathing and matters of simple hygiene. She recalled her recent moratorium on these acts and again was struck by her foolishness. She felt the humbling power of illness, and cared for him more tenderly than she thought she thought possible. He spoke very little of his own life, and she respectfully stopped asking. But only after making it clear she was interested in knowing more about him, not just the outside world in which he had walked. But he continually declined to share that part of himself, and she let it fade away.

The severe winter came harshly with nary a month of autumn weather to soften the blow. There was little time for the thin skin and raised capillaries created by the heat to recede to firmer ground buried in the safety of muscles and fat in preparation for the cold. Gloria was chilled for a month solid, her body never quite seeming to catch up with the frigid onslaught brought by the absence of heat.

Bugsy had not improved like she hoped, and the darker days of winter seemed to be pulling him farther and farther away. He rarely bathed at all any more, and often he stayed in the same clothes for days at a time. Gloria offered to help, he declined. He was mostly taking in liquids. She strained his soup, juiced his fruits and vegetables, she did what she could, but his weight continued to drop. Their conversations grew less animated; there were more moments of silence between them.

They had spoken very little on this particular day and she was surprised when he said he had something to tell her. He explained. "This is what you have been asking about all these years. I finally see the power it holds for you, and I cannot pretend to spare you any longer." She sat up with focused intensity wondering what he could possibly have to say that hadn't already been discussed in the previous weeks of conversation. "This is serious," he said, "your life will never be the same."

"I'm ready," she replied.

He began. "Before you, I had really only been close with two other people. You're the first I'll leave behind. I'm not sure which is worse, watching someone go or being the one to leave. But I know death brings out a part of life that until then hadn't existed, wrongs can be made right, and sometimes unimaginable secrets need to be revealed. And my only wrong is the secret I've kept from you for so long."

Gloria's heart began to pound, her mind went blank. She knew this was larger than any quick speculation she could make as she waited impatiently for him to continue. She felt her mouth go dry, she smacked her lips.

Noticing her response he gave a little laugh. "I know, the moment you've been waiting for is finally here, almost unbearable," he said. "I hope it doesn't disappoint."

Somehow she was sure it would not. "Tell me already," she said, overcoming the initial shock of the impending disclosure. "You're liable to kick the bucket before you get through it," she halfheartedly joked.

"Oh, I see, once I tell you I'm disposable, is that it?" he smiled.

"That's it old man. Now you get to it," she joked. She felt for a moment they were back to their old selves, not the girl who lost her mother, or the man with only a short time to live, but two friends sharing a laugh.

They calmed, he took a small sip of water and settled into his chair. "Gloria, I must preface this by letting you know I'm not entirely sure I should be telling you what I am about to say. It will undoubtedly prove very disruptive to everything you believe. And if your mom was still alive I would not be saying this now. Her death has made me fear for your safety… Sometimes the grandest of dreams are the most combustible."

"Do you know what happened to her?"

"I can only suspect. There will be so many questions my child. Now you must listen." She nodded as he continued. "I have spoken briefly to you of my boss, and you have some understanding of what she meant to me. What I have not mentioned is what she meant to other people, her place in the world." He paused and took a small sip of water. "The woman who became my closest and dearest friend was not a woman who lived only in the private sphere. You see, my boss was a very important woman, my boss was Maggie Pelt, the former First Lady of the United States of America."

Gloria's eyes grew wide with amazement. She opened her mouth, thought better of it, and waited quietly as Bugsy took another small sip of water.

"I know." he continued. "I'm just as surprised as you. I'm still wondering whether it was real even though we spent twenty five years together. I was very young when we first met, nineteen, I was in the army and had been badly injured. I was in a coma for weeks, she heard about my story. My drill sergeant, even though he was facing troubles of his own had written to her. She visited me later, after my time in a coma

160

when I was still recuperating. I couldn't believe it, the first lady coming to see me. But that's the way she was, she cared deeply for people, she did whatever she could. She told me she didn't think it was a good idea for me to go back to active duty and wondered if I had a place to go. I said I did not, but I would find a place. She looked at me with her kind, soulful eyes and said, 'I want you to come with me, get better,' she said. She had a job for me. 'No obligations, stay if you want, go if you like,' she said

"So that's what I did when I was well enough. I boarded a train to D.C. and headed for the White House, me, Charlie Lisack, on the way to the White House. I got there expecting to be told there had been some mistake, that they had never heard of me and I should go back to where I came from. But do you know what happened?" he said, sitting up in his chair. "They let me in. They showed me all around like I was somebody important. I walked through the same halls and same rooms as former presidents. I couldn't believe it, nineteen, never been nowhere, the first time I left my hometown was to join the army, and there I was, a poor, dumb small town kid walking around the White House. They eventually took me to her office, she was nice as could be, humble, kind, made me feel completely welcome, I just couldn't believe it.

"At first I did some odd jobs, you know nothing much, she didn't seem to need me. I thought, well it doesn't look like things are going to work out, but I still felt great, I felt so lucky, like now I could be whatever I wanted to be. Then I started driving for her and traveling with her. She had some driving troubles of her own, so she brought me on. I couldn't imagine life getting any better. To spend so much time with the greatest person I'd ever met, who treated me with respect, like I was somebody, like I mattered, it was unbelievable. She gave me a second chance at life, and I'm not the only one," he said, looking squarely into Gloria's eyes.

"She cared about the suffering of all people. You've probably read about her International human rights work. And you certainly know about the atrocities committed by Hitler's Germany during the time her husband was in office. Maggie felt the plight of one was the plight of all. I wasn't aware at the time, not until years later, I found out in a scenario much like this, she was nearing her death and there were things she wanted me to know, but she put into practice the principles she held so dearly. She was horrified by the complacency of world leaders in their response to Nazi Germany. You must understand Gloria, people in positions of power like Maggie's husband knew about Hitler's intentions for a long time, years before the war started, and many, many, years before U.S. involvement. They hedged their bets hoping Hitler would not become powerful enough to see his plans through, or that someone else would step in and defeat him. Well, no one did, thus enabling the herding and massacre of millions of people.

"Can you imagine, rounding up people from all over Europe, imprisoning them, and killing them without intervention? Governments, civilians, watching millions of frightened people marched through the streets. Hitler ran a massive campaign of terror and intimidation, I'll grant that, but one country, one leader, rendering

161

so many powerless? It is not possible without a collective condemnation of the persecuted. No one cared enough about the Jews to stop it. Only when their own safety was threatened did they stand up and fight.

"Maggie was determined to do something, what little she could. First ladies up until that point, rarely, if ever, played a role in the political process. It was a testament to both Maggie and her husband the influence she was able to maintain at the White House, and therefore, what she was able to accomplish as a protector of the people. It is quite likely the full extent of her influence, and what she was able to accomplish, will never be known.

"Today, I share with you information that no more than a dozen people outside theses boundaries have ever known. The secrecy of what I am going to tell you is the reason for the programs continued success and must be maintained. Gloria, if you were to share what I tell you it would be the end of Larkspur, do you understand?"

She nodded.

"In the late thirties and early forties, when it became clear they would not be protected at home many Jews attempted to flee Europe. The U.S., along with many other countries would not allow them to emigrate; essentially the Jews had nowhere to go. Maggie devised a plan to allow some refugees into the country, certain, special refugees, who would never know of their background."

Gloria leaned in expectantly from her perch atop the table. Bugsy took a slow long sip of water then continued. "The nineteen thirties were very difficult years for this country. The roaring twenties, a time of free expression and revelation was slapped down by the economic fallout of the depression. Our country was suffering greatly; many had difficulty looking past their own struggles. There was enough sorrow and hardship in their own backyard, few cared or even knew about the problems going on in Europe. During this time there became a great need for social welfare. Policies were enacted, Social Security, the New Deal, President Pelt exhibited great leadership. But there were many forgotten victims of the times, the poor, the children, especially the children, who have no ability to care for themselves, abandoned, found dead from starvation; there was little that could be done.

"The plight of the children during the depression left a lasting impression on Maggie Pelt. She was determined to advocate for those who were most vulnerable to human failures. As the crisis in Europe escalated she knew something must be done, and it was the children, the most innocent victims of all, she devised a plan to save. She began convincing her husband something had to be done, if not for all Jews, then at least the children. She believed every life was valuable, but choices had to be made, not everyone could be saved, she did what she could. You see Gloria, a program was implemented, Larkspur, a top secret military base created solely to raise Jewish refugees. The travel restrictions placed on the people of Larkspur are not because of radiation, but because no one even knows you exist, not even the people who vote to fund the program."

"My parents?" Gloria asked.

"Some of the first refugees to arrive."

"Raised by the military?"

"Yes. They tried to recruit married military couples, but most were strangers thrown together in a project they couldn't get out of."

"What about their families?"

"Efforts were made to take recruits from broken homes, ones who would get the most out of the opportunity, but it was one of the great moral dilemmas facing Project Redeye. The families of the recruits involved were told they perished in the war."

"Redeye?"

"Named for the method used to transport the children, secrecy maintained, shrouded in the darkness of night."

"What do people think is going on here?"

"They don't know, it's entirely top secret. There are many projects rubber stamped by the oval office that no one in the government knows the true nature of, projects grandfathered in like this one. The government signs off on it blindly; the suppliers and infrastructure support believe they are maintaining military operations, which is accurate, but not the whole truth. The government seems to operate well with half truths, nobody is truly responsible, so no one interferes. Everyone involved with the creation of the project has since passed on; the few who knew the whole truth took it to the grave."

"But why? Why can't we just be set free?"

"Because you don't exist. Imagine if people found out the government has been keeping a secret this big from them for fifty years. People would have to wonder what else the government was capable of; a serious credibility issue would emerge, there would be outrage. Hundreds of thousands of people manipulated into staying put, long lost Jewish refugees unaware of their family ties, the fallout would be immense. The wounds would cut deep; the damage to the country's reputation would be incalculable, far greater than the damage to those whom without the Redeye Project would not be alive remaining unaware of their history."

"Whoa," she said in the way only a teenager can, "this town is crazier than I thought."

"This town is an extraordinary place to live. It's like the noble premise and all the thought put into its inception insulated it from the evils of the country. People enjoy more freedom and peace of mind here than anywhere out there."

"How could you say that? It's all a lie, no one here is free, no one here knows who they truly are, or what the rest of the world is really like. We don't want to be insulated; we want to fight the evils and help make the world better."

"I know Gloria, but they won't let you. Of the many lies told about this place to keep its secrecy, one is that it is a quarantine for a blood disease yet to be introduced into the general population. They will not let you leave because they have been told you are a danger. Supposedly, everyone will be kept here until they find a cure. Any threat to the safety of the population is to be disposed of."

"Like my mom?"

"Like your mom, and possibly you too. That is why I had to tell you, you will never survive here with your attitude."

"I don't want to just survive, and I don't want to stay here."

"I know Gloria, I'm going to help you. Please, let me go on… I don't want you to think Maggie was a terrible person for what she did."

"I don't."

"It was a very complicated issue, she did the best she could and was tortured by her decisions every day until she died. She never stopped trying to figure out a way to set you free, she could give you life, but she could not give you freedom."

"How many people, how many babies did she save?"

"A hundred thousand. Who went on to have hundreds of thousands of children, including you."

The bright orange light of the setting sun began to pour through the windows. Bugsy coughed and adjusted slightly in his chair. "I think that is enough for one day. We'll talk more tomorrow."

Gloria jumped down from the table and gingerly gave the sick man a hug. "Bye Bugs, thank you," she said tenderly. She quickly kissed his forehead and skipped away.

She leapt into the twilight with bliss swimming through her head, the curious feeling of lightness that comes after a lifetime of suspicions confirmed. The euphoric acknowledgement that the persistent paranoia she felt was not delusional, but in fact elemental to the understanding of her surroundings. Her intuition had always known there were great mysteries to Larkspur, and the more disbelieving she was of the eerie feelings inside her, the more hopeless she had felt. She would never have to question her skepticism again, she had been vindicated. Too relieved to be troubled by all she had heard, for that would surely come later, she marveled at the beautiful enchantment of the evening. The snow, as vast in its pure white undertaking as the blue of a bright cloudless day, dominated the environment. She abandoned her usual route home and headed into town.

The half light of the setting sun hung over the town in a state of suspended animation, with the crystal blue of the day undaunted by the looming darkness of a sun deprived night. The horizon, with a thin wisp of green under an aqua blue brightened by the gradual transition from darker blues to violets, rising to blacks, so starkly contrasted the still white of the ground it seemed as if she was temporarily of two different worlds, each with its essential presence, but neither entirely comforting. The familiarity of the snow covered land which helped shape her but left little potential for greatness, and the translucent multicolored sky spread before her, intrigued and tempted, but also frightened with its mercurial nature. Bright stars hung low, enchanting the legend of the endless possibilities of the unknown. Anything could happen in the land beyond the horizon, moments as bright as day and as dark as night. She knew every dark sky had its bright stars,

164

while sometimes hidden behind clouds or masked by surrounding light, they wait patiently to once again burn glorious in time.

The snow brought a certain quiet to the town, unburdened by the clusters of people coming and going. She walked through downtown with a newfound respect for what had been built here. The simplicity of the town now made sense to her. What once seemed boring and unimaginative now seemed practical and responsible. The little shops with quaint personal touches, industrious people, self-sufficient and determined. They had built a life here, maybe not the one they had originally hoped for, but an adapted life with new hopes and dreams. She now saw their loyalty and belief in Larkspur as an affirmation of hope, not the complacent lack of desire for more she had convinced herself of for so long. People, who knew by circumstances beyond their control that they were limited, and still they managed to carve out a great life. The same mundane buildings which once symbolized the town's lack of desire to reach beyond the general realm now intoned strength of character, dedication to a project, the preservation of life with great sacrifice to their own.

How could she not have known of the righteousness of the people who built this place? She had so lost herself in the displeasure of her encasement; she had despised everything and everyone around her. Her own eyes blinded by ignorance, creating a harsher landscape than need exist. Possibly it was necessary, the rejection of Larkspur entirely, to fuel her passion to leave, to bring her to this moment where she might now be able to flee. If she had embraced the people, the culture, maybe she would not have fought so hard for independence, but still, she had her regrets about the contempt she had showed for the town.

The night grew colder, pleading with her to return home, but she would not. She indulged in the town built upon empathy and compassion; and she now understood Bugsy's passion for it. Despite the solitude, she felt more connected to the people of Larkspur walking down the empty snow covered streets than ever before. In her mind she heard the laughter, pure and true, saw the smiling faces, the new families, a welcome contrast to the death that could have befallen them. She imagined the townspeople now, in their homes, sharing stories, warming by the fire, engaging in the simplicity of life. She re-familiarized herself with the place of her birth, transforming the trauma of her discontent into the purpose of her existence. She grappled with the knowledge that every baby that had come to Larkspur during the war was a gift taken from those who loved the child most. How could a world allow such suffering, the tenderness between a parent and child betrayed? What is left when we disavow the purest parts of our existence, when the loss of life is no more than the means to an end? The immeasurable magnitude of the lives almost lost spurred her on. She fell deeper and deeper in love with her hometown with every passing step, and surer and surer she must leave to help ensure there would never be a need for a place like Larkspur again. The blurring of certain distinctions should never exist, kindness or condemnation, freedom or life, truth or death. The questions raised by a community built in secret to protect those no one else was willing, are ones that should never have to be answered, she thought. The only question she kept asking herself is why are there lives we choose to ignore?

She never did return home that evening, preferring to take in the brisk fresh air of a town reborn. She did leave a note for her dad at his classroom where he was scheduled to teach that morning. She could hardly endure the thought of inflicting more damage to the grieving man's frayed nerves, which a night away from home was sure to do, but she could not rest with all the thoughts running through her head, and she dare not attempt to keep her new knowledge from him until she was more settled.

She came upon the small adobe with black smoke pouring out of the chimney just after dawn with a new found understanding of Bugsy's warnings about the outside world. She lightly knocked on the door before she entered. He sat in his chair, bright eyed and alert, sipping tea, a welcome sight. She greeted him warmly, hugging him, placing her cheek on his. "I see you managed to get the fire going again this morning," she said. The first time he had been able to do so in weeks. Usually, she arrived and started the fire, allowing the place to warm for an hour before he felt comfortable enough to leave his restful cocoon. She would blend him some fruit, turn on some peaceful jazz, and finally, the fire properly stoked, he would be lured from bed.

Today, he was ready for her. "Yes, my body seems slightly competent, an unexpected delight for a body I thought no longer held any capabilities other than pain," he said.

"But your mind has remained sharp," she replied.

"The sick and twisted humor of death, so often not coming until a bright mind is enslaved by a decaying body or the willing body incapacitated by the lost mind. I can't say I'd prefer either, quick and painless with all faculties still remaining that's the only merciful way to go."

"That seems the cruelest of all, still so much possibility," she countered.

"At least you don't have to suffer the degradation of ability, becoming as dependent as a child after so long on your own."

"We should all be so lucky to complete the full cycle of life, from birth to an aged death, a return to our innocence."

"Do I look innocent, dear?"

"Why yes, you do, quite innocent."

"Don't confuse incapable with innocent."

"I'm not. You're sharing your truth in its most pure state, no pretension, no distortion, you are exactly who you are."

"Because there can be no other way. I can't be anything other than this dying sack of bones."

"You see the innocence of it?"

"I see the brutality of it."

166

"Brutality is not what's motivating you to finally tell me the truth about Larkspur."

"Maybe it is, maybe you'll wish you'd never known?"

"The truth still exists whether we know of it or not, still influences, affects and determines, regardless. This process, dying, has stripped you of all that clouds your judgment, all the extraneous components found in meaning. This is your pure state, your state of innocence, and this is what you have chosen to do."

"I guess we should continue then?"

"I think it would be wise."

"Where was I?"

"You were defending the first lady, but we can move on from there, I can make up my own mind about the morality of her decision. I know you trust and love her, that's all I need to know from you. I want to know what happened to my mother."

"I can't say for sure. Maybe it was a tragic accident."

"She blew herself up? I don't think so."

"No, I don't either, but it is within the realm of possibility. Much more likely, as I've intimated, she became a threat and they disposed of her. Gloria, I know your desire to know what happened to your mother is strong, but I fear you will never know the whole truth. Not all of us get the peace of mind of knowing how our loved ones left the earth. As strange as it sounds, there's comfort by simply knowing some of the circumstances surrounding her death. You will carry the burden so many have carried before you, an incomprehensible loss for unknown reasons. There are many who never heal from a wound like that, but carry on anyway. Whether or not you find the strength to overcome your mother's death is up to you. Tragedy comes for us all, whether in the form of neglect, the painful silence of isolation, abuse, the devastation of the mind and body by another, or loss, and the longing for someone whom may never return. No great person is without their tragedies, and you are no exception. Her death may torment you, but do not let it take you. There are great things yet to be done, whether all whom you would want to share your life with are there or not. So what happened to your mother, my child, her brilliant life was stopped short, but not yours, my dear girl, not yours."

"There's so much we never did, never talked about."

"I know. Every achievement will have a whisper of sadness, every loss all the more painful, and you will spend the rest of your life reconciling the time you did and didn't have with your mother. Maybe you'll blame Larkspur, maybe Maggie, maybe me for not telling you sooner or warning her of the danger, but all those thoughts keep you looking backwards, your life is ahead of you, Gloria, never let the past keep you from your future."

"What is my future?"

"Ah, now that is what we should be discussing. I've told you about one dear friend, now let me tell you about another. Our meeting was as a result of another kind act of compassion by Maggie. She was a little sneaky this time because she felt the circumstances demanded discretion."

167

"She was a little sneaky in the case of Larkspur, as well," Gloria said smiling.

"Yes that's true. We can safely say she was a woman willing to do what it takes to do what she felt was right."

"Sure, we could say that," Gloria said, giving Bugsy a little bit of a hard time.

He smiled at her wryly, conceding her supposed suspicion, but recognizing her willingness to be open to possibilities. "This is quite different from Larkspur," he assured. "All she asked me to do was pick up a man just arriving to the States after many years, and make sure he safely arrived to his destination. She did leave out a few key points, but I surely would not have agreed had she not; and as usual, her intuition did not lead her astray. I met John just a few years before Maggie's death. Again, it was a letter which precipitated the clandestine coming together of intertwined lives. The simple act of writing a letter has had a profound impact on my life, never underestimate the power of words, true, heartfelt words, they can change the world.

"John had also been in the army; he fought in World War II, but deserted his troop shortly before the end of the war. He spent nearly fifteen years living modestly in a small village in France. He was unable to return to the States for fear of court-martial. The army never forgets a deserter; it forgives and forgets many crimes, but never those who decide to leave. John enjoyed his simple life in France, he worked on a vineyard, made wine, he had not planned on returning. Everything changed when he got a phone call from the one man in the army he kept in touch with. The man had served with John and was a loyal friend who helped get letters and communication to John's family. This time, he called with news of their former sergeant, he was in an army hospital in Virginia, the son of a bitch was dying, he told John. Their sergeant had not treated his men well, but something about the sergeant's declining health made John want to come back to face the man he had run from so many years earlier."

"I don't get it," Gloria said perplexed.

"It's the power of death in the eyes of those who cherish life; nothing looks the same when you face it. John could no longer ignore the past. You see, Gloria, he had let the past decide his future. He wanted his life back, and for him that meant going through the sergeant. John wrote Maggie, he said she was the only person he could imagine who might care enough and be able to help him. Maggie said she received only one other letter which had moved her so, and that was the one written about me, and look how well that turned out. So she talked to some people, she was very well respected, and still had some very good friends in both the military and the White House. John was honorably discharged, a free man, and I was there to meet him at the airport. I'll spare you the details, but we became close, loyal friends."

"You don't have to spare me."

"Perhaps I spare myself, but I am an old man, I've had far too long to think about my own life. This is a story with purpose, let us not get distracted."

"I would listen you know, to your story, anything that might have happened to you, I would listen."

168

"Gloria, some things are best left unspoken, even between friends, no good can come for you, or me, by discussing some of the frailties of my life. I lived through them, I had my great moments, which is all you need to know, I am at peace."

She reached out to him from her location seated on the floor by his feet, a gentle reassuring touch on the hand, she started a bit. "You're cold, let me get you a blanket," she said. She got up and grabbed a quilt from the cupboard.

Bugsy smiled. "Aw, Maggie made me this quilt. I only bring it out for special occasions, this will have to qualify." Gloria glanced at the oddly shaped patterns and crooked stitch work. He noticed her sideways look and added, "she took to needlework late in her life. I dare say she wasn't very good at it," he said laughing. "She never did have the patience for sitting still inside, a restless spirit that one…" he looked longingly out the window for a moment. "Anyway, John, that's who I want you to see when you leave here."

A big smile came over Gloria's face. "You're going to help me get out of here?"

"Look at me child; I am helping you do nothing. You have to get yourself out of here; I'll give you a place to go."

"Sounds good to me," she said smiling.

"John now lives in the central coast of California, wine country. He owns a ranch and vineyard." Bugsy pointed over at his record collection. "Look in the Joni Mitchell album, Blue, there's a letter in there for John and an envelope full of money for your travels."

She pulled out the album cautiously, like any misstep and she would wake up from the trance that was leading her towards freedom. She found the letter and the money; she placed them on the table. "What should I do?" she said.

"I'm sorry to say I don't have some brilliant escape plan for you. You're going to have to rely on good old-fashioned guts and grit. You're going to have to hike out of here."

But of course, she thought, it made perfect sense. She knew the desert better than anyone, how to survive in it, hide in it, it was perfect. "But where are we? I mean, I think I know, but I'm not quite sure."

"We're in northeastern New Mexico. You have John's address on the letter, find your way there and you'll be safe. Don't ever tell anyone about Larkspur. You need to make up a back story, nothing major, just enough to get by."

"What should I do when I'm out there?"

"My dear, that is for you to figure out."

"Thank you, Bugsy."

"It's time you see what you're made of."

Gloria arrived at dawn the next morning eager to hear about John in California. There was no smoke rising from the chimney, it will be freezing inside she thought. She lightly knocked on the door and entered, the pale blue light of dawn reflected off the snow leaving a soft white light hovering over the room. "Good morning

Bugs," she called as she headed to the fire. She opened the door to the small wood stove, stirred the ashes with the poker, no red in the embers emerged, only the dull gray and black of extinguished coals. She crumpled up some paper, placed kindling on top of it and lit the paper. After a few moments spent waiting for the pieces of wood to catch, she placed a couple of small logs on the burning kindling. She closed the door, left the flute open, filled up the kettle with water and placed it on the stove. "What shall it be this morning," she called up to Bugsy, "a little Joni?" she said, not waiting for a reply.

She took a couple of steps towards the records and stopped dead in her tracks. She had been bustling about in her normal routine, but now she sensed something was different. There was no stirring in the cocoon, no sniveling or groaning. She scampered up the ladder to find a tangle of books and blankets, no Bugsy, she felt the sheets, they were cold. She backed down from the perch, slowly now, deliberately placing each foot on each rung. Her heart began to thump madly inside her, her vision narrowed, her hands shook. She said nothing as she lightly tiptoed over to the bathroom. She took a deep breath and peered in through the open door. There, Bugsy awkwardly lay, with his chest and face pressed against the floor, his hips turned sideways, and his legs slightly bent lying on top of each other. She fell to the floor and scooped his naked torso into her arms. He was stiff and freezing cold as she held him. Her warm tears rolled down her cheeks and onto his body, they passed between the crevices left by the hundreds of small circular scars that covered him. Her tears wound down his chest, the raised bumps providing a canal in which they streamed, they pooled gently in the dimple of his belly button until they filled the small indentation and tumbled over the side, again finding their stream within the scars.

Gloria grabbed a blanket from his cocoon and rolled him into it. She dragged him by the fire to warm him. The tea kettle bubbled vigorously and began the underpinnings of its high pitched whine. She swiftly removed the kettle from atop the stove not wanting to be subjected to the evil scream. She found his favorite thick, soft navy cotton pants, and his navy turtleneck. She always thought he looked like some strange sailor in this outfit, his uniform she called it. She pulled his pants over his slightly bent knees, she was unable to get his legs completely straightened, but managed to get his pants on without much difficulty. Navigating his upper body proved more difficult. She propped him upright, bringing over his favorite burgundy chair to support him. She sat in the chair behind him, straddling his upper body as she tried to dress him. She felt the smooth cold bumps of the scars against her arms. How could she never have noticed them before, for surely they hugged, she must have felt them. It must be too far out of the realm of possibility she thought, she could not possibly have suspected the terror that covered him.

She could not help but feel the scars as she pulled the shirt sleeve over his arm, they were so soft and smooth, so far from the rough and grotesque actions that must have caused them. She pulled the turtleneck over each arm, and then his head, finally pulling it down to cover his torso. She grabbed the quilt, the one that Maggie

170

had made, still resting on the back of the chair. She laid it down beside him looking at it in its entirety for the first time. It was beautiful in its own awkward way, a foot long yellow crescent moon lay at the center of the dominantly white quilt. There were oddly shaped navy and turquoise stars strewn about the quilt, variously shaped and colored planets, one resembling Saturn with rings. It was in this soft, warm, celestial body that Gloria wrapped him, careful to leave the moon directly on top of his midsection. She grabbed Bugsy's sewing supplies and tightly stitched the sides shut, then proceeded to snugly stitch him in above the shoulder leaving just his head poking out of the blanket.

She spent a few moments looking around the comfortable adobe, remembering all the wonderful times there. She noticed light glimmering off a tiny metal object in the corner; of course she thought as she rose to retrieve the shining object, she placed his dog tags around his neck. She kissed his forehead then walked over to the stove. She shoveled embers onto the top of the large mahogany table. She grabbed kindling, then logs, and built a large fire. She placed embers in his bed, building a fire there. In the far corners of the room she also built fires. She knew the adobe itself would not catch fire, but she proceeded to burn the entire contents inside the home, including the body of her best friend, never to be laid eyes on again.

She walked away from the charred remains of the adobe without the deep sadness she had expected. There was a comfortable stoic sense of purpose that had overtaken her at the first sign of trouble. She had simply slowed herself to the moment, recognizing her duty as his friend to protect him during his final moments on earth. She had never given it a moment's thought, what she would do if he died, but she acted swiftly, with ease, confident he would be proud. The scars on his body had terrified her, the profound intimacy of the divulgence nearly shocked her out of action, but quickly her desire to do right by him overtook her. Help had so clearly not been afforded him all too often. The language of a life left marked communicated sadness and struggle no book or experience had ever taught her. The sight of her beloved friend pocked, naked and tortured, instantly made everything he had ever said to her more meaningful, his warnings more important. The shedding which had begun with the death of her mother was now complete with the utter exposure of her friend. Her previously thin and soft skin was replaced with a thick, tough exterior, hardened by the rigors of loss and betrayal.

The brisk air cooled Gloria's cheeks as she slowly walked home. Her icy skin welcomed the warm liquid tumbling from her eyes. She felt every hot streak, each quickly turned vulnerable by the cold wind, exposing her sensitive flesh to tingles until warmly covered again. She arrived home, covered in a gooey mixture of tears, new and old, intertwined with a running nose. She didn't even bother to wipe her face as she pushed open the door. Her father, seated by the window reading a book, lifted his head. "Gloria, what's wrong?" He rose to meet her, using the end of his sleeve to clean her face as he took her into his arms. "What's wrong my child?" he asked. She didn't answer, only cried as he held her; she cried and cried and cried.

It took only a moment before Marty realized Bugsy was gone. All the residual anger and fear from two nights ago when she did not come home melted away. He held his firstborn daughter tightly in his arms, something he had not done, she had not let him do, since she was a very small child. He felt her convulsing with the exertion from crying, her last moments of childhood falling away before him, draining from her, the vestige of innocence leaving her with every tear. He knows she mourns for her mother, for Bugsy, and the innocence of a life past. He feels her slipping further and further away with every moment of closeness they share. He understands these are the waning moments of his role as a father to her, there is no protecting the initiated, she now walks alone in the world of suffering.

He knows he must let her go, he knows she will go anyway, and he would only be a stubborn fool to try and hold on. He must accept the reasons she must go are far more compelling than her reasons to stay. As pained as he will be to see his sweet Gloria leave, he knows he would be far more pained if she stayed. Her endless suffering if she remained would be too unbearable. In the light of his child unable to live her dream, he knew there was only one option. He would have three other children to stay strong for and a life with an extraordinary wife to look back on. Marty had never felt like a man of ordinary plight and circumstance, all the great moments he has known came with burdens he must accept.

Gloria had quieted now. Slumping slightly in his arms, she looked up at him. "Dad, I need your help."

She led him through the snow, the bright midday sun reflected harshly off the white ground cover. "I want to show you what I've done," she said. She knew the town needed to know, there would be questions. She wanted no part of the process; hopefully her dad could deal with it. She felt guilty for bringing him into this, but death always had to be dealt with in some official capacity, and she knew she could not muster one ounce of official behavior out of herself.

They made the two mile trek away from town with heavy thoughts thickening the air, each brooding over their presence in the dramatic unknowns of the new future. Gloria had watched her dad fight through sorrow without displaying self-pity, she'd watched as his world crumbled down around him, and he sifted through the rubble, rescuing the viable parts, discarding the unusable. He kept the family going, nurturing his wounded kids, catching them when they fell. And he was there for her now, she had pressed the limits of his loyalty, and he had always returned as willing as ever to prove his love.

She wondered how he continued to give, asking nothing in return. Was it the indisputable duty of a parent, or did he excel, a grand example of a man dedicated to a cause greater than himself. Surely a man who loses his wife can be pardoned if he, in his despair, let's his children's pain linger with his own. But after those first moments of shocked sorrow at the news of the explosion, he had not stumbled openly once. He had tried to make sure his kids lost only one parent, not both.

Gloria had needed every bit of his strength. With him there leading the family, she was able to fall, as hard, and as far as the time necessitated, and he remained capable and ready for whatever her sorrow may bring. And she needed him now, for that slight relief the reliance on another can bring, he was there for her, standing by her side, willing to do anything she asked of him.

The smoldering Adobe, with smoke leaking out its crevices, lay before them like the sunken remains of a vessel brought to the surface only to be burned and disposed of. The thick clay of the structure acting like waterlogged wood stubbornly refusing to succumb to the heat of the fire. Marty walked up to the shell, placed the palms of his hands on the glowing warm building, welcome heat after the frozen journey. The snow around the Adobe had melted away, leaving a ring of exposed ground. The wooden door burned away, they peered inside. Grotesque, melted records covered the floor and the burned spring remains of the chair smoked. The smell, something between the scent of human hair burning, and the toxic noxious fumes of burnt plastic, crossed with the plain smell of a campfire, wafted from the opening. Marty glanced down at the blackened human figure on the ground. "Was this necessary?" he asked his daughter.

She turned away from the smoldering scene. "It was dad, I'm sorry. Secrets carried a lifetime only to be exposed in death, by the neglect and lack of protection by those left behind, damage the life already lived. The indignity he suffered in life, the torture of what he kept hidden, would be trivialized had I not acted. The preservation of the spirit is equally as important in death as it is in life, only in death we must rely entirely on others."

"I understand Gloria," he said kindly to his daughter. "I will speak with the council."

"Thank you dad," she said as she hugged him.

Chapter 15

Bugsy was a revered teacher, controversial, and for the most part a loner, but well respected for his passion and commitment. His funeral was attended by hundreds of former students and their parents. Gloria did not go; she felt no connection to the town's relationship with Bugsy. She needed no ceremony, no kind words; her time with him was complete. She did, however, appreciate the town's gesture. Their kindness brought her closer yet to the people she was just opening herself up to. Her father, who did attend, said it was a lovely ceremony and they gave her friend a wonderful sendoff.

The harsh snows of winter ceased. The lush white landscape hesitantly gave way to the tan, red and brown rocky terrain. The first few colorful flowers peeked out from in between the rocks, tantalizing with the oncoming presence of spring. Sounds of life filled the air again as nature hatched the year's new brood. The giggling of children playing lingered again in the wind. The undercurrent of life's activities swelled with the new mixture of longer days and warmer air. The spring equinox, an ushering in of the new, the letting go of the past, had arrived. Marty sensed the shift, the air purpose laden after an aimless winter. The time changed like that, one hard winter of loss and sorrow, and now new life set to begin.

Marty watched as his sleepy daughter emerged from her bedroom, her long curly brown hair tousled by a night, he hopes of dreams, but fears of nightmares. The same nightmares that have plagued him since Ava's death, the desperate longing that arises in the unprotected state of sleep. She raised an arm, yawned, and stretched mightily. "Good morning," he said lovingly.

"Morning dad," Gloria replied.

"How did you sleep?"

"Well. Thank you"

"No nightmares?"

"No, I only dreamt of the ocean. I could feel the mist on my skin, and taste the salt on my lips. It was one of those dreams that seems so real, when you wake up you wonder for a moment where you are."

"I love those dreams," he said sincerely, quite sure he could not remember the last time he had such a dream, and afraid he might never again. "I was hoping we could go on a hike together today," he said. "The weather is warming up, I thought it would be nice. Just us, none of the other kids, you and your old pops exploring together. How's that sound?"

She looked up at him, slightly skeptical, but she quickly softened. "Sure."

"We'll leave after breakfast then."

"Okay. So where are you taking me anyway?" she asked happily.

"You'll see," he said. She was in fine spirits today, he thought. She rarely wanted to spend time together in the morning, generally fraught with the fear of a troubled night. But the sound night's sleep had done her well, he was sure today was the right day. "Something more than a smoothie today?" he said in reference to her usual habit of blending banana, papaya and almond milk together. Tummy settling and easily digestible was almost always the order for the day for Gloria, sometimes oatmeal, but mostly the subtle engagement of blended fruit eased her into the day. Fresh fruit all year round from the town's greenhouses, one of the many perks of Larkspur.

"How about that tofu scramble you used to make mom, the one with basil and sun-dried tomatoes," she said.

There were maybe a handful of times each year she strayed from her breakfast regiment, and today he took it as a good sign she felt well enough to do so. Another indicator today was the day. "Sure, you want some potatoes?" he asked.

"Yeah."

"Toast?"

"Sourdough."

"Whoa, toast and everything, you must be feeling good," he said to his daughter, smiling.

"Shut up," she said sheepishly.

Beaming inside, he turned away not wanting to make too big a fuss and alienate her, but unwilling to let the moment pass without a little fun. He pulled the seasoned tofu out of the fridge and went to work. He enjoyed the rich deep colors of the food as he chopped, the dark red of the dried tomatoes, the green of the basil against the deep blue of the countertop. He took his time, savoring the moment, enjoying his eldest daughter seated at the counter watching him prepare the food. He fried up some potatoes, then baked them for a little added crisp. He warmed the tofu scramble and toasted the bread. He was full of the comforting feeling of taking care of someone, the feeling he had enjoyed so often with his wife, and now revisited with his daughter. He was rarely able to indulge his nurturing side anymore, with his wife gone, and the boys too busy for that sort of thing. Only Audrey still needed him that way, and she had grown complacent with her expectant ways. He buttered the toast, placing it on top of the warm toaster to let the butter melt while he dished the rest of the meal. He placed a glass of room temperature water in front of his daughter, water only, no O.J., no coffee, ever, they were too

175

much, too influential on her sensitive system. He then placed a steaming plate of food in front of her.

"Aren't you going to eat?" she asked.

"I already did."

"You made this just for me?" she asked surprised.

He wondered for a moment how she could have any doubt. Did she feel like this was too much to ask, a simple breakfast from her father? "Of course I did," he said.

"Thank you."

"You're welcome, sweetheart," he said, slightly pausing before sweetheart. He had almost said sweet love, the endearment he used for his wife. He missed Ava so, and knew he would miss Gloria just as much.

They headed due west, away from the center of town, the fresh spring air alive with aromas and sounds enchanting them as they walked. They walked leisurely, a pace both of them were unaccustomed to. Marty pointed to a blooming flower, naming it, describing its characteristics. Gloria listened, interested, but not wanting to break the silence of a thoughtful mind. She studied her father as they walked, noticing his easy agility and the skill with which he navigated the terrain. He was lean and strong, full of the love of nature. A slow, warm feeling grew inside her, she was proud of him, she always had been, in his pursuits, his gentleness; she admired him, his skilled and competent ways, his confidence, his stability. She used to think it was weird, his obsession with plants, but now it seemed to her to be a fine choice for a life's work, there were few finer subjects than plants, she thought.

Gloria watched her father, with his dark hair flecked with gray, not old; he was only forty-five, still with the gleaming exuberance of a young child becoming aware for the first time. He stopped and leaned in close to his latest find, smelling and examining it. "It's early for Bluebells to bud," he said. She noticed his quizzical look, the curiosity he brought to everything, how lucky she has been, she thought, an upbringing engulfed in passion. She thought of her mother, and the silly way her parents interacted, flirting playfully, full of love and humor. How hard it must have been for him to lose her so young, with so much life left to live. Yet there he was, smiling, still in love with life, strong and proud, holding his family together. She remembered the way he would look at her mother, the way he held her, and stroked her cheek, time altered for all those around, a moment greater than the past or the future, a moment when time stood still.

"Dad," she said, stopping him in his tracks.

"Yeah," he answered.

"You've done a good job, I mean since mom died, well with everything."

He looked her in the eye, nodded and smiled, and continued walking.

They spent the next half hour hiking in silence. Eventually, it occurred to Gloria their direction was not aimless; her father knew exactly where they were going. She rarely came out this way, preferring the eastern hills overlooking her mom's lab and surrounding Bugsy's adobe. She knew those trails well, now she found herself studying hard trying to orient herself. She looked for landmarks, oddly shaped rocks or cacti to familiarize herself to the area. She noticed the shadows were different, on her right instead of left, laying due west.

She had watched the sun set out over these mountains hundreds of times from her vantage point in the east, often painting until the last wisps of light left her. She hadn't painted since her mom died, hadn't even thought of it until now. The time alone with her easel now seemed like the enchanted world of a naïve little girl looking to exert power over her surroundings in the only way she could, the creations of her mind. Now, she was beyond that, with her hands firmly placed in the exposed guts of life, moving towards the life she envisioned, one full of intrigue and wonder. The peril, the taunts and torments, the sacrifice, she wanted it all, not in essence, or notion, but the grind, the reality of the complicated and troubled world that so infuriates it must be held onto tightly to catch the brief moments of gold when the glory and brilliance of existence shines above all else.

"We're almost there," she heard her father say.

"Where?" she replied.

"The place your mother and I fell in love."

Ah, she thought, a sentimental jaunt with her sappy father that's what this is. Her anticipation over their arrival subsided as they continued on. She had felt the special tone in her dad's voice since he first said good morning, she hadn't been able to place its source, but now it seemed clear, a lesson on her parents love. She was up for it, she thought, her dad's devotion, it was a beautiful story to share after all, and he had so few with whom to share it. "You fell in love all the way out here? Why am I not surprised," she said.

"You aren't the only one who liked to wander these hills, my dear. Don't forget you were born from two restless spirits, the forces that drive us, drive you, and they can prove difficult to contain."

"I don't want to contain them."

"Neither do I," he said as they turned a corner around a large boulder unveiling a beautifully arched opening. "That is why I brought you here," he said, motioning to the dark hole.

"What is it?"

"It's our secret hideout, your mom's and mine. We found it when we were kids, no one else knows about it."

"Cool," she said as she lowered her head to go inside.

The arch was plenty tall to accommodate event the tallest of individuals, but something about its shape made newcomers bow upon entrance. Marty and Ava had done so for years before finally realizing it was not necessary. He was curious to see if Gloria would enter the same way, she did, he couldn't help but smile.

They entered the dimly lit, thirty by forty foot, cavern. Marty lit some candles; the light exposed a few of Marty and Ava's things left in the cave. A couple of old wooden folding chairs surrounded a small fire pit with a tea kettle sitting atop a wire mesh structure. There was an old school desk with a small chair connected to the metal frame, the desk Ava had spent so much time studying at. The items, child sized and dusty, spoke of a life since passed. Gloria grabbed a candle and examined some of the artifacts more closely. She trembled slightly as she pictured her parents, young vibrant beings finding their way, coming here to escape town and be free to collude on any number of endeavors.

"This is Mav's Hollow," her father said proudly.

"The first parts of your names, m and av, Mav's Hollow, oh, too cute."

"Hey, we were young; it was very bonding this secret place we created together."

"I'm sure it was," she said coyly, with possibly a hint of sexual innuendo.

He looked at her sharply, she made a silly face feigning innocence, he smiled. Right then, he knew his daughter was an aware sexual being. He had spent a great deal of time trying not to think of her burgeoning teenage hormones and what it would mean out in the world. "Oh brother," he said.

Gloria gave him a wry smile and giggled. She returned to examining the cave. She brought the light up to the dark reddish-brown walls; she felt the smooth, cool slabs as she moved past. "I love it here," she said.

"So did your mom and I," he paused, suppressing the lump in his throat. "Your mom wanted me to bring you here," he said. Gloria looked up at him intently as he continued. "She felt it was important for you to be aware of Mav's Hollow and what it meant to us."

"She told you that?"

"She did."

"Like she knew she might not be around to tell me?"

"Yes," he said, tears welling up in his eyes.

Gloria leaned back against the edge of the cave; she let out a heavy sigh, turned and kicked the wall slapping the stone with her hands. "Why did she have to keep doing it then? Why didn't she just stop doing whatever it is they wanted her to stop?" Gloria said, pleading.

Marty walked over to Gloria, taking hold of her arms gently. "She couldn't sweetheart, it was too important to her."

"And you just let her?" she said angrily.

He averted her eyes and turned away. He cried now, unable to bear the weight of all he had endured, losing his wife, feeling the brunt of his daughter's anger, and knowing he must watch her go, knowing there will be so much left unanswered, so many things he cannot explain.

"Oh, dad, I'm sorry," she said wiping away his tears. "It's not your fault."

"No, it's okay," he said lowering her hands. "I know there is nothing more I could have done. I'm just sorry I'll never be able to fully convey that to you."

"But you have dad, I'm sorry. I know it wasn't your fault. Mom always did exactly what she wanted to, I know that."

Marty picked up the now unlit candle Gloria had thrown to the ground, and relit it. "Here, take this," he said, slightly recovered, handing her the candle. "It's time you know exactly what your mom was doing."

He led her around the edge of the cave to the small, partially obstructed gap between two rock walls. Gloria followed, watching him squeeze into the wedge leading to the small hidden room. The black with red trim backpack was leaned up against the wall. Gloria picked it up and immediately put it on. "This is nice," she said.

Her father, with a slightly fearful look on his face, reached out both hands. "Careful," he said, "it's dangerous."

She removed the backpack and placed it on the ground. "Mom's great contribution, small enough to fit in a back pack," she said sarcastically.

"That's part of the beauty; her efforts would have been in vain if they were not made portable," he replied.

Marty opened the flap of the pack, pulling out three loosely wrapped eight by six inch metal cylinders. He reached into a side pocket and pulled out a tiny, quarter size remote control with two buttons, one white, one red. He removed the wrapping around the cylinders and placed them on the ground.

"Gloria, your mom spent her entire life creating this machine, she was willing to die for it, and there was nothing I, or anyone else, could do to stop her. The truth is, I didn't want to stop her." Gloria looked painfully at her father as he continued. "This meant more to her than life itself, and until you know why, nothing about the way she lived will make sense."

Marty picked up two spheres and rotated them together, they clicked and interlocked tightly, he attached the final piece. Marty held out the remote and pressed the white button. The two ends of the device rotated a half turn in the opposite direction and locked into place, a deep purple bulb illuminated at the center of the device. He pressed the red button, the ends unlocked and rotated, the light went dim.

"You see, red for blood, white for peace," he said.

He detached the ends and pointed to their grooves, an etched out plain in the metal which allowed each end to attach to the center piece. "It attaches here, give it a little twist 'til you hear a click. When you've got them both, hit the white button and it's armed, the red to disarm."

"What is it? Some bomb," Gloria asked.

"No. It's the anti-bomb. Red for blood, white for peace, when it's armed it keeps people safe, when it's not, people will die."

"From what, what does it do?"

"It prevents nuclear weapons from detonating."

"You're telling me this little thing will stop a nuclear weapon?"

"Yes. Now you see the beauty in its size."

"Now I think you're crazy. Is this what mom's been working on, some delusional mad scientist bullshit?"

"Gloria, watch your mouth."

179

"I don't want to watch my fucking mouth. You guys are nuts, both of you, the dead and the living."

"Gloria, I've seen it, it works. Why do you think it can't be done?"

"Maybe because it's never been done before."

"Every great accomplishment was at some point a first."

"I'm supposed to believe mom toiled away in that podunk lab and created something no one else in the world has been able to create."

"First of all, your mom created an incredibly sophisticated physics lab. She designed her own equipment, she collaborated with Ipstein until his death, and she conducted experiments that had never before been conducted, and may never be again."

"She worked with Ipstein, how?"

"Through letters. She had great opportunity; the community was very supportive at first. She was given complete autonomy. They hoped she would create something great for everyone, and she did, except for the people using the bomb to hold onto power, so she kept it to herself. They never knew what she was doing; few people in the world could even understand the formulas."

"But they grew scared of her?"

"They did."

"And she wouldn't stop?"

"She wouldn't."

"Why, when she had already made what she wanted?"

"She was developing a way to travel through the radiation."

Gloria's heart sank, but there was no radiation it was a lie, she thought. "A simple well sealed motor vehicle," Gloria said.

"Too cumbersome, too costly, decontamination sites would have to be built, qualities the government would not go for."

"So, she was trying to leave?"

"Of course she was trying to leave. She wanted to bring her device to the world."

"Why not just arm it and leave it here?"

"They would find it, track the heavy matter, they would destroy it, and the science behind it would never be shared."

"Mom made this, some revolutionary device, she just did it?"

"Sometimes, when you care about something with all your heart, and you put everything you are capable of into it, the extraordinary can be accomplished. Everything came together, many extreme circumstances played in her favor, Larkspur for one. Maybe it was her fate, but she did what she set out to do with only her faith to guide her. Gloria, what we create as people and as a society is what we are willing to invest in, the ideas behind the world we want. This device couldn't be made out there, because nobody really wants it. No one dared to dream it could be done. We are only limited by our vision of the future, and your mother envisioned a future without the tyranny of nuclear warfare."

180

"So this is serious, you're serious?"

"Yes."

'Why are you telling me?"

"Because she asked me to."

"What am I supposed to save the world now, complete the legacy of my mother's unfinished life?"

"She wanted you to know why she spent so much time away, how important her time away from you was. She wanted you to know she never took her absence lightly, not from you, or your brothers and sister."

"Why not tell them, why me?"

"You always cared the most about everything, what she did, what she didn't, you felt it all. She thought you should know. What you do with this information is your choice."

"Oh yeah, no pressure, just a little dead mother daughter sharing."

"It would have been nice if your mother would have lived through your teenage years, your angst is wearing me out," Marty said exasperated.

"Sorry dad if I didn't have the response you wanted."

"It's not that Gloria. Your mother and what she brought to life is untouchable. What you do, or don't do, will never change the power and beauty of her vision and what she was willing to do to pursue it. What you are not getting is this is your life now, not your parents pressuring you to do this or that. Take a step back for a moment, nobody is trying to hurt you, or ruin your life. Yes, it's heavy, it's a big deal, this is your life, these are the circumstances you face. Now what are you going to do about it? You can keep acting like a kid upset at everybody for everything, or you can accept what's really going on, the magnitude of it, and what role you play in it. I wish you didn't have to know this now, you're not even sixteen, but this is the way it is, deal with it."

It pained him to speak this way to his daughter, to push her away, faster and farther than he wanted and she was ready for. But she would have to know what she was made of if she were to leave Larkspur. He knew it wouldn't be easy, and she would not survive with the reasoning of a child.

"Okay," she said with a hurt look on her face, "I just need a minute to take it all in."

"I understand," he said, less authoritative but still sharp. "I say none of this without a heavy heart. You were a child born into a predicament not of your asking. And certainly your parents' choices are not yours to keep, at least not forever. But there is some unmistakable quality in you which leads me to believe your mother's story is not that far from your own, that you share the same spark that can keep a fire alive through the darkest times. Your mom thought you could handle knowing everything, maybe she was wrong, maybe I should have waited, but you can't leave without knowing the whole truth." Gloria looked up at her dad. "Yes, I know you are leaving," he said. "I don't know when or how, but I couldn't take the chance of you leaving before I brought you here. This may not be the complete picture you've always searched for; you must fill in the rest on your own. Know that we love you, we trust you, and we believe in you."

Gloria looked down at the ground and then over to the disassembled machine. "It's rather extraordinary."

"It is."

"How does it work?"

"I could never tell you exactly, only your mom knows for sure." He reached into another side pocket of the bag and pulled out a notebook. "It's all in here. She said a good physicist, one who really knew what he or she was doing, could build her machine from scratch with the knowledge in this notebook. From what I know it creates a negative space, a black hole, which traps all surrounding matter, then vanishes."

"Won't it suck up everything?"

"It's only activated in the presence of particular nuclear matter under specific conditions, and for only a brief period of time. Very little of the surrounding atmosphere is lost."

"Brilliant."

"I know."

"The purple beam of light?"

"Yep. It travels at the speed of light, the fastest human made object in existence. It's so the device can reach a nuclear weapon anywhere in the world."

"How does it sense the weapon?"

"I have no idea really, something to do with the change of electrons, the instability of the matter, and the velocity, or something. I must say there was no way to verify the range of the machine, except for the science, we only tested it once. The device worked perfectly. I myself find it a little hard to fathom a weapon on the other side of the world could be detected and disposed of in the blink of an eye. But your mom said the science was sound, that's enough for me, one mile or a million, she said, the process is so fast it doesn't matter."

"What did they do when you tested it?"

"They came and looked for us. They weren't sure what happened, if it was your mom, or me, or some freak thing, but we cooled it for a while, had you guys. Then, as you know, your mom went back to work."

"We're the experiments between experiments," Gloria said half jokingly before continuing. "So she finished this before she had kids?"

"She was twenty-one."

"When did she start working on it?"

"There was never a time she didn't want to change the world, but I'd say five, when they dropped the bombs. She listened to the radio for days, the accounts, the descriptions, she was never the same."

"So a child, as a child she decided she was going to stop nuclear warfare?"

"Yeah, she never knew any different, it was her whole life until you kids."

"And you, you were her life too."

182

"Yeah well, I got there before the bombs, she was stuck with me." They both smiled. "Why don't you go ahead and pack it up, it's time we get going," he said.

Gloria looked at the machine then back at her dad. "All right."

She bent down, grabbed an end cylinder, and instead of wrapping it, she attached it to the center piece, turned it until it clicked. Then she attached the other end, she grabbed the remote from the ground. "White for peace," she said as she armed the device.

The slow walk home seemed more like a dream than reality. She couldn't feel her feet hit the ground, only the effortless state of perpetual motion leading her where she needed to go. Her mind was so full of wonder, every thought she touched upon seemed like a vast pool of endless mystery. It was as if the haunting theories constantly swimming in the back of her mind now completely immersed her, she was lost in their enormity. The ground passed by, she saw the browns, greens and grays only peripherally, her sight unable to accurately display the external world. The flood of internal stimulation overwhelmed the processing of her surroundings. She noticed her father in the foreground, familiar but undefined, nothing was sharp; only present somewhere she no longer was. Her reality had shifted; how she integrated this new information would change her forever. But now, it was as if she knew nothing, only scraps of ideas that led to unknowns. Scattered and scrambled, she walked in a malaise of uncertainty, she felt eternally distracted, unable to get her mind to ease into a direction, the blurred terrain, the noises in her head, she grew dizzy with a delusional terror. She slowed to a more manageable pace; she held her arms bent away from her body to steady herself. She eventually lingered so far behind her father came to check on her. "How are you doing Gloria, feeling okay?" he asked.

"Ah, just kind of slow," she responded in a daze.

"Come on," he said gently grabbing her hand, "I'll help you." They walked the last mile together, hand in hand.

Once home, she went to her bedroom, undressed, wrapped a towel around her and walked to the bathroom. She turned on the shower, waiting for the water to change from cold to hot; she leveled the hot to warm and stepped in. The warm water reigned over her; the pressure from the stream indented her skin, prodding her to feel. She brought her face to the water, letting the pressure and the warmth relax her tightened jaw. She had hardly spoken since leaving the cave, barely breathed, with only shallow short gasps able to force their way into her lungs. She calmed now as she was able to feel her blood begin to quicken and her alertness begin to return. The comfort of the warmth began to draw her out of the recesses of her mind. She let the water run over her hair, pour over her scalp, the back of her neck, her mind slowed with every soothing moment. What had just happened, she thought. She had anticipated some upheaval with the truth, but the events of the last year had proven revelatory. What should she do? All she ever thought about was leaving, anything after that seemed secondary, manageable, now she had burden, the torch of an unfinished life.

It was too soon to answer all the questions popping into her head. She leaned against the shower wall and again relied on the same simple comfort that restarted her mind after her mother's passing, a state of quiet recollection. Removed enough from the processes going on inside her, but not so removed she could not function, she attempted to regain her focus. It would take time to understand her place within the new realm of existence. She was unsure if she would be able to leave in a month, the next full moon, like she had planned. But not everything must always be clear at the moment of inception. She knew patience and calmness would bring her understanding. Finding the strength and composure to allow for serenity would be the challenge. She must return again to painting, her meditative state, where the underlying emotions to all she felt were engaged and explored without judgment. She settled in the safety of a near future filled with the redemptive quality of painting. She washed her hair, scrubbed herself clean, resumed with the practical part of her life. She spent a quiet evening reading with her dad and sister, a little music, a little dinner, a lot of reflection.

The next day she packed her painting supplies, strapped a canvas to her back, pulled on her favorite brown leather boots, and headed into the hills. The cool morning air, just warm enough to enliven instead of devastate, reminded her of the changing weather on the horizon. She had grown accustomed to the burning and tingling of her cheeks, lips, and nose on her many winter walks to visit Bugsy. But now the air was invigorating, the temperature that makes its presence known with a refreshing cool bite, but still invites one to stay with its moderate subtlety. The severity of the extreme lows seemed to have subsided for now, and a few minutes into the walk the air felt nothing but pleasant and fresh.

It had been some time since she had walked with her paint pack into the hills with no particular agenda. She had forgotten how simple and pleasurable this singular creative exercise was. She had deemed it trivial and indulgent after her mom died, but now it seemed peaceful, healing, and essential, an uncluttered day devoid of the masks of constant activity. Coping by ignoring, or overlooking, would only distance her from the elemental agonizing truth of loss. To neglect one's deepest sorrows is to turn away from life's greatest lessons, entirely possible, and maybe easier in the short term, but why settle for a year or two of shallow protection when there can be a lifetime of the knowledge of depth. So, for now, the quiet and simple will serve as a platform on which to stabilize the tumult and terror which engulfed her.

Gloria enjoyed using her body, feeling the strength in her legs as she walked from rock to rock. She tested the limits of her balance and endurance, pushing herself to go farther, faster. She fell into a heavy rhythmic breathing, short, swift and efficient, new air in, old air out, the constant cycle of life. Sweat dripped down her temples, the warm sun and heat from her body combined, trapped by her full hair tied back in a single braid.

Nearly two hours into the foothills she ventured upon a beautiful clearing overlooking a valley. There were Prickly Pear, she knocked off the spines and sliced the pad open with the knife she carried strapped to her calf under her pants. She drank the temperate refreshing liquid, tasting its subtle sweetness, a liking developed after years of growing accustomed to the cacti's bitter beginning.

She set up her easel and canvas and prepared her palate. She felt the bold, burgeoning colors of spring breaking free from the mundane drab of winter. She mixed yellows and greens, pinks and purples; the valley floor was filled with little pockets of color. The composition, the execution, she was lost for hours in the hearty field laid out in front of her, the smooth wind eroded rocks, the ancient gnarled cacti, the timeless sand of the desert. She stopped painting only briefly for a light snack, an apple, a few nuts, a berry or two off a cactus. She painted until the sun hung low in the sky. As the light wanes she packs up, expertly leaving her fresh oils untouched, secured by the frame of the canvas, left free to dry in the desert evening breeze. She heads back with an hour of daylight left.

She had hoped to be home by sunset, her father would be comforted by her timely arrival, but the day had slipped away from her and she hurried now. Not that she minded walking home through the dark; she quite liked the feeling, especially under a large moon as tonight. Even without the glowing moon, she had keen night vision and always managed to make her way through the dark. But she felt her father needed her home at night, if she wasn't there, he couldn't be sure she was ever coming back. And she longed to spend her last evenings with her father in the comfort of her childhood home.

She approached the hill behind her house as the last wisps of color left the sky. The brilliant pinks and oranges of the sunset bouncing off the high puffy clouds led her home in a fanciful color saturated state. Practically running, the two hour hike turned into just over an hour return trip. She was dirty and panting when she arrived. She placed her painting, along with the hundreds of others, in a shed her dad had built for her. She must retrieve her paintings from Bugsy's she thought, they were unharmed by the fire. Amazing she hadn't thought of them at all when she decided to burn the place. She walked onto the deck and opened the sliding glass door that led into the house. She saw her dad reading by the fire. He looked up at her and smiled, she returned the happy gaze.

"Hey dad," she said flying by him. "I'm going to shower. What's for dinner?"

"So you're going to be here for dinner?" he asked simply.

"Yeah, I'll be here."

"Roasted veggies, and salad."

"Great," she said scampering off to get cleaned up.

Gloria reemerged light and fresh, her boisterous curls bowing to the weight of her wet hair. "Where's everybody else?" she asked her father who was in the kitchen getting the meal together.

"Audrey's at class, the boys, I don't know, they're out running around."

"You and me," she said cheerfully.

"You and me," he replied.

They sat together at the round wooden table large enough for six. She loved her dad's salads with little bits of energetic flavors, the creamy tang of goat cheese, the crisp of celery, the sweet of the raisins, and sometimes the surprising spice of pepper. The roasted vegetables were warm and hearty: potatoes, yams, carrots and beets, nourishing and filling. She was satisfied after a long day out in the elements. "Gloria," her father said, pulling her away from her taste bud bliss. She turned to him as he continued. "I don't want you to tell me when you are going. I know it will be soon, just don't show up for dinner. I want to treat everyday as if it is our last together."

She swallowed a final bit of carrot. "Yes dad."

"So it will be soon then?"

She smiled at him as she thought, it's not that he didn't want to know, it's that he didn't want to have to believe it was true. She didn't want to get his hopes up or let him linger in uncertainty. It would be in a month like she had planned. "Soon, but not immediately. I will be home for dinner until then," she said.

He looked at her, nodded his head in acknowledgement and looked down.

"Dad, there are some paintings outside Bugsy's in the bins, they're of all sorts of things, landscapes, abstracts, portraits... portraits of you, of mom, some of you two together, I think you'd like them."

"Are there any of you?" he asked.

"I don't feel I know myself well enough yet to paint my own portrait. Maybe one day?"

"Must you know everything so well before you paint it?"

"I at least want to know exactly how I feel about what I'm painting. How I feel about myself is never exact."

"That's a high standard."

"It's a hopeful goal, to know exactly what to do at the right time, to be completely sure I've got it right, to do the best I can... I'm not that person yet, I don't know if I'll ever be, but that's what I would want to capture. Until then, spending so much time looking at myself and analyzing everything sounds dreadful," she said with a self effacing laugh.

"I see what you mean," he said smiling. "But life is not about perfection."

"Perfection is such a loaded word, like the pursuit of perfection is hopeless because it is so obviously unattainable. But, of course, perfection is what we should strive for, the ultimate state of being. We should always work towards that goal regardless of the monumental difficulty of the task. Should we be pursuing pretty good, not too bad, mediocre, great? Is great good enough, when the implication is that there is better? It's the pursuit of perfection I live for. I don't mean dotting all your i's and crossing all your t's. I mean harmonious, thriving culture filled with joy and spiritual abundance in the context of living peacefully with one another and being respectful of our surroundings. Perfection is never a pursuit for the solitary. Perfect is attainable, we look so terribly beyond its implications. It is in the sublime simplicity that perfection lives. We make perfection seem larger than life.

Nourished and fulfilled, that's what I want, not just for myself, but everyone, that is life's perfection."

Marty looked at his daughter thoughtfully. "Your mother would be proud."

"Well, I'm proud of her. I'm just sorry I never got to show her."

"She knows, she always knew. Everything that you are, she saw it. Everything you felt about her but wouldn't express, she knew it deep in her heart, a place above logic and experience, buried in the grand synthesis of everything one knows. There is not one ounce of your mother that left this earth that didn't know how much you cared for her, and she for you. Never forget, she lives on inside you, as do I, we are very proud of you and always will be. I hope you find what it is you seek, and those in pursuit of your same ideals. For one can move many, but many can move mountains."

"I shall not be alone dad. I am not leaving here to whither away in intellectual isolation. People are what I am interested in, their lives, their glory; it is with them I shall live."

"You are leaving a family and a community, they are not easily replaced," he warned.

"I shall never replace them, only build upon."

"You will have to be strong."

"I will be, dad. I wouldn't go if I didn't think I could handle it. I wouldn't leave you unless I was sure."

"That is what I needed to hear. I love you, my sweet girl."

"I love you, too."

He cleared the table. She put on some music, the Beatles, her dad's favorite. She joined him in the kitchen to help with the dishes. He was crying a little, a wayward tear occasionally slipped down his face dripping into the full sink below. Gloria started singing along with the music. "I wanna hold your haaaaaannnnd, I wanna hold your haaaaaannnnd," she bellowed loudly.

Marty joined in, at first timidly, then joyously, enjoying the singing antics with his daughter. "Very sweet song, innocent," he said to his daughter when the song finished. "life isn't always so innocent."

"I know dad."

"I mean sex. People aren't always so nice about it."

"People aren't always nice about a lot of things, why would sex be any different? Bugsy's warned me dad, he lived out there, he's been trying to make me paranoid for years about the 'predatory mentality,' as he called it. Believe me, I'm afraid. But I'm strong, and I'm smart, I'll look out for myself. But I can never know what is lurking in every corner. And if the threat of rape is as pervasive as Bugsy says it is, I will always be vulnerable and unprotected, until, like Larkspur, there is a societal condemnation of the practice. I am going into a culture where rape is permissible, or at the very least not properly condemned. I must still pursue my dreams regardless of the undue harm I face."

"Be careful."

187

"Dad, I will try to surround myself with good people, that is all I can do." She paused for a few moments. "So, you're not worried about sex in general?"

"No, you'll figure it out. It's your body, your mind, you'll figure out how you want to be treated. It is an exploration, a deep physical and emotional exploration, you're thoughtful about such things, I'm not worried."

They finished up washing the dishes. "Hey, I want to show you something," he said, with the slight embarrassment of a child not sure if he was allowed to talk about the subject. Marty walked her over to his desk, small next to the tall lean man, a simple roll top dark wood desk with drawers on both sides, with a plain wooden chair. He unrolled the curved jointed roll top to expose an orderly workspace. There were papers neatly stacked on the desktop, a pencil, a calculator, an eraser, and a couple of reference books. Pushed towards the back was a letter sized bound leather notebook Gloria had seen her dad working in many times. "I have something I want you to take. Who knows, it may be of some use out there?" She picked up the leather notebook, opened it, and flipped through it as he continued. "You know your dad's no slouch, I know a thing or two about plants, somebody might find this interesting," he said as he shrugged.

She laughed. "Mom isn't the only one who's got something to offer the world, hey?" she kidded.

"Possibly not."

She came upon the last page of his notebook where she found a picture of the six of them, recent, within the last year, her parents and all the kids together in the backyard. "I remember that day," she said. "We were all doing our own thing, mom reading, you gardening, I was painting, the boys playing catch and Audrey looking for attention. You grabbed the camera and made us come together for a minute, we all complained. I like it, we all look like ourselves."

"I thought it might be nice for you to have," he said.

"I love it, thank you."

Over the next month Gloria painted by day, planned by night. She had detailed maps of the areas topography that she used to determine her likely route. She hoped to quickly drop to lower elevations to avoid the cold nights brought on by high altitude. She would then try to find a town, railroad tracks, or a road, some sign of civilization in which to disappear. She could not find recent maps of railroad lines, only turn of the century details that showed the nearest tracks to be several hundred miles southeast in Texas. This she deemed unsuitable both directionally, the opposite of her goal, and distance wise, far too long for her to travel through the desert. She studied the tracks patterns and locations relative to the terrain; she hoped to be able to anticipate where new tracks may have been built.

Her decision about which route to take proved far less complicated than what to bring. She formulated two plans, one with her mother's device, one without, still unsure if she would dedicate herself to her mom's creation. She had a waterproof warm down sleeping bag her father had given her several years ago when she first started spending the night in the hills. She would also bring a knife, soap, a small pan, binoculars, matches, compass, flashlight, maps, money, her dad's notebook, some nuts, dried fruits and a canteen. Other desirables including a tent, book, towel, extra clothing and shoes, and extra food and water were contingent upon her decision to bring her mother's device. Her mom's pack wasn't heavy, maybe thirty pounds, but she knew it would be enough to slow her down. The less she brought the better, the faster she found a town, the better her chance for survival. Not that she thought for a moment she wouldn't survive. Nonetheless, there was no room for arrogance or carelessness. In reality she was far more scared about life after the desert pass than the desert pass itself.

Her extreme certainty that she must leave was matched in equal intensity by her fear of life beyond Larkspur. She was traveling into a new culture where she knew no one, and she would have to completely reject her past. She would never be able to speak to her family again, and would have to lie about her origins; she knew she faced devastating difficulties.

Her paintings had become dark and despondent, trapped in the doubt and insecurity of her impending endeavor. Gloria painted muted, colorless, scenes. Gone were the hints of spring, the sparks of life, she fixated on blues and grays. She was angry, lonely, hurt and scared. The loss of her mother infiltrated every part of her life, but she knew everything she was feeling was only the beginning. It would take years before she had a chance of feeling whole again. She was meant to suffer on her own, that she truly believed, so she could extract every bit of meaning out of her experience and one day be able to translate the universalities of loss to others, to fully engage with the many who speak the language of suffering.

She had the time to indulge her sorrow, for the mourning she must do now, only struggle and coping would comprise her near future. All her fear, anguish and hate breathed onto the canvas. She disliked these paintings so, they sickened her to look at them. She would slice them when she finished, smash them against the rocks, leaving the ugly drips of the still wet oils marked on the earth's surface, a lasting imprint of her ferocity. Her adrenaline booming, she would rush home in an urgent panic to make it back before sundown. She raced aggressively through the terrain, brushing against cacti and scraping against rocks. She would arrive home tattered and bleeding with spines embedded in her skin reminding her she was still walking within a life full of pain with much more was yet to come. She learned pain was not something she could rush through, or outrun, that would only keep the feeling from being resolved, she must sit within it, every tortuous breath, before it slowly dissipated. Her rage, her frustration, proved futile, a desperate exercise of the wounded. But still, she had nothing but destruction to offer her mind and body, a racing whir of out of control thought, indulged until its last moment.

Her father tenderly cared for his torn and hurt daughter, removing the spines, cleaning the affected area with antiseptic. He cooked for her, hoping to nourish her for the travails she will face. He checked on her when she was sleeping, returning the covers she had thrown off in a fitful spate of emotion. He watched as his daughter delved into the bitter pit of despair, taking its wounds, its misery. And he grimaced as she continually returned for more, her last self-destructive gasps before her harrowing duty of complete self-sufficiency. He watched her test the limits and boundaries of her pain, and then push farther, time and again marveling at her body's ability to endure.

He calmed some, as the rapid pace of her descent slowed after a couple of weeks. She began to pull out of the death drop, leveling in an unseemly low. But soon, ever so slightly she began to bring herself back. She began to arrive home after a day of painting, calmer, clearer, less frantic, less out of breath and less injured from the return. He no longer had to remove debris from her hair, or spines from her body. Her perilous journey into the face of pain was coming to an end. He knew she had learned what she needed to; overcoming the guilt of leaving her family, the tests of her worthiness, the honing of her skills. She was an animal hunting down the prey of her determination, circling it, smothering it, until she had extracted every last bit of its marrow.

Gloria sat in the mild spring evening air staring at the nearly perfect circle of the moon, the craters and shadows of a full life in the universe were visible. Her entire family was home, they had decided to have dinner on the patio in the warm open air. She gazed into the evening, playing the constellation game with her sister Audrey. Gloria knew them all, but would sometimes feign ignorance until Audrey could come up with the right name. She had spent so many nights looking into the same sky she could almost close her eyes and plot every star, including variations for new seasons. Tonight, Leo and Virgo hung prominently in the spring air sky.

Gloria heard her father and brothers discussing the most recent town Council meeting, the state of the travel moratorium. She heard her brothers' frustrations and her father's quiet attempts to assuage them. But mostly, she took it all in, the sights, the sounds, the smells, the way the warm breeze carried the fragrance of lilac through the air, the buzzing of the newly born insects, the occasional shooting star. She lingered in the backyard for hours, she and her father, after the others had gone in, they sat in silence together in the perfect mountain spring air.

The morning came quickly upon her. She soaked in a nice warm bath and had breakfast with her father. She headed out like usual giving her dad a hug and a kiss on the cheek. Only this time instead of her painting pack strapped to her back, she had her hiking kit. Maybe her father noticed the change, but he did not say anything, and as he requested, neither did she.

She left the yard feeling calm, serene and full of purpose. She walked directly into the hills avoiding town. She was sure her father could ward off any interest in her absence for quite a while, until she was long gone from Larkspur. No one would come looking for weeks; they were used to not seeing her for extended periods of time. She would be off without a trace before anyone would be the wiser, and even then, they would most likely believe a mishap or suicide, before desertion.

Chapter 16

Gloria headed west, the same direction her father had taken her that day, into the open land full of mystery and intrigue. It was an hour before she saw anything she was sure she recognized, but the odd oblong rock was such a welcome sight she smiled with delight. The first of hopefully many successes in navigating released a little pressure from the overwrought girl. Now, she began to relax and enjoy her beloved mountains like she had so many days in the past. She reached Mav's Hollow before the high sun of midday. Calmly, she spent a few moments looking around the cave for the final time. But she had little time for sentiments now, she was on a mission, and today was a new day with contracted emotions and purposeful pursuits.

Gloria squeezed through the rocky entrance to the hidden room in Mav's Hollow. She pulled her sleeping bag and a few other items out of her pack, she incorporated them into the red and black hiking pack with the device her mother had left her. The pack was quite comfortable, snug and stable. She shook her head at her mother's insight, anticipating so many parts of the plan to make the execution easier. She loaded up, walked confidently through the arch way, and didn't look back.

Her intention was to travel southwest while staying within a days trek, twenty miles or so, of water. There were three lakes in the hundred mile region, and Gloria hoped to find a town near one of them. She would come across the first lake in about sixty miles; she hoped to be there by the end of the third day. Her elevation was near ten thousand feet, and she needed to drop about eight thousand feet to find the lake.

Her pace was consistent, swift and controlled. Gloria knew maintaining her stamina was far more important than pushing herself to go faster. She followed the ridge line from the valley below, traversing peaks only when necessary, attempting to make her way down through the crevices between the peaks. She kept an eye out for Agaves, Pincushion, and Prickly Pear cacti, slicing them as she found them, drinking the juice and attaching their pads to her pack. She also dug up Bush Morning Glory for their precious edible roots, hoping to conserve as much food as possible. There were long stretches of flat valleys followed by climbs over high peaks. She couldn't be sure about the rate of her decline, but she was satisfied she was making good time.

As night began to fall she continued to walk under the orange sunset speckled clouds. She felt strong, calm, undaunted by the journey ahead. She debated hiking into the night but found a beautiful serene bluff overlooking a large open valley and decided to camp there. She gathered some dried twigs and debris, the carcasses of plants that had succumbed to the dry desert air. The spring rains had yet to begin so there was ample kindling. She started a fire, cleaned cacti and roots, and squeezed their liquid into her small pan. She added a little water and boiled the plants. She snacked on the bitter yet satisfying meal, not wanting to tap into her fruit and nut reserve unless absolutely necessary. Eventually, she leaned against a rock by the fire and relaxed as the warm flames fought off the nips of the night chill. Subdued by the warmth and peaceful desert air she stared into the night, the familiar stars, the moon with just a small sliver still missing. She had chosen to maximize the bright nights just before the full moon. Her eyes grew tired, heavy under the strain of the day. She put more kindling on the fire, unrolled her sleeping bag and faded off into a sweet deep sleep.

She awoke to a strange rumbling echo and lay for a brief moment trying to figure out the origin of the sound. Even before she could identify the noise she realized it meant trouble. She immediately stamped out the remains of the fire, rolled up her sleeping bag, tied it to her pack, and quickly headed for jagged terrain. The sound grew louder and more ominous; she saw a bright beam of light pouring over the ridge behind her. She began to run from the beam as a helicopter appeared on the horizon. She wedged herself between some rocks under an overhang, the aircraft emerged overhead, deafening with the whining reverberations of its blades. The fire, she thought, how could she have been so naïve, smoke in the middle of the desert, a sure way to attract attention.

The helicopter searched frantically with its high-powered beam, hovering and circling, locating her campsite, homing in on her direction. A voice boomed over the loudspeaker. "This is a restricted area, you must surrender yourself immediately. This is a restricted area…"

She watched the chopper sink into the valley a hundred feet below, leveling, and then lowering for landing. They were coming for her. She un-wedged herself and began to climb straight up the mountain. She worked the crevices the best she could, straining to see, hoping to avoid a sheer face. She heard the men disembark from the chopper and the thudding sound of their feet running over the terrain.

Gloria climbed and climbed, hoping to put as much distance between she and her pursuers as possible. Gripping the rock forcefully, she pushed solidly off her toes, keeping all her momentum headed upwards, not stopping to think or look at what was below. She reached a peak and peered down the other side, she gasped at what she saw, a large well lit military base with runways and hangars, as out of place in the barren landscape as a baby on a battlefield.

There were hundreds of planes, fighter jets, and helicopters lined up; several massive rectangular buildings covered the desert floor. She lingered for a moment wondering where to go. She stayed on the base side of the ridge and began to move parallel, navigating the steep terrain just below the peak. She headed west, listening for the men on the other side of the mountain. Frantic but focused, she moved endlessly until dawn, one thought, one purpose, keep going, keep going.

As the sun began to rise she decided to traverse the peak again to stay out of view of the base. She momentarily paused at the top of the peak, surveying the terrain below. She hadn't seen the men for hours, and couldn't see them now. She moved out of view from the base and continued on. A few moments later she heard the low rumble of a helicopter again. She watched as it flew over a ridge. The helicopter landed in the valley near the other chopper. The men converged and the first chopper departed. She tucked herself in under some rocks and watched the first helicopter head back over the ridge to the base. The men from the second helicopter formed six groups of two and headed out in all different directions. She sipped a little water from her canteen and kept going. Gloria hoped her altitude and distance from the men would keep her from being spotted. It was too risky to return to the base side of the ridge, her only hope was to stay as hidden as possible and outrun them. There appeared to be no other open areas to land a helicopter, so this looked like a foot race, one she was determined to win.

"Gentlemen," the commanding officer said to the returning crew of a dozen men as the blades from the helicopter slowed to a stop. The group walked together off the tarmac into a locker room. The commanding officer continued. "Where is the trespasser?"

The pilot, and highest ranking officer among the men, a compact, well-built, stocky, red faced, fair-haired man replied. "We were unable to bring the hiker in," he said.

"How's that sergeant?"

"He was really quick, long and lean, like a gazelle in the mountains. We lost sight of him. He couldn't have gone far, sir."

"Twelve men chasing one, I'm disappointed gentlemen."

"Sorry, Captain."

"I'm also a little dumbfounded about how a hiker could end up in our backyard undetected. We cannot rule out secret op."

"Yes, Captain."

"The base is on high alert, we will find the infiltrator," the Captain said.

"Captain, we've been performing routine checks of the area and saw nothing suspicious. What secret op canvases the desert for weeks to find our base, gets there, and then lights a fire, seems crazy?"

"You're sure there was nothing suspicious?"

"Plain old boring desert air, Captain. I mean Captain, we're fifty miles from the nearest town. No one's traveling fifty miles without us knowing about it."

"What about twenty?" the captain asked.

"You mean the base; you think it's one of our guys, captain?"

"Possibly AWOL."

"It's possible, captain, an experienced hiker could get here in a day."

"We've never had a security breach before; it's the only thing that makes sense."

"But why the fire, captain?"

"Nobody has any idea we're here, probably thought he was home free. Listen, this is still a very serious situation, let's find him. Regroup, get some rest, report back at eighteen hundred hours."

"Yes, captain. Sorry, captain," the sergeant said humbly.

"Hey, we'll get him. I'll talk to Larkspur, find out if any of their men are missing."

"Yes, captain."

Not sure of Gloria's whereabouts, only four of the six pairs of soldiers were headed in her general direction, with just two pairs, she surmised, with a possible chance of catching her. One duo started straight up the peak a few miles behind her. There was no telling whether they would turn her direction once at the top, regardless, she felt confident she could maintain her lead. The second, and most troubling threat, came from the duo making up time on her by running on the flat ground below. If they spotted her, they would be able to overtake her and force her back into their reinforcements. Her best chance was to avoid being detected.

Her tan, heavy cotton pants and off-white t-shirt, while great for staying cool and blending in with the desert sand, left her visually vulnerable in the dark red peaks. Large gray clouds loomed low, darkening the sky, making her light colors even more apparent. The crumbling steep rocks made traction difficult, forcing her to be thoughtful and concise with every step. The men below on flat ground seemed to be traveling twice her speed, in just a few minutes they would be only a couple of miles behind her.

A huge rod of lightning flashed in the sky. An immediate tremendous clap of thunder shuttered, seemingly shaking the earth below her. Gloria froze, checked her balance, felt the oncoming presence of her pursuers, and decided to take her chances on the base side of the peak where they may be less alert than those below. Gloria again made the difficult traverse to the other side of the peak hoping to buy more time in anonymity.

She settled into the motions, foot placement, balance, step, she no longer attempted to maintain covered within the terrain and began picking up speed. Perspiration poured down her neck, dripping from the captured heat of her hair in a tight bun wrapped underneath her cap. She pushed forward, teetering between slipping, losing her grip on the earth and tumbling down, and gliding safely just above the surface, immune to the danger. She heard her breathing, steady and strong, she was so focused the sound ruminated inside her head, as if she was aware of every action her body would make the split second before it happened. She felt her legs, strong and sturdy, completely under her control. She was able to spring when she needed to, and stop immediately when necessary. She felt completely prepared for this moment, her skill and agility honed perfectly for this fight. The culmination of a life of cultivating her instincts, the endless thinking, planning, and preparing, left her free, in the moment, not stifled by doubt. More lightning flashed through the sky, followed by heavy thunder. This time she did not stop, did not need to balance herself with the changing elements, she had become one with them.

The sky grew darker, heavily laden with thick, deep, dark, purplish-gray, moisture filled clouds. Gloria could see where just ahead the peak turned into a gradual decline, returning her to the narrow crevices between ranges, and then eventually a valley. She would soon lose her altitude advantage, and the hunt would turn into a flat out chase.

This time, Gloria immediately recognized the artificial rumble that began to fill the air; her stomach lurched as she grew concerned. They had spotted her; three helicopters filled the sky below. She heard the plops of the heavy drops and saw water marks darken the red rocks around her. She looked up for a moment and felt the clean rain on her face. She tried to take cover between the rocks as the helicopters approached. It began to pour; the first rain of the spring welled up, biding its time, waiting for its moment to finally arrive. Immediately, small streams of water began pouring down the face of the mountain. Her years in the desert made her familiar with the way even very little rain would collect and pour down to the rock hard valley floor, making movement nearly impossible. Now, the heavy downpour altered the landscape dramatically as she gripped the rocks to keep from being washed away.

She listened to the cacophony of sound, the heavy rain, the proliferation of streams, the boom of the thunder and the drone of the helicopters. She watched the helicopters draw closer, then a sudden flash illuminated the sky, sparks pitched like fireworks from the lead helicopter. The chopper wavered and began smoking, it angled sideways towards the ground as the thunder rumbled, then recovered, straightening out, turning back towards the base. The rain grew stronger still; flashes of light filled the air. The remaining two helicopters fanned out in large u-turns in opposite directions and headed back towards the base.

Shocked by what she had seen, Gloria paused for a moment, collecting herself and catching her breath. She steadily climbed to the top of the peak and looked down upon the valley below. Water was gushing down the mountain in every direction, leaving the men who were traversing the face clinging to the rocks. One of the men had been washed down a trail and swept into the valley. The others struggled to hold their ground against the swift tide of water. Gloria left the base side of the mountain to return to the side occupied by the struggling men, and continued forward.

The rain lessened in severity but continued to fall for nearly an hour. Companions lightning and thunder appeared sporadically, affirming their presence often enough to keep the helicopters grounded. The current of the rushing water pushed the men further and further behind her. Gloria followed the ridgeline west until a plateau, she turned due south, away from the northern base down into the foothills.

The rain left the desert floor in a state of impassable mush. The type of mud which creates such suction boots are ripped from feet, lost to the desert floor forever. Gloria could no longer count on the luxury of dictating her direction, she was at the mercy of the terrain, where the terrain proved passable, she would follow. Determined to walk as long as the lightning persisted, she kept an eye out for shelter to keep her out of sight for when the helicopters returned. She walked until mid-afternoon, struggling to make progress, moving along the bottom of the mountain just above the muddy floor. She was forced to walk at a forty-five degree angle on slippery wet rock, clutching crevices with her hands to support herself, like a rock climber moving parallel to the ground which was only a couple of feet below.

As the lightning subsided, and she feared the helicopters would return, above her, maybe twenty feet or so, she noticed an indentation in the rock. She climbed up to investigate. There was a small oblong overhang in the rock, approximately six feet wide, seven feet high, and ten feet deep, tall enough to stand up in, and long enough to stretch out. She pulled herself into the quiet cavern and fell exhausted to the ground. She had only slept a couple of hours since leaving Larkspur nearly thirty hours ago. The great exertion of the hike throughout the night and the heightened awareness brought on by the chase caught up with her as she collapsed heavily onto the earth. She lay face first on the cave floor for a few minutes, too tired to make herself more comfortable. She deliberately tried to bring her breath to a state of relaxation, focusing on long deep inhales and long smooth exhales. She could worry about nothing else, not the men chasing her, the difficult conditions of the soggy desert, or where she was headed, for now, all she could do was rest.

She rolled over on to her side and wriggled out of the pack. She was relieved by the removal of fifty pounds of added weight. She sighed, rubbing her strained and weary shoulders. Gloria untied her sleeping bag, rolling it out against the rear most wall of the cave. She removed her trusty old waterproof boots, and her mostly dry socks. She pulled off her heavy wet pants and laid them on her pack. She removed the customary long shorts she wore beneath her pants. A habit she got into as a painter, she preferred long pants for hiking, but would remove them once settled in for a day of painting to allow her bare skin the freedom of fresh air and sun. She took off her hat and pulled her soggy shirt over her head. She slid an arm into her sports bra and slipped it off relieving the pressure of her confined breasts. In the course of the years between twelve and fifteen she had gone from completely flat-chested to rather bothersome full round breasts. They were manageable, a C cup, but she feared any larger and they would begin to pose a hindrance. She pulled off her shorts and her white cotton briefs, and laid the clothes by her bag. Lastly, she removed her hair from the tight stifling bun, freeing her long curly locks. She quickly crawled into the dry sleeping bag and began to warm. She snuggled into the sleeping bag, and fell fast asleep.

Gloria woke as the soft light of dawn peered though the cave's opening. The dry discomfort of her mouth alerted her to her thirst. She reached for her pack, found the canteen and took three small sips of water. She was cautious with her water supply, not sure when she would be able to traverse through the flatter, life sustaining terrain of the valley floor. She squirmed out of her sleeping bag, shivering in the cold. She walked to the opening of the cave, squatted, stuck her bum over the edge, and peed down the side of the mountain. She quickly huddled back in the warmth of her sleeping bag and nibbled on a few pieces of dried fruit and nuts. She drank a little more water and waited for the sun to rise higher in the sky bringing warmth to the day.

The peaceful energy of the cave poured over her, the same soothing comfort that had greeted her upon entering Mav's Hollow. In the harsh open land of the desert, sometimes being buried in the bowels of the rocks is the only comfort left to be found. Gloria loved the external sensory deprivation of the cool stone walls, the internal intensity which comes from the depletion of the major senses, investigative sight and sound replaced with thoughtful wonder. The silence could be petrifying, overwhelming in its own right, the constant attention to the thoughts in one's head. But she was too focused to entertain the paranoia of terrible possibilities. She welcomed the quiet protective cavern, happy to be temporarily removed from the outside world. She checked in with her body, sensing the areas she was tight, then gently rubbing them. Her legs were heavy, scraped and bruised, her shoulders were stiff, but she felt healthy and strong. Her body had begun to notice the lack of food and water; but it was too early to be overtaken by her body's doubts when her mind was still so eager and capable.

Gloria pulled her damp clothes over to her, burrowing them down to the bottom of her sleeping bag to warm them before putting them on. She lazily dreamed and dozed for a couple of hours until the warm rays of the sun began to penetrate the cold earth. She shuffled through the clothes at the bottom of her sleeping bag and began to assemble again for another day. She lay for another twenty minutes in her sleeping bag, fully clothed, trying to keep her body temperature up. She knew with the slow difficulty of the terrain, and with the temperature still lingering in the forties, it would not be easy to stay warm. Finally ready, Gloria rolled up her sleeping bag, pulled on her boots, strapped on her pack, and climbed down from the cave. She surveyed the muddy ground, it would take at least a full day of sun to be passable, she surmised.

She continued on for hours, climbing the peaks and valleys of the rocks which rise and fall before her, all the while following the steady stream of the runoff. Mid afternoon she stopped for a little sustenance. Still not within distance of cacti or plants, she drank and ate very little. She started again, slightly weary under the weight of the pack, but not discouraged. The mountain flowers popped up inexplicably at all sorts of angles and directions from the steep crevices. The first spring rain had turned the dull, lifeless mountain, into a lively colorful speckled backdrop overnight. She welcomed the sight of her bright beautiful flower friends, a little drop of inspiration to help her on her way.

The day after a heavy rain the air always smelled sweet and fresh, Gloria thought, cleaner and clearer than the day's preceding. She in turn could see farther and deeper into the desert sky. She had been gaining ground on a large peak ahead of her all day. A fine opportunity to look for a lake, or railroad tracks, or possibly even a town. She summited the peak in a couple of hours, weakened, bent over, she recovered from the exertion before finally removing her pack. Gloria was startled to see the large base far off in the distance; she had traveled farther than she thought. She pulled her binoculars from the pack; turning south she was heartened by what she saw. Directly below her the mountains rippled away in progressively smaller descending ridges. In a valley between the last of the peaks lay a small lake which must have formed during the recent rains. Farther beyond the lake lay a seemingly endless horizon of the flattest land she had ever seen. There were cacti and plants galore, and she couldn't be sure, but shimmering in the light looked to be the metal line of a railroad track. She assessed, she was probably still up around four thousand feet and the lake was still several hours away, but she suddenly felt better. Where there was water there was life, and it seemed she was narrowing in on civilization.

She descended into the first of four valleys leading to the lake. The day grew cooler and cooler as she passed from the last of the sun's rays into the shadows of the canyon. She had been hearing the distant sound of helicopters periodically throughout the day, and as she dropped farther and farther into the valley the reverberations of the blades grew stronger. She wasn't sure if they were coming nearer, or if the echo off the rock walls only made them seem closer. Taking no chances, she tucked under a jagged rock protrusion and hid from the skies above. She remained there as the setting sun turned the sky a pale purple. She fixated on the small patch of purple sky visible from her hiding spot and fantasized about a free future. All the limits and peril of the situation only made her focus harder on the pursuit of an unfettered life. Curled up under a rock, shivering in the cold, hungry, thirsty, she held onto her dream harder than ever, willing her belief to carry her through. The helicopters never did come any closer; even so, her body demanded rest. She pulled out her sleeping bag and decided to remain in the thin crevice for the night. She snacked on some fruit and nuts, drank a good portion of her water. She was down to a quarter of the canteen, but hopeful she would reach water soon.

The night grew so cold she awoke in the heart of darkness, teeth chattering and her face numb. Gloria pulled the sleeping bag over her head and tried to warm her frozen face, but her mind would not be appeased. She was ready to get moving again, dead of the night or not. She packed up and emerged from her hidden depression in the earth. The stars nearly took her breath away, she had missed them last night, sleeping through the darkness, there plentiful beauty startled her. It was as if she was seeing the sparkling darkness for the first time. Altered by her struggle and the bitter cold, her near delusional state left her unguarded, easily swayed by the enormity of her surroundings.

The great light from the moon and stars poured into the canyon, easing her passage. She started out quickly, eager to get her circulation moving to help her warm. The quiet, still night far better suited her contemplative state than the hectic chaos of the last thirty-six hours. She loved simple uncomplicated sound, her boots hitting the earth, the sniffles of her cold nose, the patterns of her breath. The lack of terrifying accompaniment made her enjoy the moment even more. When something cherished is threatened, it becomes enlivened and new again. She was again gliding like a gazelle, rock top to rock top, heavily engaged in one of the activities she loved most.

Gloria hiked for three hours, out of one valley and into another, before the first softening of the darkness from dawn appeared. She was deep into her heightened state of being, controlling every movement, alert, warm and agile. The soft pinks and purples of the sunrise, similar to the sunset of the night before, warmed her even more, a sign of good things to come, she thought.

She did have a relatively easy day of it, stopping a couple of times to take cover from the sound of distant helicopters, but she cheerfully arrived at the lake early afternoon. Her pursuers seemed to have underestimated her pace, and hadn't come within miles of her. She felt safe enough to take a quick dip in the clear fresh water. She removed her clothes, grabbed her small worn bar of soap, and plunged into the cool liquid. The cold from the water forced the air out of her tightening chest. She emerged from the icy depths panting heavily, shivering, but invigorated. She swam directly back to the shoreline, not standing despite the shallow water, the slippery rock bottom too difficult to balance upon. She pulled herself from the lake, stood in the open air, lathered up, and returned to the cold water. She scrubbed again at her dirty hands and face, rinsed again, and left the water for the warmth of the sun.

She realized she had found a natural reservoir wedged between two cliffs catching the runoff from melting snow and heavy rain. Her decided luck, the reservoir would surely have been dry if not for the recent rain. She smiled at her good fortune. She drank the rest of the water from her canteen, refilled it from a running stream by the lake, and lounged. No helicopters, no sounds of pursuit whatsoever, she relaxed and reveled in the unadulterated glory of naked flesh basking in the sun. Gloria gave herself twenty minutes, twenty minutes of complete luxury.

After the enchantment of naked sunbathing, she put on her dirty, crusty, clothes; she tied her hair back, and headed to the top of the final ridge. Gloria reached the peak quickly. Rested and reenergized from her mini vacation she moved easily, her young body seemingly recovered from the fatigue. She again looked over the vast plain, this time from much closer. Her hopes raised by her previous first glance, were now quickly dashed by a second look. She saw no railroad tracks, only rocks, cacti and uncovered flatland. Yes, she could pass through, but she could be easily spotted from above. She would have to remain in the relative safety of the low-lying mountain terrain and slowly continue south. She would have access to the edible desert plants, so food would not be a concern, but she still had a long way to go. How long she could not be sure, but for a moment her heart sank, just slightly, for the first time she was dismayed.

She reached the bottom of the last ridge, foraged the place for edibles, returned to the low-lying rocky terrain and continued south. She walked well into the night, now feeling a sense of urgency. She slept little, three, maybe four hour's, and continued on before dawn. The helicopters no longer filled the air, and it was just now beginning to be like she thought it would, just she and the desert. But now her nerves were frayed, and after three days she seemed to be getting nowhere.

Another day, and then another, Gloria continued to hike. She developed diarrhea from the lack of sustenance and her energy was waning. She was not sleeping at all now, not wanting to prolong the foreboding hopelessly lost feeling which had settled upon her. Sleep became an unwanted distraction from her only desire, civilization, living, breathing, free, civilization.

Finally, on the sixth day, she saw a narrow two-lane highway and a rectangular building with a couple of gas pumps. She exhaled deeply, not able to fight the instantaneous tears welling up in her eyes. A few tears spilled over and slipped down her cheeks, she wiped them away as wandered toward the road.

It took her three hours to get to the building, all the while she worried about her presence in plain sight. Time drifted by interminably slow, the heat soaked, wavy horizon agonized her weary vision, seemingly her destination floating farther and farther away from her with every belabored step. Her mouth dusty and dry began to throb. The hidden aches and pains of her body began to divulge them self in the presence of a resting place. She slumped under the weight of the pack, her feet heavier and heavier each moment. Exhausted, she was basically left to shuffle and lean, trying to keep her balance, trying to keep moving forward.

Gloria finally staggered up to the shabby structure which had become her oasis. She opened the door to the faded white and turquoise building too exhausted to anticipate what awaited her. The thick stink of smoke first greeted her upon entry; she nearly gagged with the toxicity of it. Two windows surrounded the entrance of the building, but other than that it was a windowless dive with a couple of patrons seated on stools at the counter. She couldn't have been happier, she smelled food, she saw drinks, and was confident they had a bathroom.

A weathered, red haired lady from behind the bar spoke to her first. "Can I get you something little lady?" she said kindly.

"A glass of water please," Gloria responded, trying not to seem too desperate.

"Sure, have a seat. You from around here?"

Gloria panicked slightly, realizing she would have to come up with something to say. "No, just traveling through, my car broke down a few miles up the road."

The bartender eyed the ragged teenager. "Looks like it's been a rough trip?"

"Yeah," Gloria said sheepishly, looking down at herself. "Do you have a bathroom I could use?"

"Sure do, straight back on your right," the woman replied.

The bartender placed the water on the counter. Gloria took a small sip as not to arouse suspicion, but brought the glass with her as she headed to the bathroom.

"You hungry sweetie?" the woman called.

"Yes ma'am, I am."

"We have hamburgers or hot dogs, no fries, just chips, take your pick."

Gloria rarely ate meat but the thought of anything other than cacti made her mouth water. "I'll take a hamburger," she said.

"Want cheese on that?"

"No, thank you," Gloria said as she walked off to the bathroom.

After Gloria left the room, one of the men at the counter immediately got up and walked over to the pay phone.

"Don't you do it Saul," the lady behind the bar said. "That ain't whose they're talking about."

He picked up the receiver. "Those men said to call if any hiker show up. Now she looked like she come straight out of that desert, I don't care what she say," he said.

"You go ahead you old fool, they gonna laugh at you, wonder why you wasting their time with some silly teenage girl," the bartender responded.

"They sure might, but they might sure gimme that reward money." He dialed the number on the card he had shoved away in his pocket. "We got a hiker here..."

Gloria entered the small bathroom. There was a dingy gray toilet with murky brown water, faded white tile on the floor, and a tiny rust stained sink with a small rectangular cracked mirror above it. She dropped her pack heavily to the ground toppling over with it. She pulled herself up and turned on the tap try to clean herself up. Dark brown water flowed for a moment before settling on a light orange tinge. She gulped down some more water from the glass, and looked at herself in the mirror. The crack running through the mirror left her face disjointed, one side higher than the other. She pulled off her cap, cupped her hands, collected the tinged water and splashed her face with it. She took off her shirt to wipe herself dry, then she pulled off her boots, socks, and pants, leaving her in only shorts and a sports bra. Gloria used her wet shirt to wipe down the rest of her body, examining the bloody gashes and wounds that covered her legs. She slowly began to adjust to the presence of shelter, the sun and wind blocked. She rung out her wet, dirty, bloodstained shirt, deciding she'd have to do without it for now. Her pants were hopeless, a crusty mess of dirt stains, various needles and debris. She undid her hair, releasing its tight pull on her face. Gloria then gathered up her things and walked out to get her food.

The two men stared at her as she walked up to the bar. She put her bag under the counter and laid her clothes over it. The bartender looked up from the grill and smiled. "You look better sweetie, hamburger's almost done," she said.

"Thank you," Gloria replied.

The bartender brought a pitcher of water and placed it on the counter. "Help yourself, sweetie."

"Thank you."

The man who made the phone call spoke to Gloria from across the bar. "So where did you say you're from?" he asked.

"Texas."

"What part?"

"Down south, little town near the border."

"That right. What are you doing in these parts all alone? Seem a little young to be traveling by yourself."

"Oh, Saul, leave her alone," the bartender said as she handed Gloria the burger.

"Thank you," Gloria said sincerely.

Gloria picked up a small crinkled potato chip and popped it into her mouth, a little stale, very salty, not bad, she thought. She went for the burger, the warm soft sponge dough bun, lettuce, tomatoes, thick greasy meat, her heart raced as she bit into the juicy mess. A warm sense of relief came over her, there was something about the first bite into warm food when you've spent so much time not sure when your next meal would come. Her stomach gurgled with eager anticipation as she chewed. She chewed slowly and thoroughly hoping not to shock her system. She washed the food down with a sip of water, enjoying the fullness of the mass entering her system, giddy with the promise of more to come. Her dad would be more than amused, she thought, her sitting in a sports bra, barefoot, eating a burger, a moment more casual, and totally dissimilar from any in Larkspur. Walking through the desert for six days leaves few rigid rules in place. Survival, the ultimate trump card, left her in a position to only follow her immediate needs. The selective reasoning of a comfortable controlled environment could not be less relevant at this moment in time.

Gloria smiled to herself slightly. She could not have known what her first encounter with the outside world would be. Now, in a dirty little bar in the middle of nowhere, she smiled with amazement.

"How's your burger sweetheart?" the kind lady behind the bar asked.

"It's great," Gloria replied contentedly.

"Eat up, you're just a tiny little skinny thing."

"Yes ma'am," Gloria said, smiling as she took another bite. The chips, the burger, the water, her perfect little rejuvenation kit. She needed the protein the most, the deprivation had left her foggy. Her brain sharpened with the integration of the essential fuel. Gloria began to playfully dangle her feet back and forth from the high barstool, the foreboding peril of the desert passage subsiding. Maybe she would be okay, she thought, a rougher beginning than she had hoped, but things were looking up.

No sooner had she completed her hopeful internal diatribe than she heard the familiar rumble of a helicopter. She tried to stay calm, hoping not to alert the patrons to her worry. She finished chewing the food in her mouth and innocently asked, "what's that?"

"That's the military, they got a base somewhere over the mountains. They been looking for someone." The bartender gave a slight wink as she continued. "Don't worry hon', they ain't looking for you. Saul seems to think so, he's the one that called them up, he wants that reward."

"Reward?" Gloria repeated.

"Yeah, the government will pay you if you help them get their man," the bartender said looking squarely into Gloria's eyes.

The door to the bar opened, a dozen men filled the room. Gloria, whose back was to the entrance, swiveled around clumsily swinging her feet with the burger in her hand. A red-faced, stocky man looked at her and then over to the bartender as he stepped forward. "Got a call about a hiker," he said to the woman.

"Yeah, that's her," she said pointing at Gloria. She nodded at Saul. "He's real eager to get that reward," she said downplaying Gloria's presence.

The soldier sighed slightly. "Hello ma'am," he said to Gloria.

"Hello," Gloria said cheerfully.

"May I ask you what you are doing here?"

"I'm on spring break."

"Spring break in the middle of the desert?"

"I got stuck here. I'm a plein air painter. The desert has the most serene, beautiful mountainscapes, I mean it's a little scary with the snakes and vultures and all, but I like the colors, so I come out here to paint when I get a chance. I'm an art major at the University of Texas. Go longhorns," Gloria said, holding up her free hand with the symbol of the horns. "Got my supplies right here in my pack."

Gloria wanted to kick herself the moment she brought up the pack. She was so accustomed to traveling with her art supplies she tried to mix a little truth in with her lies. But with her inexperience in the ways of the deceitful she gave them an easily verifiable opportunity to poke a hole in her story.

"Show me something," he said.

Not sure if he was talking about her pack, Gloria grabbed a napkin off the counter. "Can I borrow your pencil?" she asked the bartender.

The woman took the pencil from behind her ear and handed it to Gloria. Gloria quickly sketched a miniature reproduction of Mount Rushmore, complete with the tiny detailed faces of the four presidents: George Washington, Thomas Jefferson, Theodore Roosevelt, and Abraham Lincoln. She turned and held it up to the men.

"Hey, that's pretty good," the stocky man said, grabbing it from her hand for closer inspection. He handed the napkin to the other men who looked at it and passed it around. The stocky man spoke again. "You know it's not such a good idea for a young girl to travel around alone," he said.

"I'm starting to get the idea," Gloria said sincerely.

"You haven't by chance come across any hikers have you?" the man asked.

"No, sir," Gloria replied.

"All right, ma'am. Sorry to bother you." He turned over to Saul. "Better luck next time, pal. Hey, if a six year-old comes wandering in, call child services, not us," he joked. Saul shrugged and took a sip of his beer. The red-faced man turned back to Gloria. "Good luck to you young lady. You be careful now, ya hear."

"Yes sir, thank you."

"Come on guys, let's go," he said turning to the men.

They filed back out of the room, boarded the chopper parked in the open field, and took off.

Gloria sat for a moment on the stool; she was bewildered and badly shaken. They were right here and hadn't recognized her, she couldn't believe it. Her pent up anxiety mushroomed, she felt her stomach rumble and her face flush. "Excuse me," she said to the woman. She hurried to the restroom where she proceeded to regurgitate her first taste of freedom into the murky brown water of the toilet bowl. Gloria kneeled over the bowl until her nerves eased and her stomach settled. She lifted herself up stiffly from the hard tile floor; her legs wrought with tension seemed to be defying her wishes. She turned on the sink; the water was mostly clear this time, she splashed some on her face, rinsed her mouth and wiped herself dry with the back of her hand. A light knocking came at the door. "Hon', you all right in there?" she heard the bartender call.

Gloria unlocked the door. The woman opened the door slightly and peered in. "Yeah, I'm okay," Gloria said weakly.

The woman came through the door and grabbed Gloria by the hand. "Here, come with me girl, we can't have you in your skivvies wandering around the desert."

The woman led Gloria through a door across the hall. Inside was a small room with a bench dissecting the room between two wall mounted lockers. There was one small window at the end of the room allowing in the strong midday light. Gloria looked over at the old time punch machine on the wall. The woman noticed the girl's curiosity. "This place used to be busier before they built the tracks through here, but that was a long time ago," the woman said forlorn.

"A train?" Gloria asked.

"Yeah, they move cargo through here. There's a pass a couple of miles from here," the woman said. A couple miles Gloria thought, it seemed such a monumental distance after everything she had been through. The woman continued. "Come on sweetie, let's get you dressed. I got a spare change of clothes here in case I go out after work, which almost never happens, but that doesn't mean a girl can't be prepared, you know what I mean?"

"Sure."

"Now, they might be a little big on you. You wouldn't know it, but under here I still got a pretty good figure, looked a lot like you when I was younger."

"I can tell," Gloria said kindly.

"You can, thank you sweetie. Here put these on, you might have to take those shorts off."

"I'd prefer to leave the shorts on if they'll fit."

"You go ahead and be shy hon', that's fine."

Gloria pulled on the jeans, a little baggy at the waist, but not a bad fit. She snapped up the plaid brown and white cotton cowboy shirt the woman gave her.

"There sweetie, that's better, you look just fine."

"Thank you," Gloria said, as she felt the new clothes.

"Don't mention it. We women got to stick together," she said to Gloria, straightening the girl's collar. "That train pulls to a near stop when it turns to go around the mountain not more than two or three miles from here. Stay on the north side, they won't see a thing. You here me hon', it's best you get going. Them army boys dumb as rocks but they sure are persistent, best you get a move on."

"Yes, ma'am, and thank you." Gloria said, as she stepped toward the woman to give her a hug.

The woman, stiff at first, relented to the embrace. "You're welcome, sweetheart."

Chapter 17

Gloria headed back into the dry desert air, boots on, pack strapped, a new adventure lay ahead. She felt more like a tourist now, trying to assimilate and pass as the typical traveler, not someone with secrets to hide. She hoped to leave her secret laden existence behind in the mountains. She moved forward hoping to make it on her own, unhindered by all that came before. The eventful hour and a half in the bar made her days in the desert seem like a distant memory. The only thing that crossed her mind now was making it on that train, if she could do that, she was sure her life would begin anew, the life she had dreamed of for so long, an anonymous existence in a vast and complicated land full of possibilities.

The hike across the flat land to the tracks was not nearly as bad as she thought. With less fear of pursuers, and the promise of machine propelled transportation, she took each stride nice and easy. Her legs had begun to stiffen with the inactivity, and she welcomed the slow, gentle pace of the leisurely walk. She begrudgingly sliced a few cacti pads to bring on the road, hoping to never bite through their tough bitter exterior again.

Spirits lifted once again, she began to reconcile with the heavy pack strapped to her back. Just like the rest of her body, the pack became essential, albeit an aching and annoying, nonetheless, she knew she couldn't live without it. She took pride in the trouble and burden of life on the road, proud she decided to take on the challenge of the device. At her moments of greatest weakness, her time traveling high up on the peaks with the voices of those chasing her echoing through the canyon, it was her mother's strength and her mother's dream that helped her get through. To be caught would no doubt be a great personal disappointment, but to be caught and lose her mother's achievement, that would be entirely unbearable. So she pushed on now, despite her blister torn feet, shooting pains in her lower back, nausea, headache, and blinding exhaustion, she continued forward like she did in the mountains, and like she will continue to forever, because she must.

Gloria arrived at the bend in the tracks just before dusk. The evening had begun to cool and the light soften. According to the bartender there hadn't been a train all day, which bode well for one's speedy arrival. Spending another stress filled night in the valley of her pursuers evoked preemptive nightmares.

She rested by some rocks at the base of a cliff mostly hidden from the tracks. She no longer yearned for food. The burger and the subsequent stomach troubles had dulled her appetite. She still suffered from the lack of nutrition, but she would have to wait until morning to try and ingest anything again. She hoped by then her stomach would be sufficiently settled, and she would be in a safe locale to get a decent meal.

She gazed into the sky as the sun lowered, watching the first twinkling stars magically appear in the soft blue light. She thought of Larkspur, and how long ago her life there seemed, how distant the simplicity of the young girl wandering through the hills, painting away the days, felt from the assertive and complicated days of the present. She knew she had needed that time, that silent reflection, but now she couldn't imagine living that way, couldn't imagine how she could have been so still for so long. The endless disengagement of her youth in Larkspur seemed sad and lonely. She was without purpose, without challenge, it now felt as if the safe and structured life she left behind was more dangerous to her existence than this life fraught with tumult and terror. She had always felt she was rightly cautious in Larkspur, not endangering her body or her mind, but her lack of challenge had left her numb and alone. Now, she realized she loved living on the edge, alive with suffering and determination.

Stars began to fill the sky; she watched the sweet subtle fading of day into night. Her familiar companion, Leo, dazzled in the night above her. She felt comforted by the presence of the constellations, like old friends keeping her company on her voyage. The distant whistle withdrew her from the stars and she turned east to see a train approaching. Her heart leapt with joy as she watched the dark smoke plume rise into the air signaling the approach of the vessel that would carry her into her future.

She jumped to her feet, feeling stabs of shooting pain she regretted her quick action. She recovered, grabbed her pack, and prepared herself to board. She wasn't quite sure what to expect from the train, open cars, locked doors, or whether she would be able to gain entryway, but she knew she needed to try. She feared having to ride up on the roof of the moving train, a tiresome way to travel she hoped to avoid. The thought of staying alert, no sleep, and contending again all night with the elements tumbled her already fragile stomach.

She peered from behind the rocks as the engine passed by. The train began to slow significantly as it needed to make a sharp left turn to circumvent the mountain. It was a thing of beauty, the massive wheels, the axle system propelling the enormous mass forward. She relaxed as she saw the enormity of the train, the line of cars went back for miles, and she was sure boarding and finding a comfortable spot to rest was likely. She watched the characteristics of the first cars go by, if there were places to grab hold, how the doors were fashioned, she gathered the necessary information before making the plunge. Some cars were flat, carrying large tree trunks which were tied down. A few cars carried other building materials out in the open air, but most were cargo cars with doors fastened shut. At worst, she thought, she could lie among the logs, wedged in safely. She noticed the dark rust colored cars, as opposed to the green or beige cars had a particularly long and sturdy ladder riding not too high off the ground. It also looked like the ladder was within arms length of the latch of the door. She decided she would try for a rust color car near a load of trees, and if she couldn't make it inside she'd traverse to a flat car and ride with the trees.

Noticing the type of car she was looking for, Gloria sprang into action. She sprinted the twenty yards from the rocks to the tracks, agonizing with every heavy step as the aches and pains of the previous days screamed with the exertion. She came alongside the train, measured its speed, faster than she thought, she struggled to match it. She grabbed a rung with her left hand, leapt onto the ladder, and stabilized herself with her right. She adjusted her footing, steadied her balance, and leaned out to open the latch. She reached, first able to get her fingertips on the handle, then a full grip, she pulled, and the door slid open, she pulled it further and was able to leap inside the car.

The car smelled terribly, but was mostly empty save for a few crates. There were twenty crates stacked in the corner, each with a white feathered clucking occupant, the source of the smell she thought, as she smiled. She left the door open for a few minutes and watched the land as it went by at an unusually accelerated pace. She watched as the edge of the cacti blurred with the speed, and how at first the cacti looked to be standing still, and then a quick spill sideways, and they were gone. She looked at the open sky above the mountains and knew somewhere past those mountains was the hometown she would never see again. She sat and watched the passing of the land until the chill of the night spurred her to pull the door shut. She could not latch the door properly from the inside, but the large metal doors were heavy enough to stay together despite the force of the train's momentum.

The chickens calmed in the enclosed space, quieting and nesting. Gloria quite liked their presence, companionship of the living, regardless of the animal, dulled the edge of loneliness. She had always felt a kinship with animals, whose existence was entirely determined by the whims of their owner. She recognized the unyielding restraints of a lack of autonomy, they were born into a life of total control, measured only by degrees, their existence always in another's hands. She never understood people's seeming obsession with eating meat, as if no good meal could exist without it, as if there was no compelling reason to not eat another living being. Occasionally, eating meat, that was one thing, we are all part of the food chain after all, but we have so many choices, how could the utter disregard for an animal's life still play so prominently into the equation. It was not an animal's death she struggled with, it was the way they were treated while alive. "Don't worry, I won't hurt you little chickens," she said to the resting birds.

She took off her boots, unrolled her sleeping bag, and cozied in. The heaviness of her exhaustion flattened her into the hard floor. She was asleep in moments, not to stir until the slowing of the train the next morning.

Gloria could see light breaking through the crack in between the doors. The chickens were restless with the oncoming of a new day seen through the bars of a cage. The train was blowing its whistle and seemed to be coming to a stop. Sleepily, she pulled open the doors a few inches. Peering through to the outside she saw several tracks running parallel below her. It appeared she had arrived at a large train depot. "This is my stop," she said to the chickens.

She pulled on her boots, packed up her sleeping bag, opened the door, and hopped off the train. The sound nights sleep helped prepare her body for further travel, she landed the leap, strong and balanced. She quickly navigated through the tracks, and ran to escape the view of the station.

There was a large, slightly dilapidated, rectangular wooden structure with a huge opening, almost like an airplane hangar, the trains were routed through. There only seemed to be a handful of men around the station, and none had noticed her. It appeared she was still in desert terrain, although she sensed the air was heavier with the lower altitude and increased moisture. She shielded herself behind a stopped train on a far outlying track. She looked for a place to wait and gather herself before deciding her next course of action. There was nothing in the way of shelter or cover other than the train depot, no structures or rocks, only open desert. She decided she would have to make her way carefully to the side of the building to try to hop a departing train before being detected.

There was a gap of about fifty yards before she reached the building where the tracks veered into one before entering the station. She would have to run for it. Her position, a hundred yards to the side of the building, would hopefully keep her from coming into the men's view. She readied herself, waited until the men seemed occupied, and bolted, running parallel not towards the building, but alongside of it, hoping to cut in at an angle out of view. She felt twinges of pain in her legs, and they weren't quite as responsive as she was accustomed, but she was quickly out of sight without causing alarm. She arched around, coming to rest along the outside of the building. She could not stay in the open, anyone could mistakenly happen upon her without much effort. She would have to get inside and hide amongst the machinery, awaiting a chance to board again.

Gloria heard some of the men preparing to examine the cargo of the train she had just arrived on. She scurried to the opposite end of the building where the trains departed. She listened for a moment, hearing nothing, she nervously poked her head around the corner to survey the situation. There were old dusty and greasy idle machinery in the near corner she could sit behind which would leave her in a good position to board an exiting train. Out of the corner of her eye she noticed the workers cars parked on the other side of the exit, she looked more closely, California plates, she exulted inside. She heard the men's voices grow louder on the other side of the building, they were outside. She quickly turned into the building and tucked herself in the corner behind an old forklift. She sat down, pack still on, and leaned against the wall. California, she thought, I've made it to California. She knew she still needed to get further west, ideally all the way to the coast, and plenty farther north, but she was well on her way, and she felt elated.

It appeared the men were briefly inspecting the train she arrived on and then it would continue. The conductor sat on a bench chatting it up with a few of the workers at the front of the building, out of sight, but within earshot of Gloria. They talked about the land, their families, and the haul the train was carrying. They were kind and good natured with each other, some sweet teasing; it seemed as if they had been performing this same ritual for many years. She liked the railroad men, jovial and hard working, the type of men who needed a few good moments with their buddies and they were satisfied with their day. She liked sitting there listening to the camaraderie, quite a fine way to pass the time as the train was readied. She hadn't heard men talking like that very often; there wasn't a lot of that in Larkspur, the simple nonsensical joking of fellows having a good time.

The train seemed ready rather quickly. She had just grown into a comfortable state of relaxation listening to the men when they began to say their goodbyes. As the conductor headed to the front of the train she got the sense the men were genuinely sorry to see him go. But they were professionals first, not dawdling, they had a schedule to keep, their time regulated, enjoyed, but fleeting. She rose as the train started slowly moving past her. The workers were no threat, on the other side of the tracks and two hundred yards away, she focused on safely boarding.

She tried to locate the same rust colored car she had traveled in before. She thought she recognized it, sandwiched in between two flatcars carrying tree trunks. The car was nearly halfway down the train; she waited as dozens of cars rolled past. Her anxiety began to increase as the time to jump the train approached. She felt her heart pumping rapidly through her chest. Although this boarding was much less complicated than the first, aided by proximity and experience, her body grew nervous with anticipation. Possibly it was the very real awareness of her closeness to civilization? Maybe she was worried about coming this far and making a silly mistake? Either way, as she prepared to run towards the ladder, her heart racing, she was more entirely aware of her terror than ever before. She sprinted, grabbed hold of the ladder, expertly opened the doors, smooth as could be she was inside. She pulled the doors closed, said hello to the chickens, sat down, and took a huge sigh of relief.

She leaned against the side wall of the car, listening to the rhythm of the swift moving wheels underneath her. She noticed the chickens were particularly calm, there was feed scattered below their cages; bellies full, they rested contently. She again thought kindly of the men back at the station, a peaceful group of hard workers, whom despite her perilous situation, she had felt safe near. Not safe enough to expose herself, for she was still riding the train illegally, but safe enough that she felt no real harm would come to her if they had found her.

She sipped on her canteen, it was midday, and for the first time since the previous afternoon's hamburger she felt the pangs of hunger. She wasn't worried, although California was a large state, it was tall and skinny, if they continued west they would probably be at the coast in a few hours. She also knew California was highly populated, and anywhere the train was likely to end up would have ample resources. She relaxed and looked forward to the next stop, knowing she would be able to stop running, anonymous, with new opportunity.

She dozed off some time in between her daydreaming about the future and the delirium of her hunger. The train jolted slightly as it slowed, she awoke, instantly tasting and smelling the salty moisture of the air, the first time she had experienced air away from the arid desert. Gloria hopped to her feet. Eager to see what was outside, she opened the doors and immediately noticed a strange tall silhouette. A lean pole with a bushy top was outlined against the sky, a palm tree, the ugliest tree she had ever seen she thought. Never had she been so happy to see such an ugly sight. She smiled broadly as she looked at the urban scene around her. The train was pulling into a large station, one that handled passengers as well as cargo, surrounded on either side by large industrial buildings. There was a slightly perceptible pulse to the environment; she sensed far greater energy and action than that of Larkspur. There were cars and trucks, movement, and life, she rejoiced in the populated surroundings. Unable to wait a moment longer, she grabbed her pack and jumped off the slowly moving train.

She was shocked by the sights and sounds, the cars whizzing by, there were not many, but they drove fast on a wide smooth highway the likes of which she had never seen, two lanes on each side with a lane in the middle. There were paved roads and rectangular buildings as far as the eye could see. She marveled at the prevalent funny shaped skinny trees looming over the road, like the sharp pointed finger of a scolding teacher. She walked no more than twenty yards from the tracks to a beautiful, perfectly smooth cemented sidewalk beside a wide road. She followed the sinking sun and turned west.

After a few minutes of walking it was clear she was in a strictly industrial area, no restaurants, no houses, no shops. Her hopes were not dashed entirely, lost in an urban industrial center was quite different from being lost in the desert. But the disappointment of being so close to everything she wanted, and not quite knowing exactly where to go was emotionally difficult compared with the determined searching required in the desert. Her current quest called for a new resolve, confusion the obstacle instead of the elements. All directions looked the same, there were no ridgelines to follow, she couldn't read the vegetation to find a water source, she had to guess, west was her only guess.

She walked as the shadows from the buildings grew long. Any city must have a restaurant within an hour walk, she thought. She made her last push hoping soon she would indulge in a proper meal. She had little energy, she shuffled along, barely able to lift her feet off the ground, unable to truly evaluate the entirety of her surroundings. The generic rectangular buildings dismayed her; she was expecting a vast architectural departure from the plainness of Larkspur. She continued forward, no longer looking around, but up into the sky occasionally, the only intriguing sight, as she awaited the emergence of the evening stars.

There was very little daylight left; she thought it odd the lack of celestial appearance. The only star visible as the last wisps of color from the receding sun faded was the dependable North Star, the brightest star in the sky. The humming of the streetlights introduced her to their presence. She looked around; dusk had brought an overwhelming artificial illumination to the street. The buildings were lit up, the streets, the signs, everything, as if nothing manmade should go unseen. In fact, despite the setting sun, there was little evidence of a transition into darkness. The stars could not compete she realized, drowned out by the well lit concrete masses. Fewer cars drove by, the last stragglers of a workday long over, none of them noticed her, not even a curious turn of the head. She felt invisible in a large world, like she was separate from the perpetual movement of those whom belong.

She wove herself out of the maze of the industrial zone. Night fully set in, she looked up, trying to imagine her lost twinkling companions. She plotted the sky with Orion, Virgo, and Cassiopeia, imagining the strong shapes and the countless number of people who have turned to them in times of despair looking into the celestial night for comfort. The buildings grew smaller, more diverse, a Laundromat, an auto body shop, a strip club, the type of businesses that lay on the fringe of a residential neighborhood.

Her heart swooned as the first of the run down houses began to merge with the businesses. The outside of the small homes appeared to be neglected, the paint, formerly bright neon and pastels, pinks, blues, purples, faded and cracked from years in the sun. The warm glow of the light through the windows and the lusty, mouth watering smells which filled the air told another story, one of a rich home life within the shabby outer walls. The aromas, not entirely unfamiliar to Gloria, hinted of spices and the sweetness of corn. Her stomach grumbled, hopeful the enchanting smell of warm food would lead to her own nourishment. Her pace slowed as she grew weary, surrounded by the teasing allure of comfort.

She heard the sounds of laughter, and saw some children skipping rope in their front yard. Gloria watched as three young girls tried to guide a small boy through the hopping process. He dutifully complied, attempting the task although he was clearly too small to manage jumping the rope. The girls playfully giggled when he became entangled, and lovingly picked him up when he fell. One of the girls, the oldest, in little pink shorts and a faded lilac shirt, turned to Gloria, her long ponytail blowing in the breeze. "Como estas?" she asked.

Gloria, entranced with the kids' game, took a moment before realizing the girl had addressed her. "Ay, bien, nina, y tu." Gloria responded. Spanish was part of Gloria's early education in Larkspur, a fact that she had always found ironic until now.

"Bien. Que es este?" the girl said, pointing to Gloria's pack.

"Mi ropa," Gloria replied, sad she had to lie to the nice girl.

"Como se llama?" the precocious girl asked.

"Gloria. Y tu?"

"Evelyn. Y mi hermanas Maria, y Carmen, y mi hermano, Jose."

"Como Estan," Gloria said to the now interested group.

"Hola," the little boy replied, with the other two girls appearing quite shy.

The front door to the house swung open. "Ninos, comida," Gloria heard a woman's voice call. The three younger children immediately turned and ran up the front stairs into the house. Evelyn remained with Gloria. "Evelyn, que es?" her mother asked from the porch.

"Gloria es muy hambre, mama," the girl replied.

"Esta bien, comida con tu amiga."

"My mom says you can come to dinner," the girl said in English, without the hint of an accent.

"How'd you know I was hungry?" Gloria asked the little girl.

"I could just tell."

"Thank you."

"No problema. Mi mama makes the best tamales this side of the border."

Gloria followed the little girl up the steps into the house. The moment she stepped into the home she felt as if she left behind the cold harsh world and entered the warm security of a loving family. The beautiful smell of the food intensified her happiness, but it was the small shrine in the corner of the room that quickly drew her attention. A three foot tall gold statue of the Virgin Mary beamed, proudly displayed, surrounded by several glass candles wrapped with colorful paper images of saints. Rosaries hung from the virgin's bent arms of prayer.

"She looks out for us, no?" the young mother said.

"It's very beautiful," Gloria replied.

"Welcome to our home, you can leave your bag here. Now, it's time to eat."

"Thank you," Gloria said with a supreme earnestness.

"No problema. I'm Constantine."

"Gloria."

Constantine led Gloria through the small living room into the dining room, and motioned for Gloria to sit. Gloria remained standing unsure which seat to take as Constantine continued into the kitchen. There were six high backed, armless, wooden chairs surrounding an oval wooden table which was covered with a beautiful ivory lace tablecloth. Evelyn and her two sisters emerged from the kitchen and expertly set the table. The girls returned to the kitchen and reemerged moments later carrying platters of food. Constantine entered, followed by little Jose, and placed two large platters on the table. "Sit," Constantine said. The kids promptly filled their spots. Constantine sat at one end of the table and motioned for Gloria to sit at the other. "My husband is working," she said, "please sit."

As Gloria seated herself, she was immediately greeted by the outstretched hands of Evelyn and Maria. Constantine addressed her eldest daughter. "Evelyn, because you have a special friend joining us this evening, why don't you say grace?"

"Ingles?" the little girl asked.

"Yes," Constantine replied. "We don't usually speak English at home," she explained to Gloria.

"That's very kind of you, my Spanish is basic at best. Thank you," Gloria said.

Constantine nodded at Gloria, and then at Evelyn. The child bowed her head as everyone clasped hands. "Dear Lord, thank you for this food we are about to eat. Thank you for my brother and sisters, y mi papa, y mama, and thank you for bringing our new amiga, Gloria. Amen."

"Amen," the rest of the family said together. Gloria remained quiet. She smiled at Evelyn when the little girl lifted her head. The kids quickly dove into their respective nearby platters, grabbing tortillas, tamales, chicken and pork, scooping up beans and rice, it was a veritable feast. Gloria did not go near the chicken or the pork; she took a green chile and cheese tamale, tortillas, beans and rice.

"No meat girl? You look like you could use some meat," Constantine said.

"Weak stomach," Gloria replied.

"Be careful, that's very spicy," Evelyn said, as Gloria scooped some salsa onto her plate.

"Most gringos don't like it," Maria said, quickly followed by little Carmen's giggling.

"Maria," her mother said in a thick Spanish accent, "cuidado, m'ija."

"Mom doesn't like it when we call white people gringos," Evelyn explained.

"You don't want people calling you Mexican all the time, or treating you differently because you are Mexican. We don't treat people differently because they are white."

"I don't see what's wrong with being Mexican?" Evelyn said.

"No m'ija, of course nothing is wrong with being Mexican. It's about making people feel different. It hurts people's feelings when you assume they are one way because they are Mexican or white, you understand?"

"'Cause we are all people, which is bigger than being Mexican," the little girl said.

"Yes, we treat all people with respect and kindness," her mother replied.

"I'll be careful though," Gloria said reassuringly to Evelyn. "Thanks for the warning."

Gloria raised the first bite of the tamale to her mouth, the warm soft, sweet corn melted around the spicy, cheesy center. She chewed slowly, savoring the contrast of the spice and sweet, wanting to extract every last bit of flavor from the tantalizing morsel. "This is very good," she said to Constantine after swallowing.

"Good m'ija, I'm glad you like it."

Gloria's cheeks turned red at Constantine's endearing inclusion into her brood, m'ija, my daughter. Gloria related far better to the young mother, most likely not yet thirty, than she did the young children. And she was surprised and honored when Constantine established a maternal nature. Gloria was struck by a heavy burning in her chest, the flooding pain of her own lost mother overcame her, she fought to hold back tears as they welled up in her eyes. Constantine noticed the blush and then the pained look of sorrow in the teenager's eyes. She reached over to Jose and tickled him under his arms. The little boy let out a squeal and then giggled mightily as he nearly fell out of his chair trying to avoid his mother. The girls laughed, Gloria smiled, regained her composure, and they all continued with their dinner.

Gloria helped Constantine with the dishes as the kids got ready for bed, Gloria washed, Constantine dried. "Where are you going, m'ija?" Constantine asked.

"To a friend's in northern California." Gloria thought for a moment. "Where am I now?" she asked.

"Chula Vista."

Gloria stared at her blankly.

"San Diego," Constantine clarified.

"Is the ocean near here?"

"Not far, twenty or thirty minutes." Constantine paused for a moment, then looked over at Gloria ponderingly. "Have you never seen the ocean?"

"I never have, well, I mean, pictures, but not the real thing."

"Oye, nina, we shall get you there. I can show you how to get there in the morning. You can sleep in the kids' room or on the couch if you'd like."

"Thank you, that would be wonderful," Gloria said, relieved to have a safe place to sleep for the night. They washed the remainder of the dishes in a comfortable silence.

Evelyn, dressed in a pink princess nightgown, wandered into the kitchen. "Mama, can we play with Gloria before bed?" she asked.

'Sure, m'ija, if it's okay with Gloria."

Evelyn looked up at Gloria with her big dark chocolate brown eyes. Gloria dried her hands and took Evelyn's hand in hers. "Let's see this room of yours," Gloria said. The little girl skipped away merrily, Gloria in tow.

A pastel pink paint covered the walls of the medium sized room. There were two bunk beds on opposite sides of the room. The three smaller kids were engaged in various states of play on a brightly colored rug in the center of the room. A child sized white vanity with children's make-up and hair accessories neatly arranged leaned against one wall. A large trunk full of toys and dress up clothes was against the wall adjacent to the door.

'What a wonderful room," Gloria said.

"You can sleep here if you want," Evelyn said somewhat shyly to the teenager.

"That sounds like a pretty cool idea to me. You know what we should do if it's okay with your mom? I think we should build a fort."

The kids eyes lit up. Evelyn ran to go ask her mom. She came back a moment later. "She said it was okay."

"Okay, the first thing we need to do is gather all fort building materials, this includes blankets, sheets, pillows, chairs, and anything else you think might work."

The four eager kids began stripping their beds, bringing everything to the middle of the room. They all helped to assemble a canopy over the bunk beds. The toy chest, along with a couple of chairs, and several pillows were used to make a wall and entrance way. Inside the fort they laid some sheets and blankets down to sleep upon. After they finished building the fort they all settled down. Gloria read the four kids some stories. The children quickly grew tired. The two little ones, Jose and Carmen, slept on the bottom of each bunk. Gloria, Maria, and Evelyn slept on the floor.

Gloria woke to little Jose's hand on her shoulder. The faded white light of dawn subtly illuminated the windows. The fort had lost its shape during the night, everything a jumbled mess on the floor. Jose patted Gloria's shoulder gently as she opened her eyes. She leaned back from her position on her side and looked up at him. He jumped down from the bed into her arms, bear hugging her. Jose snuggled in between Gloria and Evelyn, resting quietly for some time.

As more light filled the room, the children began to stir. There were a few giggles and tickles before the smell of fried eggs and potatoes drew them to the kitchen. Constantine was busy at the stove as her brood flooded in.

"Buenos dias, sleepy heads," she said. They each kissed their mother and then grabbed plates and lined up for food. Gloria followed suit, except for the kiss, and soon all six of them were seated at the table enjoying breakfast. The kids contentedly swung their feet and ate their food. Gloria, again overjoyed with the chance to eat such delicious food, rejoiced in sharing another meal with the family. After a few moments of concentrated chewing Gloria raised a question to Constantine. "Where's your husband?"

"He's working." Constantine replied. "He came home after you were asleep and left again early this morning. He cooks nights for a restaurant, and on the weekends he cooks breakfast for another. I'm sorry you missed him, he welcomes you. He's going to come meet us at the beach later."

Gloria's face lit up. "We're going to the beach?" she said. All of the children cheered with glee.

"I've never been to the beach before," Gloria said to the kids as they were all piling in to Constantine's old maroon, with a wide gray stripe, Dodge minivan.

"You've never been to the beach before, it's so fun," Maria said.

"You get to go in the ocean and build sand castles," said Evelyn.

"Will you help us build a sand castle?" Maria asked Gloria.

"Sure," Gloria said excitedly.

They drove for twenty-five minutes, Gloria in the passenger seat, the four kids in various kid safety contraptions in the back. They arrived before ten, parking in a large lot next to the beach. Gloria was surprised by the wide expanse of sand leading to the ocean, not the rocky, cove like beaches she had most often seen depicted in pictures. They grabbed blankets, coolers, buckets, shovels, towels, and toys then ran the fifty yards to the ocean. Gloria looked at the deep blue mass glistening in the sun. She set down the things she was carrying, took off her shirt, dressed in her sports bra and shorts, she ran to the water.

She anxiously tiptoed through the rising and receding water of the ocean's edge.

She was shocked by the chill of the water. "Oh, it's cold," she said to the jumping and dancing kids around her.

"You need to get used to it," Evelyn said, after screaming at an oncoming ripple. The kids ran up the beach with the water nipping at their heels, then turned and chased the water as it pulled away, only to repeat the same tidal dance over and over.

Gloria slowly introduced herself to the ocean, her cold feet and ankles finally acclimating, then her legs and knees. Her shorts grew heavy as she continued to risk going deeper and deeper. She swirled in the whitewash, now over her waist. She quickly realized how easily the tumbling water could knock her off stride. Wanting to go deeper, she readied herself then followed the tide out, diving into a small clear wave. The cold water rushed passed her face and torso. She broke through the surface, took a deep breath and let her weight pull her back down to the sandy bottom. She pushed off the ocean floor, springing herself out through the surface again.

She dipped underwater many times, exploring the ocean's underbelly with eyes wide open. She couldn't see far, mostly just murky blue/green water with a rippled grayish sandy bottom floor. Rather plain in sight, but the feeling of total submersion, that was something. The way time seemed to slow, as if filtered by the thick water, the slight gentle rocking accompanying the ebbs and flows of the tide. She heard only a subtle soothing white noise fill her head as she felt her senses adapt to the new environment. She felt so still, immersed within the elements, she dipped and floated without fear.

A large swell formed on the horizon. She swam quickly to dive under a barreling wave before it crashed on her. She swam farther to meet the next several large waves in succession. She felt the surge of the powerful rush of water as she dove through each one. She was far from the shore. She looked back at the children playing in the whitewash, the smiling faces relishing their playful moments. She waited for the waves to die down before swimming in and rejoining the kids. She was panting with the effort of swimming in against the tide, the voluminous strong living liquid mass left her humbled by its power.

"You're a good swimmer," Maria said to Gloria as she and Evelyn took hold of her hands and walked with her to the blankets.

"It was more difficult than I thought," Gloria said to the girls, "cold, and lots of current."

"Yeah, one time Maria got swept in and mommy had to pull her out. The ocean is very powerful," Evelyn said.

"It sure is," Gloria replied.

They spent the rest of the morning digging in the sand and building various forts and castles. The group was famished by noon; they feasted on the previous evening's leftovers, and resumed playing. Fernando, the children's father, joined them around two. He splashed, dug, and chased, at some point carrying each child out into the ocean dunking them. A short, rounded, jolly man, he matched the boisterous energy of the children.

Constantine took the opportunity of Fernando's presence to nap peacefully on the blanket. Fernando eventually woke her as he was leaving, flinging his wet hair on her, then kissing her as she giggled. He waved, calling back to his wife and children as he left to work.

The family played until the sun grew low, cold and exhausted, they all schlepped back to the mercifully sun-warmed van. Everyone quickly fell asleep during the car ride home, safe with Constantine at the helm, even Gloria, drooling and all.

The kids bathed while Constantine and Gloria warmed up dinner. Gloria reveled in the warm exhausted sleepiness after a full day at the beach. She noticed there were salt crystals dried crisply on her arm hairs. Her thick full head of long hair, curled even tighter from the ocean, had bits of seaweed wound within the curls. "I don't even want to shower," Gloria said to Constantine. "I want these reminders of the ocean to stay with me always."

"Moments you love stay forever in your heart," Constantine replied.

"I hope that's true, there are many feelings, and many people I never want to forget."

Constantine took the opportunity to learn more about her guest. "Why are you here Gloria, alone, on your own?"

"I could not stay where I was," was all Gloria said.

"You said you were on your way to northern California?"

"Wine country."

"Do you have money?"

"I do."

"Because, you are welcome to stay here as long as you like," Constantine said.

"Thank you, Constantine. I have loved spending time with you and your family, but I don't think I'll feel settled until I get to my destination."

"I understand." Constantine replied. "There's an Amtrak that goes all the way up the coast, tickets are relatively cheap, we could drop you off tomorrow morning on our way to church."

"That would be great."

Just then the kids came piling into the kitchen, squirrelly and squeaky clean. Constantine ordered them to the table as the women brought out the food. They enjoyed a wonderful meal together with warm nourishing food, laughter, and playful conversation.

The kids were extremely tired, their sun-browned faces and heavy eyes displaying the exhaustion of the full day. Gloria showered, her first in over a week, as Constantine put the kids to bed. As the warm water washed away her salt sealed skin, she again was drawn to the peaceful stillness of the underwater world of the ocean. Her time in the gravity defying supportive mass was such a contradiction to the perilous peaks of the mountains she had spent her whole life trying not to fall from. To encounter such weightlessness, with its slow, prolonged descent, the type that could be controlled, and avoided, brought her a sense of assuredness. The world opened to her anew, full of a natural balance that her previous experiences had left dangerously skewed. She tapped into the center of her strength, where any known fear could be undone with the right experience. She was silly to think for a moment she needed the particles of the ocean to stay on her to continue to feel their effects. She would always remember the simple, easy feeling of the unusual presence of being surrounded by heavy liquid, and the comfort of the slow-motion propulsion of a body immersed. The serene ocean, even with its currents and liveliness, had rounded some of her rougher desert elements, a homeostasis of natural elements occurred within her.

She stepped out of the shower refreshed, feeling clean for the first time since leaving Larkspur. Constantine knocked on the bathroom door as she dried off. "Gloria?" she said as she opened the door a crack and held out a beautiful off-white hand embroidered shirt. "Una camisa para ti."

"Gracias," Gloria replied as she took the shirt from Constantine. Gloria pulled on the shirt over her wet head. Light brown, large, thick stitching lined the short sleeves and the plunging V-neck of the cream colored shirt. A large flower shape in the same large stitching blossomed over the center of her chest. The shirt was light, soft, practical and beautiful. Gloria smiled at the sight of herself in the mirror.

Gloria exited the bathroom to an awaiting Constantine. "Bonita, Gloria, muy bonita," Constantine said.

Gloria smiled and blushed slightly. "Thank you, I love it."

"I'm glad you like it. I made it you know."

"It's beautiful. Is that what you do, make clothes?"

"No, not for work, I'm a housekeeper for a family in La Jolla."

The two moved into the dining room to keep from waking the kids. "They are a really nice family," Constantine continued. "I've been working for them for almost twelve years, just after their first was born. Now they have four."

"Before Evelyn was born?"

"Yes, I was nineteen. Fernando and I had only been in the country a few months. They've been very good to me, very kind. They paid for me to take English classes."

"I was wondering, your English is excellent," Gloria said.

"Thank you, lots of classes, and the kids help. The family I work for encourages me to speak Spanish to their kids to help them learn. And, if my kids aren't in school for some reason, and I can't find somebody to watch them, they allow me to bring them with me. I get there early, before their kids wake up, see them off to school, then clean until early afternoon. I'm usually back by the time my kids get home."

"So you're gone before your kids wake up?"

"Fernando takes care of them weekday mornings, he works nights, it works out."

"It must be hard, not seeing your kids in the morning."

"It is, but they are fed, clothed, and able to get an education. They are all citizens, born here. They have the opportunity to be whatever they want."

"They seem like great kids, happy and playful."

"I do not think they suffer, one of us is usually around. Fernando and I, we may suffer a bit, but any parent must go through some suffering for the betterment of their children."

"Yeah, I'm just starting to realize the sacrifices parents are forced to make."

"Your parents?"

"Yes, they were both these amazing, freaky, researcher types, who gave up what they loved to have a family."

"I doubt they would look at it like that, giving up. They chose to have a family because there is so much love shared, hard times too, but unsurpassed love."

"Yeah, well, my mom didn't give it up forever, she went back to work, and it ended up killing her."

"I'm sorry, Gloria. You are far too young to have lost your mother."

"I never really had her. She was always consumed with her work. I understand it now more than I did. The crazy thing is, I know she felt she sacrificed so much, but I feel like my whole childhood was sacrificed. Family is nothing but sacrifice."

"Sometimes I feel like I'm here first to shepherd them as best and safely as I can into the next part of their life, here for them only, you know." Constantine said. "But I know they could do it without me if they had to. I do believe parents are instrumental in their children's future, and all the ways their influences play out unfold over a lifetime. Mostly, we do the best we can, and usually we have our reasons. Sometimes the farther we are removed from our family, the more they make sense," Constantine said reassuringly.

"Yes, I understand my mom had very good reasons for being gone, I don't fault her, it just has an impact, you know, like you're not wanted. I know she loved me, and my dad was great, very supportive, always there, but I always felt something was missing."

"Maybe what's missing has nothing to do with your mother? Because parents and family are such a huge part of childhood we tend to think everything we feel is somehow related to them. I'm sure it hurt when your mom wasn't around, but she's not the source of all your hurt."

"No, there's plenty of hurt to go around," Gloria said lightly.

"Let me tell you something m'ija, it is usually those who feel deeply at a young age who end up doing great things in the world. Because those unsettled from the beginning work until the end to find peace. They also tend to have great compassion, and an understanding of others suffering that cannot be taught. I know you have sorrow, that's why my kids are not afraid of you, and you were immediately welcome in our home. And I'm sure your sorrow feels like a great burden, being all you know, but it will serve you well if you find a way to be free within it. You're young, you will rise above it, and a life full of determined trying will be a tremendous one indeed." Gloria looked at her slightly skeptically, but appreciative of the faith. Constantine continued. "I do not know why you have left your home, but I do not see a damaged, hopeless person. I see a strong, powerful young woman waiting to be an instrumental part of the world. Whatever has come before, it will hinder you in moments, but you have the ability to overcome. It is ability I see most when I look at you Gloria, and that is a quality that can take you anywhere you want to go."

"Thank you Constantine," Gloria said shyly, leaving her head down.

"Now get some rest, m'ija. I left some pillows and blankets on the floor in the kid's room, or you can sleep on the couch if you like?"

"I'll sleep with the kids."

"See you in the morning." Constantine stood and motioned for Gloria to rise. She embraced the modest teenager. "Sweet dreams, m'ija," she said.

"Thank you, you too," Gloria replied.

The kids stirred shortly after dawn, joining Gloria on the floor. They didn't play for long before Constantine came to the door. "Breakfast niños, we must leave early for church today, we are dropping Gloria off at the train station," she said.

"No," the kids groaned in unison.

"I know you want her to stay, but she has things she must do," their mother replied.

They grudgingly walked into the kitchen. There was just cereal for breakfast this morning. Constantine explained. "After church we have a nice big brunch at the restaurant where Fernando works, it's a special treat," she said.

"Sounds nice," Gloria replied.

"Eat a little now; I've packed you some food for the road."

"Tamales?" Gloria asked hopefully.

"Tamales," Constantine said enthusiastically. "And a few other things. If the train breaks down you'll have plenty of food."

"Thanks, Constantine."

"You're welcome. Niños, hurry up, it's time to get dressed for church," Constantine implored the still sleepy children.

During the brief conversation, Constantine had braided two long braids in her youngest girl's hair. She wrapped each braid into a bun on each side of Carmen's head and bobby pinned them into tight balls. Constantine worked on Maria's hair as the girl finished her breakfast, expertly weaving the hair then swooping it into a bun. They all finished breakfast, and Evelyn helped the little ones get dressed as Constantine gave her oldest the same hair style as the other girls.

Jose wore a sharp little navy suit and red tie with soccer balls on it. The three girls wore beautiful thick white dresses covered with colorful embroidery of flowers and birds. The kids waited quietly in the living room as Gloria gathered her things, including the rather large sack of food Constantine prepared for her. Their mother readied herself in her room. Gloria joined the three waiting kids in the living room. Evelyn hugged her and the others followed, all finding a part of her to cling onto.

221

"I'm going to miss you all. I've had so much fun playing with all of you," Gloria said, lovingly.

"We're going to miss you, too," Evelyn replied, sadly.

Constantine came into the room wearing a smart light cream pant suit with a lavender blouse, smelling of roses. "You look pretty mama," Maria said.

"Thank you, sweetie."

They all headed to the car. Gloria was struck by the sadness welling up inside her. It had only been thirty-six hours, but she had grown very attached to the loving family. The car ride was quiet, silent preparation for the goodbye. After twenty minutes they pulled up to the same train station Gloria had arrived at not long ago. They parked, then Constantine and the kids accompanied Gloria to the ticket counter. They waited patiently as she selected a route and purchased a ticket.

"Do you have to wait long?" Constantine asked.

"No, only an hour," Gloria replied.

"Good."

The kids ran up to hug Gloria, followed by Constantine. "You take care, m'ija. If you need anything, you call. I put our phone number and address in with the food," Constantine said.

"Thank you," Gloria said tenderly. Constantine wiped away tears as they broke the embrace. "You've been so kind," Gloria said. "I will never forget you."

"I know you won't, we won't forget you either."

With that the kids gave their last hugs goodbye, and then they were gone, Gloria was alone again.

Chapter 18

Gloria felt odd as a genuine paid passenger. She belonged in the nice cushioned seat by the window just as the other riders belonged. The sparsely occupied train was comfortably efficient, a trim padded seat, an armrest and some foot room, the quintessential people mover. She sat facing north, next to a window at her left. She didn't dare lose sight of her pack, she laid it on the floor below her and propped her feet on it.

She had bought a book and a map at the gift shop at the train station. She was extremely curious to view a more accurate representation of the United States geography. She spent the first couple of hours of the train ride gazing at the ocean and studying the map of the country. Not surprisingly, there was no mention of Larkspur anywhere. She was surprised that the map did mention a top-secret sixty square mile portion of the desert, Area 51. Although in Arizona, the area seemed relatively close to her surmised location in New Mexico. The disclosure indicated the government's propensity to have top secret locations. The information struck her as both honest, more than the leaders of Larkspur would admit as they were happy to not exist to the outside world, and absurd, a secret everyone willingly chooses to accept. All in all, the map held little new information. The transportation infrastructure was far more extensive than she had imagined, but the maps she had access to in Larkspur were more or less accurate, only edited for sensitive information. She dozed off looking out over the glistening water, under a pure, cloudless, powder blue sky.

The train slowed to a stop, gently stirring Gloria from a deep sleep. She relaxed, steeped in the warm sunshine pouring through the window. The signs indicated they were in Santa Barbara, she was half way. Few passengers disembarked and even fewer boarded. The ones who did board seemed very young, not much older than her. They too, these young travelers, had hiking packs on their backs. A young woman sat in the row in front of her, looking at the same stunning ocean view. The train started again on its way, the motion quickly put Gloria back to sleep.

"Hey, hey," she heard a voice saying softly. Gloria felt the light touch of fingertips on her arm; she woke to the sun shone silhouette of a young woman turned around looking over her from the seat in front of her. "You're talking and twitching all over the place," the girl said.

"Oh, sorry," Gloria replied, sitting up in her seat.

"Sorry to wake you, but you seemed very agitated, not the ideal conditions for sleeping," the girl said.

"No, I don't suppose so," Gloria replied.

"There was some explosion, in your dream, you cried out and kept jolting."

"Sorry."

"No, it's okay, I mean, I'm sorry, it seems very traumatic," the girl said.

"No, I'm okay really, it's just a dream."

The girl climbed off her seat, grabbed her pack and joined Gloria sitting in the seat next to her. "Do you mind?" the girl asked.

"No, go ahead."

"Where you headed?"

"Danville."

"Me too," the girl said cheerfully. "My family owns a ranch up there, horses, cows the whole bit. I'm on spring break from the UC; I'm a freshman, a political science major."

"What does a political science major study?" Gloria asked.

"Oh, I don't know, different governments and policies. I just declared so I haven't taken too many classes. To be honest, I don't really like school that much."

"Me either."

"I like politics though. What about you, do you like politics?"

"I guess you could say that."

They sat quietly for a moment settling into their new proximity. "What happened anyway? I mean the explosion, it seemed pretty real," the girl asked. The blood drained from Gloria's face, she looked away turning towards the window. The girl raised her hand and put it on top of Gloria's. "I'm sorry, I didn't mean to make you uncomfortable. You don't have to talk about it. I just thought, I don't know what I thought...sometimes it's nice to have someone to talk to," she said.

"Yeah," Gloria managed to say softly.

"My name is Nancy by the way," the girl said, extending her hand.

"Gloria."

"Pleased to meet you Gloria. Firm grip, I like that, means you're forthright."

"Not so far."

"Even forthright people have things they don't want to share."

Gloria turned and took a good look at Nancy for the first time. She had light brown, long, wavy hair, dark olive skin, striking green eyes and a beautiful smile.

"How old are you anyway?" Nancy asked.

"Fifteen."

"You seem a lot older, a lot different from the college kids I hang out with."

"How old are you?" Gloria asked, feeling more anxious about the girl as the conversation progressed.

"Eighteen."

"Where's your ranch?" Gloria asked, gathering information.

"It's out Red Fox Road. Where are you going to be?"

Gloria reached into the side pocket of her pack and pulled out the envelope Bugsy had given her. "1187 Maple Road."

"Oh yeah, that's just down the road from me. You should come over; I'll show you the place."

"I will."

"Good," the girl smiled. "Are you on spring break too?"

"No, I'm going to live with a friend."

"Do you go to school?"

"Not really."

"What do you do?"

"I'm a painter."

"Oh, a painter, that's cool. My mom's pretty into painting, I mean, it's more of a hobby she took up in the past couple of years, but she loves it. She converted an old rundown barn into a studio. You can meet her."

"Yeah, okay." Gloria said shyly.

"I mean, if you want," Nancy said backing off a little at Gloria's hesitation.

"I mean, I haven't even met the guy I'm going to stay with. I have no idea what it's going to be like."

"What's his name?"

"John Finch."

"Oh, I know John, he's a sweetheart, he's been a friend of the family for years. He makes really good wine. He's great. You'll have a good time there, but watch out, he's going to put you to work."

"I don't mind work," Gloria said. "I just hope to feel welcome."

"Oh, don't worry, he's very kind. I'll have my parents invite the two of you over for dinner tomorrow, it'll be great."

"Sounds good."

"How long are you staying with John?"

"I'm not quite sure, probably a while."

"What about your parents?"

"My mom's dead."

"Oh, I'm sorry."

Gloria was surprised when she felt the tears well up in her eyes. She was even more surprised when they tumbled down her cheeks.

"I'm so sorry," Nancy said tenderly as she reached over to wipe a tear away.

Gloria turned toward the window and cried silently for a couple of minutes. She composed herself, cleaned herself up, and returned to the conversation. "I lived in a really small town," Gloria began. "I wanted to leave basically since I was born. After my mom died, and my best friend Bugsy died, the one who told me about John, my dad knew I wanted to go, we said our goodbyes, and I left."

"Wow, that's really brave."

"Brave or stupid," Gloria said, managing a laugh between sniffles.

"Sometimes they're one and the same, but bravery usually takes commitment, time will tell."

They sat for several moments in silence watching the small flower filled rolling hills go by. Gloria was shocked by her confession. She had not planned on telling anyone anything about her life, let alone the second safe person she had a conversation with. She felt totally open and vulnerable, a feeling she was unaccustomed to. She was surprised, but comfortable, Nancy's kindness was so disarming her fears melted away. She didn't want to berate herself too much over the experience, but she had better tighten the reins if she wanted to stay anonymous. After a few minutes Nancy broke the trance of the passing landscape. "I'm sorry, Gloria, that I pried into your personal life like that," she said.

"No, it's okay. I guess I needed to talk about it. I could have deflected the question, but the emotions must have been lying close to the surface looking for a time to come out, and this was the time."

"Well I appreciate you being so open with me. It's a great gift to share true sorrow."

"I must've known you'd think so."

"You must have. I'm going to go back to my seat now; I'm a little tired myself," Nancy said.

"Okay," Gloria replied.

Gloria stared blankly out the window for a few minutes then brought out a book to read. Gloria could scarcely concentrate on the story between the peeks at the countryside, the anticipation of arriving at her destination, and the sound of the soft whirring of Nancy's breath passing through her pursed lips. She could see Nancy's slight forearm and tender wrist through the space between the seats. She had to stop herself from peeking over the top of the seat to make sure the girl wasn't sleeping awkwardly. A strange feeling arose inside of her, she hoped they would become friends, she had never had a friend her own age before, it might be nice, she thought. It bothered her some that Nancy would be heading back to school so soon, but a week of friendship was better than nothing. And now she actually knew someone, knew someone in the real world she might get along with.

Gloria hoped the slowing and lurching of the train would wake her new friend, a little company with Constantine and the kids, and now Nancy, made her realize how nice it was to have people to share with. There were a couple short stops when she thought Nancy might rouse, but she stayed soundly asleep.

The sun hung low in the sky as the train ride neared its completion. The terrain was mostly farmland now. There was an occasional field of cows, but mostly agriculture: artichokes, strawberries, and vineyards. Nancy still slept, a couple of hours had passed since their conversation, and she had hardly stirred. The large red setting sun glowed over the ocean as the train sped forward. It seemed like an eternity since Gloria had left Larkspur, but here she was, a week and a half later, moments from her new home, watching the sun set over the ocean for the very first time. The soft golden reflection off the ripples in the water reminded her of the glistening mountaintops of the desert. The few small high clouds picked up the vibrant reds, and casted a soft orange glow through the air. She leaned back, head tilted to the side resting comfortably, utterly satisfied with this exact moment in time.

"Beautiful isn't it?" Nancy said peaking at Gloria from between the seats.

A slightly startled Gloria responded. "Yes, very."

"That's the main reason I chose UC Santa Barbara, to be by the ocean. I almost went to Santa Cruz, but that was a little too close to home."

"How far is the ranch from the ocean?" Gloria asked.

"Thirty, forty miles. We never really go out there much, my parents are ranch folks, not beach bums, there's a big difference."

"You want to come back and sit here?" Gloria asked sweetly.

"Sure," Nancy replied. The girl eagerly skipped around the end of the aisle and plopped down next to Gloria.

Gloria touched an indentation on the side of Nancy's head. "You have a mark from sleeping."

"Oh, probably from my jacket. I curled it up to use as a pillow," the girl said, turning slightly red on the apple of her high cheekbone. "I was pretty tired."

Gloria was comforted by Nancy's slight embarrassment; she wasn't the only one who was shy. "Yeah, you didn't even wake up when we stopped."

"How many times did we stop?"

"Twice."

"We're next, we're almost there. Say goodbye to the ocean, we're about to head inland. The train lets off about twenty-five miles from where we live. Do you have a ride?"

"No, John doesn't even know I'm coming."

Nancy looked over at her surprised. "Oh, well, don't worry about it, we'll give you a ride," she said.

"That'd be nice."

The train made a large arcing turn to the right and pressed forward into the sparse, dry flatland. Nancy returned to her seat as the train began to slow, gathering up her things. The last pale light of the gloaming lingered on the horizon as the train's wheels stopped churning. "I see my parents already," Nancy said as she leaned sideways to get a better view out the window.

"Where are they?" Gloria asked, joining her in the lean.

"In the jeans, my dad's got a brown cowboy hat."

"They're cute, waiting for you."

"Yeah," Nancy said slightly embarrassed again, "I'm the baby."

The doors opened, they stepped onto the platform. Nancy's parents approached her, arms wide open. Her father gave her a big bear hug, lifting her off her feet. The large man, around six feet five, two hundred and fifty pounds, swung her around like a rag doll. Her mother attacked her with kisses as soon as her father relinquished her, planting them all over Nancy's head and face. She then gave her daughter a long tender hug. The two were nearly identical in height and physique, five seven, maybe five eight, broad shoulders, narrow hips. Nancy, bright red at this point, turned to introduce her parents to Gloria. "This is my friend Gloria, I met her on the train. She is staying at Finch's place for awhile."

"Hi there, Gloria," Nancy's mom said holding out her hand. "I'm Beth."

"Tom," Nancy's dad said, also shaking her hand.

"I brought the truck," Nancy's dad said as they approached the parking lot. "probably too tight to squeeze the four of us in the cab, you two won't mind riding in the back I hope?"

"That'll be fine dad," Nancy assured her father.

They hopped in the old brown and white Ford pickup. Gloria and Nancy laid their packs in the bed of the truck, leaning their backs against the cab, staring out toward the road behind them. They were knee to knee, occasionally knocking into each other during the bumpy ride. Nancy put on a sweater, warding off the night chill of the breezy open air ride. She noticed the goose bumps on Gloria's arms, still dressed only in her jeans and the light embroidered shirt that Constantine had given her. "You're cold, do you have something warmer to put on?" Nancy questioned.

"I'm okay," Gloria assured.

"Don't be silly," Nancy said as she reached into her pack pulling out a faded navy zip up hooded sweatshirt. "Wear this."

Gloria put on the hoodie and relaxed back into her spot. She hadn't imagined being attached to anyone, especially so quickly. So when they arrived at John's, and her heart dropped as she jumped out of the back of the truck, she took a millisecond to notice, but tucked the feeling away deep in the folds of all feelings impractical. The cheerful, reunited family waved as Gloria walked away. "See you tomorrow night," Nancy called.

Gloria nodded as she backed away, then turned to approach the house she had worked so hard to arrive at. She walked towards the house with thoughts full of the last few hours, the horrible nightmare which started it all; funny how sometimes moments of terror lead to times of splendor. She had dreamed of that moment often, the startling explosion, and the internal upheaval which followed. This was the first time she felt okay about it, like she was subconsciously processing emotions that she should carry into her waking life. If persuaded, as she was today with Nancy, she could delve into the lingering tragedies within her. The release felt nice, the crying, she wasn't even that embarrassed, she felt lighter. She walked up to the door feeling calm and confident; things might work out after all, she thought.

She pressed the small, round, glowing button of the doorbell; beautiful melodic chimes alerted the inhabitants to her presence. It wasn't too late, eight, maybe nine. There was the flickering of candlelight towards the back of the house, other than that the house was dark. The home was a simple one level ranch house, not so different from her house in Larkspur, except the walls were made of logs. She waited a couple of minutes after the chimes died down, hearing nothing, she walked along the side of the house. She came upon a large back deck with a big brick fireplace built into the outer edge. The fire was blazing and crackling away, that must've been the flickering light she saw, she thought, the inside the house was completely dark. There were a few old tree stumps surrounding the fireplace, she took a seat warming herself, then pulling out the letter Bugsy had left for John.

She reached out her hands, rubbing them together near the flames, soothing the chill that had seeped in during the truck ride. She felt the soft sweatshirt Nancy had let her borrow. She had not given the cold another thought after the sweet smell of the sweatshirt surrounded her until now, the warm fire made her realize her body's distance from comfort. She put her boots up on the brick ledge in front of the fire and let the heat seep into her toes. Better and better she thought, this day keeps getting better and better.

"What are you doing here young lady?" she heard a deep voiced man say, making her jump.

Surprisingly, she hadn't heard him approach at all, engrossed in the enchantment of fond memories. "Hi," she said, standing, placing her hand on her chest to both comfort herself and appear non-threatening. "I'm a friend of Bugsy."

"I don't know any Bugsy," the man said.

"Sorry, Charlie, Charlie Lisack."

He put the quarter rounds of wood he was carrying by the fire, and reached out his hand. "Welcome, sorry if I startled you," he said. "I don't get too many visitors out here. I'm John Finch."

"Gloria," she said, shaking his hand firmly.

"Nice to meet you, Gloria. How is Charlie, he's got to be getting up there by now?"

"He passed away recently, I'm sorry," Gloria said tenderly.

"He'd done his time."

"Yeah, he was ready."

They both paused for a moment, outwardly unsentimental, but the loss of a loved one, no matter how merciful, was never simple. "He wrote you a letter," Gloria said after a few moments.

John grabbed it and opened it eagerly. He took a stump by the fire and read. Legs spread, elbows on knees, he held the letter in both hands close up to his face. He sighed deeply a couple of times as he read, a tear came to his eye, he quickly wiped the tear away as it fell. "He was a very kind man," John said as he finished the letter. "It seems he loved you very much."

"We were very close."

"I'm sorry for your loss. He says here your mother recently died."

"Yes."

"I'm sorry. You are welcome to stay here as long as you like," John said.

229

"Thank you, I appreciate that."

John stared intently at the letter, then crumpled it up and threw it in the fire. She looked at him surprised. "He asked me to," was all he said. They sat in silence, both remembering the past.

"You know, I only knew Charlie for a few years before he left," John said finally.

"I didn't know that, there was so little time, we didn't get into all of it."

"He was the best friend I ever had," John said.

"He named you as one of the few friends he ever had."

"He says the same of you."

"Imagine that, Charlie's only two remaining friends here together by the fire. We are so connected, people, so much more than we ever know," he said.

Gloria smiled, made herself comfortable, I'm going to like it here, she thought. They spent another hour together sitting by the fire, getting used to being in each other's company. Gloria occasionally looked into the night. Comforted by the presence of her constellation companions, relieved to see many more stars out in the relatively rural farm land, she felt at peace.

"We better get in," John said eventually. "You're probably tired after your trip."

She grabbed her pack and followed him inside. He flipped on the lights exposing elements much like the outdoors, wooden beams and stones. There were many windows, plants, and natural materials throughout the home. "This place is beautiful," Gloria said.

"Thanks, I built it myself. Every bit of stone comes from the property. The wood and the beams are reclaimed from old local cabins and farm houses. You'd be surprised how much good material is out there unused or unwanted."

"I really love it," she said. She looked around at the warm tones and the deep rich grained wood. There was a circular stone fireplace in the middle of a large room which comprised the kitchen and living space.

"I like open spaces," he said. "I wasn't interested in too many walls. I wanted to feel like you were still outside, but protected from the elements. There are a couple small bedrooms over here, one bathroom; I never saw the need for more. I don't have any children or anything, never married. There are also a couple different workers' cabins I built on the property out by the vineyards; you may want to stay there. Let's get you situated here tonight and we'll see how things work out."

"Sounds good to me," Gloria said.

They continued to the front of the house and walked down a small hallway. There was a door on either side of the hall leading to each bedroom, and a bathroom at the end of the hallway. John opened the door into the bedroom on the left. Gloria noticed a bank of windows on each corner wall, and a large bed with white sheets and a fluffy white down comforter on a dark wood rectangular platform. Against the wall at the front of the bed was a dresser. There was a long mirrored closet on the wall to the right, and a simple night stand with a wooden lamp and small shade by the bed. "I made the furniture myself, even the lamp. I got a shop outback. It's simple, but it will do," John said.

"Thank you, I think it will work out just fine." Gloria said as she opened the closet and threw in her pack.

"I'm going to head back out to the fire and let you get situated. I'm not much of a sleeper, so at night that's usually where you can find me."

"Thank you, I appreciate you letting me stay here."

"Don't think anything of it, you are more than welcome. Goodnight, sweet dreams."

"Goodnight."

Gloria, overjoyed at the thought of a sound night's sleep in an actual bed, went into the bathroom to brush her teeth before curling up. She saw the beautiful porcelain claw foot tub and couldn't resist the allure of soaking in warm water, deciding to prolong her anticipation over climbing into the cozy bed a little longer. She turned on the tap allowing the water to warm as she brushed her teeth. She got into the tub as the bath continued to fill, adjusting the temperature to just the right state of soothing heat. The tub adequately full, she leaned back and felt downright joyful at her good fortune. First the lady in the bar, then Constantine and her family, Nancy, now John, people had been wonderful thus far. But it was Nancy and their dream like time on the train her mind kept returning to. A friend, she thought, an actual girlfriend my age, it opened up a world of possibilities to explore. She lay comfortably relaxed, soaking in the tub for twenty minutes. She grew tired, picked herself up, and headed off to bed in her new home in a new land.

The next morning she woke early and met John in the kitchen. "Morning Gloria," he said as she appeared.

"Morning, John."

"Sleep okay?"

"Great, thank you."

"I'm heading out in a few minutes if you want to grab a quick bite and come along? I'll show you around the land."

"I have this food from a friend," Gloria said, holding up the sack Constantine prepared for her. "I'll throw it in the fridge, grab one of these bananas if you don't mind, and I'm ready to go."

"Take anything you want, you don't have to ask. We grow most everything in the kitchen out here on the farm."

"Self sustainable, I like that."

He smiled. "Me too."

They rode around the farm in a small open-air dune buggy. "A solar/electric combination, I made it myself," John explained. "I'm still installing solar panels around the place. I hate relying on the grid if you know what I mean."

Gloria was starting to get the idea. He showed her the fields of various produce, the orchards bearing all kinds of fruit, and the vineyards. The ranch was large, over two-hundred acres. John said he bought the land in the early sixties after Charlie moved away, dirt cheap he said, only a couple other family farms around at the time. He had dug several large wells that were able to meet all the farms water needs the first couple of decades. As the farm grew, he created sophisticated water entrapments and cisterns to reclaim rainwater.

"How did you learn how to do all this?" Gloria asked

"Oh mostly just getting my hands dirty trying things out, tweaking things as I went along. I spent some time in France on a farm when I was younger. Wonderful old farmer taught me a few things," he said.

They drove up to the workers' cabins and got out. There were three, sixty foot by forty foot long, cabins with front and back decking, outdoor fireplaces, and several picnic tables surrounding them.

"I built these with some of my first workers back in the seventies when we really started growing. One is for families, one is for women, one is for men. Couples can live together in the family cabin if there's room, if not, separate cabins, that's the rule. Mostly illegals here, a few wayward college-age kids, but most everyone is Mexican or Central American. They get a good wage and can eat any of the food off the land. Believe it or not, a bus comes out here and picks the kids up for school. I have great loyal workers, I'm lucky, it's back breaking work tending the land, you have to be dedicated and strong," John explained.

"I expect to do my part," Gloria said.

"I expect you to as well. I'll give you the same starting wage as everybody else, raises based on time worked, if you can't hold your weight in the field we'll find something else for you to do. If you like, I thought you could stay in the house with me for awhile. I wouldn't mind the company to be honest, but if you'd feel more comfortable you are welcome to live in the women's cabin."

"I feel very comfortable in your house. Let's see how it goes though, I don't want to alienate myself from everyone by living apart from them."

"Oh, I don't think they'll mind. I've never seen an ounce of jealousy out of any of my workers, only kindness and respect. But if you begin to see it as a problem, by all means come stay in the cabin."

"We'll see how it goes. I couldn't get a good feeling for how many people worked here when we drove by."

"Nearly a hundred."

"You must be proud."

"I'm honored really, to help people live decent lives, feed people, work the land, it's a great life."

They ate lunch out in the fields with the workers. At midday all the workers came together under a large open air wooden structure shading several long wooden tables. They grilled up carne asada and boiled pork. It was as if every afternoon they held a small outdoor party. John, the workers said in their Latin accents, making the J silent and emphasizing the last syllable, who's she, they asked. Gloria introduced herself, shaking hands, immediately trying to create an independent identity away from John. Her name with a G, another letter that got the silent treatment, was quickly supplanted with a nickname, "la nina bonita." The beautiful girl.

After lunch they drove over to the stables. John explained. "Horses for transportation and because I love them, chickens for eggs, cows for milk, goats for milk and grazing. We don't slaughter animals, I get way too attached. The workers buy their meat in town. I'm not a big meat eater, I don't make a big deal out of it, if the occasion calls for it, I'll partake."

"I'm the same way," Gloria said.

They both heard the sound of a horse galloping up behind them at the same time, and turned to see the bouncing brown locks of Nancy approaching in the distance. "Oh, here's the Clintock's youngest, Nancy," John said.

"We met yesterday on the train," Gloria told John as Nancy arrived.

"Hey you two," Nancy said cheerfully. "My parents want me to invite you both over for dinner tonight."

"That sounds good," John said. "That all right with you Gloria?"

"Yeah, that'd be great," she said, trying not to sound too eager.

"Great. Also, Gloria," Nancy said making eye contact with her, "I was wondering what you were doing for the rest of the afternoon, if you might want to go on a ride with me?"

Gloria looked over at John. "Don't look at me, you're not on the clock yet," he said.

"Uh," she stammered, "I don't know how to ride a horse."

"Oh, don't worry about that," John said. "I'll let you take old Betsy, she's as sweet as pie, she'll keep you safe."

"All right, I'll give it a try."

"Yee haw," Nancy hollered with a country twang. "let's get that girl on a horse."

John led them to the stable to meet Betsy. He began to talk with the old horse as if she were a child, introducing her to Gloria, explaining the details of the day. He showed Gloria how to put on the saddle, how to mount, and how to use the reigns. "You'll be fine," he said. Nancy and John must have seen the fear on her face because they both reassured her she'd be okay several more times before she mounted the horse. Betsy was a small, coarse, grey and white mare. Late in years, she was docile and accommodating. "Sweet old girl," John kept calling her. "Not much to look at now, but in her day she had those stallions jumping fences to be with her. Finally had to separate them entirely, wouldn't leave her alone," John said.

"So, she's not going to run off with me?" Gloria asked.

"At this point, you could probably outrun her," John replied. "Go on, hop up there."

Gloria mounted the horse tentatively, checking her balance as the saddle shifted. Nancy made a clicking sound prompting the horses to start moving. Gloria hunched into the horse, wide eyed. Nancy and John laughed. "I'll go ahead and meet you two later for dinner," John said with a smirk on his face.

"Okay," Nancy called back. Gloria sat, eyes facing forward, too nervous to reply.

They slowly made their way along a fence at the perimeter of John's land. They didn't say much, primarily just Nancy checking to see if Gloria was okay. Nancy would look back to find Gloria white knuckled, hanging on for dear life. Gloria wasn't exactly sure why being on a horse scared her so much. She certainly respected their power and independent minds. She wasn't used to having another animal play a role in her fate, apparently it was a little upsetting. "How you and Betsy doing?" Nancy asked.

"So far so good," Gloria managed.

"Want to go a little faster?"

"I don't think so."

Nancy chuckled. "Just messing with you. You're doing well. We'll go as fast as you feel comfortable," she said reassuringly.

"I feel comfortable on my own two feet," Gloria quipped.

"I grew up with horses, I feel as comfortable on the back of a horse as anywhere else, give it time.'

"I'll try. Where are we going anyway, how long are you going to make me ride this thing?"

"Be nice, you'll hurt Betsy's feelings."

"Sorry old Betsy," Gloria said as she patted the horse gently on her neck.

"We're going to my favorite spot as a kid. At the bottom of the hill there's a creek that's swollen at this time of year, thought we'd go swimming."

Gloria gulped, realizing she hadn't worn her shorts under her jeans because they were so dirty, and because of her travels she hadn't worn underwear for days. "I don't have a suit," Gloria said.

"I don't either, it's okay, it's totally secluded."

Except for you, Gloria thought.

They had to maneuver down an uneven narrow path to get to the bed of the creek. Gloria was scared, then petrified, as Betsy seemed to wobble and lose her balance. "Ah, I don't know if she can do it," Gloria called out.

"She's just being careful. She's slowed down a little in her old age."

"Seems to have lost some of her vision and balance as well."

"She's fine, so mistrusting, Gloria, only perfection for you."

Gloria recoiled a little bit. She didn't think she was being overly harsh on the horse, just cautious, concerned there might be a mishap. She was not the type to perceive something and not speak up. Gloria expected to tumble at any moment, a few slips, a little wavering, but they made it to the shores edge.

Now what, Gloria thought. She had grown quite warm riding under the unadulterated California sun, but swimming naked in front of someone else, she wasn't so sure. Nancy, however, had no reservations. She hopped down from the horse, stripped to the buff, climbed a ridge, unhooked a rope from a tree, swung out over the creek and dropped in the water. Her dramatic entrance was followed by a large splash springing from the surface.

Gloria, still sitting on the horse, mouth wide open, could hardly believe her eyes. Nancy stayed underwater for a while. Gloria could see her silhouette through the translucent surface, gliding her way confidently from point to point. For the first time since she climbed aboard Betsy she had no desire to get off her, the thought of joining Nancy in the water was far more terrifying. Nancy eventually surfaced near the water's edge, supporting herself on her hands in the shallow water, head up, laying on her belly, her white bottom glowing through the water. "You don't feel like going swimming?" she said to Gloria.

"Not really," Gloria replied.

"The water is great, clear and fresh, not that cold."

"I'm still thinking about it."

"All right. You're missing out though, the rope swing is great, my older siblings put it in before I was born. I have five brothers and sisters. I've been coming here since I was a baby; pardon my indiscretion if it has made you uncomfortable."

"Ah, well you know," Gloria said, shyly. "I've always been a little shy about my body."

"That's all right, I understand, people are used to being covered, it can be disconcerting. Would you feel more comfortable swimming in your underwear?" Nancy asked.

Gloria turned bright red, entirely perceptible even from Nancy's compromised vantage point. "I don't have any on. I mean I have a bra on, but I've been traveling, so you know," she said, mortified.

"Don't worry about it. At least come down here and stick your feet in."

Gloria obliged, awkwardly dismounting the horse. Betsy gave a grateful whinny. Gloria took off her boots, rolled up her pant legs and waded into the creek. She could clearly see the outline of Nancy's slender body beneath the surface. She looked away, looked at anything other than the naked girl wading so comfortably in the water. Gloria spent a few awkward minutes with her feet in the water then sat down on the shore. Nancy swam a little longer, taking water in her mouth, squirting it about, frolicking and playing like a child. Gloria put her head down as Nancy exited the water and walked past her. Nancy climbed onto a smooth large stone. "I'm going to sit here and dry off a little and then we can go," Nancy called.

"Okay," Gloria said without lifting her head. They remained there quietly, soaking up the sun, mind adrift in the leisurely landscape of the rippling water. Gloria forgot a moment about the naked girl basking behind her. She reflected on all she'd been through the past week and a half. She was just beginning to feel truly calm after the travails of the trip. She knew this was in part because she was already so consumed with her present life, worried about what Nancy thought of her, and life at John's. She had come through the harrowing transition, and now the slow painful progression of entering a life away from Larkspur was free to occur.

The travel had been difficult, unexpectedly risky when the soldiers appeared, but she did it. A small smile came over her face, she was proud of herself, she had found out more about what she was made of, and she liked it. All fighters are one punch away from being knocked out, when it comes, it is always a surprise, but a true fighter takes the opponent's best shot, gets through it and keeps going. She wasn't sure what would take her down, but she knew she took a pretty good shot and persevered. The gut check had shown plenty of fortitude, and until one is faced with terrifying peril, one never really knows how they will respond. So far so good, she thought.

"What are you grinning about over there?" Nancy asked, noticing the silent musings.

Gloria turned unafraid. Nancy, knees bent, resting back on her hands was still seated on the rock, her skin already tinting a deeper bronze. "Just thinking," Gloria said.

"I do wonder what goes on in that head of yours."

Gloria's smile grew, happy Nancy was acknowledging a similar curiosity about her. "Just thinking about my trip, there were some wild moments," she said.

"Naked pool parties I'm sure," Nancy joked.

"Not wild like that, just some interesting people, some interesting events."

"You'll have to tell me all about it," Nancy said as she got up and walked towards Gloria to retrieve her clothes. Gloria looked at Nancy for a moment then turned away. "You sure are shy," Nancy said. "It's all right, it's sweet."

Gloria waited until Nancy was clothed before heading over to Betsy. The two horses had been chomping on some reeds near the shore after taking a few sips of water from the creek. "Nelson," Nancy called.

"Come here Betsy," Gloria called, following suit.

"I'm not sure Betsy will make it up this hill with you on her back. Hop on with me, we'll lead her out," Nancy said.

"No way, your horse is huge," Gloria quickly replied. It was true, Nelson was nearly twice the size of old Betsy, a big strong stallion.

"Come on, we'll both fit. Nothing's going to happen."

Gloria thought for a moment, not really wanting to get on the horse, but it did seem rather practical. "All right," she said.

"That's the spirit. Shy, scared…things of the past."

Gloria smiled as she nervously approached Nelson. "I'm not really afraid of much, you'd be surprised," she said.

"I'm sure," Nancy said as she helped Gloria get her foot in the stirrup and propelled her up to the saddle. "Okay, scoot up, I'm going to squeeze in behind you and reach around you to hold the reins." Gloria hadn't realized exactly what riding together would entail, her throat tightened, nervous about the contact. Nancy hopped up easily. They were snug, the two of them sharing the saddle. Nancy wrapped her arms loosely around Gloria and grabbed the reins. She made a sound to get the horses moving forward to make the slow trot up the narrow pathway.

"Not too bad, Nelson is a sweetheart," Nancy said.

Gloria looked down at the rocky ground a good five feet below. "it's all right," she said. Truth was she did feel safe, Nelson seemed strong and confident, and having Nancy support her eased her mind. Gloria noticed Betsy stumble and struggle, she was glad she decided to ride with Nancy. She had thought about walking, but it seemed rude, or at the very least exceptionally wimpy. They traversed the path in a few minutes, and waited for Betsy who lagged behind.

"She looks beat," Gloria said.

"She does. Tough day for the old gal," Nancy replied.

"I would feel bad climbing on her back and getting a ride."

"Don't sweat it, stay here, Nelson and I don't mind."

"You sure?"

"Yeah. This is how we used to ride with my parents all the time, we're used to it."

"All right," Gloria said, as they slowly carried on.

Gloria grew more relaxed on the horse, loosening her stiff and rigid body. Nancy in turn loosened her grip on the reins, letting her forearms rest gently on Gloria's thighs. "I feel very lucky I got to grow up here," Nancy began. "So many kids never get to experience animals, or the land, or even hardly see their parents. I got to see both my parents all the time, play outside, explore, you know, be a part of nature."

"Yeah, I grew up sort of the same way, except the parents part, my mom worked a lot," Gloria said.

"And then she died," Nancy said plainly, but with a clear invitation for Gloria to broach the difficult subject if desired.

"Then she died," Gloria repeated plainly.

"Must be tough."

"Yeah, I'm tough, you have no idea," Gloria said, trying to lighten the mood.

"I can tell you're tough, but you're guarded, why, I don't know."

"I probably don't know all the reasons either. I've been on guard ever since I can remember, can't seem to get past it."

"We'll work on it," Nancy said flatly.

They rode for a few minutes in silence, jerked about by the movements of the horse, but mostly rounding comfortably into each other. Gloria was surprised at how easily she had grown accustomed to having Nancy pressed up against her. She tended to keep her personal space private, with the exception of her dad's frequent hugs, but now she felt the power of changing environments and letting herself be more open to new experiences. "Maybe I'll swim next time. I don't know why I made it such a big deal. I mean, I swim naked alone," Gloria said.

"No, it's okay, we'll bring some shorts or something, it doesn't matter."

"We'll see, I mean, I just left my home, traveled thousands of miles alone, you'd think a little skinny dip in a creek would be no big deal."

"It's a big deal until it's not. See how you feel."

Gloria was quiet for a moment. "Thanks for understanding, and not making me feel silly," she said, finally.

"Hey, everybody has their own relationship with their body for their own very personal reasons. I want you to feel comfortable. I don't want you to feel bad just because I'm little miss free as a bee. Don't let me warp you, not everyone swims naked, do what you want."

"I will."

"Good. Now hold on, I'm going to set Nelson free a little bit."

Gloria felt Nancy tighten her thighs, tighten up the reins, and give the horse a little kick. They bolted forward; not exactly a sprint, but a good trot. Gloria let out a frightened yell and held the knob of the saddle tightly. They were jostled and knocked about, but Nancy had a good hold on her, and she never seemed off balance. The run was brief, only a hundred yards or so, but Gloria's heart was beating fast as she felt simultaneously afraid and exhilarated.

"You okay?" Nancy said as she slowed Nelson down and turned back to rejoin Betsy who had continued her slow trot.

"Yeah. You could've warned me."

"The anticipation is worse, just do it, and then you know it can be done, you don't have to worry about it. That's what my parents did with us."

"Trial by fire."

"I hope it wasn't that bad, I was pretty easy on you."

"No it wasn't that bad, pretty amazing actually, all the power."

"All right," Nancy said joyously, "afraid, but willing to face her fears."

"Not all at once," Gloria warned. "That was quite enough for today."

"All right," Nancy laughed, momentarily feigning disappointment. "We're almost to my house anyway."

They took the horses to the barn by the house. Nelson and Betsy were each given their own stall, equipped with oats, hay, water, and a couple of carrots Nancy gave them as an extra treat.

"This place was built in the sixties," Nancy said as they approached the home. "Good old solid construction, not that imaginative, but it's functional. And the two different sections of the house," she pointed to the two identical peaks at either side of the house, "kept the eight of us sane. My parents and the youngest two kids, including me, kept to the left, the older hell raisers were on the right. There are two stories, and there's a hallway in the middle of the second floor connecting the two sides. It's that way on the first floor too. The house is kind of like a horseshoe, with plants and a seating area in the middle outside, like a hacienda or something."

"That seems pretty imaginative to me, I've never seen a building like that," Gloria said.

"Yeah, it's about being able to support a lot of people and still have some semblance of privacy." They entered a door on the right side of the house. "Now that everyone is gone I stay on this side of the house," Nancy explained. "There are two bedrooms down here, a bathroom, and a little game room or whatever." They ascended a staircase to the second floor. "There are two more bedrooms up here, a bathroom, and a really cool deck."

"The house is huge."

"Yeah, lots of space out here. My parents always wanted a lot of kids, so when it came time to build the house, they went for it."

Nancy opened a door on the right side of the hallway. "This is the room I stay in when I'm here. Check this out," she said, as she opened the French doors that led onto a large deck. "Faces east, the sunrises are amazing, and it stays pretty cool out here in the summer." They stared out over the horizon lined with rolling foothills dotted with bushes and trees. "We should probably get ready for dinner." Nancy said. "You're pretty dirty, not swimming and all, you can shower if you want? It looked like you didn't have very many clothes with you," Nancy continued, as she opened the door to her closet. She pulled some items onto the bed. "These are things I left behind when I went away to school. Good clothes for the ranch but not necessarily college. You can borrow them if you want, I mean while you're around, I don't mind."

Gloria looked at Nancy, nice, giving, and totally unpretentious. She felt comfortable accepting her offer. "Yeah sure, thanks," she said.

"Great. Let me show you the bathroom." Nancy opened another door in the room. "This goes straight through to the bathroom. That door there," she said pointing to a door directly across on the other side of the bathroom, "goes to the other bedroom. There's everything you need, shampoo, conditioner, soap, here's a towel, enjoy."

"Thank you."

Gloria pulled off her dirty jeans and cowboy shirt the woman at the bar gave her. Dirt and grime had formed a ring around her neck and encrusted her nostrils. She happily got into the sparkling white shower, again overjoyed at the opportunity to bathe.

Clean and refreshed she came out of the bathroom wrapped in a towel, expecting to find Nancy there, but the bedroom was empty. After not hearing anything for a few moments, she began sorting through the clothes Nancy had left on the bed. There were a couple pairs of jeans and a light tan sturdy pair of cotton pants, not too unlike the ones she left behind at the bar. These will work nicely, she thought. She grabbed a navy button-up shirt, and pulled on the pants.

Nancy came in as she was finishing buttoning her shirt. "Oh great, everything fits nicely. I was going to leave some underwear for you, but I thought that would be a bit too much," Nancy said.

"This is fine, thanks," Gloria said, becoming more familiar with Nancy's playful ways.

"I just told my parents we were here. They said to come down whenever we're ready. I'm going to rinse off and get changed; you can hang here if you want."

"Okay," Gloria said.

Nancy entered the bathroom. Gloria heard the shower begin to run. She looked around the room a little, there wasn't much, simple floral wallpaper, a ruffle and lace bed. Gloria smoothed the bedspread and felt the softness. There was a nightstand with a picture on it. The picture was a group of six, the siblings she presumed, kneeling on each other's back, forming a pyramid, four girls, two boys. Nancy looked young, eleven or twelve, innocent and sweet, Gloria thought. Gloria headed out to the deck to get some fresh air, taking a seat on an old faded wooden bench. She took in the sweet evening air, closing her eyes, listening to the unfamiliar sounds, different birds, different bugs, she recognized a few, crickets mostly, but everything else was entirely new.

Nancy peered around the corner of the door. "Ready," she said.

"Oh, you're done. I didn't hear you. Yeah, I'm hungry."

"Great."

They went downstairs and joined Nancy's parents on the patio between the two wings of the house. "Hello again, Gloria," Nancy's mom said.

"Hello, Mrs. Clintock," Gloria replied.

"Beth, I prefer to be called Beth."

"Okay, Beth."

"We're eating outside if you don't mind," Nancy's dad said from behind a large propane grill.

"Sounds good to me," Gloria replied.

John strolled out onto the patio. "There he is. Let me get you a beer," Nancy's dad said as he left the grill. Tom walked over to John, gave him a pat on the back, and shook his hand. "How ya' doing Ace?"

"Ace. Why do they call you that?" Gloria asked.

"They don't," John said.

"Aw, he's just being modest; this man's a legend in the army," Nancy's dad said. John put his head down and squirmed, noticeably uncomfortable. "He doesn't like to talk about it," Tom continued. "He was a great soldier. I served in the same platoon just a few months after he left, thank God the war was already over. I heard some stories, a fine soldier this here Ace. Lived here for twenty years before I found out he was in the army, took another five to get him to talk about it at all. He'll never tell you himself, but he's a hero."

Gloria looked over at John who shook his head slightly. "I'll take that beer now," he said. The two men turned and walked into the house. Tom put his hand on John's back. John turned to him, smiled, and shook his head shyly.

"It's funny," Beth began, "my husband tries to deal with his time in the army by talking about it, bringing it up you know, and he hated every moment. Ace deals with it by never saying a word. Sometimes I wish my husband would shut up and John might share some of his feelings. Seems he's been traumatized into silence. I think that's what Tom's doing in his own misguided, sweet way, giving John a chance to open up. But a man like that has carried the burden of silence so long he can't find his way out."

Sounds like Bugsy, Gloria thought, before adding, "sometimes it's best to leave a man's story unspoken, to die when he dies."

"Sometimes those are the stories that need to be told the most," Beth replied.

"Mom," Nancy said interrupting the conversation. "Gloria is a painter. I told her you might show her your studio."

"Sure, Gloria honey. I'm really not very good, but I'd love to talk with a real painter."

"That'd be great," Gloria said.

"How old did you say you were?" Beth asked.

"I'm fifteen."

"You seem so much older."

"Come on, let me show you around the yard a little bit," Nancy said to Gloria.

"Okay."

"Don't go too far, dinner is in fifteen," Nancy's mom said.

"Okay mom," Nancy called as they walked away.

"Sorry about that," Nancy said to Gloria when they were out of earshot from her parents.

"Oh no, it's fine."

"They're goons."

"They're nice. I'd rather hear exactly what someone thinks than nothing at all."

"Well you've come to the right place, not a lot of holding back here."

"Good."

"I'm not sure if John is so comfortable."

"I had a friend like that, burdened by his secrets."

"Aren't we all," Nancy said.

"I guess we are," Gloria replied.

"Let's not have any secrets," Nancy said. "I mean the past, that's one thing, share what you want, but from this moment forward, no secrets."

"My life is pretty complicated," Gloria said.

"I don't think keeping secrets makes it any less complicated."

"Depends on the secret."

"Don't you have some say in what secrets you choose to keep?" Nancy wondered.

"Sometimes the past shapes our future more than we care to admit."

"All right, Gloria. I'm just letting you know you can trust me. You don't have to keep everything inside. I will listen, and will never betray you."

"That type of trust takes a lifetime to build."

"Or it's there, intrinsically, between two people from the get-go."

"We'll see." Gloria said.

"We will," Nancy replied confidently. "Come on, let's eat," she said.

Dinner was great, quite jovial with the talkative group. There were kebabs, both with meat and without, warm bread, salad, a spinach and tomato quiche, and fresh baked Marionberry pie. The earlier slightly awkward exchange between Tom and

241

John did not accurately reflect the deep profound respect and love they seemed to have for each other. The table was full of the warm enjoyment and the ease of people who have known each other for a long time and revel in each other's company.

The adults eventually got a little tipsy and loud. At one point Beth laughed so hard at her husband's antics, beer came out of her nose; an extremely pleasant occurrence for everyone at the table, with the possible exception of Beth, although even she didn't really seem to mind. The evening wound down, the plates were cleared, they gathered by the fire.

"What's with the outdoor fireplaces?" Gloria asked when they were settled.

"It's a California thing. The weather's nice year-round so we spend a lot of nights outside," Nancy said.

"Also," Beth interjected, drunkenly sticking her pointer finger in the air, "most places just dig a hole in the ground, call it a fire pit, and they're on their way. But, because it seldom rains here, there's a fire hazard three hundred and sixty-five days a year, so we need proper chimneys for the sparks," she said proudly.

"Thank you for clarifying, mom," Nancy said sarcastically.

"You're welcome," Beth said, somewhat triumphantly, not catching Nancy's sarcasm.

Gloria yawned quietly, turning her head in an attempt to go unnoticed. Nancy stood up. "We're going to go." Nancy declared. "Mom, if you don't mind I want to show Gloria the studio?"

"That's fine honey."

"It's okay," Gloria said, "we can stay."

"Oh, believe me, we aren't being rude." Nancy said. "They'll be out here for hours, partying all night, and still up at the crack of dawn. I don't know how they do it."

"Jeesh, you'd think we were the ones in college and her the adult," Nancy's dad said.

"You guys, once you hit your fifties became some freaky sleepless monsters," Nancy replied.

"Fifties, that was a long time ago, I can't remember my fifties," Tom said, laughing.

"My point exactly," Nancy said with amusement.

"All right, you girls have a good time," Beth said. They began to walk away, Beth called after them. "Oh honey, if Gloria wants to stay the night that's fine."

"I have Betsy," Gloria said.

"I can take Betsy," John said.

"We'll see," Nancy said.

"We will," Gloria said quietly, turning to Nancy.

Nancy smiled. "See you guys in the morning," she called to her parents.

"Goodnight," the group called in staggered intervals.

The pair walked west on a dirt road leading away from the house. The night had grown cool, not cold, only a forgettable brisk chill cool enough to remind the girls of life outside their head, if only for a moment. The short night stroll did well to calm Gloria's nerves after the evening of activity. Since she had left Larkspur the world seemed to be moving at a break neck pace. These short quiet moments helped her to recount some of what she had experienced, a fleeting attempt to catch up to a life so far out in front of her she could not possibly know yet what it all meant. She liked that Nancy didn't feel the need to talk all the time, that there was room for quiet contemplation alongside companionship.

As they approached Beth's studio the old barn seemed spooky to Gloria, darkened and isolated, it had the air of an abandoned ship in plain sight. The loud creaking of the wide split door as they opened it did nothing to assuage Gloria's haunted thoughts. "It's not as creepy as it seems," Nancy said, sensing Gloria's apprehension. "I keep telling my mom she should get a light for out here, a motion sensor or something, but she won't hear anything of it. She likes the idea of the barn dead to the night, a black space for her to bring her energy to. I say, man it's only a light, you know, so other people are more comfortable. She says, exactly, like she's long since done compromising for other people. Post traumatic child-rearing syndrome, I suppose."

Gloria laughed a little, thankful for Nancy's little rant, the mood noticeably lighter as they entered the dark space. The barn smelled strongly of hay, and slightly musty with the dampness and the dust that accompanies old structures, and then another barely perceptible smell lingered through the more dominant ones which caught Gloria's attention. A smell possibly only perceived by a painter accustomed to the tools of the trade, the bitter, pungent, resin smell of Gloria's past, her favorite medium to paint with, the smell of freshly painted oils.

Nancy flicked on a lamp; a soft golden glow illuminated a portion of the room, leaving the remainder to the shadows. "My mom paints during the day." Nancy explained. "She only likes soft, non-intrusive light at night, preferably from the fire or candles. This probably wasn't the best time to bring you out here, you won't be able to see much."

"It's okay," Gloria said, touching Nancy's arm reassuringly. "Show me where she paints."

"Up here," Nancy said, leading Gloria to a plain exposed wooden staircase against the wall. They entered the second floor loft space where a glowing wall of windows appeared. Moonlight poured into the upper level, casting a blue glow over the room. Hidden from the floor below, the windows changed the entire feel of the space. Gloria, now entirely comfortable, spoke confidently. "I can see why she paints here."

"The only change she made to the original building was these windows on the north side, and a fireplace, and electricity of course. No water though, she carries that in from the well."

"When the moon's full I bet you can paint by moonlight. I used to do that back home, paint under the open stars."

243

"You can do that here," Nancy said as she struck a match to light a candle. Nancy lit a series of candles which gave Gloria a better look at the room. The barn was not large, maybe twenty five feet by thirty five feet, but the high ceiling made the interior seem expansive. The northern wall of windows spanned the entire thirty five foot length of the barn, and appeared around fifteen feet high. The west wall of the loft was comprised entirely of a large stone fireplace, surrounded on either side by large stacks of wood. In the center of the loft was a very large easel. A palette lay on a large wooden table adjacent to the easel. There were a couple small wooden chairs surrounding the easel, and several blank canvases resting against the railing which overlooked the bottom level of the barn. Nancy opened the built in drawer below the table. "Her paints," she said, exposing the many misshapen tubes of color. "She wanted a room big enough for her easel. The barn seemed like a logical choice."

"It's perfect," Gloria said. "Almost as nice as being outside."

"Do you do all of your painting outside?"

"So far. But I never had an indoor space as nice as this."

"I'm sure my mom would be happy to have you around, you could show her a few things."

"Maybe, we'll see, I'm going to be working for John, I probably won't have a whole lot of time to paint."

"Maybe my mom will show you around the place a little more tomorrow and you can talk about it then. When it's light you'll get a better sense of the place."

"That'd be nice. There's this piece I want to do for the family I stayed with in San Diego, maybe tomorrow…"

"Yeah," Nancy said, yawning. "Now I think I need to go to bed."

They blew out the candles, closed the old, lonely, rickety barn door and headed back to the house. The girls were exhausted after the long day. The time approached midnight as they entered the side of the house to return to Nancy's room. Nancy lent Gloria shorts and a t-shirt to sleep in, which Gloria changed into while Nancy brushed her teeth. Nancy opened the bathroom door and motioned for Gloria to follow her through the bathroom into the spare bedroom. Nancy turned down the bed for Gloria. "There are a couple of books on the nightstand if you like to read before bed," Nancy offered.

"Thanks, I'm probably too tired to read tonight."

"I know, I'm beat, must have been the horses," Nancy said coyly, recalling the earlier terror of Gloria's day.

"Yeah, yeah," Gloria said, smiling and tilting her head back.

"Oh, there are glasses for water by the sink in the bathroom, and you can use my toothbrush if you want."

"Thanks."

"Goodnight," Nancy said, practically waving as she backed out of the bathroom.

"Goodnight," Gloria said, with a slight wave in return. Gloria waited a few moments for Nancy to get situated in the other room before going into the bathroom. She filled up a glass of water, brushed her teeth with her finger, too shy to share Nancy's toothbrush, and went to sleep.

The pink glow of the rising sun softly tinted the room through the fine lace curtains covering the windows. Gloria had slept impatiently, ready for the next day to begin. Despite her exhaustion, the temptations of her new life left her eager with anticipation over the direction of upcoming events. So, when the light peered through the window, she could no longer spend another minute in bed. She threw off the covers, hastily made the bed, and quietly went to use the restroom. Hopeful she could catch the rest of the sunrise, she opened the French doors out onto the shared deck. To her surprise, Nancy was already seated on the deck cozily wrapped in a blanket. "Oh, good morning," Gloria said.

"Oh, hey, I thought you'd be sleeping awhile longer," Nancy gently replied.

"I thought the same about you."

"Nah, didn't sleep so well last night."

"Me neither," Gloria said wistfully.

"Plus, I love the sunrise, besides my family, I thinks it's what I miss most."

Gloria stood there, skinny boned, in her T-shirt and shorts not really sure what to say next. Goose bumps forming, oblivious to the cold, she looked around for a seat. The chairs were all covered with a light film of dew from the cold morning air. "Here, sit with me. I covered the bench with a towel," Nancy said, lifting the blanket to make room for Gloria on the bench. Gloria sat down next to Nancy. "Get in, you'll freeze," Nancy said, as she wrapped Gloria in the blanket.

Gloria felt the warmth from Nancy's body left on the blanket. She cozied her bare feet, burrowing them into a warm spot. "Thank you," she said. The two girls sat in silence wrapped together in the warm blanket under a pale pink sky ringing in the glory of a new day.

After a few minutes Nancy began to sniff the open air. "Mmm, I smell breakfast. See, I told you, late to bed, early to rise, they're freaks," Nancy said, standing to go inside. Gloria, sad to have the vapor lock of warmth broken, waited a few seconds before moving. "Are you not hungry?" Nancy asked.

"No, I am. Just enjoying the last moments of the sunrise."

"Oh," Nancy said excitedly, jumping back into the warmth of the blanket, wrapping her arm around the seated Gloria, giving her a squeeze, then curling herself up in a ball snuggling into the blanket. "I've acted too hastily," she said.

Gloria looked sideways at the giddy girl and shook her head. "I take it you're a morning person," Gloria said flatly.

"Can't help it," Nancy said cheerily, "grew up on a farm, day starts when light appears."

"Okay," Gloria said a few moments later as the pale blue light finally took hold, "now I've had enough."

245

Nancy pulled the blanket off and ran into the bedroom, Gloria followed. Nancy pulled on jeans and a hoodie, Gloria did the same, and they headed downstairs.

"Hello girls," Tom said kindly as they entered the kitchen. Nancy ran up behind her dad and leapt a little as she gave the tall man a kiss on the cheek. "Sleep okay?" He asked.

"Couldn't have slept that great if we're down here at the crack of dawn with you," Nancy quipped.

"I slept fine, thank you," Gloria said almost apologetically.

"I thought you missed me so much you couldn't wait to get down here to see me," the big bear of a man said to his daughter.

"Yeah right, dad," she replied, squeezing him around the side.

"I'm finishing up some eggs and potatoes, Gloria, will that be all right?" he asked.

"That would be great."

"I gathered from last night you're not a big meat eater, like John."

"That's right."

"John's got me good and trained, don't you worry. Before I met John I would've looked at you cross eyed if you turned down warm sizzling bacon in the morning, but I get it, I'm not that way, but I get it."

"That's very noble of you dad," Nancy broke in.

"My child, my biggest skeptic," he said, rolling his eyes.

"That's very sweet of you, thank you," Gloria said. Again the sincere turn to Nancy's joviality.

"Sweet as apple pie you are little one," Tom said to Gloria.

"She's not that sweet dad, don't let her fool you," Nancy said playfully.

"Sit down you little busy bee. Always were energetic in the morning. Had to send her to milk the cows first thing just to keep her occupied, she'd drive the other kids nuts otherwise. Not everyone's so spry in the morning, hey Nancy?"

"All right," Nancy said, taking a seat next to Gloria at the table. "Where's mom?"

"She headed out to her studio. Said she awoke in a moment of inspiration. She said you girls should head over there after breakfast if you like."

"Dad, hurry up already, I'm starving."

"Sheesh, I do recall you wolfing down a big dinner last night. What are you eating for two these days?"

"Dad," Nancy said, turning bright red.

Gloria laughed at the embarrassed come down of her higher than life friend, and the freedom with which her dad commented on her sex life.

"I always told my girls, do what you want, because we all know guys only want one thing, just use a rubber."

"Dad," Nancy yelled again.

The large man wearing oven mitts and an apron laughed loudly as he shoveled potatoes and eggs onto the plates in front of the girls. Nancy smacked him hard on the butt as he walked away.

"What?" He said innocently. "You're in college now, don't act all naive with me."

"That's none of your business, that's all."

"Oh yeah, my kid getting knocked up is none of my business."

"I'm not getting knocked up. I haven't even had sex," Nancy said shyly.

Gloria felt relieved by this admission. She didn't want to be expected to be experienced.

"I didn't think so," her dad said calmly. "You never were one to go running around with boys, not like your sisters, golly, the gray hairs I got when they became teenagers. But a father never stops worrying."

"Well, you don't have to bring it up like that, when I'm joking around with my friend."

"Sorry if I embarrassed you sweetheart."

"It's okay," Nancy said resigned, clearly long since passed believing she could change her father's behavior.

"I found there is never a better time than the present to talk with your girls about sex, it's always uncomfortable, but always necessary."

"Great advice, I'll remember that when I have kids. Maybe I'll hand my daughter's prom date a condom like you did with Sally."

"Did you really do that?" Gloria said laughing.

"I tried to give it to Sally, she wouldn't take it."

"She was mortified," Nancy said, "her father the pimp."

"Oh come on, it's not like Sally was miss innocent, parents talk, we heard the rumors."

"Oh God, dad, you wish, up and up on all the gossip."

"I'm just saying, you got to be prepared. The parent who thinks by not bringing up sex their kids are less likely to have it is a fool. Bring it out in the open, be frank, that's what I say."

"Dad, please, can we change the subject, I haven't even had breakfast yet."

"Sure, you girls enjoy. I'm going to head out." He paused. "Glad we could have this little chat," he said, smiling.

Nancy rolled her eyes and shooed him away. "Sorry about that," Nancy said to Gloria after her dad had left.

"No, I don't mind. I think he's right, it's important to talk about things."

"So, did your dad talk about it with you?"

"Right before I left, I mean there was no need before that, I was clearly not on that path, but he told me to be careful."

"I know, you have to fend them off, guys are horn dogs."

Gloria looked down. "Well, I don't know about that, but he said to be careful."

"Guys can be really aggressive," Nancy said authoritatively.

247

"I'm not that interested to be honest, I mean, I'm sure I will be one day, but for now there are many things I'd much rather do."

"I understand that," Nancy replied.

They finally noticed their breakfast and began to eat. After breakfast they rinsed their dishes and made their way to Beth's studio.

Beth was heavily engaged in a massive, ten foot by six foot, portrait of a horse when they arrived. "It's Nelson," she said, as they came to the top of the stairs.

"Nice mom," Nancy said with a possible tinge of sarcasm, but Gloria couldn't be sure. Gloria had noticed the slightly combative relationship Nancy seemed to share with her parents, reminding her of her own tough times with her mother, the wasted futility of hostility. Gloria looked at Beth's rendition of the large horse, a luminous figure glowing from a stark, dark background. "I just started," Beth explained. The horse was still in a rough sketch form, with only the warm golden glow of his light brown hair filled in, little detail, little distraction.

"I like it a lot," Gloria said. Nancy, somewhat surprised, looked over at her. Gloria continued. "The colors, they are very loving and positive. The power of the horse and your feelings for him jump from the background. It is a very strong piece."

Beth turned from the painting to look at the two girls, she smiled. "I like you," she said to Gloria. "Why don't you pull up a chair? There's another easel behind the canvases, stay, paint a while."

The soft light pouring through the windows, mixed with the slightly toxic smell of the paint proved an irresistibly alluring combination for Gloria.

"Do you mind?" Gloria asked Nancy.

"No, not at all, my mom will love you forever. I'll go show Nelson how much I adore him by taking him out to roam," Nancy said, chiding her mom again.

"Stay, please. I was hoping to paint you," Gloria appealed.

Beth cheerfully interjected. "What a wonderful idea, but Nancy will have to get that sourpuss look off her face."

"Mom, focus on the horse."

"We'll take Nelson out later. Come, sit," Gloria implored.

"Okay," Nancy agreed.

"I didn't bother starting a fire this morning I was so eager to paint, but now that you girls are here I think it's a must," Beth said excitedly.

"Excellent. Sit by the fire," Gloria said to Nancy.

"All right, but this better not take all day," Nancy warned.

"No problem, a quick portrait," Gloria replied.

Beth had the fire raging in no time, Nancy pulled up a chair. Gloria, hands trembling, visited the inner world of painting for the first time since joining the outside land. The wall of light cascaded down over the quaint scene, giving a sense of subtle importance to the air. Nancy's casual manner and simple jeans and T-shirt seemed to Gloria to perfectly capture the unpretentious nature of her new friend. Gloria sketched the silhouette of the scene, the characteristics of the barn, the windows, the fire. Gloria was so moved by the aura of the surrounding environment, Nancy became but a player in it, not the sole focus, but a part of the whole.

"I might peek over your shoulder," Beth said, as Gloria started to mix her paints.

"Feel free," Gloria said kindly. "I'm not sure if my technique is proper, I have no training, but the accepted techniques are usually people's best guesses at representing some master's particular style. I'm more of a find and enjoy your own style kind of girl. Freedom, fun, and focus, that's why I paint, things that distract me from that, I avoid."

"I'm glad to hear you say that, because I think I worry too much about what other people think," Beth said.

"Some things are best left to a singular vision. There's a time and a place for other people's concerns, the creation of art is not one of them. Conversation and analysis are great, but save that for later, now, do what you like. I mean, really, you're here in this beautiful space removed from everything, let yourself be."

"Heartwarming really, but can we please get on with it, my ass is going numb," Nancy interjected.

"Charming Nancy," her mother replied.

"Just here to please, evidently."

"Well, I'll keep quiet for now, but I can't make any promises. I never get to talk to anyone about painting, this is a real treat for me," Beth said.

"Mom, you're so syrupy sweet you're in danger of sticking, back off, give Gloria some space."

"You mean you want her all to yourself, rather possessive of you."

"Mom, just chill. She's staying, I'm going, you two will have plenty of time together."

"All right, all right, I guess I have been a little overzealous. I'll leave you to paint in peace," Beth said, putting her hand on Gloria's back.

Gloria had been painting, ignoring the banter between mother and daughter. She now found herself rushing through the elements of the background, as beautiful as they were, eager to get to the fine details of Nancy's face. The light from the crackling fire and the flood of light pouring through the windows gave Nancy's features a clear and radiant look. The unpleasantries Nancy shared with her mom did nothing to detract from the peaceful gleam of the twinkle in her eyes. She was more mischievous than angry Gloria thought, pushing her mother's buttons in a somewhat controlling way, but also playful and slightly insecure. The action of a girl with wants half expressed and not totally understood, a perilous quandary when parents were involved.

The pure heart of her new friend was never more evident than now, with her feisty spirit basking under the unadulterated perfect light from the north. The energetic melee of the contentious conversation disappeared, slowly transforming the lingering tension into quiet harmonious focus. Beth worked away on her portrait with no obvious attempt to interfere, as Gloria fully immersed herself into painting.

Gloria rejoiced in the abstract concentrated immersion of transcribing a live scene to a flat canvas. The interplay between environment, subject and painter, created numerous opportunities for emotional translation. Gloria was in a constant state of examination, the intriguing light, the serene setting, and the mysterious girl, played out in front of the watchful eyes of an engaged mother. A peculiar painting scene Gloria was less than accustomed to, it led to some preoccupation, not the unconscious release typical of her time painting. But as emotions calmed, and each woman became more themselves, the painting began to emerge before her.

As the painting took shape, Gloria was surprised by the volatility bursting forth from the tranquil scene. There was a puzzled wandering communication between observer and observed, an unsettled component of mistrust and caution transmitted within magnetic curiosity. The mild spell cast over the room, hindered by triangular conflict and touchy nerves, lasted little more than an hour. That will have to do Gloria thought, looking down at the unsatisfying portrait fraught with inconsistencies and poorly explored subtleties; textures left shallow, colors left hollow, emotions left lingering. "Enough for now," Gloria said, releasing Nancy from her frozen moment of ogle.

"Thank goodness," the reluctant model declared.

"I'm sorry, I couldn't get totally into it," Gloria said, as Nancy came around to view the painting.

"I like it. It's me, but it's not me. It's you wondering who I am," said Nancy.

"It's closer to the person you're going to be than who you are now," Beth said.

"I'm pretty serious," Nancy said.

"No, I think that's me," Gloria replied

"I think it's both of you," said Beth.

"I don't think I was ready to paint you. I mean, I really wanted to, but there are too many unknowns," Gloria said.

"Well you two just met. You'll feel more confident as time goes on, but I think it's a wonderful likeness Gloria. The Nancy of the future as only a truly insightful mind can see her."

"I like it, I like it a lot," Nancy said. "But these fumes are making me dizzy. I think it's time we leave you mom," she declared.

"All right girls. Thanks for stopping by, you two have a good time."

Gloria began disassembling her painting station.

"Don't worry about that honey. I'll clean up, you two go have fun," Beth assured.

"Thanks a lot Mrs. Clintock."

"Beth," Nancy's mom said, again imploring Gloria to call her by her first name.

"Beth. Thanks for letting me come in here and paint."

"Anytime."

"Bye mom," Nancy said, as she began clomping down the stairs.

"Bye," Gloria said, following her.

"Bye," Beth called after them.

The moment they stepped out of the barn into the fresh air Nancy let out a large sigh of relief. "What do you say we pack a lunch and have a picnic by the creek?" she said.

"I like that idea a lot," Gloria replied.

They walked quietly to the house, letting the tension of the morning confinement dissolve. Inside the house Nancy pulled together a simple meal; fruit, nuts, cheese and crackers. They went up to Nancy's bedroom where she gathered towels, T-shirts and shorts for swimming. Nancy threw on a backpack and they were ready to go.

"We can walk, or take Nelson. I'm not sure we have any horses you'd feel comfortable riding by yourself, they're all pretty big."

"Let's take Nelson. He'd probably like the exercise," Gloria said.

"All right," Nancy said excitedly, happy Gloria was willing to get back on the horse.

The ride together was comfortable and uneventful. Gloria, much less petrified than the day before, let her mind wander, taking in the sights and sounds of the surrounding beauty. The landscape wasn't exactly lush, but compared to the desert, there was an abundance of diverse plant life, shrubs, and the occasional tree. Oaks mostly, interspersed among the shallow dips and rises of the slow rolling hills. As they strayed further from the mundane flat farmland, the nooks and crannies with pockets of more luscious habitat revealed themselves. And as they approached the water, the landscape grew greener, taller and more diverse. A jungle oasis far different from the stark reality of everything Gloria had previously known. Nancy clung to Gloria tightly as Nelson navigated the uneven steep terrain leading to the creek. Gloria hardly noticed Nancy was there anymore, she was simply part of the landscape of her new life.

This time, Gloria knew she would swim. They changed from their jeans to shorts, shielding themselves on either side of the horse. Shy, but undeterred, Gloria efficiently exchanged her heavy, dusty clothes for the lightness of the swim attire. They both, Nancy clothed this time, eagerly ran down to the water's edge, ungainly splashing and flopping into the water. They swam, giggled and splashed each other. They launched off the rope swing, attempting more creative aerial acrobatics each time. They lay in the sun, munched on snacks, a perfectly simple, blissful day; idle chatter, playful banter, and lighthearted musings. Gloria allowed herself this respite, this time away from both the loss of Larkspur and the craving for a new society. For a moment, time ceased to exist, with the girls engulfed in a world of humor filled understanding and pleasure. Life the way they would want it, if they didn't spend so much time thinking about it.

They changed back into their ranch clothes as the day wound down, this time out in the open. Gloria had grown more comfortable than a little exposed flesh could undo.

"I should probably check in with John," Gloria said as she finished dressing.

"Yeah, I was thinking that," Nancy said somberly. "I'll take you back."

They situated themselves on Nelson, Gloria in front, Nancy snuggled in behind her. They rode in quiet contemplation, senses stoked, minds ablaze.

Nelson strolled up to John's place as the sun disappeared behind the hills. John was seated by the fire on the back deck. He called to them as they dismounted. "Hey girls, you have fun?"

"Sure did," Nancy replied.

"She taking good care of you?" John asked Gloria.

"She is," Gloria replied.

"Good. You girls hungry? I got lasagna in the oven."

"Thanks, but I should probably get back," Nancy said. "My parents begin to whimper like lonely puppies if I'm gone too long when I come to visit." She cupped her hand to her ear. "I think I can hear the high-pitched whine now," she joked.

John chuckled. Gloria watched as Nancy's tough exterior quickly hardened. Gloria touched Nancy's elbow and said, "I'll see you tomorrow?"

"Yeah. I'll probably hang with my parents some. We'll touch base at some point."

"All right. Thanks for taking me swimming."

"Yeah sure, no problem." Nancy hopped up on Nelson. "Bye John," she yelled. "Bye G," she said, smiling, looking down at Gloria.

"Bye," Gloria said, returning the smile.

Gloria joined John by the fire.

"How you doing Gloria?" he asked politely, an open ended invitation to share.

"I'm okay."

"A lot of upheaval recently," he said more pointedly.

"Yeah, I haven't even begun to catch up with it all."

"I'm not sure we ever give justice to the great times, tragic or momentous, that befall us. We carry on, sometimes heavier, sometimes lighter, but always moving. You're young though, without the responsibility and complexities which come with a long life of speculative decision-making. Take the time if you can, but don't let the past burden you to the point you lose your future."

"Is that what you did?"

"For quite some time, yes. I hid out, removed myself from everything. I was close to never returning. But I learned no matter how hurtful the past is, the only way to free yourself from it, is to one day revisit it, integrate it into who you are now, and love yourself despite it. I don't know if it's reconciling, or accepting, or what? But your past is no reason to hate your future."

"It complicates everything though," Gloria confided.

"It does. But if you allow it, the past can simplify. You're able to know what you stand for, what you want, experiences define us. And to have powerful experiences so young allows you to continue with a stronger sense of self."

"Or a shattered one, like you... like Bugsy."

John folded his hands and looked into his lap.

"I'm sorry, I didn't mean to hurt your feelings," Gloria said comfortingly.

"No, you're right," he said softly. "Charlie suffered, probably his whole life. And I let my sorrow rule my life for far too long. But you know who helped me through, Charlie, and there are people who will help you too. You've found yourself here for a reason. Charlie has helped place you in an environment where you can overcome, but the work is yours. The demons of a haunted past will always come for you, whether or not you fight them is up to you."

"Why does it always have to be a fight?"

"Because life is worth fighting for."

"It would be nice to not have to."

"It would be nice, but that's not your plight. Leave that life to others, that is not your place in the world."

"I don't have a place in this world."

"You must make one. Some are born into it, but they never know what it truly means. Some manipulate their way, but they will never be satisfied. Those who truly earn their way, those are the ones who find true purpose in life, and for them the struggle will have been worth it."

"But you never know when you're in it whether it will be worth it."

"You never know, but you try anyway. The only times in my life which still trouble me are the times I didn't try my best, not my failures, not my faulty judgment, but the times I gave up and accepted the situation before me was greater than I could manage, the times I quit before I had exhausted all options. Only my inaction troubles me, never my action. Everything I did I gave my all, it's what I didn't do I wish I could change."

"I've already done things I regret," Gloria said.

"Because you do not believe in yourself yet. You don't believe it is acceptable to be flawed."

"The same could be said for you. You must believe that what you didn't do was valuable and for good reason."

"Yes, but there is a difference, knowing something is wrong and not acting because you are afraid, and acting, sometimes poorly, despite your fear, they are different."

"Yes, but you can't blame yourself for your fears and hold your adherence to them against yourself."

"We all have fears, judgments that stop us from acting, that's what I'm saying, when I let those get the better of me, that's when I have let myself down. To stumble in the face of fear, is to still be strong, but to have never attempted at all, for that I'm sorry."

"So we should face all our fears? I'm afraid to be bitten by a snake. Should I force myself to keep close proximity with snakes?"

"I'm talking about a collective sense of purpose, a greater sense of good. When others are involved, or principles, things that matter, or should matter to all people, and if they really matter to you, you will act. And for you, this is the time, the time to find out what really matters to you, and if you will act."

Gloria sat looking at the relative stranger somewhat skeptically. "I can see why you and Bugsy are friends," she said "You both believe in life's great potential."

"Despite it all," John said, rising to go into the house. He returned a few minutes later with two heaping plates of steaming lasagna, accompanied by a grand green salad.

"Thank you," she said, taking a plate from him and placing it on the ledge in front of the fire. The night grew dark and the fire crackled loudly as they ate dinner.

"This is really good. I love spinach in my lasagna," Gloria said warmly.

"I try to work spinach into anything I can," John replied.

She was glad they could talk like this, about silly regular stuff after such an intense conversation. The conversation had certainly piqued her curiosity further about John, and in turn, her dear friend Bugsy. She gathered her thoughts as she decided to inquire about the new man in her life after dinner. They both settled in by the fire after the nourishing meal, complete with berries and crème fraîche for dessert. The mood was relaxed and comfortable, Gloria felt respected and welcomed, relieved to be settling in. But there were definitely things she wanted to find out to better fill in the picture of the people around her.

"John," she said with slight trepidation, "I understand if you don't want to talk about it, but what made you run? What made you leave the army?"

He sat up and ran both hands over his short gray hair. "Sometimes with an institution there are such gross injustices one must choose to fight the system, or leave the institution. I believed my only option at the time was to leave. Looking back, I should've fought. I should've fought hard the first time, and every time travesties occurred."

"Do you think it would have made a difference?"

"For some of the people who were harmed, maybe. For my conscience certainly. I did what I could; I was very young, still wet behind the ears. But I would've never wanted to stay in the army. We were at war, I had to go. I believed in why we were there, but what the military power structure allows for people who wish to abuse it; the devastation can become unstoppable. It was clear I would have had to give my life to remain and fight against an unyielding system easily corrupted by scoundrels. Death for a battle I could not win, I chose to leave. The decision nearly killed me. For a decade I was in a stupor, sure I could have done more.

"There are causes I would die for," he continued, "disgusting acts tolerated by fragile, scared men in uniform is not one of them. What happened? An abuse of power silently condoned by those around, until a living breathing monster overtook the soul of a human. A man intoxicated by hatred and entitlement, unchecked by men, like myself, made to feel powerless in an arbitrary ranking system, he became an American-made maniac preying on those he was sent to protect. What happened? No one cared enough to stop it, not even me, not soon enough. I ran scared. I'm

254

ashamed I turned the other way. Because the moment you let injustice go by, it propagates, and then you have become a part of it."

"You're so hard on yourself. I'm sure you did all you could at the time."

"It wasn't enough. I should've spoken out, persuaded the other men to turn against him, they respected me, there was a point they would have listened."

"Sure, one person can stand up against the hierarchy of the military," Gloria said skeptically.

"Before there's one, there is none, and until there's one, there will never be two."

"Mr. Clintock says you're a hero."

"I was a good soldier, I fought hard for this country, I was no hero. We have been so tainted by corruption and incompetence, proper decency is confused as heroism. If more people maintained a sense of decency, true heroes would be uncommon and noticed by all. As a soldier I did what I should, as a person I did not. I'm no hero."

"I'm sorry this has tortured you for so long."

"There are reasons there are things we never forget. I'm always reminded of those reasons, and they make me who I am today, whom I might add, I like quite well. I was a shy, stoic, principled kid, I didn't really enjoy anything. Charlie broke me of that; I enjoy life now, because if he could, anybody can."

"What do you mean, what happened to Bugsy?"

John paused for a moment, undeniably trusting of Gloria, but worried about betraying the honor of his friend. "How much do you know?" he asked.

"Nothing about what happened to him. I know he worked for Maggie Pelt who took him in after some incident, and I've seen the scars..."

"He never discussed the scars with me, but I have my suspicions they are from childhood which he also never discussed. With Charlie it was always what he didn't say that mattered as much as what he did. How he acted, and who he trusted, it spoke volumes. He was a man who had been through things that were written on his face and with the marks left on his body, and you knew he would never treat anyone the way he had been treated, that's strength, strength few people can comprehend."

"And he was alone, fighting alone, virtually his whole life," Gloria said.

"He had Maggie, she helped restore his faith."

"What happened, why did she step in?"

"Because she wasn't willing to turn the other way. Things happened to Charlie that she could not ignore. It's funny who walks into our lives and what brings people together. I'm looking back and there's this chain linking us all, you, me, Charlie, Maggie, and the grotesque events that helped bring us together." He paused and looked for a moment into the sky before he continued. "I'd heard about Charlie long before I met him. I served a decade after Charlie; my commanding officer had been in Charlie's platoon back when they were in basic training. I didn't know all this until much later, some twenty years after they served together, but Charlie and I shared the same foe."

They both sat back for a moment and regrouped. By the intensity in John's voice Gloria wondered if she should be hearing this. She wasn't sure she would be the same afterwards, but knew she needed to know.

John continued. "Sergeant Pierce was his name, a true asshole from day one. There were a lot of assholes in the army, but only a few like Pierce did everything they could to separate themselves from the pack. He wanted to make sure his boys never stepped out of line, and never forgot he was in charge. He would tell the story of what would happen to a soldier if he didn't play the game. Some men didn't believe him, they thought he made it up, or it was something he heard, but I always knew it was true. It was the gleam in his eyes as he told the story that convinced me, he was proud, like a new father, like he had accomplished something great."

"What did he do?"

"It's unspeakable. Charlie would not want you to know. They nearly killed him, body and spirit, but he survived. His body healed, I don't think his mind ever did, yet somehow he carried on, and he was good, a good man to all."

"Did Maggie know this, that the same guy was involved in both your lives?"

"She did, she brought us together, she didn't tell us, but it soon became clear."

"How so?"

"Did Charlie tell you about the hospital, seeing Pierce?"

"No, this is the first I've heard of Pierce. Bugsy told me you came back to face things, you wrote Maggie and she worked it out, she sent Charlie to pick you up, he said you were lifelong friends from then on, that's all I know."

"Pierce was sick, that's why I chose to come back. I went to see him in the hospital, he was forty-five, he looked eighty, cirrhosis, the guy basically drank himself to death. He was this pathetic person, this shriveled up, scared, dying person. He didn't even know what he'd done. He wasn't angry or violent, he was weak and hopeless. All those years he had this power over me, the shame I carried with me, and I saw him, and I realized he was nothing; a sad, lonely person I gave power by giving him importance in my life."

"Did Charlie see him?"

"He did. He was waiting for me in the hall and heard the nurses talking about Pierce. He didn't know who I was seeing; he came in to see if it was really him. You know what Charlie did when he went in there, seeing this man who had tortured him again for first time, a man that he would never be able to forget? He sat down by the bed, he held the man's hand, and he comforted him. He said, 'my name is Charlie Lisack, do you remember me?' The sick man nodded. Charlie said, 'I forgive you.' Pierce cried, Charlie held his hand as he cried. The next day Pierce died. We were all changed forever, everybody in that room, but just two of us got to live on. Charlie and I were bonded forever in that moment in time, actually earlier, but we didn't know it. I realized he was the man I had heard about, everything had come full circle."

256

"Wow, he forgave him, like that, no thought, no apology."

"He was free of it. He didn't need anything from Pierce to make himself feel better; he did the work on his own. To wait for those who harm us to help make us better is futile, to rise above, despite them, that is the real power. And Charlie knew we are all forgiven in death, death is the great equalizer."

"Did you talk about what happened?"

"There was nothing more to say. We became friends, we'd fish, simple stuff, we let go of the past."

"And then Charlie left."

"A few years later. He said he had a great opportunity Maggie set up for him. Her final act of kindness for her dear friend."

"And you never saw or heard from him again?"

"Until now."

"Did you wonder?"

"Of course, I missed him. Our relationship was the most complete of my life, he knew more about me than anyone, more about what I had been through than anyone. But he said he had to go, that's it."

"No questions."

"No questions. He knew I cared, he knew I wanted what was best for him. Some things better left unspoken. He had my support, that's what I could give him."

They were quiet for a few moments, Gloria in a state of astonishment, John in remembrance. She got up, walked over to the seated sullen man. She noticed flecks of red hair interspersed within the gray flickering in the firelight. "Thank you," she said, kissing him on the temple. "Goodnight," she said. He remained seated, quietly staring at the fire.

Once inside she bathed, and calmly reflected. She felt guilty for feeling bad about her life for even a day. She'd been through nothing compared to these men. The loss of her mother and her friend, of course she could mourn that, but she was embarrassed by the self pitying indulgent days of her youth. She felt like a fool. But mostly her heart ached for Bugsy and all he'd been through, a lifetime of torture, no wonder he had been so harsh about life outside of Larkspur. But even he had found a way to love life and people he enjoyed. It was horrible, but not forever, and if he had given up he would have never lived to see the day when he felt peace and happiness. She left the bath, twisted by the terror of the people's lives that she loved, but resigned to the perfunctory necessity of sorrow. Without the hardships those in her life would have never found their way to each other, and life after all is entirely about the people we share it with.

Chapter 19

The rest of the week was a blur. Nancy was around some, but Gloria was untouchable, lost in the realm of the clash between old and new. She was sad to see Nancy go; sure however, they would be in each other's future, but keenly aware there was no room for Nancy in her life for now. Shortly thereafter, John put her to work. She loved working the land, and greatly enjoyed the people she met. Her Spanish improved tremendously.

Occasionally, Gloria would visit Beth and paint. She painted a portrait of Constantine, Fernando and the kids and sent it to them. She painted a portrait of her family from the picture her dad had given her, and hung it in her room. She thought of Larkspur, her mother, and Bugsy, but mostly she grew up, leaving the childhood of her discontent behind.

As the years passed she and John established a quiet respect, seamlessly coming together when appropriate, and still maintaining distance to lead their separate lives, perfect housemates. She never did move into the workers bunks, preferring the privacy and quiet living with John afforded her. As Gloria's eighteenth birthday approached, she felt it was time for a change. She had traded one sheltered town for another, and she knew there was more out there waiting for her, and it was time she went out and found it.

Life had progressively grown less tainted for Gloria. The sting of loss eased as time and experience clouded fading memories of old. Her mind swirled with anticipation and trepidation. Leaving John's was so different from leaving Larkspur, she knew she would be safe, but she would be on her own again, no network, no link to her past.

Christmas was coming, a big deal she had come to learn, her birthday was a few days later, the twenty-eighth, she would leave at the beginning of the new year. The Clintock's were throwing her a birthday/going away party. She had decided to move to the bay area, a college town by the ocean, she thought she'd try Santa Cruz. Gloria hadn't seen Nancy for a couple of years, various travels and exploits had kept Nancy away, but she was expected back for the party. Gloria was looking forward to seeing her friend. There were many people on the farm she enjoyed, but none with the easy casual intimacy she and Nancy had so quickly shared.

Nancy arrived by train on Christmas Eve. For the first time in ten years all Nancy's siblings would be together at her parent's house for Christmas. Gloria had met two of Nancy's sisters over the years. This time, nieces, nephews, the whole caravan would be there. Seeing Nancy in her childhood role should be interesting, Gloria thought.

Gloria came over to the Clintock's the day after Christmas. It was the last day the whole family would be there, and the first day she didn't feel intrusive. The distance between she and Nancy had grown to the point where thoughts of their reuniting left heavy overtones ringing through her head. It was clear Nancy felt rejected by Gloria after being shunned for the remainder of their initial week together. Now they would have a chance to heal those old wounds. Gloria hadn't really worried much about their relationship, always confident it would be repaired, but now with her departure from the ranch, the time was pressing. She was sweating as she knocked on the front door. Gloria found the California weather to be varying degrees of warm, a heat wave had overtaken the last part of December, she wiped her palms on her jeans as the door began to open. A small child, five, maybe six, opened the door. "Hi is Nancy home?" Gloria asked.

"Yes, she's on the patio," the little boy said.

He ran away, leaving the door open. Gloria anxiously stepped through the door making her way to the patio. "Gloria," she heard a voice call. Gloria turned to see Nancy coming out of the bathroom. Gloria nearly gasped at the woman standing before her. Nancy's face had narrowed and elongated, her hair darker, wavier and longer, framed her deep, soulful green eyes. Nancy stood taller and straighter, proud and confident; she approached with the grace and spirit of a tiger. They embraced, cheek to cheek, both smiling with the warm exchange. "I was wondering when you'd show up, my girl of perpetual intrigue," Nancy mused.

"I wanted to catch your family while they were all still here."

"Come on, they're outback, I'll introduce you," Nancy said, leading Gloria out by the hand.

Nancy's family were all very warm, friendly and playful. They ribbed Nancy often, being the youngest and all, but it was obvious they all tremendously cared and looked out for her. Gloria found herself gravitating towards playing with the kids. Nancy joined in, being the favored cool younger aunt, they all had a blast. Any tension left over from their time apart flew away with the playful laughter and interactions with the children. They played tickle monster, running and chasing the half-dozen kids wildly. They wrestled and played chase, the physical activity left the women elated.

The evening calmed, with exhausted kids put to bed and weary adults chatting by the fire. Gloria observed more than participated, enjoying the energy of so much shared history. A polite question was thrown her way now and again, but the time was mostly for teasing and reminiscing, playful laughter with loaded undertones, the language of hurt, love, and loyalty specific to family.

Gloria was surprised by how little a roll Nancy seemed to play in the family, adored from afar, the object of their affection and misguided advice, but no voice, no tenet of action. It was strange to see her boisterous, engaging friend swallowed up by the dynamic she was born into. She and Nancy occasionally shared comforting glances, Nancy worried her family's careless portrayals of her would affect Gloria, Gloria assuring her they would not. Gloria occasionally wondered if Nancy's family had gone too far and Nancy would be hurt, but Nancy seemed to shrug it off convincingly.

The conversation continued well into the night, the group happy to feel the collective emotion of reunited family, and yet, still bracing for the fallout of misperceived intentions and hurt feelings. Gloria laughed and grimaced, longing for her own family at times, and glad to be gone at others. Gloria excused herself near midnight, reflecting about the evening on the long walk home in the warm night air, under the heavy starred sky.

Gloria was soundly sleeping when she was roused by the voices in the hall. She wondered a moment if she was dreaming. She listened closely, John's deep voice, and a soft female voice, curious she thought. There was a knocking at her bedroom door. "Yeah?" she said.

"Gloria, Nancy has come to see you," John said.

It was early, not long after sunrise. Gloria sat up in bed, anxious but not alarmed, she got up and opened the door. There stood John, sleepy eyed after the late-night gathering, cozy in his T-shirt and boxers, and Nancy fully dressed and alert, casual, but full of purpose.

"I thought I would be able to come in and talk to you without waking up John," Nancy said. "Sorry, should have known an ex-soldier is always on alert, even in sleep."

"I am going back to bed," John said, rumbling off.

Gloria opened the door widely to let Nancy in.

"Sorry to wake you, most of my family got up early, I saw them off. Thought I'd come over, we haven't really had a chance to talk, and you're leaving…"

"It's fine, come in," Gloria said, as she climbed back into bed and propped herself up on the pillows. Nancy sat down on the edge of the bed. "Was it nice to see your family?" Gloria asked.

"Yeah, it's intense to be around everybody. I loved seeing my nieces and nephews. But I don't feel like I can totally be myself, they don't take me seriously."

"The baby."

"Yeah, I've changed a lot, there are things they don't know about me, it's hard."

"Like what?"

"Well that's part of the reason I wanted to come over here. There's something I need to tell you."

"All right."

"I mean it's big, it's personal, it's something I'm pretty nervous about, I'm not sure how people are going to take it."

Gloria grew concerned. "What is it, is everything okay?"

"Well, yeah. Well, you know how most people fall in love and get married and everything?"

"Yeah."

"Well I want to do that too...with a woman."

"You're gay."

"Yeah."

"Oh, I was worried there for a moment. Yeah we totally had gay people where I grew up, it's no big deal."

"You mean you're not upset?"

"Why would I be upset?"

"Well, some people don't like gay people."

"Well, I'm not one of those people."

Nancy scooted up on the bed and gave Gloria an exuberant hug. "I was so worried. I thought you might be mad or hurt."

"Don't be silly. Have you told your family?"

"No, I'm going to tell them before I leave, probably after your party."

"I'm sure they'll be fine with it."

"I hope so, I mean, I know they love me, but they don't really know any gay people."

"You're their daughter."

"But parents have some idea about how they want their kid's lives to go, and being gay isn't it."

"Yeah, I don't get that, like there's one prescribed life everyone is supposed to lead, and if they deviate from it all chance at happiness is lost. Don't parents realize being ostracized from your family is the biggest loss?"

"Well, society isn't too keen on gays, lesbians, whatever, parents don't want to see their kids suffer."

"I grew up in a very accepting place, we would never dream of making people feel bad for being gay, that would be cruel. I guess I'm not aware of how this country feels about gay people."

"Well, it's not good."

"Have you told your friends?"

"No, you're the first, except the girl, you know, that I liked."

Gloria felt her face grow warm and she worked hard to ward off the signs of the oncoming blush. "So you like somebody?" she asked.

"Yes, I mean, no. There was this girl, it was nothing, just confirmed what I had suspected, that my attraction to women can be more than friendship."

"I think it's great. Any time two people are lucky enough to love each other it is something to be celebrated. I'm glad you know what you're looking for and in turn feel comfortable enough to express yourself. I'd imagine it's not easy."

"No, it's not easy."

"I'm glad you told me."

"Did you ever wonder?" Nancy asked cautiously.

Gloria thought for a moment. "Not really. I mean when we first met everything was so new to me I had so much going on, it never occurred to me."

"And now?"

"Now I'm happy for you."

"Do you think it's weird, being friends with a gay person?"

"No."

"So you're not going to feel weird or anything?"

"No."

"Good. You think you might want to hang out later, I mean at a more decent hour?"

"Sure."

Nancy leaned over and kissed Gloria on the cheek, then rolled off the bed and left the room. Gloria rolled onto her side and pondered about what had just occurred. She couldn't believe Nancy was so serious about telling her. Gloria laughed to herself as she rolled over and fell back into a deep sleep.

Gloria woke again around nine, the latest she had slept since becoming a worker on the farm. The bright sun burned her eyes as she pulled opened the curtains. She wandered out into the kitchen where John was sipping orange juice reading the paper. "The early morning visitor go?" he asked.

"Yeah, she didn't stay long; she just wanted to tell me something."

"Good news I hope."

"Yeah, good news."

"You two going to hang out later?"

"Yeah."

"You can take the dune buggy if you want."

"Really?" Gloria said excitedly.

"Sure, I won't need it."

John had taught Gloria how to drive the dune buggy and even occasionally let her take the truck into town. She was hesitant at first, not liking the feeling of heavy metal around her moving at unnatural speeds, but he had encouraged her, she grew competent. A day in the dune buggy with Nancy sounded like fun.

She pulled up to Nancy's house, the solar power engine of the buggy humming lightly. She walked through the front door to the back patio where she found Nancy and her parents.

"Nancy was just telling us she's a lesbian," Tom said loudly.

"She was worried we wouldn't love her anymore. Like we didn't already know," Beth said, almost yelling to the approaching Gloria.

"So you told them," Gloria said to Nancy, walking over to her and putting her

262

hand on her back. Nancy looked up at her blankly from the lounge chair, still in shock.

"Oh, you know?" said Beth to Gloria. "You two aren't," she paused, "lovers?"

"No, mom," Nancy yelled out, annoyed.

"Of course not, Gloria hasn't quite come into her sexual awakening."

"Mom!" Nancy yelled horrified.

"What?" Beth said innocently. "I think it would be great."

Nancy stood up and began to walk away. "We're leaving," she stated. Gloria looked at Nancy's parents, shrugged, and followed her out the door.

"We're taking the dune buggy," Gloria said to Nancy, catching up with her. Nancy said nothing, clearly still in a huff not wanting to talk, but obligingly climbed in.

Gloria had done a lot of exploring of the land in her year's there, and decided to take Nancy to a place she had found way out on the other side of the valley. They drove with the warm open air blowing over them and the bright sun pouring down. It was nearly an hour before Nancy appeared to grow less agitated. Gloria watched as Nancy transformed her rigid posture, stretching out her legs, leaning back and finally seeming to enjoy the ride. Gloria reached over and gently squeezed Nancy's knee. Nancy, distractedly, momentarily placed her hand on Gloria's and turned away, again staring at the terrain. Gloria returned her hand to the wheel and continued on the dusty road.

They pulled up to the mostly barren ridge, save for two trees close together located on the top of the rise. Gloria stopped the buggy about twenty feet below. "Come on moper, I want to show you something," she said, nudging Nancy on the shoulder.

Gloria walked up the ridge and proceeded to climb one of the trees. Not high, about five feet from the ground, there was a little nook where three large limbs grew away from the trunk, a perfect place to sit. "Go on, get up there," Gloria said, nodding at the other tree a few feet away to the still silent Nancy. Perched in the protected shady locale, they were able to look miles and miles into the valley. At the very tail end of the valley, there were the perfectly aligned rows of different colored rectangles that made up a town.

"I found this place last year, this is the first time I've been back, seemed lonely all by myself with the second tree and all," Gloria said.

"It's nice," Nancy responded in a low tone.

"I thought of you when I found the place. How fun it would be to bring you here," Gloria said. It was true, Nancy was the only person she imagined doing anything with, if she imagined anyone at all.

"I like it. I've never been out this far before," Nancy said, breaking out of her funk a little.

"Little far for horses."

"Yeah."

"There's no place to swim or anything, but the view's nice."

"Makes the world seem huge."

"The world is huge."

"Right now I feel as if it's all caving in on me," Nancy said.

"I know this is a really big deal for you, but it's going to be okay," Gloria said reassuringly.

"I just don't want people to treat me like I'm different."

"I know, and they might, because to some people you are different. But that's no reason to be afraid. We're all different in our own way, some people just get ganged up on. Try not to let the bullies bother you, but fight when you feel you need to. Know that you are loved, and nothing, certainly not this, is going to change that."

"Do you really feel that way?"

"I do."

"Thank you."

"You don't have to thank me, it's not like I love you for no good reason, pity or obligation or something like that, I think you're extraordinary, I always have."

"It's hard to tell, you're pretty distant, you definitely have your walls."

"Really? I feel like an open book, I feel like my emotions are swirling so forcefully in the air around me it's embarrassing."

"Maybe at first, like a day or two, but overall you're pretty hard to read."

"Really?"

"Yeah."

"You don't understand, Nancy, I mean I haven't been close to hardly anyone, you are my first friend my age, and the first girl I could ever relate to. I feel like I've been very open with you."

"But there's so much you don't say, like you have a whole life you don't talk about, it's intimidating."

"I feel like I'm totally honest."

"You are at the time. You divulge the pertinent information for the moment."

"I told you about my mom, and leaving my family."

"Yeah, when we first met, then it was all business. After that one day you painted me, we had a great day swimming, and then you closed up."

Gloria remembered the conversation she had with John later that night, the one that changed her mind about her own suffering. "I just stopped feeling sorry for myself. I didn't want to talk about that stuff anymore."

"Sorry for yourself? You're nothing but hard on yourself. You never give yourself a break, you expect unyielding perfection."

"It's not like I've been mistreated or abused, some people have real, horrible things happen to them."

"Like their mother being killed in front of them," Nancy said. Gloria looked intensely at Nancy. "That's what happened isn't it?" Nancy asked. Gloria hadn't told anyone the full story. She was surprised to hear it thrown at her without ever divulging the truth. She looked away and said nothing. Nancy continued. "You were a neglected loner whose mom died, then your only friend died, and you left home

264

alone at fifteen. And you never talk about it because you don't want to feel sorry for yourself, that's insane. You can't pretend it never happened, or that it doesn't affect you."

"I'm not pretending."

"You're hiding."

"I'm moving," Gloria yelled exasperated.

"Do you know what you're doing, do you have a plan?"

"Listen, I'm trying. Yes, all those things affect me, and I'm not sure what I'm doing, or where I want to go, but at least I'm not making a big deal out of nothing."

"Like me?" Nancy said, hurt. "You have no idea what it's like Gloria. Wait until you get out into the real world, you'll realize people are cruel, and some will take any chance they get to feel superior. Now, because I'm gay, any yahoo can get their rocks off on me whenever they want, anyone can degrade me anytime they want."

"Why would you let those people affect you?"

"Because I'm not stone like you try to be. I'm flesh and blood, and people thinking badly about me hurts my feelings no matter how wrong I know they are."

"You give people too much power over how you feel."

"You don't give people enough, walking around unaffected, it's alienating."

"I'm not unaffected."

"Could've fooled me. You said I'm making a big deal out of nothing, well you don't make a big deal out of anything. When are you going to start putting yourself out there? I know you have all these really strong feelings, and this wealth of power and strength, but it's like you left it behind on the road somewhere between your hometown and here, and now you're happy to stay here and do nothing."

"I'm leaving."

"You'll leave but you will never really go anywhere because you ignore so many parts of yourself."

"Why are you so mad at me?" Gloria asked.

"Because, I love you, and I see your greatness, but you're too afraid or too hurt to really express it."

"Express what?"

"Exactly. You're not even trying to find out."

"What do you know," Gloria said, angrily jumping down from the tree. She walked down to the buggy, Nancy followed.

They drove the nearly two hours back to the ranch in silence. Gloria pulled up to Nancy's front door, not even bothering to cut off the engine.

"You know," Nancy said after a brief moment, "I didn't mean to hurt your feelings."

"What did you mean to do, enlighten me, help me overcome my problems?"

"Gloria, I'm sorry. I don't know why I got so mad. I don't think you're unmotivated, I think you care very deeply about things, you just…"

"I just what?"

"You just don't know what you want."

"And now that you do everyone else must also. I don't get it, you tell me this big thing that you're really nervous about and all I do is be nice and supportive and you go and yell at me."

"You're right. I don't know what my problem is, I'm just freaking out right now," Nancy said, hoping to calm Gloria down.

"Well I don't appreciate it. You know I'm leaving, I have things going on too."

"I know, I guess it's a hard time for both of us."

"I was really looking forward to you coming back, and now I just want you to go. I don't want to have this stupid party, I just want to leave."

"Don't say that, my parents would be devastated. I'm sorry I hurt your feelings. I don't want to fight anymore."

"I never did want to fight," Gloria said softly.

"I'm sorry," Nancy said. She hopped over the side of the car. "I'll see you tomorrow," she said hopefully.

"Yeah, you'll see me," Gloria said, with more than a hint of irritation.

Gloria spent the next day by herself. She woke up early, strapped on the painting supplies she had purchased in town, and headed into the hills for a hike. She needed the peace and quiet to clear her head. She was distraught over Nancy's harsh questioning of her the day before. Up until yesterday Gloria had been feeling quite good about the direction of her life, after all she was about to be eighteen, most people her age had no idea what they wanted to do, surely Nancy's anger was unjustified. Then again, Gloria wasn't in the habit of being like the other kids her age. Had she stopped pushing herself since leaving Larkspur? What did she want to do? There was always the persistent pressure of her mom's invention, the nagging question she had thus far managed to ignore.

Her options were limited, no Social Security number, no documents of any kind. She was invisible in the eyes of the government, and unsure of herself in her own mind. She had money, almost an embarrassing amount at this point, with what Charlie left her, and three years of continuous labor on the farm. She could support herself without employment for many years if need be. Finding herself and her place in the world was not something she could rush; she had to trust the process. Despite the cage rattling by her friend, she decided to carry on with her plan to move.

She continued on her hike, alone with her thoughts, now realizing she was following the route to the swimming hole. She wondered why Nancy's sexuality had never occurred to her. Why she had never thought about Nancy's sexuality at all? She lived a life so far removed from the social rigors of teenage hood, the hormones, the experimentation; she'd given very little thought to sexuality in general. She realized her own sense of sexual identity was nonexistent, she didn't feel comfortable calling herself a gay, straight, or otherwise. Again, not something she felt she had to rush, but the wheels were set in motion. Yesterday's conversation with Nancy had her head spinning, and there were things she could no longer ignore.

266

Nearly stumbling with her preoccupation, she traversed the narrow, uneven pathway that led to the creek. She set up her easel on the shore, hoping to capture her vantage point from that first day, the first time Nancy brought her to the water. She smiled as she remembered the way Nancy boldly swam, unafraid of anything or anyone.

The party was to start at six, and the creek was a nearly two hour walk from the house. She only had a short window, three, maybe four hours to paint before she had to head back. She thought about putting herself in the painting, which made her recall one of the last conversations she had with her dad, when they talked about why she hadn't painted a self-portrait. She had been worried she wouldn't like the person she was through her critical eyes. She had worried a portrait of herself could never live up to her own standards. She was sorry now she hadn't left him a portrait of her, that she had let her fear of being imperfect prevent her from acting.

She missed her father now most of all, the way he always made her feel better, worthy of love. He always believed in her, he saw her as great even when she was so very far from it, never a doubt. Yesterday's conversation with Nancy placed that troublesome seed of doubt in their relationship, possibly a seed long since planted in Nancy, but not in Gloria. The innocence and adoration was lost, it would either be rebuilt, replaced, or simply a fond memory. Gloria hoped it was not the end between them.

She painted now with an edge. An eerie abstract quality seeped its way into the idyllic scene at the water's edge. Gloria was not one for realism, but her embellishments generally touched on a romantic, fanciful quality, unlike the starkness of today. She brought grays into the water to replace the blues. She dulled the greens, leaving the scene murky and uninviting. She had intended to more closely re-create the wonder of that first day, but she had a bitter taste in her mouth, and a hollow feeling in her gut, and with her paintings she never lied. She finished the painting feeling slightly dulled, glad she had decided to come out and paint, slightly less conflicted, but still agitated. She packed up, careful to tie the canvas by the frame, leaving the still drying oils exposed to the open air.

She arrived at John's, quickly showered, dressed, and headed to the party a few minutes before six. She was running late, but decided against hurrying through the two mile walk, instead choosing to enjoy possibly the last time she would walk the familiar worn route that joined the Clintock's and John's place. She was nervous about seeing Nancy, but the sheer number of guests, the entire staff of the farm, would hopefully deflect any awkward energy between them.

Music blasting, smoke rising, she stepped into the backyard seemingly unnoticed. She looked around for Nancy, but before she had a chance to find her, she was swept off her feet into the air. Two men from the farm, Manny and Juan, lifted her onto their shoulders. "Manny," she screamed, looking down at the smiling, cheering faces of the partygoers. The partygoers immediately burst into a Spanish rendition of happy birthday. Gloria turned bright red, and wriggled, until Manny and Juan finally put her down.

She was greeted with countless hugs and kisses. So began a whirlwind of an evening when Nancy and the troubles of the past were a distant memory, and the intoxicating mix of food, music, and friends transformed her into the smiling playful girl buried deep inside her.

The party was an all night raucous affair, with many revelers wandering home as the sun signaled the oncoming of a new day. Gloria lasted until four in the morning. She had sipped on some tequila, a little, not much, enough for a head change, and an easy entry into the festivities. She'd slipped out quietly, John and the Clintock's talking by the fire, Nancy playing poker with the workers, she wandered home under the sweet, soft moonlight.

Nancy went back to school the next day, something about a big New Year's Eve party. She had stopped by John's to see Gloria for a quick, shy goodbye. John drove Gloria to the coast on New Year's Day. A quiet, solemn drive. They had grown quite fond of each other, John was stoic and calm, but it was clear he would mourn her absence. They hugged, a warm kiss on the cheek, and Gloria couldn't be sure, but she thought she saw him wipe away a tear.

She was renting a furnished room in a house from a middle-aged woman who took in students to supplement the mortgage. It was a nice place, an old Victorian home a half a mile from the water. Gloria settled in and tried to figure out what she wanted to do with her life. She went about trying to engage more in typical American culture.

She realized quickly Santa Cruz was too small, too liberal, and lacked the diversity necessary to truly sink her teeth into the flesh of America. So when Nancy showed up in town that summer and said she was going to graduate school at U.C. Berkeley, was moving to Oakland, and that they had a room open in the big house she was renting with a bunch of her friends, Gloria didn't hesitate to go with her. The move to Oakland, and the reuniting with her friend was just what she needed.

Chapter 20

Gloria immersed herself in the creative and vibrant culture of the Oakland community. Their house, six of them lived there, Nancy, Gloria and four guys: Ronnie, Phil, Lee and Christopher, became hangout central for all sorts of artists, musicians, writers and students.

Oakland was just the city Gloria needed; rich, poor, black, white and everything in between, surrounded by the rich diversity of the greater metropolitan area of San Francisco and Berkeley. There was a street culture, a drug culture, and many more left behind by the country's practices. There were those who strove to rise above, writers, poets, rappers, passionate people of all types, exchanging ideas. It was the country she always thought it would be, complicated, full of struggle and endless potential.

She finally got to see the problems she had always pondered: race, sex and class issues. There were the downtrodden, but more often there were those with undeniable spirit, a will to reach beyond the societal problems that plagued them, and succeed despite it all. She found so much warmth and kindness, not the justifiable skeptical mistrust of people oppressed she may have imagined, but a willingness to talk and share, a desire to reach out and form relationships across boundaries. She made many friends, but it was the poets, writers and rappers she was most intrigued by, the ones combating the malevolence with their words.

Nancy was often busy. She was in the Political Science Ph.D. program at U.C. Berkeley, a commitment that greatly diverged from the underground culture with which Gloria walked. Two of the other housemates were also in Ph.D. programs at the university, Phil in government, and Christopher in physics. Rounding out the roommates was Ronnie, a poet, and Lee, a sax player who played gigs with several bands around town.

Gloria spent most of her time with Ronnie and a loose gang of writers who shared their work at various clubs. Ronnie and the gang often performed on stage at open mic nights. Gloria was in the infancy of her self expression and wanted nothing to do with the stage. She listened, absorbed, drew inspiration, but had much more to take in before she would feel comfortable enough to synthesize and release. Ronnie and his friends were steeped in the culture about which they spoke; she was a recent transplant, naïve to the subtleties and intricacies that shaped directions and actions. She had not experienced so many of the themes they discussed; poverty, racism, low expectations, disrespect, and general disregard. She had faced isolation, neglect, loneliness, and loss. She could empathize with their plight, but it was not her own.

Gloria chose to walk with the empowered, those working for change, into the lands that shaped them, their streets, their homes. At first there was a casual introduction to the group, then as relationships strengthened, she met families and attended gatherings. Ronnie, an Oakland native, had many friends throughout town. A white man, he was part of a diverse group: Blacks, Asians, Latinos, they all found common ground.

Ronnie's best friend, Trey, lived in a rundown part of town with his large extended family. Trey shared a small three-bedroom house with his mom, grandma, auntie, and two young cousins. Warmth and welcoming dominated the overflowing home. Much of Trey's extended family lived on the neighboring blocks, and his house was a constant destination for activity and get-togethers. Gloria and Ronnie could often be found over at Trey's place, barbecuing, playing dominoes, talking about the state of affairs. By night there was no sense of hardship in the small home, yes, they struggled, bills didn't get paid, jobs were lost, healthcare nonexistent, the days were trials, but by night, there was a profound love of life, and a deep unwavering love for those who entered their circle. Violence had touched them all, guns, muggings, robberies. It was a place where one found out quick whose one's friends were because decisions of life and death were made on a regular basis. Trey's circle's loyalty was unyielding; they would die for each other, tried and true.

Gloria was living it, the heady life of strife she had imagined. Her stomach churned with the painful moments of the struggles of the sick and homeless. And her heart soared with the joy when members of her extended community achieved long hoped-for goals, landing a job, college acceptance, critical acclaim, rare and fought for, never taken for granted. It was a life where every achievement was earned, the roadblocks placed before them shattered by perseverance. She saw the ugliness of the human psyche Bugsy had spoken of. The disturbingly pathetic way black people were perceived; thugs, or mercenaries, far from the kind loving people she had come to know. She saw the dangerous blurring of expectation and perception into reality, the psychological pitfalls of constant degradation. She saw the seedy underbelly of societal practices destroy the futures of many, leaving them locked up, desperate, hungry, the antithesis of American ideals. Her eyes wide, her heart open, she barreled into a community full of every complicated human emotion. Every part of the visceral spectrum represented, it was a crash course on an ethnically, racially, economically diverse America, the country she had always dreamed of, the country that would never leave her purposeless again.

Within a few months of being in Oakland she began volunteering on a regular basis. She cooked and served at a homeless shelter, she worked with kids at a Boys and Girls Club, she picked up trash, planted gardens. But most importantly, she talked with the people; she heard their stories, their experiences, what they had been through, and what they would change. For the first time she became political, rallies, protests, smalltime stuff, but the fire was stoked.

The first couple of years in the Oakland house flew by for Gloria, she was in over her head the whole time, and she loved it. She grew more independent in her thoughts and writings, and more connected to her group of friends, who had become family. The thought of the sleepy ranch town where she had first settled, and the counterculture coastal college town she transitioned to, were very far from her mind, passed over and pushed back by the heights of the thriving urban culture in which she was now immersed. So when Nancy asked if she wanted to come along to visit her parents this Christmas she was inclined to say no, addicted to the energy of new experience, but she reconsidered, the time away, and the time to reflect might be needed she thought, her constant fast-paced life in perpetual motion had left many thoughts lingering, she agreed to go. They would take the train, the great reminder of the inception of their relationship, time for them to be still, together, headed in the same direction.

The Clintock's were more than pleased to see their baby girl get off the train, unpretentious smiles, hugs and kisses abound. There they were, the two girls riding in the back of the truck, five years later, not an ounce of insecurity between them. They had seen a few things by now, in life, and of each other. There were the times of excessive intoxication, Nancy's crying drunken stupors, Gloria's heavily stoic withdrawals, petty arguments about cleanliness, parental like concerns over safety. They had watched the other live from near and afar, living within the same walls, seeing the most intimate aspects involved with sharing a home, but an unspoken distance was maintained. They had an undeniable vested interest in each other, but there were parts of each other's life they left alone.

Nancy, the academic, was far more structured than Gloria. Occasionally their lifestyles clashed, unbridled freedom without clear intent against controlled instruction within defined parameters. A degree, a bona fide accomplishment to Nancy, a course strictly for others, to Gloria. Gloria would not have been allowed to enroll in school, lacking documentation, even if she'd wanted, but never enjoying the confinement and prescribed thinking, their different courses had worked to alienate the two friends from each other. Now, as they bounced around in the back of the truck, all that disappeared, they were two girls temporarily away from the cares of the world, smiling broadly with a twinkle in their eyes.

Gloria could not come back to the ranch and not stay with John. She was happy to see he was in good health. They shared a warm embrace, it reminded her very much of the love she felt with her father. Three days, that's as long as Gloria wanted to be away from life in the city, three days of simple, kind love, nature and reflection.

The first night they all had dinner together at the Clintock's. Gone was the tension between child and parent. Nancy was very much her own person, a young woman with her own perspective. They talked politics, about family, school, and the city, they were equals sharing an evening together. The night broke up early, ten-ish, a tame affair.

Gloria and John walked home together under the cool, clear winter night. The evening left a warm sense of belonging in Gloria's chest. She felt her chest open even more as she walked back to the house with the man she respected so.

"It's nice to see you," he said, echoing her thoughts.

"It's nice to see you, too," she replied warmly.

"You seem well, happy, intrigued."

"There is so much, I never knew there was so much, I mean, I thought, but to see it all before my eyes, to feel it myself, I have the full life I always wanted, it is a dream come true… well one of my dreams, the first in a succession."

"You want it all."

"I want everyone to have it all, or at least the opportunity."

"It's hard not to want to help."

"It is."

"What are you going to do?" he asked.

"I don't know yet. I've been writing some, mostly my thoughts, no real form, but that's so removed, I like the collective energy of people, you know, the force of so many people's will united in purpose."

"That's hard to find."

"It is."

"What are you passionate about?"

"Everything really. It's been really hard to see the struggles of the poor, the people in society who are dumped on, mistreated and exploited. But then I'm also really interested in our role, the U.S. I mean, in the international landscape. We seem to be such an egotistical bully. We have an opportunity to help so many, but have too often asked what's in it for us. To lead with the express interest of securing one's fortunes will eventually make us an enemy to all. Our nuclear policies, both for energy production and war are a danger to us all. I'm not proud to be a citizen of the only country to use a nuclear weapon on people, one of the most atrocious acts throughout history as far as I'm concerned. It's hard to reconcile the idea of America, and the actions of America."

"I've struggled with that myself," John said.

"There's so much more we could be doing around the globe, and here at home. I just want people to believe again in the power of their actions, and the role we all play in deciding the fate of this country. The people of this country were handed the power, and we abdicated."

"Lulled into submission is how I like to put it."

"There's all this talk about the American dream, we've lost sight of the American reality. Today, what life is like today, and how we can make it better?"

272

"Our priorities seemed to have been lost along the way," John furthered. "We are placated by our food and material goods. We meet our needs without meeting the needs of others, or asking one simple question, do I really need this?"

"It's a Catch-22 because we are such a great country, with so much opportunity," Gloria began again. "America really is a place where most everyone can achieve their goals. But at what cost? The price some people have to pay is so great. I see kids who get up, make their ailing parents breakfast, go to school, then work, and then do homework. Little kids who care for their families. There are so many poor in such a constant state of struggle; it's the rare few who actually complete their high school degree. The stress, the burden, where's our country then? Why are so many left on their own with the fear of sickness, violence, and starvation?

"Then there are those who never give any of that a second thought, have every possession they ever wanted, doors are opened everywhere, the right family, the right color, the money to pay the price. For them the dream comes easy. We are still very much a country willing to leave people out in the cold, with some who only notice long enough only to make sure they don't muck up their view. I understand these are the actions of humans, and we are all flawed, but where is the push to improve? Where's the voice reminding us of our ideals and how they are within our reach, that we must try, that we must act to combat the ills of complacency?"

"I think the voice is right here," John said. Gloria stopped walking and looked up at him as he continued. "The power to inspire is a rare gift, and only the determined prevail, are you determined?" he asked.

"No one would take what I have to say seriously," she said.

"Have you tried?"

"No, but..."

"Then it is you who does not take yourself seriously. And I'm sorry if that is truly the case that cannot be overcome."

They strolled the last few minutes in silence, then parted warmly as they entered the house. Gloria went to her bedroom, John to the fire, each alone with her thoughts, imaginations blazing with the heat of engagement.

The next morning Gloria visited the workers' cabins to say hello to her old friends. A warm, bright sunny day, many of the men were engaged in a soccer game. Off for the holiday, kids were playing, the women were chatting and preparing food, the mood was jovial. The men stopped the game momentarily as they saw her approach. They were waving and whistling, happy to see her.

She joined the kids in play, and the women came and talked to her. Her Spanish was still sharp, exercised often with her volunteer work in Oakland. Gloria was overwhelmed by the love she was given by her former coworkers. She stayed for lunch. They feasted on chile rellenos, tamales, beans, rice, and the various meats the others enjoyed. As difficult as U.S. racial relations seemed to be on a large scale with the systematic oppression of minorities, Gloria was continuously surprised by how easily relationships seemed to form based on kindness and respect on the small scale. Any ill will society built crumbled in a matter of moments. All relationships, she had come to learn, were based upon honest, open interactions. Volatility occurred when one was unwilling to share, whether it is because of prejudice, fear, disdain, or shyness. Gloria felt all people had the chance to relate if given the opportunity, and when given a common purpose, prejudices were almost always overcome. Gloria was thankful for her many opportunities to get to know so many different people with so many different perspectives. She left to hugs, kisses and good cheer, as she was perceived to be one of them; honest, kind, and full of life, dedicated in work and family.

As she walked away from her friends she reminisced about her interactions with some of the people she had met over the years, from the woman in the bar, Constantine's family, here at the ranch, and the people of Oakland, there was a trust, simple, quick and easy, she in them, and they in her. Her conversation with John from the night before played in her head. Could she have a message to share? Did she have the power to bring people together? She felt a spark inside her, maybe it was possible, she thought. She was wary of taking on that responsibility before she was sure, but for now she churned with the prospect of coming to know herself as a leader.

Gloria began to smile as she heard the clip clopping of horseshoes behind her. She turned to see Nancy confidently riding bareback on Nelson, galloping towards her. "Nelson missed you," Nancy said as she pulled alongside Gloria.

"Is that so?" Gloria replied charmingly.

"Yeah, he thought it might be nice to head over to the creek."

"That sounds like a fine idea," Gloria said to Nelson, as she patted him gently on the bridge of his nose.

"I didn't think we'd both be able to fit in the saddle, we're not little teenagers anymore, we'll have to ride bareback."

Over the years their bodies had grown more womanly, Gloria's more than Nancy. Naturally more curvy, Gloria's waist had narrowed, her hips widened slightly. Nancy's breasts filled out, she grew more muscle, but she maintained her straight, narrow hipped figure. They were still a slender pair.

"Where do I hold on?" Gloria asked.

"You can hold his mane if you want. Nelson's slowed down a step or two over the years, you'll be fine."

"How do I get up?"

"Here," Nancy said reaching out her hand, "step up on my foot, I'll pull you up facing me, then you can turn around."

Gloria stepped, Nancy pulled, Gloria swung her leg over Nelson, straddling the horse. Gloria lurched forward as she tried to gain her balance and knocked her forehead into Nancy's cheek.

"Ow," Nancy said laughing, grabbing her face.

"Sorry," Gloria said laughing. "Let me kiss it, make it better." Gloria placed both her hands on Nancy's face and gently kissed her on the cheek just below the eye.

"Thank you," Nancy said cheerily. Gloria awkwardly turned around on the horse, almost falling if not for Nancy securely grabbing her hip to stabilize her. They made their way slowly, seated casually, Gloria resting her hand on Nelson's neck, Nancy lightly holding Gloria's hips. They followed the familiar route to the narrow, steep path that led to the creek. Nelson, strong and prideful, sure-footed, guided them safely to the water's edge.

"No suits," Nancy said, as they came to a stop.

"I'm not as modest as I used to be," Gloria said wryly.

They undressed and calmly walked into the water; each girl held her head up high and looked the other in the eye. The swimming was tame, the water was cold, they both knew they could not stay in long. The thought of a warm place atop a smooth rock coaxed them out from the water after a few minutes, Nancy first, then Gloria. Gloria walked a few feet behind Nancy, waited for Nancy to choose a place on a rock, and took a seat a couple yards away.

"Only in California could you sunbathe on Christmas Eve, not every year, but some," Nancy said.

"It is strange. I grew up in a place where it snowed, I miss it."

"The snow or your hometown?"

"Both."

"You never talk about it, where you grew up, your family…"

"I always wanted to leave, I never felt like I belonged, even in my own family."

"So you left?"

"Well, it wasn't that simple."

"I'm sure it wasn't, there is nothing simple about you. I've been trying to figure you out for years," Nancy said.

Gloria smiled shyly, turning her head to make eye contact with Nancy then returning her gaze to the water. "What have you learned?" Gloria asked.

"I've learned that you have a ferocious interior full of thoughts and desires, but on the outside you seem calm, cool, and collected. I've learned you are far more apt to extend kindness and compassion to others than to yourself. I've learned you believe there is a greater purpose to life, one that reaches far beyond your inner circle. You are funny, but only sometimes, when you trust those around you. You treat everyone like they are the most important person on earth, yet no one more important than anyone else. You don't cry. You are in a constant state of turmoil. You are amazingly insecure for all your ability. You love passionately and you hurt deeply, which seems to keep you at arms length from most people. You are intense, which some confuse with intimidating or off-putting, but it allows you to walk into any situation, even ones that you know you're in way over your head, and figure out a way to make it work. You take yourself very seriously, sometimes at the expense of your own happiness. I've learned that you carry great sorrow, and quite possibly may never let it go. I know you cry out at night, and you do not sleep peacefully. I know you have no one to hold you."

"Anything else?" Gloria said, feeling completely exposed.

"I know I love you."

"I love you, too."

They looked kindly at each other, smiling.

They lay naked in the mild midmorning afternoon winter sunlight for an hour, Gloria even dozing off for a time, a testament to her extreme comfort in Nancy's presence. "We should probably get going," Nancy finally said. "We wouldn't want you to get burned."

They dressed and rode back to John's, parting ways. "Thank you for the nice day," Gloria said to Nancy as she rode off.

"Thank you," Nancy called in reply.

They didn't see each other again over the remainder of their visit, Nancy spending time with her family, and Gloria hanging out with John and the community of workers. The Clintock's drove them to the train station a couple of days after Christmas, the day before Gloria's birthday. They bounced around the back of the truck again, sitting closely, comfortably. They received hugs and kisses from Beth and Tom, and boarded the train to Oakland.

They arrived home that evening to a full house. A "Unity Through Community," meeting, a small nonprofit organization Ronnie and Lee had recently started, was convening. Twenty or so members were gathered together in the living room. Ronnie stopped talking when he saw the women return; he nodded to Nancy, and embraced Gloria. "I missed you," he said quietly in her ear.

She and Ronnie had spent nearly every day together until her recent trip. She had thought of him a time or two. "I missed you, too," she said.

"Hi everybody," Nancy said to the group, as she walked through them to get upstairs.

"Why don't you sit and join us?" Ronnie said enthusiastically to Gloria. "You always have good ideas."

"Yeah, all right," she said, putting down her backpack.

"We're talking about community activities to bring people from different neighborhoods together in hopes of encouraging people to be more trusting of each other through interaction. We are often scared of what we don't know," Ronnie said to Gloria. Addressing the group as a whole now, "and even more scared if all the information we hear about a certain group is negative. The more we talk with each other, the more we find in common, the less we talk, the more we see our differences."

Gloria seated on the floor quickly spoke up. "The two large-scale events I've always found it really easy to get along with people, are the fair, and barbecues, family settings. Seeing people with kids always breaks down boundaries as far as I'm concerned," she concluded.

"It's true, kids keep it light," a member of the group said.

"I don't know about a fair, but we could definitely have a barbecue. I could put together a group to play some music, set up a little stage, some speakers," Lee said.

"All right, let's look into that, location, permits, cost, time, etc. We'll hear your ideas next week. Thanks for coming over, see you next time, and love one another," Ronnie said, concluding the meeting.

Later that night Ronnie came up to Gloria's room. She had showered, and was in the process of unpacking. "Mind if I come in?" he asked.

"Sure, come on in," Gloria replied.

He sat down on her bed. "That was a great idea you had in the meeting."

"Thanks," she said, not feeling personally impressed by the simple suggestion.

"How was the trip?"

"Good, relaxing, got to see a lot of old friends, I'm happy to be back though."

"I'm happy you're back too. I meant what I said; I missed you, a lot."

"We're practically connected at the hip," she joked, sensing his intensity.

"I mean, I was surprised by how much I missed you. I didn't realize how much I like having you around."

"Thanks, I like having you around too."

"Cool," he said standing up. "I guess I'll let you get some rest, see you tomorrow. I made you something for your birthday, but you'll have to wait till your party to open it," he said.

"You didn't have to do that," she said, nervous about all the special attention he seemed to be paying her.

"I wanted to. Anyway, goodnight."

"Goodnight."

The next day, Gloria spent a leisurely morning having breakfast with Nancy at a café. The boys had wanted to come, but Nancy insisted it would be a quiet girls morning, assuredly followed by a raucous wild night they should just be patient. It was after all Gloria's twenty-first birthday.

The evening got underway with shots of tequila by the housemates. "Party preparation," Christian had called it. Friends of Gloria's from various walks of life came over. There were friends of the housemates, friends of friends; they all came together for the party. By ten p.m. there were nearly a hundred people flooding the rooms of the house, many spilling into the backyard on the relatively cold winter night.

Gloria drank more than she ever had before, the equivalent of about four drinks. She was different, a little drunk, a little unwound. There were many people at the party she didn't know, some belligerent and obnoxious who she would prefer to leave, but she focused on other things. At one point, her butt was pinched. Ronnie who had been following her around like a puppy dog, promptly roughly escorted the groper out. "Thanks Ronnie, I was just going to deck him," she said when he came back.

"No problem, don't want you breaking your fist on some moron's face."

"Tell me about it. Who are all these people anyway?"

"I don't know, but after ten the cops start giving out noise violations. I'm going to kick a few of these jokers out of here."

"Good idea. I'm going to go find Nancy."

"She's outside," Ronnie said.

Gloria went looking for Nancy outside. At first she didn't see her, but upon further drunken examination she found Nancy seated in a chair with a blonde girl on her lap. The pair was laughing playfully as Gloria approached. "Hey birthday girl," Nancy said when she saw Gloria approaching. "This is a friend of mine from school, Nicole," Nancy said, without either of them getting up.

"Hey," Gloria said, slightly acknowledging the girl. "I'm going to go back inside," she said, as she turned and walked away.

Nancy started to rise, Nicole stood. Nancy ran after Gloria, grabbing her by the wrist. Gloria intuitively pulled back her hand, staggering Nancy.

"Hey," Nancy said shocked. "You're not mad are you?"

"I'm not mad, I just want to go inside."

"You seem mad. Did that hurt your feelings, seeing a girl on my lap?"

"I've just never seen you, you know, being gay before. I guess I was a little caught off guard."

"I wasn't being gay. She's a friend, she's straight, she's affectionate that's it. If there's something more you want to discuss, we can take a walk or something?"

"No, it's fine, I'm just going to go inside."

"I'm coming with you."

"Fine." Gloria walked directly into the kitchen and took two consecutive shots of tequila.

"Gloria, don't," Nancy warned.

"You of all people should be happy to see me finally letting loose."

"Not like this."

"Carpe diem," Gloria said sarcastically.

The rest of Gloria's night became a blur. The movement of the people swirled around her, a chaotic dizzying mixture of energy and noise. Gloria danced, engaged in boisterous conversation, and affectionately showed her adoration to all those around. She eventually ended up face first on the cold tile floor in the upstairs bathroom, spinning and nauseated. Nancy looked after her, soothed her, and held her hair as she vomited. Nancy brought her blankets, pillows, aspirin and water. She waited until Gloria finally passed out before going to bed. The party had died down after Ronnie realized how drunk Gloria had become and began kicking people out in earnest. Gloria's birthday turned into a wild fiasco of a night, Ronnie and Nancy would never forget, and Gloria would scarcely remember.

Tensions around the house were high the next couple of days. A palatable undercurrent of mistrust and hurt settled in, straining the ease with which the housemates had interacted. There was Nancy, hurt by Gloria's distance and callousness since the party, Gloria, ashamed by her drunken stupor, and Ronnie, upset his role in the evening had been lost in the shuffle.

Gloria struggled to reconnect the pieces of the evening. She remembered the butt pinching, remembered the girl on Nancy's lap, then drinking. After the shots the event turned into a downward spiral. She danced with Ronnie, quite crazily she recalled, but few other specifics came to mind. The throwing up and spending the night on the bathroom floor, of course, annoyingly replayed in her mind over and over again.

Mostly, Gloria was puzzled by her reaction to Nancy. Was she jealous? Little else seemed plausible. Maybe it was the fact that it was her birthday that upset her, not being the center of attention, she entertained the thought for a moment, but it was highly doubtful. Had she wanted to be the girl on Nancy's lap? And if so, how could she not have known before that's how she felt? She had been friends with Nancy for so long now, she always loved her, from the very beginning, the only thing that changed was seeing that Nancy might want someone else. Whether it was the friendship feeling threatened, or something more, Gloria did not know, and for now she was too consumed with life in the city to find out.

Something did appear certain, things were changing with Ronnie. He had been incredibly present since her return, eager for interaction, complimentary, and undeniably sweet. She had always spent a lot of time with Ronnie since they first moved in together, but it had always been business, activities, a relationship based on shared ideology. It was clear things were changing in the house, and the dynamic was no longer as free and easy as it had once been.

As it stood now, the six housemates were on their way to Ronnie's best friend, Trey's New Year's Eve party. The party was more of a block party than a house party. When they arrived virtually every home on Trey's block had their door open, barbecues smoking, and music playing.

Gloria rooted herself in Trey's backyard upon arrival, not wanting to drink or walk from house to house. Ronnie knew everyone, and he made the rounds until nearly midnight. Nancy kept her eye on Gloria, still not comfortable enough to be in each other's presence, she kept a safe distance. Nancy knew few people, a couple of Ronnie's good friends who came over to the house, and the roommates, that's it. Nancy could have attended a party with her friends from school, but it was New Year's, she was going to be with Gloria, no matter how uncomfortable.

The crowd in Trey's backyard grew larger as midnight neared. All the roommates had reconvened and now occupied a corner of the yard. Besides the infrequent brief conversations with some of her extended network, Gloria had only watched the festivities. The mood was jovial, physical and playful, dancing, laughing and joking dominated the occasion. The party, a consistent thirty which now swelled to fifty as midnight approached, was predominantly black, mostly Trey's large extended family and friends. They teased each other mercilessly, each the butt of the joke at a time, all never for a moment feeling anything but loved. There was a DJ, one of Trey's cousins, keeping the energy high with plenty of dance tunes and some timeless classics that seemed to encourage spontaneous sing-alongs.

The music lowered as the countdown began, ten, nine, Gloria stood, Ronnie at her side, Nancy a few feet away. Eight, seven, six, Nancy looked at Gloria and smiled. Five, four, three, Ronnie put his arm around Gloria's waist. Two, one, he kissed her, full tongue before Gloria knew what was happening. The sound of small handgun fire popped through the air. She listened to the mini explosions as the strange sensation of Ronnie's tongue rolling around in her mouth perplexed her. "Happy New Year," he said as he pulled away.

Gloria, in shock, said nothing, wiped her mouth, then looked over at Nancy. Nancy, with a look of terror on her face, quickly turned and made her way through the crowd. Gloria took a step to run after her. Ronnie called her name, "Gloria?" She turned. "Do you think you might want to dance?" he asked.

The music pumped through her head loudly. "No. I don't know? I'll talk to you later," she said frantically. She turned to go after Nancy, but Nancy was nowhere to be found.

She didn't dance with Ronnie, or anyone else for that matter. For the rest of the night Gloria sat in the corner and moped until the roommates were ready to leave.

Nancy was not home when they returned. It would be three days before Nancy would reappear at the house when she came to pack her things. Nancy moved in with a friend from school, and just like that, she was gone.

Both women were entirely too hurt to reach out. A combination of rejection, poor communication, and downright devastation, led to months of silence. During that time a persistent Ronnie had come to take Gloria on as his girlfriend. For Gloria it seemed about time she looked into that part of her life anyway. Ronnie was nice, she liked him, trusted him, and after some initial reluctance she decided to go ahead and give it a try.

They became the power couple of the activist community, a tandem of brains and passion working for mobilization. They had gained a reputation as movers and shakers in the political world; Ronnie the more outgoing and well known, Gloria the behind the scenes mastermind. Ronnie did most of the speaking, but Gloria had recently taken to the stage and was hooked. She was gearing up for her first major appearance, a rally against nuclear proliferation in May. Gloria had quickly realized her words and ideas were best served coming from her own mouth, there was something lost in the translation of ideology and concept when she left her ideas for others to express. So out of necessity, a desire to represent the truth in her heart accurately, she realized she must find her voice and speak up for what she believed.

The political climate was volatile, the country was at war. Many countries had begun to level nuclear threats, an ideological battle was firmly at foot, and nuclear capability was the trump card those involved threatened to play. Gloria knew the time was coming when she could no longer neglect her past. She must find an outlet for her mother's invention. Her roommate, Chris, was extremely driven in the world of physics, but had shown no political nature whatsoever. She thought she could trust him, but didn't know if he could handle the responsibility. She feared Ronnie would determine to take an overly aggressive approach with the news of the device, his own trump card per se. Times were becoming more pressing within the movement. Unity Through Community had expanded beyond Oakland throughout the Bay Area, and looked to become a national force. They were young idealists wanting to make their way in the world. They were provocative, inflammatory, and brazen, not the climate which best suited the enormity of what Gloria had to introduce. She didn't know what to do, she wished Nancy was here to confide in; she needed someone she knew she could trust.

As the May anti-nuclear proliferation rally approached, Gloria worked hard to refine her speech. She spent countless hours of internal dialogue psyching herself up for her first large public appearance. She convinced herself that despite her age and relative inexperience, considering the turmoil of the country, her voice was valuable. However, she worried she lacked legitimacy, and she would be devastated if the speech did not go well. The nerve she must develop to push herself into the public forum felt like some delusional indulgence in her own talent, as if any fear or doubt would cause a paralyzing collapse. At times, she felt outside herself, pretending she was someone else not someone handicapped by her own propensity to feel others always knew more. Growing up the way she did, so removed from the world, she couldn't help but feel in any given situation there was always some essential bit of knowledge all others knew that she was not privy to. But she also felt a great sense purpose, and this purpose demanded she let her insecurities go, if only temporarily, there departure necessary for a good far greater than her own.

They came, thirty-thousand strong gathered in People's Park, Berkeley. There was a large main stage where speaker after speaker addressed the crowd during the daylong rally. The energy of the people was sometimes mind-boggling, but Gloria was amazed at how quickly the energy ebbed and flowed depending on the speaker. Distracted and aimless when being addressed by someone without a clear message or passionate discourse, the crowd would meander in a momentary dull oblivion. But get someone behind the microphone with an honest, provocative, yet practical message, the crowd would roar with approval, suddenly thirty-thousand people together on message, an unbelievable feeling spurred by the possibility of great change.

Gloria trembled as she waited by the stage, her mind clouded, she was unable to hear the present speaker, and saw very little but the ground below her. She had her speech in written form, but hoped to refer to it as little as possible believing the spoken word was much more dynamic than a message simply read. Ronnie tapped her on the shoulder. "It's your turn," he said.

Everything had happened so fast, it was just a few weeks ago she was debating taking the opportunity to speak at the rally, now, all of a sudden, she was about to head on stage to face thousands of people. She walked up the steps, somehow found herself behind a podium staring at a microphone linked to massive speakers overlooking an enormous crowd. She blinked, everything went dark for what seemed like far too long, she worried she would black out, then she began.

"First, I would like to thank you all for being here today. It is only together that we speak loud enough to be heard by those who do not want to respect our message. For it is the public will that the direction of our country is predicated on, and today we send a clear message of the will to live without the threat of nuclear weaponry."

There was a smattering of applause and shouting. She had begun to draw some of the crowd's attention after the lull between speakers.

"There is no law, no document, no declaration, or constitution, which ever gave the power for the few to destroy the many. And let me not speak metaphysically here, we are not speaking of terrorists, or the enemy of the moment, nor of combatants, communists, or religious fundamentalists, these bombs kill human beings, people just like you and me. As we know from Nagasaki and Hiroshima, a nuclear weapon does not discriminate. While not simply audacious and arrogant to impose our will through nuclear threat and intimidation, it is immoral and inhumane. There is no way to garner respect and understanding throughout the international community if we communicate with such clear disrespect."

Loud cheers and applause began to punctuate her message.

"We have been a bully for far too long, and everyone knows a bully can only go so long before someone stands up to fight, and when that happens, there is no one left willing to help the bully and there is no doubt the bully deserves the retribution that comes, because intimidation makes enemies, not friends. We are in danger of pushing around too many people, too long, with a cataclysmic weapon that no decent world citizen would dream of holding over another's head. Now, the inevitable reality of the spread of nuclear capability ups the ante. In order to keep our military dominance, we destroy any country who dares to attempt to play on a level battlefield with a bully either through economic sanctions, political coercion, or war. We choose to inhibit the rights of others that we freely enact. This is not a fight that will ever have a winner, and the sooner we see that, the sooner we will see making nuclear warfare obsolete is the only answer."

A large burst of cheers and applause raised into the sky. Gloria paused for a moment, slightly shocked by the noise.

"We the people of this great union are limited by the shortsightedness of our leaders, and their unwillingness to give up the power of intimidation. They have taken the approach it is easier to divide and conquer than unify and lead. And while this tactic has devastating consequences for all of us, it is for now our government's path of least resistance. And that is where we come in, all of us standing here today, we must become the resistance. We are the leaders, not the government, not the few who so often manipulate their way to power. They can go nowhere unless we are willing, our silent collusion enables their atrocious policies to flourish. Without the reckless disinterest of the people of this nation, those in office would not be allowed to mercilessly exact their version of justice. It is time we start speaking for ourselves."

A mad rush of applause stormed through the crowd.

"It is time the citizens of this country make their voices heard."

Loud applause again echoed through the crowd.

282

"All great shifts in political thinking come through the uprising of the people. I understand the feeling of fear and powerlessness that comes with a people divided, but there are times when the call to action is so meaningful, so life altering, we must let go of our personal reservations and do everything we can to enact change."

Thunderous applause vibrated through the surrounding area.

"For far too many of us ambivalence and apathy crawl into bed with us at night as we lay under our warm cozy blankets, with our full stomachs, after a night of watching television in our beautiful homes. The perception is we are not the ones under threat, and many are convinced we have a vested interest in being the intimidators and not the intimidated. I am convinced only a world of harmony is worthy of our pursuit, all other intentions are failures. We have settled for less, the vision of mediocre, power-hungry men, focused on lining the pockets of their cronies. We have allowed people who only look out for their own interests convince us we should only look out for our own. We can do so much better, and as people of the United States of America it is time we demand change."

Dramatic, loud applause filled the air.

"I am not under the illusion there are easy solutions to the ills which plague our country, but I do know nothing will change with complacency. And we are here today to say the status quo is not good enough. Murder in the name of power is not good enough." Loud applause... "A government acting behind cloaks and veils is not good enough." Applause... "A lack of honor and respect for the planet that houses all of us is not good enough." Loud applause... "A world where all people are free to live without the terror of corrupt rogue governments threatening their very existence is the bare minimum of human decency, one at this time I am ashamed to admit we do not uphold. A peaceful and honorable government should be the only option to lead a peaceful and honorable people. So we need to ask ourselves, are we a peaceful and honorable country?"

The loud roar of a unified, "yes," came from the crowd. Gloria's heart nearly stopped, full with the flood of emotion.

"Then we must do everything in our power to make sure we are represented as such. It is clear our government is failing us, and it is up to us to make it clear that it is no longer acceptable. When the government fails to respect the will of the people, it is the responsibility of the people to force change. Today, we begin that change by making our voices heard, tomorrow we do the same, until we are large enough, loud enough, and powerful enough to be undeniable. Today is the start of the growing force that will not stop until there is change, and we need every single one of you, we need everything you can give, because change like this does not come easy. Change like this does not come without cost. I ask you here today, do you want change?"

"Yes," the crowd roared.

"Are you willing to work for change?"

"Yes."

"Do you have the passion?"

"Yes."

"The desire?"

"Yes."

"Then today, change begins."

With that Gloria turned and calmly walked off the stage. The trembling uproar from the crowd was otherworldly, transcending the present moment into a life altering experience, feeding the hunger of a hope starved people searching for a direction now found.

"That was unbelievable," Ronnie said, hugging her tightly. Gloria was in a trance like state, not fully back in the present, she stared blankly, not really seeing anything. People came to her, congratulating her, thanking her, touching her. She saw the looks in their eyes, a mix of marvel, awe, and inspiration. She was stunned by their acceptance and desire to be near her. There was a noticeable shift inside her, she had found what she was made of, she had found what she was meant to do.

Chapter 21

The war ended nearly as quickly as it had begun. Political tempers died down, and subsequently the movement died down. There was no next speech for Gloria to give, no more rallies, just like that, her cause was deemed irrelevant. The only finer example of irrationally short term memory than that displayed during war, is the pathological repeated missteps of a country at peace. The fire that raged in Gloria was so thoroughly extinguished she grew despondent, attended less meetings, engaged in less all together. The sweet taste of triumph turned into the bitter resignation of an activist without a movement. As the months passed, she grew more and more listless, alienating herself from friends, and withdrawing entirely from Ronnie.

Gloria made the decision to leave Oakland in the fall. In her eyes, she had faced a tremendous defeat at the time of her greatest vulnerability. She had been ready and willing to plunge herself into the cause. The initial positive response had raised her hopes so high the subsequent crash had emotionally eviscerated her. Retreat was all she could manage. She boarded a train and headed back to the ranch, back to John, the workers, and the land, in hopes of healing the wounds of supreme disappointment.

She had dreamed for so long of coming to a place where everything really mattered, where there was this living breathing whole, a mass society intricately connected by prevailing beliefs. She had wanted to help shape those beliefs, she had one grand moment of greatness, and now its demise appeared unrecoverable. The one time she gave herself to the world she so badly wanted to be a part of, it was great, better than she ever could have imagined, and then nothing, she was alone, lost again to the direction that drives her left wallowing in the pit of indecision.

John picked her up in the dune buggy, no Clintock's welcoming hug, she hadn't even told them she was coming, seemed appropriate, she and John, lonesome warriors in heartache. She returned to the familiar routine of pre-dawn wake-ups, back breaking work, and evenings of painting. The routine did her good, left her less time to wallow in her under-achieving misery. She enjoyed the camaraderie shared between the workers, although at first she was reticent, concerned with her own perceived tragedy, but they quickly broke through the melancholy with their kind-hearted inclusion and warm physical affection.

She thought of Nancy often, the terrain a constant reminder of moments they shared together. She wished she had made an effort to repair the relationship, she regretted letting her go without a fight. She had been so disciplined for so long, decisions were made and enacted before she realized. The loss of Nancy, she wondered why she had let it occur, a few moments of controversy, and she ran. Ronnie was easy, he was clear; his intentions were obvious and easily anticipated. She had chosen controlled over potential strife. In her own personal life she had not taken any risks, she was guarded, measured, so worried about hurt and betrayal she had betrayed herself. Why, when it came to love, was she unwilling to let herself go, unwilling to let herself potentially fail, was it too important? Had she become a person who would not put her whole self into what she deemed most meaningful? How could she possibly take such a risk in her personal life now? She was in danger of becoming more rigid when it came to love, and even less willing to put her heart on the line.

As Christmas approached Gloria hoped with all her might that Nancy would appear to help pull her from this place of spiraling doubt and fear. She decided to visit the Clintock's to inquire about Nancy. She nervously approached the house, shivering during the mid-December cold snap. The house was empty. She walked over to Beth's studio. As she approached the barn she noticed the contrast of the orange glowing light of the fire illuminated wall of glass under the cold, gray day. Gloria knocked, pulled open the door, and called out. "Beth, it's Gloria, you up there?"

"Gloria, sweetheart, come on up," Beth's familiar, kind voice called out. "I heard you were around, I kept waiting for you to visit, two months honey, really, that's far too long." The women embraced. "Nice to see you sweetie," Beth said softly as they hugged.

"Thank you, it's nice to see you, too," Gloria said, as her stiff body relaxed with Beth's warm welcome. Her apprehension that the state of her relationship with Nancy would affect her welcome within Nancy's family quickly disappeared.

"I'm sorry about what's going on with you girls," Beth said, immediately naming the elephant in the room. Gloria blushed some, not sure how much Beth knew, or how comfortable she felt discussing it. Beth continued through Gloria's awkward silence. "You know there was a time after the war when Tom and I didn't speak for awhile. We were high school sweethearts, the only man I ever wanted to be with, but, ooh he made me so mad. You know what he finally said to me, 'Beth I can't ever undo the things that I've done. I'm either worth your forgiveness or I'm not.' He said it just like that, yes, I have a past, yes, I've made mistakes, you either find a way to carry on, or you don't. True love carries on."

Gloria was shocked, had Nancy told her they were lovers? "Beth," she said gently, "Nancy and I were never together."

"You two were always together, from day one, tighter than most lovers. I know you didn't have a sexual relationship, but all serious relationships are the same, sometimes they get broken, and those rare few are worth the struggles to repair. I hope you and Nancy come back together, you two were beautiful, as comfortable as I've ever seen her."

"I hope so, too," Gloria said sadly.

"She's not coming home sweet cheeks, for Christmas, is that what you came over here to ask me?"

"It is."

"I'm sorry sweetheart. She has a lot of work with her dissertation and all, maybe next year when things calm down."

Gloria dropped her head, noticeably defeated by the news. Beth rubbed Gloria's back. "She still loves you sweetheart. She's just hurt for whatever reason, she won't tell me why…" Beth paused and looked at the sad girl. "She asks about you."

"She does?" Gloria asked needing confirmation.

"She does."

Nancy didn't come back the next Christmas, or the one after that. Nancy had taken a job teaching in New York. It would be five more years until they saw each other again. Gloria had remained on the farm all that time, where she developed and refined her perspective. She had shared her father's research with John. He was so enthusiastic about her dad's discoveries he became entirely reinvigorated with life. Now in his seventies, John worked tirelessly everyday trying to replicate the drought resistant, oxygen replenishing plants Marty had brought into existence.

Gloria left work in the fields and focused her energy on working in the greenhouse with John. It was through this process she came to fully appreciate the agricultural accomplishments of her father. "Genius," John would say, time and time again, "pure genius." John discussed the possibility of turning back the damage done to the pollution ravaged earth. "If I die," John would say, "share this, share this information with everyone. These notebooks may decide the fate of the air we breathe. But be careful," he warned, "there are people who look to make a great deal of profit cleaning up the same mess they made. They will not look kindly on people being able to heal the environment with plants grown on their own. When you release the information, make sure it is on such a large scale it cannot be suppressed," he advised.

Gloria enjoyed the work and the creativity involved in following her dad's thinking. It made her proud; he was inventive, daring with his concepts and thoughts. She had come to realize both her mom and dad were daring. She wondered if they would be proud of her, or, would they be disappointed? She vacillated. It helped that John adored her, as she adored him, and he was always encouraging. "A life is not judged by its first twenty-six years," he would say, sensing the doubt inside her.

The news of Nancy coming home for the holiday hit her like a fist to the gut. Gloria had worked so hard to adjust to life without her, now, after all this time, she was as scared to see Nancy as she had ever been in her life. But this was no time to let fear emotionally paralyze her, that was the Gloria of old. This time she was determined to use the fear to motivate her, to assure her of the importance of the completeness of her presence, not holding back, not protecting herself, entirely frighteningly present.

Gloria was as surprised as the Clintock's when she asked to come along to pick up Nancy. As she bounced around in the back of the truck on the way to the station the lump in her throat grew so tight she had to consciously remind herself to breathe. They arrived several minutes early. There was some idle nervous chatter, but each of them were consumed with their own plight, Tom and Beth, with the unfathomable anticipation of having their daughter home for the first time in years, and, Gloria, the heaviness of facing the possible unknown of the reemergence of someone she cared so much for.

Nancy stepped onto the platform, she saw the three of them, and gave a shy smile. She truly loved her parents; she was a woman now, not the young girl running to wrap her arms around her dad's neck, but a calm, composed and powerful woman gracefully hugging her aging and adoring parents. Gloria stood still as Nancy turned to her, not sure what to expect she waited for Nancy to act. Nancy put her hand behind Gloria's neck, and another on the small of her back; she cradled Gloria into her chest. Gloria melted into Nancy as there bodies met, wrapping her arms tightly around Nancy's torso. Nancy tilted her head back and touched Gloria's cheek; they looked at each other and smiled.

On the ride back Gloria took her usual seat against the cab of the truck. Nancy remained near the tailgate, leaning against the raised wheel well facing Gloria. They were quiet as the cool wind swirled their hair and thoughts filled their head. Their darting eyes occasionally bounced off each other, shyly, questioningly.

"Stay for dinner, Gloria," Beth said when they got back. Gloria looked slightly panicked as she stared at Beth, then at Nancy, then back at Beth.

"Yeah, stay," Nancy said softly.

"Okay, thank you," Gloria said, conveying her surprise.

Gloria followed Nancy up the stairs to her bedroom and waited on the deck while Nancy unpacked. She had a chill from the ride in the back of the truck. She shivered now in the open night air as goose bumps firmly took hold. Nancy kindly came out to join her. After a brief moment Nancy said to Gloria, "you're freezing." Nancy reappeared with a burgundy corduroy shirt, throwing it on Gloria's lap. Gloria grew warm as she buttoned the shirt. She inhaled deeply, taking in Nancy's distinctive scent.

"Are you well?" Nancy asked simply.

"I am," Gloria said earnestly.

"It has been a long time," Nancy said cautiously.

"It has," Gloria replied with equal caution, each wary of losing a piece of their heart.

"I saw your speech you know, at People's Park," Nancy said, surrendering the bunker defense.

Gloria's face lit up as she looked at Nancy. "You did?"

"Of course, you were amazing."

"You think so?"

"Absolutely."

"I really, really enjoyed it," Gloria said, for a moment reliving the past.

"Everybody there enjoyed it," Nancy said.

Gloria exhaled and slumped her shoulders. "That was the only time I've let myself be heard. I so wished you were there, it was the most important thing I've ever done in my life, the first time I really felt like I accomplished something." She paused for a moment and looked up at Nancy. "I'm really glad you were there."

"You were with Ronnie."

"I was."

"How was that?"

"It was fine for awhile."

"Did you sleep with him?"

"I did," Gloria answered without hesitation.

Nancy visibly flinched at the emotional jab, but didn't stagger. "How was that?" she asked.

"It was all right. I mean, I don't know what all the fuss is about, it wasn't unpleasant or anything, I could take it or leave it."

Nancy smiled, suddenly light. "You are so gay," she said, shaking her head at Gloria.

"You think so?"

"Yeah, I do."

"Really, you think I'm attracted to women?"

"I do."

"Why haven't I dated any?"

"I'm wondering that myself."

"I don't know, I think I would've been with a woman by now? I think it's great to be gay."

"I don't think that it has anything to do with being gay. I think you're very apprehensive, to the point of sabotage, at being completely vulnerable to someone. You're comfortable relying on yourself, and only yourself."

"Do you think that's what I did, sabotage our relationship?"

"It's taken me a long time, I've been very hurt, I think you did exactly what you needed to do at the time for some complicated deep seated reasons. I understand, that's all I can say."

Gloria paused for a moment before she replied. "Listen, we've both been hurt, let's not jump into everything all at once."

"All right," Nancy agreed. "I'm really hungry," she said, easing out of the heaviness of the conversation, "let's go see what there is to eat."

"Sounds good."

The dinner was quite calm and relaxed for all the tension leading up to the meal. There were the same loud, silly stories from Tom, with comedic commentary from Beth, a perfectly in sync duet, complete with one-upsmanship, slight barbs, subtle clarifications and complete admiration. Nancy and Gloria observed, interjected when necessary, but mostly internally exulted at being in each other's presence again.

They glanced at each other when they thought the other wasn't looking, searching for the changes, the more womanly characteristics each of them now possessed. The elongation and angularity of their faces, the fine lines that had barely begun to form, the leaning of the torso, the flattening of the butt, the landscape of their evolving personas subtly taking shape. It was like old times with a new frame of mind, the fondness of close familiar friends mingling with the heaviness of knowing there was difficulty still to be worked out. The unsettledness loomed in the air just before their eyes, not obstructing their view, but still a noticeable presence in the room. Dinner wound down, and it was clear they had all had enough for one day. Gloria said her goodbyes, hugging everyone, and walked contentedly home.

Nancy and Gloria didn't see each other the next couple of days, regrouping and preparing for their next encounter. Gloria spent her time with the workers, enjoying their Christmas celebrations and traditions. The unifying power of similar beliefs was undeniable, family's together, grand rituals, there was a wonderful mood to the air. She marveled at their devotion, especially in a country where so many shared their religion, but there was so little integration. A white Catholicism and a Latino Catholicism, not even religion, it appeared, transcended race. Faith in God must be different than faith in people, Gloria thought; she preferred the latter. She loved basking in the warmth of her ranch family, still, she greatly anticipated the day after Christmas, when she knew she would see Nancy again.

Gloria walked over to the Clintock's in the cool soft light of dawn. As she thought about their first interaction in years, Gloria was slightly surprised with the undercurrent of ease she and Nancy still maintained. Despite the time, the distance, the hurt, there was still an undeniable bond. She quietly climbed up the side of the house onto the deck outside Nancy's room. She tapped lightly on the window, hearing no sound, she tried the handle of the door, unlocked, she walked in. Nancy lay on her stomach, tangled in the sheets and blankets, her exposed dark olive skin contrasted against the pale yellow bedding. Gloria crawled into bed with Nancy, stroked her cheek gently, and quietly spoke her name.

"Gloria," Nancy said surprised, blinking her sleepy eyes.

"This time I've come to find you," Gloria said softly.

"I see that."

"There are some things I need to tell you," Gloria said.

"There are some things I need to tell you, too..." Nancy said. Nancy looked gently into Gloria's eyes. "I've met somebody." Gloria stared at Nancy blankly. "Back in New York, we live together," Nancy stated.

290

"Are you happy?" Gloria asked, unmoved.

"She's very kind, she loves me."

"That's not what I asked."

"I don't know? Is it the greatest love I ever could have imagined? Probably not, but I stopped dreaming of that long ago."

"That's a shame," Gloria stated without compassion.

"More like realistic. Was I supposed to hold out hope forever, wait for you?"

"No. I'm sorry. I didn't know about how you felt, I'm sorry."

Nancy reached over and put her hand on Gloria's cheek. "You don't have to be sorry. The older I get the more I realize so much in life is about timing. You weren't ready, I understand."

They lay together for a few minutes, sensing the change. Finally, Gloria got up. "I'm going to go, but I want you to come over to John's when you get up. There's something I want to tell both of you."

"I'll get up now, I'll shower, eat a little, I'll be there in half an hour," Nancy said.

"Okay." Gloria walked over to the French doors leading to the deck.

"G, you don't have to climb down, you can use the door."

"Oh yeah," Gloria said sheepishly, blushing, she left the room.

Gloria and John were seated on the back deck when a wet haired Nancy arrived. They had a fire going to fight off the chill of the early winter morning. Gloria anxiously rubbed her hands together as she began. "As you both know, I have not been exactly forthcoming about the details of my past. But over the years, despite my trepidations, a solid foundation of trust has formed between us. Now, I realize I need help, and I need your advice and friendship to move forward with my life.

"There are some peculiarities in my past that make my life rather complicated which I feel I must share with you to move forward. First and foremost, according to the government I do not exist." Gloria paused, waiting for their reaction. They stared at her stoically and engaged, she continued. "I was raised hidden from the world in a protected town in the middle of the New Mexico desert as part of a top secret project. The project was created by Maggie Pelt to harbor Jewish refugees during World War II. I'm the only person to leave the society; I will not go into all the details now. More significantly, both my parents were inventors of sorts. John is familiar with my father's work. I have been struggling for years about what to do with my mother's creation. So, I'm telling both of you about my past now, the two people in the world I implicitly trust, because I need your help."

Gloria walked over and grabbed the red and black backpack leaning against the stone mouth of the fireplace. "My mother was a brilliant physicist obsessed with nuclear warfare. The society I lived in was extremely supportive of academic pursuits. My mother was provided equipment, and a great deal of autonomy from a very young age. She was the town prodigy, they were eager to see her accomplish, and they did everything they could to support her. I knew very little of my mother, most of what I tell you now I learned from my dear friend Charlie, whom John also knows. Charlie, at the behest of First Lady Pelt, was the only outsider allowed to live within the project other than the military that raised the first generation."

Gloria opened the backpack and pulled out the small metal cylinders. "What I am going to tell you is rather unbelievable," she said.

Nancy interjected. "Yeah, up until this point it's been totally, totally normal," she laughed. Gloria turned pale as a ghost. Nancy reached her hand out to Gloria. "No, I believe you, it was just funny, now you preface," she said, explaining herself.

Gloria managed to smile, overcoming the shock of feeling for a moment that Nancy did not believe her. She knew the trust she was displaying in them would have to work both ways, she in them to keep her secret, and they in her that the story she was telling them was actually true. Gloria continued. "My mother devoted her life to this device, and ultimately she was killed because of it," Gloria said, assembling the machine. "My mother was determined to make nuclear weaponry obsolete, this device has the ability to do so, it is capable of enveloping nuclear warheads and destroying them. I'm not entirely sure how it works, but essentially it detects the presence of nuclear matter at a particular velocity and the machine transmits a momentary black hole into the sky. The mass, from which no energy can escape, envelops the warhead and simultaneously implodes. Apparently it all happens in a fraction of a second. I've never seen it, but my father has, and I believe him."

"A portable black hole machine," Nancy said enthusiastically.

"Yes," Gloria answered.

"Are there notes like your father's work?" John asked.

"There are."

"Then we must find a way to release them on a large scale to make it replicable," he said.

"Yes," Nancy interjected, "but I imagine it would take years to build, even decades, if the government didn't find a way to snuff it out first. And with the escalating nuclear tension and imminent war in the Middle East, we need to find a way to keep this machine active, anonymous and safe, in order to give us time to make more."

"So you guys believe me?" Gloria said.

"Yes," they both said at once, almost annoyed to be sidetracked from the question about what to do.

Gloria recovered from her doubt and got back on track. "It would be nice to shape the political will, so physicists will work to make the discovery on their own," she said earnestly.

"You're delusional. That's the craziest thing you've said all day," John resoundingly declared.

"I am convinced if you help people believe in new possibilities they will work to find a way," Gloria said confidently.

"Yes, I've seen your ability to unify the collective will," Nancy said. She turned to

John. "She gave this great speech at Peoples Park, thirty thousand people sure they could change the world, it was amazing," she said.

"I read about it," he said.

"You did, you never mentioned it?" Gloria said, surprised.

"Yes, I keep up, it was big news in the activist community. I knew how disappointed you were when you came back to the ranch. The time wasn't right. Now, you need to know what they were saying. One writer referred to you as the peace prophet."

"It was really inspiring," Nancy said. "I do think that is a front you should work, but not the only one. You have a gift, that is clear, but changing attitudes is a long process, the magnitude of your mother's invention necessitates action now. We have to get them made. What about Christopher?" Nancy asked, referring to their old roommate who studied physics.

"I don't know? I was never really that close with him. I don't know what he'd think?"

"I was close to him. He's gone rather nontraditional, he works for an environmental solutions company. I'll get in touch with him, feel him out," Nancy said.

"What about NYU?" John asked, referring to the college where Nancy taught.

"I don't know about the university," she said hesitantly. "There's one woman in my department who seems rather subversive, but I don't know her very well. But Linda's father is a scientist with the Dove Corporation, they are entirely devoted to projects for peace, he might be a good person to talk to."

"Who's Linda?" John asked.

Gloria was relieved she didn't have to.

"My girlfriend," Nancy replied.

"Oh," John said, compassionately turning his gaze to Gloria. "I didn't know you were in a relationship," he said protectively, expressing the concern Gloria did not.

"Yes," Nancy replied, looking down.

"Well," John said, continuing with the discussion at hand, "I think those are some good options. I have an old buddy from the military, Todd Gunderson, he's a gazillionaire, helped found some computer company, I trust him, he would definitely help with funding."

"I've never heard you talk about any old military buddies," Gloria said, again surprised.

"I just have one. I sent him letters that he passed on to my family when I was still in hiding. He was the one who wrote me, got me to come back home. We served together, he saved my life, but he says I saved him first so I really saved my own life. He was a lost man in the army, says without me he would have never really found out what he was made of and how much he had to offer. He's become a great man and a great friend. He's proven his loyalty. He's old like me, been giving away his money for years, he's a good man, he can help us, no questions asked."

"I think you should come to New York," Nancy said suddenly.

"Why New York?" Gloria asked, surprised.

"Anything is possible in New York. Every ideology, every type of person, every hardship, every sorrow, it all exists in New York. The city breathes the very essence of existence, if you really want to know about people, New York is the place."

"That is a pretty good idea, you really haven't seen very much of the country," John said.

"I'll rent a car, we can drive back. You can't fly without an ID, especially after 9/11. I don't have to be back until the third, we can leave tomorrow," Nancy said.

"Wow," Gloria said. "I haven't given any of this any thought."

"Come, you can't do what you need to do here," Nancy implored.

"She's right Gloria, you're talking about a large scale movement. I think you should go," John said.

"You asked us for advice. This is major, hiding out on the farm won't suffice, come." Nancy stated plainly.

Gloria thought for a moment. "Okay," she said.

Nancy jumped up and hugged her.

"I'll call Gundy, talk to him about some money. And I'm sure he'll know a way to get your mom's work, and your dad's work for that matter, on every computer in a moment's notice if need be," said John.

"Sounds good," Gloria said.

They all got up, John hugged and kissed Gloria. "Thank you for telling us, it must be a very difficult secret to have to keep," he said

"It explains a lot," Nancy added.

Chapter 22

Nancy and Gloria spent the next six days in the car traveling through the heartland of America. Their route was marked by snow in Utah, winds in Kansas, rains in Missouri, clear skies in Ohio, stillness in Pennsylvania, and wildness upon their arrival in New York City. They stopped and explored when they both agreed on it, which basically meant when Nancy allowed. Nancy, doing all the driving, and needing to be back at NYU to teach, tried to keep a strict schedule. Gloria, fascinated by the diversity and beauty of the land, wanted to stop and see everything.

They arrived near midnight the night before Nancy had to start teaching. Gloria was awestruck by the skyline of shapes and lights. The energy of the city seemed to reverberate in the car. This place was different Gloria thought as she gaped open mouthed at the beating heart of the country, in another category, she thought.

They dropped off the rental car and took the subway to Nancy's Brooklyn apartment. On their way up the stairway they heard Linda enthusiastically open the apartment door and run down the stairs to greet them two floors below their sixth-story apartment. Linda hugged Nancy gleefully around the neck, covered her face with kisses, then promptly stuck out her right hand out to Gloria. "Linda," she said clearly.

Gloria extended her hand and shook Linda's hand. "Gloria," she said kindly. Linda grabbed Nancy's suitcase and marched them up the stairs.

The apartment, a good sized one-bedroom, five hundred and fifty square feet, was modern and uncluttered, a vast departure from the ranch house and the permanently messy status of Nancy's room in Oakland. There were simple, solid red, ninety degree angle chairs, and a similarly erect couch. The rest of the living room consisted of sleek dark wood furniture, side tables, an entertainment center with surprisingly a TV, which Gloria knew Nancy had never had before. The kitchen was tidy, a bar seating area attached to it separated the space from the living room. Gloria noticed the kitchen area was very clean, and there were lots of gadgets. Their bedroom was simple, a bed, dresser, side tables with lamps, but shockingly to Gloria, another television. The bathroom was white with gray and dusty rose accent, and included a much coveted New York accessory, a full tub.

Linda opened a bottle of white wine, offering each of them a glass. Gloria accepted even though wine usually gave her a headache, white less so than red, so she thought she'd probably be okay, and anyway, she thought a drink might help loosen her up. They stood around the kitchen getting acquainted and sharing stories about the trip. It was quite comfortable actually, Linda was engaging and friendly, she projected not an ounce of awkwardness. Nancy and Linda were not affectionate, at least not then, it all seemed rather copasetic. Gloria learned Brooklyn was a relatively affordable up and coming borough in the city, and landing a bathtub was a particularly wonderful feat. The fact the building was a walk up did not bother them, they preferred stairs to an elevator anyway, and they had moved in together a year ago. They adjourned the get together around two in the morning. Linda had the bedding laid out on the couch by the time Gloria was out of the bathroom.

Gloria slept until the late winter light presented itself through the eastern windows. By several minutes past seven, neither of the women had emerged from the bedroom. Gloria rose and peered out the window. They were above some buildings, and below many others. She couldn't believe the vast, large scale structures that comprised the area. Up, instead of out, so many people so close together, utterly dynamic, she thought. The bedroom door opened and Linda poked her head around the corner. "Oh, you're up, coffee?" she asked.

"No thanks," Gloria replied. Caffeine had always been too much of an upper for her, made her stomach churn.

"Nancy's first class isn't until ten, thankfully," Linda said. "She must be really tired; she's usually up at the crack of dawn."

"Ranch time," Gloria said.

"Yeah, seriously."

Linda and Gloria shared some eggs and toast. Nancy eventually rolled in sleepy-eyed. "I can't believe I slept so late," she said, yawning, hand on forehead in disbelief.

"You were exhausted," Linda said.

"The wine didn't help," Nancy admitted.

"Come, I'll make you some eggs," Linda said.

Nancy sat next to Gloria at the raised counter. "How'd you sleep Glor?" Nancy asked.

Glor, that was the first time Nancy had ever referred to her in that way. "Fine, Nanc," she said, with more than a hint of sarcasm which appeared lost on the both of them.

"Unfortunately, I have to go into work in a little bit, too," Linda said to Gloria. "There will be no one here to show you around," she lamented.

"That's okay, I love exploring on my own," Gloria replied.

"There is something about getting to know a city without any guidance, discovering

296

the hidden gems; there are a lot of them in New York," Nancy said. "That's how I got to know the city, the first month I was here, I wandered aimlessly."

"That's how we met," Linda interjected. "She was lost, she needed directions to MOMA, lost in the shadows of endless buildings…"

"Yep, a month after I got here," Nancy said.

"I better get changed," Linda said, excusing herself.

Nancy and Gloria worked on their breakfasts for a moment before Nancy asked, "Is this okay, you being here?"

"Yeah, Linda is nice, I like her."

"Good. Have a good time today, take it slow, the city can be overwhelming."

"Thanks, I will."

"You know, why don't you take the subway with me to NYU? You can walk around there. I'll show you the ropes of New York's transportation lifeline."

"Okay."

"Great. We'll leave in twenty minutes."

The slight pressure change as she arrived at the bottom of the stairs, the screeching of metal on metal, the roaring of the trains in the tunnel, for Gloria the subway was a visceral experience. She paid close attention to Nancy's habits, the way she carried herself, head-up, alert, the speed with which she traveled, the efficiency with which she navigated paying the toll, walking the platform, entering the train. The experienced travelers moved in a synched rhythm of loading and unloading, a collective unison of transport.

The train encompassed far more types of people than Gloria had ever encountered. More so even than in the Bay Area, different interests, looks, attitudes, the vibe in the enclosed space was engrossing. A man in spandex on roller blades stood next to them. Seated beyond him, a tiny black woman with short gray hair fervently read a book, next to her, a multi-pierced man stared blankly straight ahead, and a young hippie girl with a guitar sat behind them. Gloria could not begin to speculate on all the different nationalities interspersed throughout the car, but she was intrigued. The speculative trance of the subway ride ended. Gloria and Nancy bustled their way to the campus where they parted ways.

Gloria walked and walked. She marveled at a place that held so many things she had only read about. The architecture: art deco, gothic, enormous looming structures, none of which she had experienced before, fascinated her. New York really was the cultural center of the world, she thought, passing world class theatre, world class museums, the financial institution, the center of fashion. The city not only had it all, it had the best of it all. She ate at a tiny Indian food stand; marvelous rich spices enhanced her already heightened state. The noise, the people, the combination of so much energy only focused her more. She felt it would take years, possibly decades, to truly know the cadence and rhythm of the city. She wanted to take in every part, the splendor and the tragedy.

She visited the hallowed site of the World Trade Center, amazed that nearly three years after the attack the country was firmly planted in a war with a country that had nothing to do with the horror that played out before her. Funny, she thought, how outrage blinds logic and fuels aimless aggression, which spurs a cathartic bludgeoning no matter how unjustified, and somehow, people are appeased. A palatable sense of terror rose up from the grotesquely distorted foundation. Thousands of captured screams remained lingering just below the surface, the innocent victims of a delusional response to a callous and self-serving international policy that has made many enemies and shows no sign of changing. The thoughts in her head swirled, until we are not seen as economic exploiters and environmental pillagers with a greedy agenda, we, by the very nature of our passive citizenry, are the next targets of the backlash.

No scene she had ever encountered, not any hardship, not even the sight of her mother's lab being blown up, had provoked such outrage and an all-consuming desire for change as the gaping wound laid out before her in the middle of the greatest city in the country. It struck her as a visibly blocked artery in the heart of the nation, if not properly treated with major intervention, and a lifestyle change, the country's demise was sure to come. Not the rapid decline measured in human years, but a more gradual decline measured in the increments of a country's growth. It took over two hundred years to get here, and she figured we have about twenty to get us out. But never has it been more clear than now, a change was necessary, a change must come.

An unmistakable message had been sent to this country, and no matter how ultimately unjustifiable, we can do better. We can no longer hide behind the remarkable constitution with which we were founded on, but must look at our actual global practices. Who we think we are as a country, and how we actually act are a long divergent set of complicated hopes, delusions, nationalism and stubbornness. We must first be stripped of our egotistical pride before we can see how much better we really can be. The denial of our failures is our greatest weakness, preventing the growth and development beyond our shortcomings that our founders laid before us so long ago, the principles we have strayed so very far from in our pursuit of economic domination. To acknowledge our missteps is to begin to heal from their violence. We must come to know ourselves for everything we are not, and everything we could be, not simply that which we think we are. For far too long we have looked in the mirror and only seen the prettiest country in the world, and regardless of our behavior this opinion has not changed. Yet, there is no doubt, throughout time moral blemishes have occurred, here and abroad. If we leave it to others to bring us from our stupor, more marks, devastating scars such as the remnants of the World Trade Center will continue to appear. Yet, somehow, we continue to look in the mirror and see no signs of our struggle, or our growing pains as a young country. We refuse to see our fallibility. What will it take if 9/11 didn't wake us up? What will it take to have an honest discourse about the ways we can improve?

We still insist upon walking up the ladder of power on the backs of other countries, but that relationship is predicated on dominance and intimidation. Now, they grab at our heels to pull us down and pummel us. It is not too late to come down voluntarily and make amends. We have not done anything that cannot be undone, yet, but we are close, so very close, this war, the smugness of our leadership, we are quickly making permanent enemies. The choice is ours, rejoin the international community with ethical and pure intentions that benefit all, or use, abuse, and alienate, until the smell of hatred overtakes many and they band together to butcher us alive. We have chosen to escalate, firmly dig in like a child throwing a tantrum. But it is our behavior that has led to these pitfalls, and in our adolescence as a country we can choose to develop into a spoiled, entitled adult ignorant to the plight of many, or we can stop, listen to the grievances of those around us, and dedicate as fervently to the deeds of others as we do to our own.

She walked away from the site of the World Trade Center as the sun was setting. The emotions of the day left her drained, worried about the narrowing opportunity of a country off-track. Enough for one day, she thought, she must still find her way back to Nancy and Linda's apartment; she could not succumb to the daunting frustration of it all. She arrived back at the apartment an hour later, dazed, deep in thought, momentarily mentally untouchable. "Maybe we should order in," Nancy said upon assessing Gloria's condition.

The next few days were much the same, Gloria wandering around the burroughs. She took it slow, sitting in Washington Square Park, visiting the Museum of Modern Art, climbing the Empire State building. She spent the evenings in the apartment, overwhelmed by her days, she was not ready to tackle the night scene.

The weekend came and the three women decided to explore Brooklyn. The restaurants, the people, it was as if Gloria didn't really know life at all until her immersion into diversity oblivion. The three of them kept their eyes out for an apartment. Gloria, although she didn't intimate as much, was eager to get her own place. Flooded with thoughts of the city, staying with Nancy and her girlfriend was something she gave little thought, but when she did, a sickening wave of disturbed melancholy overwhelmed her. And by this point she had amassed quite a large sum of money, hundreds of thousands of dollars, most of which Nancy had put into a safety deposit box along with the nuclear interceptor for safekeeping, so getting her own place seemed the best choice. Gloria's constant work and limited expenses left her economically viable, in control of her time and direction without the pulls of employment.

Sunday she found a place, a small studio apartment in a big building across the street from Nancy and Linda. The rental agent was at first hesitant to give Gloria the place because she had no identification, no rental history, and refused to fill out any forms, but six months rent in cash appeased the agent's mind. A good size for a studio, three hundred and fifty square feet, with a partial kitchen, the essential shower with tub, located on the eight floor of a twelve story building, nothing spectacular, simple, affordable accommodations.

The deal done, the three spent the rest of the afternoon scouring through thrift stores and flea markets to furnish Gloria's new place. Gloria bought a full size mattress, an old gold crushed velvet chair, a couple of tables, one large, one small, an old stained-glass lamp, and some kitchenware. Nancy and Linda helped her haul everything up the stairs, as the elevator was not in operation. And just like that Gloria had her own apartment in New York City. Gloria smiled to herself as she lay in bed that night. Two weeks after leaving the ranch, she was in her very own place, in a city worth living up to.

Gloria tried to ignore the faint rustling sound, exhausted from the rigors of the day, she attempted to fall back asleep. As the sound persisted, she grew only more alert, she decided to get up out of bed and investigate. She followed the sound to the kitchen and turned on the light. The sound stopped for a moment, then began again. The noise was coming from one of the kitchen drawers, she opened it, a large cockroach four inches long promptly crawled out. Gloria grabbed a hammer and smashed it, cutting it in half; she stared as both ends continued to crawl in opposite directions. She smashed it again, until finally killing the resilient creature, gross, she thought. She pulled out a flashlight and investigated the drawers and cabinets. There were three separate holes in the back of the cabinets that led into the walls, tomorrow's project, she thought, bug proofing. She returned to bed, but remained restless, she was far too alert to fall back asleep deeply.

The next morning Nancy stopped by before heading to work. "Cockroaches, a way of life in New York," she said, when Gloria told her about the previous night. "It's usually the neighbors that are far more annoying than the cockroaches," Nancy warned. "But all in all, a good place, toilet flushes, shower works?"

"So far so good," Gloria assured.

"Let's have dinner tonight. Linda is having a meeting with her father, we haven't really had a chance to talk since you got here," Nancy said.

"Sure," Gloria replied casually.

They met at an Ethiopian place down the street. They chatted, mostly avoiding the topic of Linda and the complexity of their personal relationship. Nancy gave Gloria a few ideas about places to hang out where artists and activists tended to congregate. Lately, Brooklyn had undergone an insurgence of creative types, the affordability and increased safety had drawn young people and many artists away from other established colonies. She was hitting Brooklyn at just the right time Nancy said, the city ripe for change after the recent horror of the attack in their own backyard. There was opportunity to shape and lead she encouraged, let yourself be known, things will happen, she said.

Gloria saw very little of Nancy over the next few months, engaging herself in the community, and getting to know the city her only focus. Nancy was right; the collective energy of the creative community was boiling over with purpose. Gloria hooked up with the poets, painters and philosophers of the area. Her new friends were not too dissimilar from her friends in Oakland, but here there was a decided edge, an unmistakable urgency to the movement. The war, once thought to be

300

elementary in ease, was escalating in ferocity. The government was showing more and more arrogance, and the country as a whole was yet to swell with outrage. But in her small community, sentiment was strong, and they were determined to convert the complacent into a force for change.

Gloria spoke unabashedly, anytime, anyplace, to anyone; cafés, parties, parks. She quickly separated herself as a woman of great intellect, unparalleled passion, and most importantly a profound ability to communicate and reach people. Her group of activists grew in strength and confidence.

A perceptible shift in public opinion, not present during the recent elections, began to appear with the gross distaste of the reelection of the president. There was a noticeable slump in the activist community after the people failed to remove the president, a temporary depression of will, but then the movement seemed to catch fire. Post election depression turned into activist mania when it became clear no small half-hearted movement would have an effect on the rapidly downward spiral of political events.

Gloria formed the core four. She and the three most committed leaders in the region: Tran, Ling, and Sean, began planning events, protests, and rallies. At twenty-eight years old, half way through two thousand five, a year and a half after moving to New York, Gloria sensed the tide was turning. Permits were easier to attain, crowds grew larger, the unpatriotic accusations decreased. With the increased exposure, the core four now became recognized as a legitimate threat by the government. Suspicions were high, caution was taken, phone lines were checked, the core four grew tighter, more cohesive, and slightly paranoid. They were sure they were being watched, newcomers were kept at a distance, friends were scarce. The movement became Gloria's whole life, she had never been happier.

*

Back at the ranch, John's old friend, Gundy, had been more than happy to work with John on his secret project. "Reason to get off my arse," Gundy had said. Gundy flew out to John's within weeks of Gloria's departure. The companionship and purpose were both welcome distractions for John after the departure of Gloria, whom he had come to love like a daughter.

Gundy had a small computer network shipped in. John, completely unfamiliar with the machines, watched over Gundy's shoulder for months before joining in. They created a mass information release system capable of being deployed anytime at the touch of a button. Gundy created thousands upon thousands of sites where both Ava and Marty's research would be displayed in their entirety. Gundy compiled an email list of every physicist, nuclear or otherwise, at academic institutions around the world. There were many hundred of these mass e-mails ready to be sent at anytime. He created virus like information spreading programs. The goal, he said, "is to get the information stored on every computer in the world at least once." He created fake advertisements, surveys and polls, that when clicked, would lead the user to a, "site of knowledge," as he called them. In less than a year the system was complete. "They will be able to track the source," Gundy warned, "in days, possibly hours. Your life as you know it will be over, the farm, everything."

"I'm an old man," John said. "I have made preparations to give all the agricultural land to the Clintock's and the workers, everyone, should be protected. I will disappear, I'm good at that."

"I remember," Gundy replied. "And when will it happen?"

"That's up to Gloria," John said.

"Does she have an idea?"

"She hoped to have another interceptor in working order before the release."

"Is the interceptor activated?"

"I don't think so," John replied. "She only wants to turn it on if nuclear war appears inevitable."

"The day is coming."

*

Nancy and Gloria had evolved into business partners. Nancy acted as a liaison between Linda's father at the Dove Corporation and Gloria. Linda's dad, Adam, agreed to take on the top-secret project. The company's sole purpose, promoting projects for peace, could not have been more perfectly aligned with the project's ideals. With funding provided by Gundy, and information given on a need to know basis, only Adam, and the physicist involved, the most brilliant and trustworthy at the Dove Corporation, knew about the project.

The physicist, Chan Lee, had worked at the government's Los Alamos National Lab for seventeen years before so firmly disagreeing with the policies of the current administration, and fearing the escalation of war after 9/11, quit the lab. Dr. Lee showed up at the doorstep of the Dove Corporation three years ago. He truly believes he was born to accomplish the task at hand. Awed by the science and the possibilities of their conclusions, he worked eighteen hours a day, everyday. Adam had briefed Nancy twice thus far. Little progress had been made as Dr. Lee first had to build the one-of-a-kind machines Ava created before he could attempt to replicate her results. Linda was kept entirely in the dark.

Gloria had come into her own in New York, and surprisingly her life had very little to do with Nancy. Proximity could do nothing to overcome the distance placed between them by the presence of Linda. Gloria was for once more consumed with her active life than her internal life. The loss of Nancy was one she could bear for now.

Nancy, engrossed in her career as a professor, was happy to see Gloria thriving. She felt being a distant supporter was her best role. The intrusions of the heart can be the downfall of the mind. Nancy was settled in, not ready to make changes, and

Gloria was booming, changing all the time. Their trajectories were too dissimilar to cross.

Gloria had gained a reputation throughout the activist community as a brilliant speaker, the leader of the times. She had quite a few suitors, men and women, but she rejected the role of lover to anyone, too much to give to a cause she wasn't nearly as committed to as the peace movement.

A rally in Central Park was set for spring, the day before Mother's Day. Gloria and her core four were among the major organizers for the Central Park rally, fifty thousand people were expected. The nuclear war rhetoric had increased as smaller, unstable governments were testing their capability. The war had proven entirely ineffectual in achieving any semblance of stability in the Middle East. Outcry amongst the American people was becoming more commonplace.

Gloria was one of eight scheduled speakers for the May rally. Others included: the mother of a soldier killed in the war, a leading Middle Eastern policy expert, and a coup for the rally, a former CIA operative directly involved in the prewar plan. Gloria's group had devoted the last six months to organizing, preparing, and promoting the Central Park rally. She had collaborated with Ronnie to drum up support on the West Coast, as well as leaders from organizations across the country. The groundswell of support was strong, with almost a ferocious uprising created by the fervor of consistent events put on by Gloria's group. This was the type of event Gloria had hoped for since her first brief glimpse at the power of the collective human spirit seven long years ago. She had been compiling this speech for years. Broader, and more volatile than her local deliveries, her collected thoughts came to her in spasms of essential poetry, waiting to be released in the open air for people to share.

Lately, Gloria's life had become one long hallucinatory fever, otherworldly in its demand, speed and importance. She slept five to six hours a night, the only time she spent in her apartment. She spent the early morning hours walking the streets of the city, enjoying the calm, relative quiet of the dawn hours in a space so fundamentally void of either. She was soothed by the dim dawn light against the skyline, a bit of the majestic in a maze of steel and cement. She usually met her counterparts, the core four, midmorning, clear and focused after the morning walk. She inundated them with thoughts and ideas, people to contact, strategies to attempt. The slow starting group, with a dedicated nightlife, usually spent the first hour or two listening to the wound up young woman.

She had much to offer the group, complete devotion, passion and talent. And they had plenty to offer her, networking, social resources, an outlet. She was like the socially awkward mad genius who greatly excelled in their field, but needed functional support to let it be known. Everyone in the group was talented, but it was Gloria who had the ability they all wanted. She had the ability to move the hearts, minds, and souls of the masses. And none of what they were attempting would be possible without her. She was in another league and they knew it. The fact that she didn't come out with them, or participate in much of the social part of the movement, seemed fundamentally correct. They knew everything she thought about politics, gender, nuclear power, poverty, race, fundamental social underpinnings, but in some ways they knew little of her, the person away from the movement. In truth, Gloria had let go of her life outside the cause, she had staggered there for so long, this world of dedication and change had become an addiction for her; time that so far surpassed any other in purpose and meaning, she didn't even notice everything it was not. They noticed, they admired her and loved her the best they could, knowing there would be places their relationship would never go.

Gloria approached the small taqueria for her third meeting with Nancy to discuss the Dove Corporation's progress with the nuclear interceptor. Gloria ordered for both of them, in Spanish, per usual. They each had tacos and a beer, a rare foray into alcohol for Gloria, a nice icebreaker for her time with Nancy. The small, brightly colored eating spot had served for the locale of each of their meetings. Down the street from their apartment building, Gloria often frequented the small restaurant. She felt entirely comfortable tucked in the corner quietly discussing their secret project.

"The information seems to have remained confidential," Nancy began.

"No surprises?"

"None. Dr. Lee has almost completed the modifications to the heavy ion collision machine."

"Good."

"Things should pick up from there, Adam says. I mean there's not much to say... about the project at least."

Gloria shot a quick glance at Nancy, contemplating opening the discussion on the absence of their relationship. "John appears all set on his end," she said, instead.

"That's great," Nancy said, somewhat dejectedly. "Do you have any idea about the release?"

"I'm not sure yet, I've given it a lot of thought."

"I'm sure you have," Nancy said, smiling.

Gloria smiled, relaxing some, realizing Nancy was gently prodding her, not attacking her. "This administration has proven merciless with its tactics. I fear for the safety of all those involved."

"So you want to wait until they're out of office?" Nancy questioned.

"If that's an option."

"I highly doubt it will be. I mean, I'm not as involved in the movement as you are, but this administration seems determined to implode and they are looking to take someone down with them, justify their actions or whatnot. Waiting until they're gone seems like more like a lack of a plan than an actual plan."

"I just don't know yet, so much is changing all the time, this rally in Central Park is huge."

"You're still hoping the people will rise up to determine the course of history."

"I am," Gloria stated simply.

"And what if the government won't let them?"

"Not possible, it is always about the people."

"I hope you're right."

They were quiet for a few minutes, picking at their tacos and sipping their beer. "Do you still paint?" Nancy asked eventually.

"I do, in the park mostly. It's tough though, painting reminds me so much of growing up, the way I left my dad. You know he really wanted a portrait of me."

"I know, you told me."

"I did?"

"Yeah, on our road trip. You said you weren't ready, because you didn't really know yourself."

"Crazy, hey?"

"Exacting, but that's who you are."

"I wish my father could see me as a woman, doing what I love, my mom, too, but I know she's gone, and she sees me in her own way, but he's still alive, and he's missing everything."

"That's the first time I've heard you talk about heaven."

Gloria looked at Nancy oddly. "I didn't say anything about heaven."

"Your mom seeing you."

"Yeah, that has nothing to do with heaven. If there's one thing she taught me, it's that there are forces at work we are far from understanding. She was able to work in a realm previously unknown. How could I possibly say there is no chance her energy is not still there somewhere, investigating the unknown? I could never say that. I believe in the unknown, heaven is some people's explanation for it, not mine. I don't need all that oppression with my afterlife."

Nancy laughed, then stated soberly, "I'm sorry you are not sharing your life with the people you love."

Gloria looked at her suspiciously. Was this another opportunity to bring up their relationship? She again deflected. "You know they've built an airstrip at the ranch, John and Gundy, and they have a decommissioned military jet out there for when they have to evacuate. Gundy flies almost everyday to stay sharp. They're very prepared," Gloria laughed.

"They're back at war," Nancy said.

"Except now they're in charge, and have a chance for it to end peacefully."

"Is Gundy living there?"

"Yes, he took the second bedroom. Two eighty year olds, they're obsessed. At first I felt guilty about dragging everybody into this, but they're so into it, I'm happy they're involved."

"It's an amazing thing to be a part of. No one would agree to help if they didn't believe in the project."

"Thank you, I worry," Gloria said appreciatively.

"You do a lot of worrying, at some point you have to enjoy it, life isn't one big fight you know."

"It's not?" Gloria said, smiling.

"No. I know you're trying to be cute, but you always take on so much responsibility for everything and everyone, that's a lot of pressure G, it will drive you crazy."

"This is how I've always felt, like I should be working for something more, it's the only time I feel settled."

"When you're working for upheaval?"

"Yes."

"Well, just take care of yourself."

"I always do."

"You don't have to, you know, always be alone," Nancy said hesitantly.

"Why, are you going to be with me?" Gloria asked flatly before she had time to censor herself.

"Maybe?" Nancy replied.

"We shall see."

"We shall."

The morning of the rally arrived. Gloria had slept unusually well, eight hours; it was seven a.m. before she awoke. The rally started at two, she arrived at ten. She was surprised to see many people had already amassed by the staging area. There appeared to be thousands; families, radicals, picnickers, and lovers, all there early to enjoy the festivities. There was very little for Gloria to do, others were in charge of staging, sound, and security. She met the other speakers as they arrived, but for the most part she kept to herself, taking in the surroundings sitting on the side of the stage overlooking the crowd. She smiled as people continued to pour in, overflowing the wide expanses of the large open field. By noon the crowd was already a mile deep and a half-mile wide, banners and signs overhead, chants filled the air. Gloria closed her eyes, listening and feeling the energy of the people.

"This is the type of audience we have all been hoping for," Catherine Nagel, the mother of a fallen soldier said to Gloria. "Thank you."

Gloria stood and hugged the tiny woman. "I'm very sorry for your loss," she said.

"Thank you."

"I respect very much your protest of the war, the sit in, your hunger strike, huge personal efforts to raise awareness. I really think it is helping," Gloria said.

"I hope."

"Today is proof."

"I hear you're the next great leader," the woman said kindly.

"That's what they say. We'll find out today if there really is something to this movement, and if I have the capacity to lead."

"You're last to speak aren't you?"

"I am."

"I look forward to it."

"Thank you, I look forward to hearing you as well."

306

The women embraced. Gloria returned to her seat beside the stage.

The crowd grew larger and larger, a hundred thousand people she'd heard someone say. She was thankful they had not grown unruly; the mass seemed as intense and focused as those about to address them.

Ronnie tapped her on the shoulder a few minutes before the event began. "Great turnout," he said as they hugged.

After his initial anger over the breakup, they had remained good friends, and worked as collaborators. "With your help," she replied.

"I heard there are over thirty thousand people from the west coast alone," he said proudly. She looked out over the crowd saying nothing. Ronnie continued, "okay, I just wanted to say hello, wish you luck."

"Thank you," she said.

One of the co-organizers, someone from a lobbying group in D.C., briefly stepped up to the microphone. The crowd grew quiet, then roared with approval as the first speaker was introduced. Gloria's mouth went dry as the rally commenced; she located a bottle of water, her head swimming with all she wanted to say. She heard the voices through the speakers, but mostly she could not come out of her head long enough to focus on what was said. The weather was perfect, sixty eight degrees, with passing large white puffy clouds. The speakers were given five to ten minutes, until Gloria, her time was unlimited.

The crowd seemed entirely engaged as Gloria's turn neared. Miles and miles of people drawn out before her, all colors, shapes and sizes, chattered and clapped, whistled and cheered, as stories of heartache and triumph played out before them. There was weeping in the crowd as Catherine Nagel shared the story of receiving the news of her son's death, the knock at the door, the letter from him that arrived more than a week after his passing. The grieving mother delivered the speech with a determined sense of duty and purpose, unwilling to let her emotions get in the way of the message. She had tears streaming down her face as she left the stage, but she had made it through, mission accomplished, possibly one iota of the pain of war expressed.

The crowd was subdued before Gloria's introduction, emotionally worn, but immediately sparked to life as they saw her approach. "Ladies and gentlemen," the announcer roared, "New York's very own, say it with me G, L, O, R, I, A, Glorrrria." The crowd continued chanting her name to the musical anthem of another generation. At first, Gloria felt mortified to have her name spelled, then sung loudly, a goofy spectacle, she thought. But the crowd kept at it, "G, L, O, R, I, A, Glorrrria, G, L, O, R, I, A, Glorrrria." The sound of thousands of voices in unison brought the crowd to life, together, smiling, singing, rooting for her, her heart soared. She walked up to the podium under the heavy vibrations of her name ringing in the air. After recovering from the embarrassment of her own name reigning upon her, she put up her hands, immediately the singing stopped. The crowd, impressed with their spontaneous silence, burst into loud applause. The applause quickly subsided, they were ready for her.

"It is an honor to stand here before you today. It is an honor to engage honestly and openly in the democratic principles of our great country. For those of us fortunate enough to be United States citizens there is no greater gift bestowed upon our people than the right to shape our nation through the democratic process. This is a country where we can fight for one's beliefs, and not be unjustly persecuted because of it. That is a rare and precious honor indeed, one that I, and clear by your presence here today, you, do not take for granted.

"Unfortunately, there are too many things we as Americans do take for granted. First and foremost, we have for too long taken for granted that our government is inherently interested in adhering to the principles this country was founded on. But this is not a speech in which I will harp on a flawed and corrupt system, because above all, the principles of this country give the people the power to decide their own fate. Let me repeat that, the people, not the government, decide the fate of this country. The government simply makes decisions on our behalf. Throughout the world, and policies here at home, they do what they think is best. Some in government do what they think is best for their country, some do what they think is best for their state, their constituency, their friends, their cronies, or even their wallet. There are countless reasons why our representatives make the decisions they do, some good, some bad, but they all represent you. What we do too often as a society is blame the government for their bad decisions, when in actuality the responsibility lies with us.

"Today, we are here to oppose the nasty and vile degradation of human life our government calls a necessary war. Some of us claim to be mad, look at what our government has done, that spoiled brat in office, he's a fool, a buffoon, look at what he's done. But today we must shift the dialogue, and ask ourselves, what have I done? I'm not talking strictly about voting, yes, many in this country made the egregious error of electing this president not once, but twice, but the democratic process does not end there. I'm talking about each and every one of us watching these decisions made on our behalf, and not caring enough to intervene. What representation cleverly allows, is for separation, an insidious distance between us and those who make decisions on our behalf.

"For far too long, because we consider ourselves a good, kind, decent people founded on equality, we have believed that this is the framework followed by our leaders despite evidence to the contrary. Whether malicious, ignorant, or with the best intentions, we have decided to stay an incredibly minor, almost inconsequential part of the equation. Yes, it is true, at this point in our history the will of the American people has become a virtually inconsequential part of the direction of our country. Not simply because we vote with abysmal irregularity, as typically only half of us exercise our right to vote, but because the few of us who do vote, stop there, our only engagement in the democratic process.

"I would like to speak about a few of the times throughout American history when the will of the people has played a major role in the future. First, we were founded on rebellion. An unfair and unrepresentative ruler was tossed out by fed up people during the Revolutionary War. And then there was the creation of quite possibly one of the greatest documents ever written, the Declaration of Independence, written by radicals unwilling to go along with an oppressive government. Uprising brought about change. There is the Civil War. Uprising brought about change. Not to taint you into believing all change must come through violence, which I firmly believe it does not, there are non-violent examples. Look at women gaining the right to vote, the Nineteenth amendment. What did it take? Peaceful protests, speeches, rallies, the people brought about change. The Civil Rights era, a remarkable period in history. Again, nonviolent protests by brave and determined people who faced beatings, harassment, jail, and yet, they were able to create change. The Vietnam War protests, a clear example of the people telling the government their actions were not acceptable. And what happened? Change. Truly, our role as citizens is very simple, let your opinion be known, if not, people will assume they know what's in your heart.

"Here's the bleak reality if I make assumptions about what is in the American people's heart today. Domestically, sadly we are a culture that does not believe our physical and mental well-being should be cared for. For some reason we have decided money is more important than health care. It is more important for our people to unreasonably sustain our capitalistic culture than take care of our sick. We accept that our government, our representatives, have deemed our health, our healthcare, something we can live without, we as a people have accepted that.

"To black people, I'm sorry; we are not very nice to you at all. We've systematically oppressed you, insulted you, degraded you. We have done everything we could to make you feel bad about yourselves, and attempt to leave you with less opportunity than the majority. And now we expect nothing of you but to be degenerates and hoodlums. And don't you dare be mad, or anything but subservient, because we will put you back in your place so fast, because, we've thought you were good for nothing for so long it's hard to stop. We have not done anything as a society to let black people know we honor and cherish them, we love them, we are glad they are here. We continue to act as if black people were a tiresome burden, the scourge we continually have to deal with.

"If I assume I know what is in the heart of the American people by the actions we allow, I can only conclude we are a racist society. That is the only conclusion I can come to when I continue to see the devastating plight of an entire culture of people. When you treat people terribly, they are going to feel bad, me, you, we all feel bad when we are treated poorly. But treat people well, and you will be amazed by what happens. It's time we start treating black people well, look them in the eye, shake their hand, treat them with the love we reserve for our own kin. The silliest thing to me has always been white people being scared of black people. What, did they take you from your homeland, enslave you, rape you, beat you, whip you, curse you, give you no rights, treat you as if you were nothing? What we don't recognize is that black people have every reason to be scared of white people. They shouldn't trust us, for good reason, because we have betrayed them. We have betrayed them in the sickest, cruelest ways humans can betray each other, and we haven't even said were sorry, it was a mistake, we recognize the value you bring to our lives, and we love you."

There was scattered applause.

"Another assumption I can make about the American people by the practice's this country tolerates, is that we are a culture of rape. We prey upon our women and our young. Generally speaking, in my own life, nine out of ten of my female friends have been forced to commit unwanted sexual acts. Sexual violence is pervasive, and still veiled in a cloak of silence. American men, you are raping the women of this country. You are disgracefully disrespecting the mothers, grandmothers, sisters, and daughters of this nation. As women we walk in constant fear of sexual attack. Let me spell it out for you so there is no doubt about the crime we continually allow to be committed, attempted murder of the soul, that is what rape is, one of the vilest and most disgusting acts perpetrated upon people, commonplace.

"We live in a country where rape is an accepted part of life. Men don't stand up against it, and women are repeatedly mistreated for trying to fight it. Is this the America we've agreed upon on? Speak up, speak out, it is time for change. To the men who perpetrate this violence, you are pathetic, despicable, feeble people with no respect for others. To women, it is time we fight back despite the obstacles, get self defense training, be vigilant. I know the onus should not be placed on women to correct the ills of men, but as women we are powerful people. And for far too long we have accepted that we are not worthy of standing up for, that we must submit because they are stronger and we are powerless. This is a myth, a fable, entirely untrue. We do have power, we have the power to demand our bodies, and consequently our minds, are treated with respect and dignity. Men, stop raping women, it is wrong. We as a country need to send a collective message, rape is wrong, it hurts people, yes, it hurts. And women, you do not need to suffer alone in silence, we care for you, we support you, we love you.

"We are a country that accepts poverty and poor education. We use cheap, illegal workers to maximize profits, and then have the audacity to insult those same people who work to the bone to feed their families. We disrespect animals, caging them, slaughtering them, as if they never mattered at all, and then we consume them and expect not to be held accountable. But deadly morphing diseases like mad cow and bird flu tell us otherwise. We care not about our food supply, nasty preservatives, additives and sugars, ruining the health of our people, dangerous but extremely profitable. In America, money justifies all means. As a society we sit lounging in front of the television, in our XXXL T-shirt from Wal-Mart, and our size forty-six jeans, our bodies bulging everywhere, and we don't care as long as we can get our ninety-nine cent hamburger, our sixty-four ounce big gulp, and a chance to vote for the next American Idol.

"The acceptance of degrading language in this country is astronomical. We harass, insult, belittle, and condemn at will. Our abominable treatment of gays and lesbians is unnecessary. We are all people who fall madly in love with each other;

we're the same, not different. Sexual and intimate expression is similar in intensity, importance, and obsessive insanity for all of us. Until we understand we are people with far more similarities than differences we will be unwilling to accept each other. We all lose in this equation, the equation of degradation, one damaging another, one hates, one hated, both lose. We are far better together, respecting one another.

"Do you know what happens when gay people work side-by-side with straight people? They get along. When Mexicans and whites work together? They get along. When we come together, free of rigid prejudice, and engage in a shared pursuit, we come away respecting each other. I'm not talking the sociopaths and deviants of the population; I'm talking about the great many of us with extremely similar ideas for society, similar ideas for what comprises solid character: respect, decency, honesty. If we take a moment to understand the importance of sharing a general respect for all people, our similar ideals will have space to expand, all of us together. But if we limit our ideas, and narrow what we're willing to share with each other, we will be a skeptical and mistrusting society infused with fear and separation. Your preference is your reality, and thus far we have chosen separation. I say it is time for unity, time we understand the beauty of our similarities, and our differences.

"Is this an unduly harsh assessment of America? Possibly? Show me a different America. I would love to be proven wrong.

"But wait, I've only talked about our domestic policies, many are here today to protest this administration's international policies. There is a great deal of anti-American sentiment throughout the world. How dare they, many of us say, we are a beautiful democratic country that just wants what's best for everybody else. But I believe many of us have been naïve to the American impact around the world for far too long. We are seen as a country that has everything; freedom, prosperity, and opportunity, and with these gifts comes responsibility. So when we exploit workers with measly wages, poor working conditions, and the unethical utilization of child labor, we quickly fan the flame of international discontent. We have fewer reasons than any country to exploit anyone. We can afford ethical working conditions more so than any other country in the world, which is why our failures are met with particular contempt.

"Our narcissistic indulgence in the earth's resources shows nothing but disdain for the world's citizens, and the earth itself, we are disrespecting everyone's home. Americans have become far too accustomed to meeting all of their whims and desires regardless of the cost to the planet or humanity. Why would these actions sit well with other people? Do they have it wrong? We really are doing everything we can to respect the rights of others sharing the planet? Again, prove America's critics wrong; show them we truly are a good world citizen.

"And now, we are at war, why? Oil, power, religion, ideology, pride, nobility, the real reasons are never clear or simple. What we do know is something isn't right, in fact, many things aren't right. We preemptively attacked a country that was no threat to us, a policy previous administrations rejected. Not only that, we attacked with a fatally flawed strategy. Many mistakes have contributed to the state of the war today, but the greatest mistake has been the uncritical, passive tolerance of the American people. We know soldiers and civilians are dying because this administration made some atrocious decisions, but as the people those decisions are made in the name of, we can only consider ourselves co-conspirators in the war until we commit to its end.

"We do not have to let these atrocities continue because some brat was bequeathed power. We are so sure it is hopeless, a situation we cannot influence, we do nothing. We talk about what a fool the president is, oh and the VP, the scum of the earth, they are bad, bad, bad, but they still represent us. We still allow them to speak for us. I'm here to let you know we don't have to, we don't have to let the narrow, mean-spirited voice of a spoiled boy who manipulated his way to power speak for this country. It is time we speak for ourselves. This war, totally unacceptable, not one more day. We, as the American people, need to make it clear, not one more day. To truly care about the future of this country is to be willing to bare your soul for it, and be willing to stand up for what you believe. We can no longer stand idly by and let every beautiful premise this country was founded on languish in the gutter of an apathetic people.

"And certainly no government is entitled to threaten the lives of millions with the touch of a button. As grotesque as war is, there is still a shred of civility in facing your enemy in combat. The greatest of arrogances allows only the most corrupt among us to believe they are justified in controlling the fate of the masses. We have a grave problem which affects all of humanity. We have somehow let totalitarianism seep into our culture. The notion that the few can kill many from opposite ends of the world looms over the head of humanity.

"A people constantly under threat are never truly free. And whether we like to admit it to ourselves or not, the allowance of nuclear weaponry leaves us all vulnerable. At this point in history, this one form of warfare so far surpasses the ethics of conflict and justification, it should be completely eradicated. All citizens of this great nation, and people throughout the world, have accepted a complete imbalance of power. I ask you, if we can create nuclear weapons, why can't we create a force to counter them? I will tell you why, there is no desire. Certainly no desire from the government, they benefit greatly from the constant threat, but surprisingly no desire from the people. It's as if we have collectively decided it is reasonable for those determined enough to develop the ultimate killing machine to control our fate, someone else will have the bomb, we might as well too. Why are we not committing to the eradication of such outrageously unjustifiable human determinism?

"To this day we have been the only country to use the atomic bomb as an act of war. We've all seen the pictures, terrified children, melting flesh, hundreds of thousands of innocent people killed. The next generations continue to be affected, with alarming amounts of cancers in the region still occurring today. This is the history of our great country that we have accepted all too willingly, and seem unconcerned about repeating. Let me remind you, at the time we dropped the first

312

atomic bomb on Hiroshima, and then another three days later at Nagasaki, Hitler was dead, Germany had surrendered, for all intents and purposes, World War II was over. Why drop the bombs on a nearly defeated Japan? To end the war sooner? impatience? To save further loss of American troops? Revenge? I ask you, could there possibly be a justifiable reason to allow a few white men in a room to kill hundreds of thousands of people, civilians, not soldiers, literally affecting the lives of millions? I will listen to all justifications, and possibly some may prove mildly persuasive, but quite frankly, with every shred of my being, I know it was the wrong decision, and not a decision we can allow to be made again.

"The scale of the devastation of nuclear warfare is incomprehensible, and in this incomprehensible abstract form we lose perspective. In the news we hear of tragic tales of entire families gunned down in their home, murdered in their sleep, neighbors weep, a horrified community mourns. Multiply that by one hundred thousand, and we are all the neighbors who weep, we are all the communities who mourn. And whether we defend our government, believe we have the right to use nuclear bombs or not; we are all affected by large-scale murder. There's something lost in the collective world psyche, a devaluation of an individual's ability to feel their life is of consequence, the simple notion that they are entitled to live because they have been born, and as people we value the lives of others as much as we value our own. The message we are sending with nuclear warfare is be careful, your government crosses us, you working in the fields, child sitting in the classroom, man sleeping in your bed; you shall lose your life. Is this a principle we as a people want to live by?"

"No!" people in the crowd yelled.

"So I ask you, why do we allow it? Why have we as a people not acted to end this gross abuse of power? How can we let this happen in our name? As a community of innovators and inventors, we today can pledge to make nuclear weaponry obsolete. I assure you it can be done. The government will not like it, and know they will be threatened. But it is about time the people of this country threaten the government, for far too long it has been the other way around. The great talent and expertise of motivated Americans can end the threat of nuclear warfare, but there must be a will, there must be a belief that it is possible. There will be no change on this issue without a cultural shift, one that replaces the belief that a nuclear bomb is a necessary tool in squelching a particular uprising. In reality the bomb is actually an extremely divisive, threatening, and peace disrupting device. We hold the perception the bomb is a peacemaker, only in self-indulgent delusions of grandeur could a person see the killing of hundreds of thousands of people as keeping the peace, that is war, the perceived peacemaker is an act of war.

"Nuclear proliferation continues to occur, countries bargain, banter, and threaten, with the ultimate feather in their cap. The world's chess match, played by leaders, with their people's lives. The people of the world have become bargaining chips for trade agreements, labor policies, and tariff reduction. We all have become the disposable commodity in trade by egomaniac leaders. When we do not respect our lives enough to say we will not live under the threat of constant nuclear warfare, why should they? We have accepted the rules of the game which someone will surely lose. As Americans, we walk with the blind confidence that it will not be us, we are the United States of America for God's sakes, nuclear bombs don't get dropped here. Not yet, but every day we continue to condone nuclear proliferation, we're one day sooner to seeing that dreaded mushroom cloud on the American horizon.

"So how do we stop it? First, we must decide we want to, then we make a plan. Today, I propose a plan: protest your government, let your voices be heard, demand change, all magical and effective democratic processes that will result in change. And, I say don't wait for the government to change; we must make the change happen on our own. Yes, nuclear weaponry can be made, an amazing scientific achievement, and it can be stopped. We have scientists here in our own country that could render nuclear bombs obsolete. A concentrated cultural movement to end the nuclear reign must be implemented, spark the interest, fund the research, the results will follow. We can solve the problem of the nuclear threat. We are resourceful, capable, and talented people; we have the ability to create a world safer and more humane than the world of today. It is a massive undertaking, it will take time, discipline and determination, but it can be done. I believe in our ability, the only thing I question is our commitment.

"We live in a time when commitments are fragmented, commercialized, and dehumanized. First, we must become aware of what we have lost, and then we must seek to reacquire it. I argue, in the case of nuclear warfare, that we have so profoundly lost respect for human life, the world can only be divided as long as the threat remains. We must return to a time when we sought to further the welfare of all people. Possibly, that time has never truly existed, as warfare is as entrenched in the human culture as anything, but that doesn't mean that time will not exist. We must do everything in our power to unify the people of the world, show them there is nothing we want more than a safe, healthy and prosperous humanity. We can start by declaring nuclear weaponry out of the ethical sphere of a country devoted to peace. It's time decide how completely we will devote to being a country of peace. We must end nuclear proliferation today. And we must find a way to return the power balance of humanity back to the people.

"I've told you about some of the sad realities of this country, and some of you I'm sure have taken great personal offense to the berating of the country you love. Let me tell you of the America I envision, the one truly worthy of your love and devotion. I envision a country, not of great promises, but of great truths. I envision a country where our truths are so great, we are above the criticism of the maniacal, one where there is no cause for international fury or retaliation. And with that envisioned America, comes a humble, righteous, ethical capitalistic approach to policy, the financial bottom line a concern, but not the only concern. We are a democracy, and a capitalist society, but the balance of power has tilted so far to our capitalist desires, our democracy has been suppressed. Ethical capitalism is a possibility, and must be made a priority.

"We need to ask ourselves what kind of decision-making we want from our leaders. Do we as a country care about human rights? The environment? Sexism? Racism? Violence? War? Do we really care about these things? I believe we do, we simply do not know how far from our beliefs we have strayed. I believe we are a country of good, kind, hard-working people who genuinely want others to succeed, but we have lost our way, mired in the game of pessimism, misinformation, and powerlessness propagated by our leaders.

"Our government tells you there is only one option, their chosen course, all others will lead to catastrophic doom and gloom. We are cowering to our supposed leaders and buckling under their scare tactics. Now, it has become clear the doom and gloom they threaten will overtake us is already upon us, and their policies are responsible. We are living with the terror they infect us with. But don't question them they warn, because it could be worse. I'm here to say, it could be better, dramatically and incredibly better. It's time to stop being afraid it will get worse and deferring our responsibility to others. It is time we decide the future of our country. It is time we the people of the United States of America act like the country we know we are capable of being, a country that brings peace and prosperity to those at home and abroad, a country that respects a person simply because they exist, not because they look right, or have the right amount of money, a country that truly, deeply, cares about the health of its' citizens, and does all it can to share medications and techniques with all people, a country with a profound respect for morality, the golden rule, life, liberty and the pursuit of happiness.

"I envision an America committed to ending poverty, here, and across borders. A country where rape is so condemned, the ostracization of the rapist eradicates the rape disease of the culture, a country where all people, all colors, all sexes, religions and orientations are treated firstly with respect and kindness. I believe the American conscience is good, simply suppressed under greed, indulgence, and complaining. We have made mistakes, we have done wrong, but as a young country we simply embody the epitome of the human struggle. A subdued and passive people have allowed the government too much power. The founders of this country envisioned a land where the people maintained the power, it is in our laws, it is in our constitution, but it is not in our hearts. If we do not feel our power and act on it, we have none. Our power, as the people of this country, is to be a part of the America we want.

"Today, there are two Americas, the one we are assumed to be based on our ignorance and our apathy, and the America we know we can be. I believe it is time to find a way to be the best America we can be. We must walk with freedom and equality in our hearts, not just in our documents. We must as citizens accept the rights and responsibilities of our power to control our own fate. We must not relinquish the beautiful gifts of our citizenship to a great country founded on extraordinary principles. We must speak up, demand change, and realize everything we do is political. How we spend our dollars, the companies and products we support, political will we can exert. To be mindless in our actions is to be a puppet for the corrupt. It is time we understand our own impact, and realize we are the deciders, but we have stopped truly caring about our decisions. We have wrongfully concluded we are only a small part of a whole and we have little influence, little control, but nothing could be further from the truth. We are the only essential component of the whole; everything else is replaceable, powerless without us. People, individuals, dreams, and desires, they are not replaceable. Your will is the most powerful force on earth. People's will is responsible for every great human experience, as well as every great tragedy.

"As Americans we are suffering through a period of time dominated by tragedies. We can debate endlessly as to why we are here, but only the will of the people will create change. Today, we must devote ourselves to our communities, our country and our people. Let there be no mistake, our people is every one of us, every person walking this earth. We have yet to understand how positively we can all influence each other, because up until this point we have been at odds. We have allowed grievances and differences to play a larger role in our interactions than our openness and similarities. We do have the ability to get along, to learn from each other, respect and cherish each other; it starts at home, your family, your neighbor, your country, the world. Kindness is an attitude, one we have not entirely committed to. Dissension is an attitude we have not yet worked hard enough to overcome. The self-portrait of America is far from complete. If we honestly take a step forward, and look closely, we must admit we do not like everything we see, but that does not mean we are ugly, or dark at heart, it means we are human. But I ask us as Americans, are we people who want to do better? Are we committed to a better nation? If we are, we must no longer shirk our responsibility to the future, we must rise up, we must demand change, and we must not stop until it happens."

The slightly stunned, near silent crowd erupted into a ferocious, powerful mix of yells and applause. The swell of energy from the mass, approaching two hundred thousand people, sent shivers up Gloria's spine. She was not hopeful about the speech, wary of the pessimistic, lecturing tone, the lack of interspersed applause and approval lingering in the back of her mind throughout the vast majority of the diatribe. But she had let herself go, said what she felt needed to be said, we are a flawed nation with much room for improvement. If we are not honest with ourselves, nothing will change.

She would have liked to give a short rip roaring speech like the one she did many years ago in People's Park, but that had proved only a minor, temporary uptake in the heartbeat of the culture. Today, she left them with something they would never forget, perspectives they would have to mull over and come to conclusions on their own, exercise the power of critical thought. She worried she had disappointed those who had come to see her, the organizers, the movement; but the one person she knew she did not disappoint, was herself.

As she left the stage to the deafening swirl of noise, her mind was completely

316

quiet, a floating piece of serenity in a lifetime of turmoil. When she hit the bottom of the stairs, Catherine Nagel, the dead soldier's mother, emphatically embraced her. "You spoke for us all, what we all wish we had the courage to say," the woman said, wiping away tears.

"Thank you, I wasn't sure," Gloria replied.

"Be sure, you have touched the heart of the matter like few who have come before."

"Thank you."

Gloria remained by the stage in a slight daze after the complete mental engagement of the speech. A few people came up to her, congratulated her, but most stared with a cautious curiosity. The speech left her somewhere between being one of the people, and being removed from them. She made grand declarations, espoused lofty ideology, but did they trust her, it was too soon to tell. Her reputation solidly proven in New York, and in the activist community, but it was the layman, the newcomers, those were the hearts she wanted to sway.

In the last year she had given nearly one hundred speeches, small venues, a few rallies, but this was the audience that could change the movement spreading the message to the corners of the country. They mulled around now, the crowd dissipating, some lingering at the booths, some convening for discussion, a few families spreading their blankets and feeding hungry children, but Gloria they were not prepared to approach. Either they were scared of her, or revered her, possibly both? The reaction of the large crowd at People's Park had been swift and clear, their enthusiasm unguarded. Now, people were thinking, she could see it in their eyes, see it in their movements. She had challenged them, and they were debating whether they should accept.

Gloria felt a comforting hand on her back as she leaned against the stage, she turned, Nancy looked at her kindly, nurturingly. "Hey," Nancy said, rubbing Gloria's back between her shoulder blades, "you all right?"

Gloria looked at her with a distant glare her in her eyes. Nancy brought her other arm up to Gloria's neck and rubbed her gently, still keeping some space between them. "Pretty raw right now," Nancy said. Gloria looked at Nancy with the same scared and vulnerable look she had not seen since that first day on the train when Gloria awoke from the nightmare. "Hey," Nancy said, taking her in her arms, "that was the bravest thing I've ever seen in my life." Gloria relaxed into Nancy's comforting embrace. Nancy continued. "No one in this park will ever forget this day. You have given the amazing power and courage in your heart to the people. You are theirs now, but they still need you to show them the way."

"And what if I can't?" Gloria said meekly, her words muffled by her face buried in Nancy's shoulder.

"You can. But you're scared, because now they take you seriously, and to you that is unbelievably important. The intensity of your life has just amplified dramatically. You've got to bring yourself back down; you're going to be okay." Nancy lowered her head and rested her cheek against Gloria's temple. "It was good," she whispered. "You made your parents, me, and many Americans very proud."

"They were very quiet, they didn't cheer, they didn't react," Gloria responded.

"They were shocked, and then they were enraptured. You raised the bar, they were not expecting to be questioned and challenged. It's all anybody is talking about, you've left them engaged, inspired, you got to them, truly, they heard you."

"Could you walk me home?" Gloria asked after a moment.

"Sure," Nancy said, grabbing her hand.

They walked slowly, hand in hand, away from the crowd. The lowering mid afternoon sun brought just the hint of a chill to the air. The park was surprisingly calm after the recent influx and departure of so many people. "My parents are here, and John and Gundy, they flew out on Gundy's plane, they all heard you," Nancy said to Gloria.

"Wow, where are they now?"

"I told them I'd meet them back at the hotel later. We're all having dinner tonight if you want to come?"

"I would love to. Oh that's so great." Gloria said, in a state of disbelief. "I had no idea they were coming."

"They all wanted to be here."

"I'm really glad, that makes me really happy," Gloria said sweetly.

"Good," Nancy said, squeezing her hand. They walked along in a thick, but comfortable silence, taking it slow, safely entering into a new world.

*

The anti-war movement had been under the watchful eye of the American government since the beginning. With virtually unlimited domestic spying power, any up tick in anti-government sentiment was readily investigated, paranoia justified by 9/11 after all. Gloria's small cell had been wiretapped, bugged and followed shortly after the inception of the core four.

There were no less than a hundred members of the FBI, and a handful of CIA operatives at the rally in Central Park. Gloria had first drawn their attention back in the year two thousand with her speech in People's Park. Then she dropped off their radar during her time at the ranch, but when she resurfaced in New York City, they decided to keep close tabs on her.

Until her speech in Central Park, she was considered a person of interest, now, she was considered a threat. Persuading the public against its policies was something the government did not take lightly. They redoubled their efforts to find out everything they could about the girl known simply as Gloria. Their initial searches provided little information, so while Gloria changed for dinner, two members of the Department of Homeland Security were staked outside her building, and a full-fledged investigation into her background was officially launched.

They went to a nice place, a French restaurant John wanted to try while in the city. The ranch family reunion in the lobby of the hotel was a joyous affair. They showered love and praise upon Gloria. So much so, she was drawn out slightly from the insecure introspection of the post-speech doubt. She was happy they had decided to make the trip, a huge dose of love to soothe her depleted emotions. The dinner was far too posh for her taste, but the food was great and the Clintock's got drunk, which was always amusing.

They walked to an Irish pub after dinner. John and Gundy grabbed stools at the bar and immediately started a lively conversation with the bartender. Even though they were in their eighties, they showed no sign of slowing down as the clock approached midnight. The Clintock's quickly became engaged in a discussion on politics with a couple of friendly guys at the bar. Nancy and Gloria slipped away to a small corner table, hoping to slow the pace of the evening into a manageable conversation. "Crazy night," Nancy said after they sat down.

"Bats out of hell set free in New York," Gloria laughed. "How long are they staying?"

"'Til Monday. We're going to have a picnic tomorrow in the park if you want to come?"

"Who is going to be there?" Gloria asked.

"The same crew as tonight."

"What about Linda?"

"She's doing her own thing."

Gloria paused, this was very unusual for Nancy and Linda, they spent most special occasions together, and with tomorrow being Mother's Day she couldn't help but be concerned, but like so many times before, she left it alone. "A picnic, sounds like fun," was all she said.

"I don't imagine it will be too early with this crew," Nancy said, looking over at the bar. "Two-ish probably."

"It is really great they came," Gloria said again, still dumbfounded.

"You're not mad I didn't tell you?"

"Not at all, it was a great surprise."

"Good, we haven't really been talking very much, I know you've had a lot on your mind, I didn't want it to disrupt you."

"No, it's great, I'm happy."

"Me too. The speech really was amazing. Are you worried about how people will react?"

"Definitely, I'm concerned, they were so quiet."

"That's not what I'm talking about. You know, the people you are organizing against, the government. You have a lot to hide, and now you are a very public figure."

"I couldn't hide forever."

"No, I know, but what if they find out about your past, your mom's project?"

"We're working as hard as we can on that."

"But what about your safety?"

"I'm not going to be around forever, I might as well do what I can while I'm here."

"What do you mean you're not going to be around forever?"

"Nancy, I watched my mother be blown to smithereens as a result of her pursuits, and still chose to follow the same path. Let's just say I don't think I'll die of old age."

"Don't say that."

"Nancy, I've declared war on the government, true it is one of ideology and principle, and I hope that's where it remains, but on this issue I'm far from naïve. My eyes are wide open, and I'm willing."

"So you think it's worth it?"

"Yes, it's worth it. It became clear I couldn't live my life any other way. I am my parents' daughter, and also a direct result of one woman's decision to change an abysmal American policy. Revolution is in my blood, every moment I spent denying it was torture, now, I can truly be free. It's not me I worry about, it's you, those around me, there is potential for so much hurt."

"There's the potential for so much gain."

"I hope so," Gloria said skeptically.

"I know so."

Gloria looked at Nancy intently. "Where does that come from, your unwavering belief in me?"

"There is nothing I know more than the trueness of your spirit, I knew it from the first moment I met you, and everyday since."

"Everyday?"

"Everyday. The time apart, the Ronnie thing, I always knew you were true, human and frail, but true."

"I feel the same way about you."

"I know you do. I've had my doubts, don't get me wrong, but they never won."

"I appreciate that."

"It's a nice feeling to have," Nancy said.

Gloria sat back in her chair as a somber lip quivering frown came over her face. Nancy reached out and placed her hand on top of Gloria's. "It means a lot to me, having someone believe in me," Gloria said, fighting back tears.

"I know it does."

"My parents always did, but my mom I didn't really realize until after she died. My dad was the only one I've always known believed in me, until you. It's hard to do it all on your own."

"You don't have to. I'm always here for you."

Tears started rolling down Gloria's cheeks. She sniffled as she looked at Nancy with her sad, soft, tear filled eyes. Nancy scooted her chair next to Gloria and wrapped her arms around her. "It's okay G, you're not alone," she said.

Gloria wiped away her tears. "Crying in public, ridiculous," she said, halfheartedly scolding herself. Nancy leaned her temple against Gloria's cheek, the warm tears running in the seam between their faces.

Gloria spent a couple of restless hours in bed after returning to her apartment. She gave up on sleep and ventured back into the city at dawn. She brought her paints to Central Park. She set up by a tree overlooking the same spot she delivered the speech less than twenty-four hours earlier. Gloria could not seem to recall any of what had transpired outside of her head during the rally. Her thoughts, her feelings, her beliefs, they were all clear, continually running through her mind again and again, but the rest, the people, the sounds, the conversations, they were muffled indiscernible moments buried behind the locked focus of her singular purpose of expressing a new vision for America.

Today, for the first time ever, she was comfortable enough to make herself the subject of her painting. She had never before felt so powerfully in control of her emotions. She had no mirror or photo to work from, only an elemental understanding of how she saw herself to guide her. A portrait, close-up, from just above the collarbone, her dark wavy hair surrounding her proud, knowing face, a keen look in her eye, with the hint of a wry smile expressing a look of supreme ability. She painted with the most sublime sense of warmth in her chest. She felt like the person she had always wanted to be.

The picnic in the park was subdued. There was an underlying reverence for a day that embodies such a poignant reminder of loss. The Clintocks had a wonderful way of making heavy times feel light, playfully joking and cajoling their way through the afternoon. Eventually the discussion wound its way to Gloria's plans. "I'm not sure what to do next," she said. "It depends on what kind of momentum comes from this event."

"I didn't think you'd seen it," Nancy said, pulling a newspaper out of her backpack. "You're on the front page of the New York Times."

Gloria looked at the cover; there was a picture of her, arms out, speaking to the crowd. The headline read, "The voice of a generation?" Below her picture, there was an aerial shot of the crowd, the caption next to the picture explaining, "Gloria (above) last name unknown, addresses the crowd (below) estimated at two-hundred and fifty thousand people."

"Saturday afternoon, in the largest anti-war protests in the United States since the Vietnam era," the lead in to the article read, "the new leader of the peace movement, known simply as Gloria, questioned the government, and challenged the American people to rise up for change."

Gloria looked up at Nancy, who continued. "I looked online; it's the lead story in at least twenty major newspapers, including the Wall Street Journal, USA Today, the

L.A. Times, the San Francisco Chronicle and the Washington Post. I think there's considerable momentum," she concluded.

"Have you seen this?" Gloria asked the group.

They all nodded. "Seems just about right to me," John said.

"Yep, you brought us old folks out to see you, there seems to be something to it," Tom said.

"You may have even outgrown New York," Gundy added.

Gloria had a look of shock on her face as Nancy interjected. "I'm done with school in two weeks," Nancy said. "I have the summer off. Mr. Gunderson said he would finance a tour. We would travel the country by bus, speaking to a new crowd every night."

"You've already discussed this?" Gloria asked, surprised.

"It came up on the way over here. Gloria, it's one thing for people to read it in the newspaper, but to see it themselves… it's time you take your message to the people," Nancy said.

Gloria took a deep breath and thought for a moment. "You'd be okay with it?" she asked Gundy.

"I'd be honored. Money is only meaningful if it is used for good," he said.

"I mean, it's a pretty good idea, a dream really. Do you think people would come?" Gloria wondered out loud.

"Well, we plan to invite some reporters along. There's not much time to get the word out, but you're such a big story right now people will be following your every move, I think there's a strong interest, yes." Nancy assured.

"Wow," Gloria said, in a moment of incomprehension. Somehow the time she had been preparing for her whole life was upon her. "Would you come with me?" she said to Nancy. "Because, I don't know if I could do it without you?"

"First of all, yes you could, second of all, there is nothing I'd rather do."

"Honey," Beth said to Gloria, "you go get 'em sweetheart."

"Wow, okay, when do we leave?"

"Yeah!" the group cheered lovingly.

Gloria walked back to her apartment alone after the picnic, amazed at how her life of cluttered confusion had all seemed to instantly snap into place. She wasn't even scared, once she realized the magnitude of the enormous opportunity presented her, she knew there was only one choice. She had support, and people who believed in her, the tour seemed like the only reasonable option. She had come to the point in her life when her purpose had become clear, crystallized under the pressure of constant search and struggle. She felt emotion running through her from head to toe as she passed through the city so full of possibilities. Her mind calm, she felt completely comfortable among the cement masses and endless energy. She walked to her apartment with a disarming sense of clarity, as if the life she had envisioned was playing out in front of her, and she was one step ahead. She wasn't worried about the constant speeches; she had been collecting her thoughts for years. She wasn't even worried about spending time with Nancy. She thought everything seemed to be happening exactly the right way, at exactly the right time.

Nancy came over that evening. They were going to meet up later with the group, their final meal together. Nancy immediately noticed Gloria's self portrait in the corner of the room. "You did it," she said.

"This morning, figured I was ready."

"It's perfect, it's exactly how I see you, a tortured genius."

"A tortured genius," Gloria repeated, laughing.

"Yes. Someone who has the ability to know and understand the world on a deeper level than many thought possible, and is still somehow able to be simultaneously humbled and inspired by it."

"Genius doesn't seem to apply."

"Intuit, whatever you want to call it, a level of understanding about the behavior of people, society, and government, which few can comprehend. But you walk within the realm you study, no arrogance, capable yes, but highly, highly affected. I mean the look in your eyes, vast pools of sorrow, clearly, but also, clever, determined and knowing. Your smile, slight, but there, you are burdened, but happy. You love the challenge of life. I see an extraordinary person; your father would love it."

"He'll never see it."

"But with its creation he will know it exists, his daughter coming into her own."

"I hope so."

"What kind of media exposure do you have where you are from?"

"It's very filtered, they'd never know about the rally, which is probably a good thing because they'd recognize me."

"Are you worried the people who ran the place might recognize you?"

"It's possible, although I left almost fifteen years ago." Gloria paused at the recognition she had spent nearly half her life away from Larkspur. "I'm hoping the program's secrecy will prevent them from coming after me," she said.

"You're a national figure now, if anything happens to you they will have many people to answer to."

"Yeah," Gloria said sarcastically, more out of embarrassment than belief.

"You know it's true," Nancy countered.

"It's not the people involved with Larkspur I worry about."

"No, me either. I spoke with Ronnie, I told him about our plans, he's going to set up the west coast for us. He says you've been bugged for years."

"You spoke with Ronnie?" Gloria asked, surprised.

"Yeah, it was no big deal. Did you hear what I said about being bugged?"

"I heard. I know there's some interest in what we're doing. I honestly believe the only privacy we can truly expect is in the world of our mind. I don't care if they know what's going on, it comes with the territory."

"It's scary though."

"Not as scary as succumbing."

"As long as you're sure."

"I'm sure."

"All right. We should probably get going," Nancy said, ending the conversation.

"Hang on, I just want to finish this up," Gloria said, returning to the rectangular crate on the floor. She picked up the canvas, carefully placing the still wet painting into the box, and secured it tightly with ropes through the wooden slats in the frame. She nailed the top shut. The lightweight, three foot by two foot, slim case betrayed nothing of the contents inside. "I want John to have it," she said. "He's the strongest link to my past I have, and he's been like a father to me."

"I think that's a good idea," Nancy said kindly.

Chapter 23

The two weeks before the onset of her speaking tour were equally frantic, and painfully slow. There was a great deal of scheduling and preparation which kept Gloria very busy, but her anticipation about the trip left each hour a seemingly endless abyss of impatience. The tour included stops in thirty cities over three months. They would work their way through the east to the south, then to the west coast, Pacific Northwest, and back through the Midwest.

Gundy had offered them a tour bus fit for rock stars, "too much," Gloria had said. They settled on a mid-sized motor home with room to sleep six. The old, nineteen eighties, diesel motor home was converted to run on vegetable oil, an important detail for the group, which consisted of Nancy, Gloria, two core members of Gloria's organization, Tran and Ling, and a rotating member of the Associated Press. Every Saturday of the trip, twelve in all, Gloria would speak at a large rally in a major city. In between these larger events, there would be stops at colleges, festivals, and conferences, anywhere a crowd was gathering. Gloria's notoriety as an outspoken critic of the war was a good promotional tool for some regions, in others, for many, her ideology would be a deterrent.

The day finally arrived. Nancy, Gloria, Tran, Ling, and Lucy from the Associated Press, boarded the motor home and headed for North Carolina. Gloria was excited to see the country, share her message, and spend time with Nancy. Gloria was shaking as she boarded the motor home; the trip, a culmination of so many hopes and dreams. The whirlwind of pre-trip preparation had left many things unsaid between Nancy and Gloria, but they had lived a lifetime in the world of things unsaid, and both of them knew over the next three months everything would change.

Nancy started out driving, with Gloria next to her in the passenger seat. A youth spent driving farm equipment, followed by a total reliance on public transportation, had left Nancy eager to be behind the wheel. There was a seating area in the middle of the motor home, a table for four where the three passengers congregated for cards, dominoes, and various ways to pass the time. The sleeping arrangements consisted of an elevated private bed in the rear, and a seating area below with a couch that folded open into a bed. There were two cushioned benches in the front cabin which comprised the final two sleeping spots. Tran and Ling, who had been dating for several years, shared the fold out couch. Lucy and Gloria were on the benches, and Nancy was in the bed up top. Nancy had offered the bed to Gloria, but Gloria insisted Nancy have the private sleeping area. Considering she was doing the majority of the driving, and feeling like she was their specifically to support her it was the least she could do, Gloria said.

Nancy and Gloria, up front together, watched the passing changing American landscape through the large elevated windshield. They quietly settled into their car trip perspective, cozying into the comfortable, slowed, extended space. The vast glacier that had been freezing communication between them now thawed with the conversation shared, right there on the center console, the great divide that had kept them apart, was melting.

Still, it wasn't until four days into the trip, after Gloria's first speech, that the two women began to speak freely. There had been two, maybe three hundred people at the University of North Carolina Auditorium, yet, Gloria spoke her heart out, not expressing a moment's disappointment. She knew an audience of one was far better than no audience at all.

"How was it speaking last night?" Nancy asked Gloria during the mid morning drive to Florida.

"It was fun, really different energy from the large, supportive outdoor crowds. More like when I first started speaking in New York, I had to give people a reason to listen, to prove that I'm worthy of their thoughts and time. I love earning people's attention," Gloria responded.

"And what if you don't earn their attention?"

"I'll keep trying. Sometimes it takes time to unlock the mystery of the understanding we walk through life with."

"So you think everyone's mind can be changed?" Nancy asked.

"Well, to some degree every new perspective we take in changes us. If we find the perspective to not be meaningful or persuasive, we rapidly return to our own belief. If a perspective is truly moving, there is a mental reorganization that can occur. Sometimes it's one sentence that gets to people, sometimes it's time, but yes, understanding is always an evolution."

"Why aren't you sleeping up with me?" Nancy asked, out of the blue.

"There's an open space down below," Gloria said, as if the answer was that simple.

"We're picking up another reporter in Atlanta," Nancy said, not wanting to push the conversation too far.

"What about Linda, what does she think about all this?"

"Linda will have moved out by the time we get back."

"Wow, sorry, I didn't know. Are you okay?"

"I am. I realized I don't feel the way I need to about her to continue the relationship."

"How is she?"

"She's hurt. But we are very different, she will meet someone far better suited for her than I."

"Is that why you want me to sleep with you, you're available again?" Gloria asked, more honestly than coldly, but still, Nancy was stung.

"No." Nancy replied. "For so long there's been this distance, we need to talk, to be in each other's company, you know, visit. I hate you being so close and not right there next to me."

Gloria had always felt the same way, that's why their distance had always been so necessary and why she was so afraid to break it. "I can't be dependent on anyone right now," she said.

Nancy thought for a moment. "Gloria, I know you feel you can only rely on yourself. I'm not going to argue with you, ultimately it is true. But all along the way, between the time you started fighting, and the time the fight is over, there is life. Because for you the fight started at birth and won't end until you're gone. And all the emotions you protect yourself from, to save yourself for the fight, actually hurt you, because you don't have the full life you encourage people to go after. You have some sheltered, stunted life, with so much missing because the fight has always won out. Now listen, I love you, I want to spend time with you in every way possible. I feel like we have missed out on so much, and I don't want to miss anymore."

Nancy was near tears now. The three companions playing cards had quietly moved to the back of the motor home. Gloria had no more fight in her when it came to Nancy. "Okay," Gloria said after a moment.

"Okay what?"

"I'll work on the distance."

"Okay," Nancy said happily, in a sad and serious tone.

That night the two women did share the bed, they lay on their sides, elbows bent, cheek on hand, talking until they fell asleep.

The tour through the South was very workmanlike for Gloria. With smaller skeptical crowds, she had to be sharp, insightful, on task. The traveling group took in as much of the natural surroundings as possible. Time permitted a view of the Everglades in Florida, the underground mall in Atlanta, and a tour of the rich musical heritage in Memphis. Also in Memphis, they toured the National Civil Rights Museum, and visited the Lorraine Motel where Dr. Martin Luther King Jr. was assassinated.

Gloria loved every moment of the trip more than the last. To be sharing her ideas and love for the country while visiting so many beautiful landmarks, all the while freely and openly getting to know Nancy, life could not be better. For once, she carried a sense of relaxation with her throughout the day. There were no intrusive ruminating thoughts pushing her into the land of the unsettled. She was composed, with direction and purpose, a hole in her heart was filled.

Halfway through Texas, Gloria's nerves began to return. They were nearing the dreaded pass in New Mexico. Gloria had mapped a route close to where she imagined Larkspur to be, and anxiety filled her chest as they approached the locale. There were a hundred square miles almost entirely unaccounted for by the maps. Considering the mountain ranges that occupied the area, Gloria mapped out a rough sketch of where she envisioned Larkspur, the military base, and the bar by the train tracks. Nancy had studied the map intently, even made her own copy which she tucked away in her suitcase.

Gloria's nerves persisted as they drove by the rundown bar. But the moment she set eyes on the now abandoned structure, she knew she was past it. Past all the trouble of her youth, no longer a dream filled, stifled little girl, she was an empowered, accomplished woman, and nothing would take her back. Her heart pounded at the close proximity to her father, still there in Larkspur, whom she could only pass by. He'd be in his late fifties by now. She pictured him out in the yard, long and lean, tanned by the sun, showing his grandkids, the nieces and nephews she would never know, his creations. Once they passed the ramshackle in the desert, Gloria breathed comfortably again. Nancy squeezed her hand, and again they faced the road in front of them unfettered.

Two weeks into the road trip, the Department of Homeland Security had a briefing on unpatriotic activity. Gloria was first on the agenda. "Unable to sustain the momentum from Central Park," one report said. "Swallowed by the South," another said. "Increasingly irrelevant," their final conclusion.

But the tour was heading to San Diego where a large rally was set for the fairgrounds. Gloria had a brief reunion with Constantine and her family. There was an outpouring of support from the population including an extremely large Latino following, whom Gloria addressed in Spanish, which would lead to no further claims of irrelevance by the government. In fact, now they were worried. She had proven she could bring together the majority and the Latin minority. All of California continued in much the same way. With the addition of Asians, and blacks, it was clear she was speaking to the masses, no exceptions, and the government was on alert.

The trip back to the Bay Area was especially rewarding. She had many old friends to share time with, and a large, raucous, supportive crowd to look forward to. They spent three days in Oakland. Ronnie was tremendously supportive and he and Nancy interacted with a respectful ease Gloria was thankful for. People's Park, the sight of her first speech, overflowed with supporters who were now there specifically to see her. She found the time was right to praise the efforts of the community. Somewhere near the end of the first month of the tour, it became clear the people had heard her, and many were committed alongside her now. She worked hard to continue to show them the way. She spoke of community, respect, principles, and she spoke of honor, truth and justice. She spoke to the potential of people, and to the potential of this great nation.

The Pacific Northwest was equally as supportive, less diverse, but all the passion of people ready for change. Two thirds into the trip, mired in the Midwest, they were tired, coming down off a wave of the west coast support. They had fewer events scheduled and more time to get to know the land. The hectic pace of the last two weeks slowed to a tepid tour of patience, rejuvenation, and the still necessary perseverance. By the time they returned to New York, Gloria had addressed over fifty different audiences, some seemingly unaffected, others clearly entrenched in the movement. She walked off the motor home sure of her place in the world, a leader by nature no longer hindered by insecurity. The three month gestation had borne the most powerful voice of her generation. Nancy returned to work, Gloria began preparing for a large-scale march on Washington, they left each other now, knowing they would never truly be separated again.

Chapter 24

At first glance the headline was just part of the familiar refrain of a typical media pop song. "Nuclear physicists arrested for spying." Then she looked at the name, Dr. Chan Lee, arrested on suspicion of sharing nuclear secrets with China, Gloria's heart sank. She received a call from Nancy shortly after reading the article. "I spoke with Linda's dad, the FBI picked up Dr. Lee early yesterday. The FBI searched the premises of The Dove Corporation. Adam said the lab is in a secret underground location, he thinks it will be safe, but he can't be sure," Nancy informed Gloria.

"What about Dr. Lee?" Gloria asked, concerned.

"They're holding him without bail."

"This is not good."

"It's just the beginning of what we knew would come."

"Let me know if you hear anything else."

"I will...and Gloria, I'm sorry."

"Me too. I'm going to call Gundy, see if he can help with a lawyer."

"Good idea."

"I'll talk to you soon."

"Okay."

The Dove Corporation already had a lawyer, Finn Geary, one of the best in the nation. He had argued in front of the Supreme Court nearly two dozen times. He was already locked in the fight to keep the U.S. government out of the Dove Corporation's labs. The case was legally bulletproof in favor of Dove's privacy rights, Geary said, but emotionally, a totalitarian government at war; it didn't look good, he warned. He stalled them long enough, thirty-six hours, to allow Adam to destroy all of Dr. Lee's work, the machines, the documents, a non-stop frantic scramble to destroy everything they had wanted so much to believe in.

A week after Dr. Lee's arrest Nancy and Linda's father met for lunch. Later that evening Nancy met Gloria at her apartment and the two went for a walk. They headed for Central Park. Leery of followers, they idly chatted until well out into the open spaces of the park. "It appears the Dove Corporation has been infiltrated,"

Nancy began. "Adam said the government had always been curious about their operations, but after your speech here in the park things began to get really creepy, employees were approached, listening devices were found. Adam thinks someone informed them Dr. Lee had recently begun a top-secret project. He doesn't believe they have any idea what it is about, or that it relates to you, but they're turning up the pressure. They warned Dove against conspiring with 'single issue extremists,' as they put it. Dr. Lee has been fiercely interrogated about his project, and his involvement with certain anti-war organizations, including his knowledge of you. He has shared nothing with them. They've trumped up some bogus charges based on suspect evidence. We don't know how long they will be able to hold him."

"I'd imagine quite some time."

"Probably."

"The project is over," Gloria said, flatly.

"For now."

"It's too dangerous, we can't put anybody in that position again, we're lucky all they did was arrest him," Gloria said, guiltily.

"That was only their first move. They might come after everyone in your life."

"What can we do?"

"This is still a country where you need probable cause to arrest someone, and they must be given due process, we should be fine. They know we can't claim retaliation when it comes to Dr. Lee, because there's no reasonable public connection. But your friends and family, if they start going down, the media will have their say."

"Our notoriety protects us," Gloria said, somewhat amazed.

"The new version of checks and balances."

"Scary."

"Really."

"Are you worried?" Gloria asked.

"No."

"No?" Gloria repeated, surprised.

"There is no other choice, for either of us. We must demand our right to protest."

Gloria smiled. "So, you believe in the message, not just me."

"Of course, you egg."

"Egg?" Gloria said, slightly laughing at the silly putdown.

"Of course I agree with what you say."

"You just never said so before."

"Gloria, this is silly, this obsessive insecurity and constant need for reassurance. I believe in you, I believe in what you're saying."

"Okay, okay," Gloria said, backing off. "It's hard though, believing enough for everyone, sometimes I need to hear others believe, too."

"They believe Gloria. But not everyone is willing to put themselves on the line like you; they have to find their own way. You chose a lonely path. The one who leads doesn't get the comfort of being amongst the people. I understand it's hard G, I'll be your people."

"I guess you'll have to do," Gloria said, smiling.

"Shut up," Nancy said, pushing Gloria. "You ingrate," she said, feigning offense.

They laughed a moment, releasing some of the pent-up tension of the past week. "How's teaching going?" Gloria asked after the air had calmed.

"It's good. We talk about you, you know, the students are very interested."

"What do you say?"

"I don't tell them I know you or anything, don't want to be a name dropper." The pair giggled lightly at the declaration of Gloria's perceived stature in the culture. "They're very heated," Nancy continued. "Some love what you're doing, some think you're the Antichrist, a traitor who should be deported. It's the one subject where they all have an opinion."

"I love opinions, contrary or not, I'd rather they were thinking."

"Their interest is piqued."

"Good."

"Some saw you speak, those students are convinced you are going to change the world. There's something that happens when people see you live, it's like they can't help but believe, all their usual logic loopholes are filled with hope and faith. I see it in their eyes. Those are the ones who join the clubs and plan protests of their own."

"You sound like you're ready for another tour," Gloria said, admiringly.

"I am. I'm so glad we went. I can't wait to go to D.C., and then this summer I think we should go out again."

"I agree," Gloria said, proudly looking into the eyes of her loyal friend.

Dr. Lee was quietly released a couple of months later, all charges dropped. Gloria turned twenty-nine that winter; a snow filled walk with Nancy through Central Park marked the day. Gloria had become even more reclusive in the months following Dr. Lee's arrest, unwilling to endanger those who were close, and unable to trust newcomer's intentions were true. The winter had been a harsh one in New York. Sleet, snow, wind and rain had presented themselves in some combination every day since Thanksgiving. The city was growing irritable under the extreme weather, combined with the progressively more troubling political situation. As the war grew increasingly more deadly, the hostilities between the U.S. and the Middle East continued to be inflamed, and nuclear threats were wielded. Gloria began to question her decision to keep a low profile until the spring march on Washington, initially fearing her message would be lost in the scandals and propaganda of a government on the brink of losing its grip. She began to reconsider as the intense winter weather, dire global warming predictions, and terrible news regarding the war, left an angry and festering American population ready to burst by the time the snow began to thaw.

The March on Washington was scheduled for April Fourth, two thousand-six, the thirty-eighth anniversary of Dr. Martin Luther King Junior's death. Various cities throughout the East were coordinating marches on the Capitol. Nancy was on spring break and would join Gloria for the march from New York. Gloria and her core organizers spent nearly six months promoting this one event. For the first time they worked with many prominent international organizations. They were hoping to pull off the largest pro-peace, pro-democracy rally ever. There were five scheduled speakers, a former presidential candidate, an international leader, a war journalist, a former soldier, and Gloria. It seemed this spring, only months before the midterm elections, and nearly a year after Gloria came onto the scene in earnest, the direction of the country was in play. Gloria hoped with one glorious rally the future of the country would be shaped, and it would be the people who would lead the way.

The march to the Capitol was part hearty protest, and part rip roaring parade. The New York group, including Gloria and a few hundred people, left the city for a three stop tour on their way to D.C. The first afternoon they stopped in Trenton, they marched down Stockton Street to the city hall. The nerves that had been accumulating in Gloria's stomach over the months leading up to the march, began to subside as the action got underway. The caravan of cars, buses, and motorcycles were rowdy and enthusiastic as they set upon the streets of New Jersey. A few gave her a pat on the back and solemn thanks, but to most she was unapproachable. They watched closely, followed her every move, listened and cheered, even walking side-by-side down the street, but they kept her revered status clear, as if the thought she might be just like them would burst their bubble of hope.

The next day they marched to Philadelphia. They arrived at the center square surrounded by the massive, ornate, veritable shrine that is the City Hall, two thousand strong, and growing. The day after that, Baltimore, and to the beautiful baroque building surrounded by the war Memorial Plaza. Ten thousand people joined her in the streets. There were chains of more citizens making their way to the nation's capitol: Atlanta, to Knoxville, to Richmond; Chicago, to Cincinnati, to Harrisburg; Jacksonville, to Charleston, to Raleigh. The masses were snaking their way through the country, addressing people along the way, coming together for change.

Gloria left the Baltimore rally with Nancy after briefly addressing the crowd, eager to get to the capitol. It was Gloria's first trip to the center of the country's political world, and she had just a few hours of daylight to take in the city before her last night's rest before her big speech. Her first stop upon arrival at the capitol was the Henry Arthur Pelt memorial. The life-size bronze sculpture of Maggie Pelt tugged at her heart as she recalled the loyal friendship First Lady Pelt and Bugsy had built, and her secret struggle to enact the principles of the America she knew was possible. Gloria's journey had begun with this woman's decision over sixty years ago, and now as her disciple, she had come to carry on her message.

Gloria walked the grounds, visiting the other Presidents memorials, the war memorials. Well after nightfall, she came upon the Vietnam Veterans' Memorial.

So senseless, she thought, so recent, have we learned nothing? How could a government be so bold as to surround itself with the names of the many people it betrayed? Was this some silent apology? A de facto admission of the importance of every individual? Sorry we sent them to be killed, but we really do believe that life is meaningful, so much so we engraved their names in granite. This elaborate reminder of atrocity appeared to be the only step the government was willing to take in the war's aftermath, no admission of mistakes made, no policy shift, no disavowal of the event, only more open space, plotted for the inevitable additions of more war memorials. How large will the next one be, she thought, Vietnam proportion? World War II proportion? How much longer will we sit back as a country and allow these false, hollow, monuments to be created where only sorrow can grow?

Gloria and Nancy had walked quietly side-by-side for hours, taking in the loss of those so impassioned about their country they were willing to die for it, and breathing the heavy air of the disconnect between those lost and those deciding their fate. Now, as the clock approached midnight, visiting hours were coming to an end. Nancy grabbed Gloria by the hand and solemnly walked her back to the motor home. Nancy could see the distance in Gloria's eyes, the far-off internal churning living inside her emotionally intense friend.

Once to the motor home, just the two of them, Gloria sat slumped on a bench, too dejected to do much else. Nancy sat beside her; she gently placed her hand on Gloria's knee. "Come on, let's get you changed," she said to the sullen girl. Nancy grabbed shorts and a t-shirt from Gloria's suitcase. She unbuttoned Gloria's navy collared shirt, and threw the t-shirt over Gloria's head. Nancy removed Gloria's shoes, and her pants. Gloria managed to pull on her shorts. Nancy placed a pillow down; she gently positioned Gloria on her side, and pulled a blanket over her. She kissed Gloria's forehead, her cheek, and stroked her hair as Gloria quietly fell asleep.

Gloria awoke with the first bright light of dawn. She was alert, a bundle of swirling emotions. She drank a little water, used the restroom. Today, she thought, it's all happening today. She climbed up into the elevated bed to join a slumbering Nancy. She crawled under the covers and snuggled up to the dreaming woman.

Nancy roused and wrapped her arms around Gloria. "Good morning," she said sleepily.

"Good morning," Gloria said, entangling her body into Nancy's warm and relaxed embrace.

"Did you get some sleep?" Nancy asked.

"I did."

"Are you ready for today?"

"I am."

"Good."

Gloria tilted her head back slightly to look at Nancy, still half slumbering. She traced the bridge of Nancy's nose with her fingertip, then her cheekbone. Nancy

334

smiled with eyes closed at the soft touch. Gloria leaned in and kissed Nancy's cheek near the corner of her mouth. She kissed her softly below the eye. She kissed her neck. Nancy smiled wider. "I love you," Gloria whispered gently, as she passed over Nancy's ear.

Nancy opened her eyes and pulled Gloria close to her chest. "I love you, too," she said. Nancy returned the round of gentle kisses across Gloria's face and neck. She explored Gloria's soft skin with her fingertips. "I'm proud of you," she said, "because you're brave, and powerful, and smart, and care enough about everything to try and change the world." Moving Gloria's face away to look into her eyes, "very sexy," she added. They both laughed, the nervous tension of the encounter broken.

"Let's go, we've got a long day," Nancy said, pulling off the sheets. "I'll meet you back here later," Nancy said provocatively. Gloria shook her head shyly, blushing and smiling at Nancy.

As Gloria walked along the grounds of the Washington Monument later that morning, the not-so-subtle reminders of the protesters unwelcome presence laid before her in the form of barricades, police, and the National Guard. Their presence seemed silly now with just a few hundred civilians mulling around, dwarfed by the thousands of enforcement personnel. There had been government "requests," for weeks to cancel the rally, phone calls, late-night knocks on the door, the "accidental," interruption of phone conversations just in case the organizers weren't already sure they were being listened to. Strangely, Gloria had not been the target of any intimidation. Possibly they considered her beyond reproach? She worried in earnest now about the safety of the protesters. She knew peace was difficult to keep with tens of thousands of armed personnel standing by to keep people in line. She knew keeping the masses occupied would be critical. Music was scheduled to play the preceding two hours before the commencement of the rally. She hoped the crowd would remain engaged and on purpose, despite the ominous forces hovering around them.

Gloria walked to the staging area beneath the Lincoln Memorial, the site of the nineteen sixty-three freedom march on Washington. Dr. Martin Luther King's, "I Have a Dream," speech echoed in her head now as she approached the granite pillars that would be the backdrop to her own chance at changing history. She trembled at the thought of the greatness of those who had come before. Chills ran down her neck with the recognition of the enormity of the opportunity granted her.

Nancy followed at a distance, neither letting her go, nor interfering. She watched the spooky, sublime focus begin to tighten its grip on Gloria. She had heard Gloria running over some things, but she knew when the time came, Gloria would act more on instinct than thoughts rehearsed. Gloria seemed to have an innate ability to sense the mood of the crowd, answer their lingering questions, face their doubts and draw them away from fear. Now, Nancy knew Gloria was taking in the essence of the mood, the setting, the energy, her speech had to the match the subtleties of the landscape and the people.

By noon, there was a human chain linking the space between the Washington Monument and the Lincoln Memorial. For miles ranging away from the stage people swarmed every inch of the grass, every speck of usable space was covered. There was no panic, no urgency, but a focused tranquility and purpose to the crowd. It was as if this moment in time was exactly how it should be. The people seemed humble and patient, perfectly at ease with their mission, and for now it was to wait, then listen, then act.

Gloria sat by the stage and felt the power of an enormous peaceful crowd joined together to share the ideologies they hoped to live by. She could feel their presence in her breath as she closed her eyes and inhaled the concepts that unified them all, the hopes, thoughts, and fears, each individual displayed. She tried to tap into it all, gently slowing her mind, listening to the sounds of the crowd. She listened until it seemed as if everything stopped, as if now was the only moment that had ever existed.

As the clock approached one, the endless singing, chants and activity began to die down, slowly at first. Then, at a quarter till there was another slight dip in the noise. Ten till, a little less noise. And now three minutes until start time, the crowd came to a virtual hush. All eyes focused on the stage, necks strained to get into position.

Gloria remained quietly by the stage, vigilantly assessing the tenor of the crowd. She heard little after the initial roar of applause welcoming the first speaker. From then on, all the moments leading up to her speech came to her not in sights or sounds, but waves of emotion that rolled through her very being, swaying her gently with the tides of the mass. She felt their yearning to be an integral part of a proud nation, their willingness to sacrifice, work and bleed for greatness. She felt the sorrow of a people mired in mediocrity, and their desire for a new world yet to come, peaceful, loving and strong.

Her time came. She calmly approached the podium. There were no chants, only respect and hope; this was a serious crowd, full of purpose, not worship.

"I'm so very honored to be here," she began. "Not only because of the privilege of addressing the people of this fine nation, but also because of all the great history this site represents. As many of you know, this is the thirty-eighth anniversary marking the death of Dr. Martin Luther King Junior. Forty three years ago, he stood just about where I am now, and addressed a crowd not too unlike yourselves, a gathered people wanting to see the best of their great country. We are survived by the great leaders of this country, such as Dr. King. We were founded under the spirit of justice and freedom, and throughout history have looked to the courageous among us to bravely guide us through our course. There are times when this country, as good spirited and righteous a people as we are, have strayed from our noble purpose, the times of slavery, oppression of women, classism and racism. And times when the people of this great nation have joined with our great leaders in condemnation of such perversions of our society, in the pursuit of the honor and equality with which we were founded.

"I'm proud to say, I see thousands upon thousands of great leaders here today. Today, every single one of you has answered the bell to the fight against injustice. Today, we the people of the United States of America stand strong for a better and safer country, and a better and safer humanity. And I ask our government, as we stand here humbly in your backyard, as your neighbor, as your fellow citizens, I ask our country's leaders, are you listening? We have come here to ask you to stop the violence, the bombing, the bloodshed, we do not want it, we do not condone it. We ask you to lift the ever present veil of nuclear warfare which clouds our landscape. We want an unobstructed view into our future, without the fear of inhumane and unnecessary threat. Today, the American people have answered a call to action. And I ask you, our elected officials, are you listening?

"I mentioned the march of nineteen sixty-three, a different time, a different era. What many of you may not know, is immediately upon completion of the march, those involved, Dr. King and others, went to meet directly with the President of the United States, John F. Kennedy Jr. There was a respect, a dialogue, a willingness by the government to hear the ideas of its people. We find ourselves in a completely contrary era today. We are entirely ignored by a government who feels entitled to rule despite the will of its people. Sounds a great deal like a dictatorship, except for one thing, we have the power to decide who represents us. Up until this point there appeared little interest in changing the direction of our country, but I daresay, today we have made it clear there is a great deal of interest. And if you listen closely, you can hear the teeth chattering and the knees knocking of a very scared White House that knows they face a formidable foe.

"We are a good people, a gentle people, a trusting people. We want to believe in our government. And I understand why up until now we have been willing to give them the benefit of the doubt. It is a hard thing to admit that we have a failed leadership; it is a condemnation of the country and the people of this country who voted these leaders into office. I grieve with you here today as we admit we are guided by failed leadership. But the truth is, the administration does not embody the principles and liberties upon which this great nation was founded. And it is up to us to bring honor back to every American citizen.

"We stand together in unity to say our great nation is one of mercy, forgiveness, and compassion. A country where each of us has the right to walk the streets with pride in a land of freedom, free of prejudice; a land where we believe the best in people, because we know what's possible; a land where our neighbors, here and abroad, have nothing but kind things to say about us because we are a good and decent people; a land where firm handshakes and honest smiles are backed up by action, not a stab in the back; where intent and purpose are considerate of the many, not just the few. Where we ask what can I do for others, not only what can I do for myself. A land where sick people are treated, for all of us deserve to be well, because we care for each other, love each other, and want to see those around us carry on. We cannot have this land we so desire, if we cannot count on our leaders to carry through with these ideals. Then it becomes the role of the people to show those in charge the way. Today, we come here to do just that. We are here to show our leaders we want a different nation than you have shown us. We want a nation of justice, respect, and freedom. And that can only come from a leadership dedicated to equality. We are here to say, if you do not become the leaders this great nation deserves, you will be asked to leave.

"In just a few months there will be the midterm elections, that is one way we will make our intentions known. But by evidence of the strength of the will here today, we will work everyday to leave no doubt in the mind of our people, our leaders, and those around the world, how strong the will of the American people is. We join together today, tomorrow, and everyday, for a nation of justice, a nation of honorable intentions and actions, a nation of proud, noble people, with a government that represents our strengths, not our weaknesses. Because, dear government, we have seen the aftermath of your deceit, we have seen your manipulation, your greed, and we stand united here today to say we feel betrayed, we are a country betrayed, and we demand change.

"As a girl I would dream of being a part of this great land, its richness, its complexities, and its ideal pursuit for the greatest dreams in all of us. Today, for the first time, I see some of my dreams about America coming true. I see a passionate people fighting for what they believe is right, and I see a strength and will of character all people can be proud of. We here today represent the true America. The America that believes peace is the way to shape the future, not war. The true America that approaches arms opened, not fists drawn tight. A true America that does not betray those we employ. A true America where we believe in others as wholeheartedly as we do ourselves. A true America guided by the forces of honor, led by a government of strong ideals and impeccable character. I see glimpses of the true America in the hearts and minds of all of you out there today. But it is time our dream for this country becomes reality, and that reality starts with the passion and will of the people, here today we demand the reality of a true America."

There was a solid respectful applause, not boisterous, not over the top, but genuine, meaningful gratitude. This was not the naïve, exuberant crowd of yesteryear; they were worn by disappointment over the course of their nation. They wanted more than feel-good speeches, they wanted substance, she delivered, and they obliged with their solemn thanks.

The speech had not taken her to the far off contemplative lands in the recesses of her mind like previous speeches had. She was intensely present, there with the crowd, sensing their determination and pride. She greeted them openly as they came to her, thanked them for their presence as they shook hands. The divide between she and her followers had narrowed. They joined her wholeheartedly, committed, like she had asked, and she acknowledged their sacrifice. Previously she had challenged the people, and they had responded. Now, the challenge was focused on the government, a monumental shift had occurred.

As the crowd dissipated, she was at ease, comfortable with the balance of her speech, the fine line between asking more of your country, and disrespecting it. A perilous journey she had not always felt she navigated successfully. But today, she felt in tune with the message and the people, aligned in meaning and purpose.

Gloria was shaking the hand of a protester when she felt an odd, awkwardly persistent tapping on her shoulder. She turned to see a man in a suit, wearing dark sunglasses, with closely cropped hair. She smiled slightly, they're here, she thought. "Miss Gloria, your presence is requested by the White House," the man stated.

"Let's go," she replied instantly. "I'm bringing my friend," Gloria said, grabbing Nancy's hand. Nancy, noticing the out of place man who hovered near Gloria had come to Gloria's side. "Nancy, some people want to talk to me, will you come?" Gloria said to Nancy loudly.

Nancy looked at her closely, silently summing up Gloria's anxiety level. Gloria appeared calm. "Yeah, I'll go," she said.

"Follow me please," the man directed. He led them to a golf cart and transported them a few miles to the White House. They were quickly ushered into a side entrance by the Rose Garden.

Gloria's skin began to crawl as she saw the fat, bald, clammy, bespectacled man, sitting behind a large wooden desk. He remained seated, not bothering to look up. The man who brought them, whom she presumed to be the Secret Service, offered the two chairs in front of the desk to the women.

"I only want to see Gloria," the man behind the desk said in an arrogant tone.

"We're both staying," Gloria said, equally as arrogantly. Nancy shot her a look. The man raised his eyes to look at Gloria as he put down the paperwork before him. "I'm Alan Node, special assistant to the President," he said.

"Your reputation precedes you," Gloria said matter-of-factly.

He leaned back from the desk, now giving her a full stare down. "I believe we have a problem," he said.

"Many," Gloria retorted.

"You seem to be insistent upon turning people against us, let me make it clear, that is a very unwise stance to take," he said.

Gloria said nothing.

"We've had our eye on you for quite some time," he continued. "You're rather like a ghost, no family, no past, an orphan possibly, lost in the system. This is Nancy I presume," he said, without taking his eyes off Gloria. "We do know some things about you, enough I'd say. You see, Gloria, a naïve little girl in way over her head can get herself into deep trouble if she opposes the wrong forces. We've humored you until this point, let you have your little fantasy, but now it is time for you to stop your little revolt. I can assure you the war will not end anytime soon, the complexities of the situation I cannot even begin to explain, but it is in the best interests of this country to continue its current policy."

"I do not agree," she said calmly.

"Let me assure you, as someone who knows a great deal more about the situation, America would be in grave danger if we pulled our troops out. If you are a true patriot, a true American shall we say, you will no longer attempt to divide this country, especially during a time of war."

"Is that all you have to say? Because I've heard this banal rhetoric before. I believe more in what I'm doing, and the power of the people to combat a rogue government, than in life itself. I will not stop, I will not be intimidated, you have wielded far too much power for far too long."

"I'm sorry you feel that way," he said, returning to his papers. "You're right, we have nothing to discuss. Please be advised we do not take kindly to your threat."

"Thoughts and ideas are never threats, they are hopes and possibilities. You must ask yourself what kind of administration are you part of if the will of your own people is a threat. Mr. Node, respectfully and humbly, I inform you this administration has failed its people. You can either start to bring about change, or the people are coming for you."

"Gloria, you far overestimate your position. Let history be your guide when you look to your future as a leader trying to undermine the government. It is not I whom should be worried."

"And yet you are, worried and desperate, threatening a little naïve girl like me. You should be the one to let history guide you when it comes to the perils of war and the escalation of violence. I am a student of the past; you are a denier of it. Your time is coming to an end, you know it, I know it. Do the honorable thing for once and listen to the people of this country."

"You take care now, Gloria, Nancy, best of luck to both of you," he said without looking up.

The women got up and followed the agent to the golf cart. After the agent had dropped them off, and the golf cart dipped down from the horizon, Nancy spoke. "What an asshole, I swear he was part reptile."

"Yeah, no acknowledgement at all about what's going on. They don't want to talk, they want to direct. It's scary, they don't care at all about any opinion other than their own."

"You were feisty. I couldn't believe it when you said your reputation precedes you. You could feel his blood boiling under his scaly skin."

"He was rude and patronizing. I treated him with the same disrespect he treated me."

"No, I know. I think he was expecting something a little different."

"A passive, meek, girl?"

"I guess...He misjudged you."

"I don't even think he sees me at all. He can't see past his own tangled web of lies. He's just a diligent little spider trying to make a stronger web to catch more prey."

"Are you nervous?" Nancy asked.

"I always knew the stakes, a corrupt government losing its grip on power, I guess they wanted to make sure I knew I was in danger, but I've always known."

"What a day," Nancy said exhausted. "The speech, how do you feel about it?"

"Good, I liked it, it was more hopeful. I really feel like the people are unstoppable now. With the election, and their willingness to stand up for their beliefs, it seems like something has changed. I can't totally explain it."

"They've risen."

"Yes."

"They trust you, they believe in you."

"It's far beyond me."

"But you were the catalyst."

"I did my part, just like them."

"Another summer tour?" Nancy asked hopefully.

"Definitely. You, me, the motor home, thousands of people to inspire, what could be better."

"That's my girl."

"That's right."

The jovial pair returned to their shy ways upon their arrival to the motor home. Alone again, they slipped into their familiar pattern of shy smiles and subtle looks. They spent a quiet evening together, a bite to eat, a sunset walk. They were pondering the events of the day, and pondering the upcoming night. They would share a bed like they had many times before, but the fading memory of Linda, and growing confidence in their relationship, created noticeable electricity increasing in intensity between them.

Nancy, for her part, was patiently waiting, giving up all thoughts of life without Gloria. She held out hope Gloria would one day be ready for her, until then, she would love her the best she could from afar. As their intimacy grew, their physicality and affection did also. But Nancy knew Gloria was cautious, measured, focused on the sanctity of the process. She knew Gloria would do only what she was ready to, and for now, their relationship was still in its proving ground.

They crawled into bed together, exhausted after the day's activities. It was comfortable between them; a simple clarity of understanding that made their closeness in whatever form it manifested a peacefully engaged time. They had their books, but neither of them bothered to open them. Nancy lay casually on her back, arms folded behind her supporting her head. The small space of the elevated confined sleeping area added to their privacy and separation from the world. Gloria laid on her side and snuggled up to Nancy, resting her head in the fold of Nancy's arms. They didn't speak, simply melded into each other, the beating of their hearts, the rushing of their pulse.

Nancy loved Gloria's increasing affection, she longed for these moments, the intense heat of their bodies pressed together, she felt so settled, so at peace, as if everything in the world was right, if only for a moment, with Gloria by her side.

Gloria began to run her hands slowly over Nancy's body, touching the soft sensitive skin on the inside of Nancy's arm, moving down her collarbone, the line of her jaw, her face. Nancy closed her eyes, relaxing her mind within the sensation of Gloria's touch. Gloria slipped her hand under Nancy's shirt, touching the smooth bare skin of her belly for the first time. The blood rushed to Gloria's head as she explored the tenderness in her heart exacted on Nancy's body. She ran her fingers over Nancy's ribs, tracing the length of each one, dipping into the tiny grooves between them. She anxiously passed near Nancy's ample breasts, running her fingers down the side of Nancy's chest, then down further to her hip, cupping the prominent bony protrusion, then slipping her hand into the valley that formed between Nancy's hip and stomach. A particularly sexy area, she thought, marking the end to the evening's exploration. Gloria left her hand there, in the indentation just above the side of Nancy's pubic bone, and nuzzled her face further into the nape of Nancy's neck. She lay there, breathing in Nancy's scent, the trust between them growing with every bated breath. Gloria fell asleep, Nancy brought her arms down to cradle her, and joined her in a fanciful, delirious, exhausted slumber.

Chapter 25

Their separate lives in New York tore them apart yet again. Nancy, with two months left in the semester, devoted herself to teaching. Gloria's life was an absolute whirlwind. The attention and notoriety gained by the march on Washington made the response to Central Park look feeble. She now had the attention of the world, the media, international organizations, and activists all descended upon her. Requests for interviews and speeches were overwhelming. Every labor organization, feminist organization, gay organization, and minority organization wanted her to speak on their behalf. She sifted through the opportunities, all the while conducting phone interviews and meeting with heads of countless movements. Her previously paltry personal life became non-existent.

The national response to her speech was decidedly mixed. There were scathing op-ed pieces in papers like the Wall Street Journal, and the Washington Post, and pious coronations in others. The New York Times said she was, "the hope of the country." The L.A. Times called her, "the conscience of the people." The political pressure and slander also grew with the attention. TV pundits skewered her as unpatriotic, un-American, childish, foolhardy, and delusional, their unyielding criticisms were constantly flung her direction. They disparaged her harsh rhetoric as insulting, she was heckled on the street, protests began at her appearances.

There was little rest and little comfort for Gloria in the aftermath of the march. She seemed to be alone within society's adoration and condemnation. She spoke on the radio, conducted television interviews; it was a torrid pace of media saturation, too much, she thought, the message was being lost. Magazines put her on the cover, people wrote her letters, all the while she held her secrets close, and her fears at a distance.

Concerning to Gloria, for the first time in earnest, people were asking who was this woman they were putting their faith in. Where was she from? What was her story? Gloria simply did not speak of the past. She let the questions linger, deeming them unimportant, or patently personal. She was at the center of the furor over the country, and now they demanded her constant presence and commitment. She had to travel with an entourage, the core four from her original New York underground days. She spoke throughout the Northeast portion of the country. She claimed a pathological fear of flying to explain her absence elsewhere, one of the many lies she had to tell to cover her absent history.

The girl who had spent the first half of her life utterly alone, now could not find a moment of privacy, her anonymity was entirely lost. She was followed, listened in on, pulled, and prodded; which only bothered her for two reasons, Nancy, and the nuclear interceptor. Her life became less and less her own. She thought of Nancy often. For the first time, the loss of her personal life pained her, and occasionally overwhelmed her ability to work. She knew the less time she spent with Nancy, the safer Nancy would be. She hoped Nancy could live as normal a life as possible, away from the blinding spotlight now placed upon Gloria's path. She greatly looked forward to the fast approaching summer tour when they would have a chance to be together, but she worried Nancy's life would never be the same again.

Their summer tour was set, first the South, before the heat was overwhelming, and then to the west. She looked forward to the quiet intimacy she had found with Nancy, the intimacy that lay dormant within her, waiting to be sparked by the sweet smell of Nancy's body so near. This time, there would be no passengers with them on the motor home, a great relief to Gloria. They didn't need the company, support, or the exposure, they were self contained at this point. The two women even planned a short three-day excursion through Ohio, Kentucky, and Tennessee on the way to her first speech in Birmingham, Alabama. They intended on doing a little hiking, swimming, and possibly horseback riding, a much needed vacation, some time alone together to reconnect.

Long ago, when Gloria first moved to New York, and she had asked Nancy to put her money and her mother's device in a safety deposit box, she had showed Nancy how to arm her mother's invention, red for blood, white for peace. With the increased tension of the times, she asked Nancy to retrieve the pack to bring on the trip. Gloria wondered often now, during the tumultuous time, if the device should be turned on. She felt this election would decide whether the administration would feel entitled to act on a whim, and whether or not they would assume they had people's consent to use a nuclear weapon. They had gone this far, pushed the boundaries farther than any corrupt government before, and there was no response, no referendum on their policies by the people's vote. The delusion of their perceived political capital could be catastrophic. She knew there was no way to have another machine built in secrecy, and she wondered what would happen if she did release her mother's notes. She feared for those involved, everyone she loved. She still hoped the political tide would turn on its own and the release of her mother's invention would not be necessary. It was a dangerous calculation, the lives and safety of her loved ones and the future of her mother's invention, weighed against a reckless government willing to wield power in its most violent and callous form.

For now, she decided upon waiting. The swell for new leadership was growing, the message was being sent, the country wants a new direction. The government would have to stand alone in the face of pressure from the people, she hoped. Then she recalled her brief meeting in the White House. If Alan Node was any indication, the arrogance and ignorance of this administration might be impenetrable. She reconsidered arming the device, an unsettled, open question for now, gnawing at her as she tried to bring the country and the administration's perceived enemies out of harms way.

Gloria, disenchanted with the spectacular media frenzy which surrounded her, greatly scaled down her schedule a week before her trip. She wanted to get back to the people, back to the city where every principle she had ever discussed played out on a daily basis.

She left her apartment at dawn, hair back, hat on, as incognito as possible in hopes of losing herself in the masses. She explored the city again, as she did when she first arrived three years ago, this time with a slightly more experienced eye, but with the same engagement and wonderment at the dazzling potential of the alarming breadth and complexity of the human experience.

She visited the site of the World Trade Center, a slightly more manicured site of devastation, but still wholly disturbing. She was surprised by the sharp visceral reaction the site caused, like a swift blow to the sternum, she lost her breath for a moment, and felt her gut contemplate the necessity of heaving out the overwhelming emotion.

She visited the great museums. She loved Van Gogh, a complete original, she thought. She was determined to get in some painting time on her vacation, allow her mind the abstract cerebral wondering the practice provided. She took in the great structures and vibrancy of the city, the culture, the people, such a land of wonder and intrigue with new possibilities around every corner.

She loved the people of New York, the combinations, Cubans with Chinese, Filipinos with Ethiopians, Brits with Cambodians, the city of true cultural integration with all its difficulties and glory's. She loved the struggle, the hardship and the perseverance, the extraordinary ability of people to overcome. There were the determined and the disenchanted, the spirited and the heartbroken, the triumphant and the trampled. Every paradox existed in this great city, the epitome of the human experience.

She lay awake in her small, clean, uncluttered apartment. Gloria had acquired very little since her arrival to New York, and besides shoring up the cockroach situation, her apartment remained virtually unchanged. She had paintings and canvasses leaning against the walls, nothing displayed, few personal touches. She had never considered the dwelling home, just a starting and ending point for life outside its walls. She crawled out of her bed at five a.m., gathered her things, and walked over to Nancy's.

The diligent Nancy was already up, drinking coffee and eating toast. She welcomed Gloria warmly. "Ready to go?" Nancy teased knowingly. She knew Gloria was anxious about the trip, not the speaking, but the first few days, the time alone together. She saw the scared look in Gloria's eyes, so afraid to be vulnerable, such a serious focused person, reading the weight of the world into every action.

"Yeah, thought It'd be nice to get out of the city before it woke up," Gloria replied.

"The city that never sleeps," Nancy laughed, trying to be light in the presence of Gloria's heaviness. "I'll get my things."

They picked up the motor home at a long-term lot, and were riding over the Brooklyn Bridge as the sun began to rise over the city. "Goodbye, New York," Gloria said.

"Till next time," Nancy added.

They headed through Ohio, then to the deep rolling forests of Kentucky. Thankfully, it appeared no one had followed them, they were free until Birmingham.

They stopped near an old fort on the Kentucky River to explore the region and stay the night. In the morning they found a trail which led them along the river. Gloria strapped on her painting supplies, grabbing her canvas and pack, not the red and black pack with her mother's interceptor that was tucked away in a cubby of the motor home. The pair headed out into the forest together.

There had been little chatter throughout the drive. And now they quietly took in the peaceful oncoming of a new day as the sun slowly rose over the landscape. They hiked high above the river and found a beautiful vantage point upon which to picnic and paint. They spent a leisurely day in each other's company, still transitioning from their own separate worlds into the realm of togetherness. They walked slowly down the forested ridge as the sun receded behind the hills.

"It's nice to see you," Nancy said, after they had settled back into the motor home, growing more comfortable being alone together. "I know your life has been crazy, and a lot has changed. I'm really glad we're able to have this time together."

Gloria, happy Nancy addressed some of the apprehension between them, relaxed slightly and replied. "I've been nervous about being with you since the trip was planned. You're all I can think about, and the one thing I work endlessly to put out of my mind."

"I know. After an absence it's all here so fast, let's just take it slow."

"Slower than we already have? We have known each other for almost fifteen years," Gloria said, almost astounded.

"But the time hasn't been right."

"Until now."

"Until now, but not all at once."

"Do you feel ready?" Gloria asked shyly.

"I do," Nancy replied.

"I do too, but I'm nervous."

"I'm nervous, too."

"You are? Why are you nervous?" Gloria asked.

"Gloria, no one has ever meant to me what you mean to me, every emotion, every touch, every breath, is so heightened, it's as if everything stops and nothing else exists, that makes me very nervous."

"We feel the same, I feel that way too."

"I know. It is there between us, and always will be, today, tomorrow, the next. We'll feel our way through it, we'll be okay."

"Far better than okay, I'm sure."

"No doubt, far, far better than okay," Nancy agreed.

Nancy reached her hand behind Gloria's neck and kissed her then, their first passionate kiss, short and sweet, a perfect glimpse into their future of physical connectedness.

They were exhausted, overwrought by emotion and nerves. They fell asleep in each other's arms, knowing the first step in the evolution of their relationship had been taken. They slept late the next morning, soothed by the silence and isolation of the forest. It was nearly nine by the time they woke up. They smiled as they sleepily looked at each other. Only a hint of shyness remaining, they looked squarely into each other's eyes, sure of their place in each other's lives. They lingered in bed, exploring each other's bodies, not sexually, but literally, the shape of the other's legs, the small of the back, the learning of the person they had seen for so long and been so curious about, but never fully explored. It was a time of enchantment, mystery, and satisfaction, the multitude of questions they had for each other beginning to be answered.

They returned to the land. This time they stayed at the river's edge, no painting, no reading, just the two of them basking in each other's presence. They swam naked together, no apprehension, they hadn't seen another soul since arriving; they felt like the only two people in the entire world. They swam with more freedom than in the days of their youth, this time coming together, briefly feeling the slick smoothness of their naked bodies touching. They kissed, only once, building up the courage to do it more. They lay in the warm early summer sun, a hand gently placed on hip, a loving stroke upon the arm, the thought of nothing but each other, stopped in time, in a world of love and tenderness.

This time they went back to the motor home without doubts. They removed their clothes and went directly to the bed. They explored each other further now. Nancy laid her naked body on top of Gloria. Gloria's face grew warm, overwhelmed by the feeling of the full weight of Nancy's body pressed on top of her the burning heat of long trapped tears tumbled down her flushed cheeks. Nancy held her close, pressing her face to the side of Gloria's as she trembled and cried. The wave of emotion subsided. Nancy kissed the wetness from the tears away, and continued over Gloria's entire body, hoping to leave no doubt she loved every part of her. They kissed and kissed for hours, trying to express every emotion they had ever felt for each other, and everything they were feeling for the first time with the increasing passion rising through them as their tongues met.

They woke late the next morning, finally succumbing to the necessity of sleep well into the night. They smiled, kissed, hugged and loved, exercising the missing piece in their lives that was empty for so long.

They left the cool comfort of Kentucky for the friendly surroundings of Tennessee. They both wanted to see the legendary Mississippi River, and decided to spend their last night before the tour within its sites. Despite its difficult politics, Gloria had a soft spot in her heart for the South. Their first trip through the region they had run out of biodiesel, she, Nancy, Tran and Ling, and the reporter, stood on the side of the highway fifty miles outside of Nashville. A couple in a truck stopped and offered to take them to town to get some diesel. They were a friendly pair, and after they helped them fill up their tank, the group followed the couple to their house, where they proceeded to share a fine home-cooked meal. When it came right down to it, the people in the South take care of each other, they may have their particular beliefs, but if you are stranded on the side of the road, help is given, no questions asked. Gloria's heart had warmed to the South, she found Southerners kind, friendly and welcoming, slow to change, but quite a few things they would never need to.

Gloria had seen glimpses of the Mississippi out of the window of the motor home, but now being down on the shore, she could feel the life force of the rushing river's current. She stuck her fingertips in, intimidated by its strength, she would go no further. A healthy respect, a watchful eye, she admired its power, but would not test its might. The Mississippi had claimed more than a few lives, transfixed by its beauty, they did not know of its swift undercurrent lying just below the surface. She and Nancy watched the sunset from the banks of the great river. Quiet, subtle, faded pinks and oranges closed out the day and sent the women back to their shelter.

Nancy lit a few candles. The two came together again, this time no reservation, no hesitation, the fire between them at a combustible level in need of release. They kissed openly now, physically, fearless and strong. They slipped out of their clothes, breaking the trance of their locked lips only as long as necessary to remove their shirts. They climbed into the bed and met again forcefully, letting their unbridled passions flow. They left each other's mouths for a moment, taking turns aggressively lunging their mouths from body part to body part. The slowly moving storm that had been brewing between them finally exploded with an otherworldly outpouring of physicality and emotion. Gloria could stand it no longer; she reached her hand between Nancy's legs. Gloria's insides rushed and pulsed as she felt the soft wetness of Nancy's body. She slowly found her way, savoring the sensual newness of the sensations. Nancy pulled closer to her, giving herself entirely to Gloria. They kissed, the intensity grew, Gloria followed the rhythms of Nancy's body, feeling the vibrations and changes, her rapid breathing, the sounds of pleasure, until the final gasp of release and exaltation.

They continued to kiss deeply, coming down together, until slowly parting to look into each other's eyes. Gloria knew she would never forget the serene peacefulness and love softly pouring from Nancy's eyes as they looked at each other for the first time with no boundaries placed between them.

Gloria's body was raging with desire, but her mind was perfectly still as they began to kiss again. Nancy's touch raised Gloria's body to new levels of passion. She felt completely in tune, body and mind, entirely engaged and open in the pursuit of supreme interaction. As Nancy brought Gloria closer and closer to climax, Gloria clung onto the woman she loved, hoping never to be far from her again. This was the closeness she had always longed for, the feeling that made any other attempt at a relationship not worth it. It was everything she knew it could be, the trust, the freedom, the passion, driving them together to find new heights. As her body finally found the key to unlock its release, Gloria moaned with pleasure, a deep soulful sound she had never heard from herself before, the sound of emotion languishing in oppression finally freed.

They lay together, intertwined, kissing, touching, entirely in unison, no distinction between them. They calmed and cooled together, into a sublime state of intimacy only found between two people who have shared everything together, holding nothing back, an exposed soul embedded in another's exposed soul. They left everything they had ever experienced behind. Now, they had confirmation that the possibilities which previously only existed in their head could become reality, moments in life really could be better than imagined.

"That was the first time I've done that," Gloria said, eventually.

"Been with a woman?" Nancy replied.

"Had an orgasm."

Nancy pulled back to look at Gloria. "Really? Not with Ronnie? Not with yourself?"

"No. My mind had to be completely at peace, safe and nurtured, this is the first time I've felt that way."

"I'm honored."

Gloria lifted her head to see if Nancy was being sarcastic, although entirely sure she wasn't.

"I'm serious," Nancy said earnestly. "I've never felt more powerful or more human than here now with you. Something extraordinary happens with the combination of our energies, I understand this is what you need to take you there, you don't settle for anything less, never have, I'm honored to be a part of it."

"You're more than a part of it, you are the entirety. You are everything I could ever ask for, and that entails quite a few things," Gloria said, smiling.

"I'm sure it does my master thinker. You ain't so bad yourself."

"It was okay, I did okay?"

"G, come on, do you have any doubt? It was spectacular, mind blowing, other worldly, don't get insecure on me now."

"I just have no idea what I'm doing."

"Yeah you do, you pay more attention, and try harder at everything you do than anyone I know. You're a great lover."

Gloria smiled and snuggled in. Nancy squeezed her hard. "I'm just going to take for granted I'm great, being the first and all," Nancy said, laughing.

"Yeah, yeah, yeah, you're a superstar," Gloria said, taming Nancy's play at arrogance.

"All right," Nancy said, taking the teasing. "You know, I'm not confident either."

"Well, you should be."

"Good, glad to hear it."

"Yeah, I'm happy."

Nancy tenderly touched Gloria's face. "Thank you for being here with me entirely, giving me all of you, I've been asking, sometimes pushing, I thank you."

"I'm only here because of you. I'm only able to be this open because of you. I would have gone through life without it, I was prepared, I'm that stubborn."

"That wounded maybe?"

"It's just difficult for me to feel loved. I see all the reasons to not like me, all the ways I'm difficult and demanding. I'm intense and exacting, and it's not that fun for other people," Gloria confided.

"You are a little complicated, not for the faint of heart, but the reward is so great. You live your life on this higher plain, yes, it's tough and demanding, but the highs are so, so great it becomes the only way to live. To get so much out of life, yes, there are struggles and heartache, but the overwhelming sense of pure emotion, I love it. And to be with you is to have an opportunity to see what life is truly capable of, it's always worth it."

"I believe you," Gloria said. I believe you would rather be with me than without me, and you're the only one who is able to make me feel that way."

*

They were due in Birmingham mid-afternoon, a labor rally for the nurses Association. The rally was scheduled to occur outside the Birmingham Civil Rights Institute, located across the street from the church where four young black girls were killed during the 60's by a Ku Klux Klan bomb attack. They spent the morning hiking above the grand Mississippi before getting back into the motor home for the two-hour drive, saying goodbye to the river of plenty.

They arrived early at the Civil Rights Institute to tour the grounds and meet some of the board members, some of the greatest living leaders of the civil rights movement. Gloria felt an instant acceptance and camaraderie when she shook the hands of the three aging black men. She looked deeply into their eyes, seeing their struggle and pride. They reflected the same look of respect back to her as they greeted her warmly. She was amongst her wise elders, those who fought the same struggles, faced the same dangers, and survived to see some of the changes brought on by their sacrifice. She listened to the men with great reverence as they viewed

350

the Institute's exhibits. They shared and explained some of their experiences and history. They recounted the day the church was bombed, youth day, a particularly difficult blow. How they had felt deep in their heart they were not respected as people, and their desire to rise up only grew stronger. That's what they said to her, the more scared the enemy becomes, the more desperate they become, hold on, rise up, the people will overcome.

She asked them what it was like after they lost their leader. They said they grew stronger, more determined, nothing would stop them. Dr. King's great sacrifice meant failure was not an option. They lost a leader, but the movement lived on, because the fight for justice shall never die. Any true leader, they said, and Dr. King was one of the greatest, creates something far more than any one individual, they create hope, determination and expectation that cannot be ignored. The men expressed, while they had not achieved everything they had hoped, mainly the inherent respect the majority is granted, they were far better off. But the struggle never ends, their passion never dies, they have the gift of passion, and that gift carries them through life.

"Amazing men," Nancy said, as they spent a few quiet minutes in the motor home before the rally.

"Truly."

"Those are your people. You know how you say it's difficult for you to feel loved, you need to be around people who have sacrificed everything for their beliefs, they are able to understand the depths of your emotion."

"They are very kind, but they have a lifetime of experience together, fighting side by side. I am not part of them, yet, I haven't earned their wisdom, yet, I'm still on the front lines, a lonely, lonely place."

"One day you'll be surrounded by your fellow warriors, an unbreakable bond."

"This is my day, Nancy, here with you now, this is all I ever wanted. I know the limitations of my life, the relationships I did not, and will not have, my family, long-term friends. I'm a child born into revolution, born alone, to die alone, a life lived for others, with a few glorious moments in between, and I've had them, I've had more, I've had you. I've been able to do everything I always wanted, and for a brief moment I wasn't alone."

"The people have always been with you."

"Better, they're with the ideas, they're with future."

A large courtyard, with a long rising staircase, surrounded on either side by brick walls, led up to the entrance of The Birmingham Civil Rights Institute. A large green domed structure sat on top of the building, ornately marking its historical significance. A long row of people filled in the large column down the extended stairway before her. The dome loomed behind and above her, with the tall brick walls on either side encapsulating the people spread out before her.

The three walls surrounding her provided a noticeable echo amplification only slightly eased by the open air of the perfect powder blue sky above them. "Ladies and gentlemen please welcome Gloria," an announcer said. She was momentarily distracted by the strange sound of her name reverberating in the air, before the echo was drown out by loud applause. There were many women in the crowd, a sight she was happy to see, somehow, revolution still seemed to be a man's forum. Gloria turned and smiled at Nancy standing a few feet to the side as she reached the podium. For a brief second it was just the two of them there, trapped in the intensity of true love.

Nancy's heart filled with pride as she watched her love turn to address the crowd. Nancy startled for a moment as she saw Gloria's knees buckle, she thought Gloria might fall, then she seemed to regain her balance. Nancy stepped to approach Gloria as she staggered again. Then again, Gloria staggered back, leaning to the side, exposing the blood beginning to flow from her neck. Nancy heard the loud pop, the violent echo of the sound between the walls. She saw Gloria lurch again and tumble to the ground. She heard the screams, and then she understood.

Nancy ran to the crumpled figure lying on the ground. She knelt and held Gloria in her arms, frantically trying to cover the wounds in her neck and chest. "Help!" Nancy yelled, "help! we need help!" There was a scattering and bustling of activity. Nancy neither heard nor saw anything other than the continually shallower rise and fall of Gloria's chest. Gloria did not respond to Nancy's calls, her eyes glazed and rolled unsettling away. Blood poured out everywhere. Nancy pulled Gloria closer to her chest. "I love you, I love you, I love you," she cried into Gloria's ear.

"They've killed her, they've killed her," Nancy screamed into the phone when her mother answered.

"No, baby, no, not our Gloria," Beth cried into the phone.

"She's gone mom, she's gone."

Beth began to cry, Tom grabbed the phone out of her hand, John stood up. They'd been eating lunch in the Clintock's backyard when the call came. "What happened?" Tom said into the receiver.

"Gloria's dead," his weeping daughter said.

"We'll be there as soon as we can."

"We're in Birmingham."

"Alabama?"

"Yes… Dad, there's something I have to do. I won't be back until tomorrow, there doing an autopsy, I'll meet you here tomorrow."

"Okay, Nancy, be safe. I love you."

"I love you, too," she said, before hanging up the phone.

Tom turned to John, his tear filled eyes spilling over. "It's Gloria," he said. John covered his hands with his face, the old man shrunk into himself, collapsed with sorrow. Tom wrapped his arms around him. "I'm sorry," he said.

"I must go," John said, picking himself up. "I love you both. Send Nancy my love."

John raced the dune buggy to the converted barn that housed the computer system where Gundy was working.

"It's happened," John said as Gundy stood. "They killed her. Now's the time."

John grabbed the package and the note Nancy had given him in New York, he quickly read over it,

Dear John,

 This is meant for her father, if it becomes necessary, and if at all possible, will you try?

Affectionately,

Nancy

He unfolded the roughly sketched map which he had used to research the area, learning everything he could. Gundy implemented the computer plan. They gathered their gear and drove the buggy to the airstrip they had built for just this moment. They put on their flight suits, parachutes, helmets, and goggles, and boarded the old fighter jet. John tied the package Nancy had given him with a rope around his waist so it dangled slightly by his side.

Gundy at the helm, they were quickly speeding through the sky, and a moment later approaching mach speed on their way to the New Mexico desert. They planned to avoid commercial flight paths in hopes of staying away from radar detection. They knew the heavily secured and restricted flight zone of their destination would be a test, but they were determined to complete the final mission of their long and nearly complete lives.

As the men were flying over the skies of Arizona, Nancy turned the motor home onto the highway towards Tennessee. Gloria had left behind the dreams of her mother, and Nancy drove to complete her final act of her loyalty. The fact that Nancy had spent hundreds of hours behind the wheel of the motor home helped her now. She went into autopilot, not even conscious she was driving, hoping to make it to her destination. Her paranoia kept her constantly checking the mirrors for trailers. She noticed the make, model and color of every car she saw, but all eventually faded from her view as she continued on her way. Tears streamed down her face, she no longer bothered to wipe them away, they rolled down her bare chest. She was in the small white tank top she used as an undershirt; her blood soaked blouse lay on the passenger seat next to her. She wept and wept as she drove back to the Mississippi.

The men passed through Arizona just below the Utah border and entered into New Mexico. Within minutes of entering northern New Mexico's flight space, the radio began to sound. "Warning, you have entered a no-fly zone, immediately change course or severe action will be taken. Warning..."

"Ignore them," John said to Gundy, "every second matters."

"I'll bullshit them, try to buy time," Gundy replied. "Hey ho, what's the problem," Gundy said, bellowing loudly into the receiver.

"You are in a restricted no fly zone, turn around immediately," a voice ordered.

"Who are you to talk to me that way, sonny," the eighty-two year-old scoffed into the radio. "This is Warren Thatch, the United States Senator from Utah. We're on our way to the President's ranch. I don't think he'd like it very much if you made us late." Gundy stopped the transmission, turned his head and snickered.

"You're an ass," John said from the back seat.

"Sir, I don't care who you are, no one is allowed to fly through here. You should notice two F-16s on your wing in a matter of seconds. I suggest you change course."

"Yes, sir." Gundy threw the plane into a quick right dive.

"Not that way sir," the worried radio operator declared.

Gundy was done playing games with the radio operator. He was in full tactical flight mode. Two F-16s appeared high on the horizon.

"Ten seconds, John. I'm going to level off, slow, pop the hatch, and you're gone."

"Thanks, Gundy,"

"It's been fun."

The two F-16's swooped down, still miles away. Gundy leveled off several hundred feet off the ground at the base of the foothills. They spotted a town. "That's it," yelled John. The hatch flew open, John sprung out of the plane, the seat fell away, he opened his shoot. He noticed a lush garden in the middle of the desert town; he pulled his rigging, guiding the shoot towards the beckoning green. Out of the corner of his eye he saw Gundy eject and pull his shoot. He focused now, like the days of war, knowing the closer he landed to his target, the far greater chance he had of accomplishing his mission. A gust of wind blew him sideways and threatened to topple him, he pulled hard on the rig, leveling himself. He zeroed in on the desert oasis. He pulled both handles hard upon landing, a slow gentle kiss as his feet on the ground. "Army training finally came in handy," he muttered. He took off his shoot, and untied the package tied to his waist. He wiped his brow, and calmly walked to the front of the luscious garden house.

"Hey," he heard a voice call. John turned to see a lanky, tanned man of about sixty poking his head out of an open gate. "You've come to see me?" the man said.

"Are you Gloria's dad?" John asked.

The man paused, looking almost pained at hearing the name of his daughter gone for so long uttered. "I am," he answered.

John went through the gate to the yard. "Your daughter wanted you to have this," John said, handing him the package.

Marty opened the package and witnessed the self-portrait of his daughter capturing her proudest moment. Tears came to Marty's eyes as he looked at the adult daughter he hadn't seen for fifteen years.

"She changed the world," John said.

"I never had a doubt. Did she find love?"

"She did."

Marty continued to look at the painting. "She's dead isn't she?" he asked.

"People like Gloria never die, she will live on forever."

"Thank you," Marty said, crying now, as several cars came skidding to a halt outside the house.

"I think it's time for me to go," John said.

"Thank you," Marty said again.

John turned to approach his fate, then turned to Marty again. "Oh yeah, your research, your wife's research, every person in the free world will have access to it. Gloria's final gift."

Marty raised his head to the skies and smiled.

Nancy approached the spot she and Gloria had inhabited mere hours before. She pulled the motor home into the secluded area, smiling at the memory of their time together. She grabbed Gloria's red and black backpack and put it on her back. Making sure she was alone, she set out on the same trail they had walked earlier that morning. She went high into the foothills above the mighty Mississippi, farther than they had gone together, higher and higher up. The sun set behind her as she pushed herself deep into forest. She hiked well into the night, miles and miles from civilization. She selected a ridge scattered with trees and rocks overlooking the river. She put down the pack, pulled out the three metal spheres; she connected two, then the third. The deep purple light turned on. She took out the tiny remote, and as she pushed the button, she declared, "white for peace."

Acknowledgements

Like many independent artists I asked my friends and family to do for free what others would only do for money.

To those I have affectionately dubbed team typo: Jeanne, Nicole F., Cate, Robin, Nielson, Gretchen, April, Layla, Jen, and Brendan, thank you.

A special mention to the brave souls who made it through the first draft and offered their kindest analysis and criticism: Myron, Colleen, and April, your advice was invaluable.

My dear friend, Nicole Smitt, who translated the image in my head onto paper. The book is far more beautiful because of you. Thank you.

My brother Brendan who so graciously put up my website and answered all my questions about starting a business; may your dreams come true. Jordan, thank you for everything you do for the family.

To Stephanie, my wonderful sister, I can say without a doubt this book would not have been published without your unwavering support and kindness. You helped me with every stage of the process, talked me through every rough moment, and gave me the confidence to see the project through. I feel lucky to have such an extraordinarily talented and insightful sister who stood by my side when I needed her most.
I will always be thankful.

Keely, you are loved and remembered.

Mom, this is for you.

www.ingramcontent.com/pod-product-compliance
Lightning Source LLC
Chambersburg PA
CBHW050540260626
47157CB00002B/375